# THE *Treasure*

## IRIS JOHANSEN

BANTAM BOOKS
*New York*

2009 Bantam Books Mass Market Edition

Copyright © 2008 by Johansen Publishing LLLP

Published in the United States by Bantam Books, an imprint
of The Random House Publishing Group, a division of
Random House, Inc., New York.

BANTAM BOOKS and the rooster colophon are registered
trademarks of Random House, Inc.

Originally published in hardcover in the United States by
Bantam Books, an imprint of The Random House Publishing
Group, a division of Random House, Inc., in 2008.

ISBN 978-0-553-57182-0

Book design: Catherine Leonardo

Printed in the United States of America

www.bantamdell.com

2 4 6 8 9 7 5 3 1

Cover design: Yook Louie

# THE *Treasure*

# Prologue

MAY 3, 1196
FORTRESS OF MAYSEF
NOSAIRI MOUNTAINS
SYRIA

HIS POWER WAS WANING, fading like that blood-red sun setting behind the mountains.

Jabbar Al Nasim's fists clenched with fury as he gazed out at the sun sinking on the horizon. It should not be. It made no sense that he should be so afflicted. Weakness was for those other fools, not for him.

Yet he had always known it would come. It had even come for Sinan, the Old Man of the Mountain. But he had always been stronger than the Old Man in both mind and spirit. Sinan had bent before the yoke, but Nasim had prepared for it.

*Kadar.*

"You sent for me, master?"

He turned to see Ali Balkir striding along the battlements toward him. The man's voice was soft, hesitant, and he could see the fear in his face. Nasim felt a jolt of fierce pleasure as he realized the captain had not detected any loss of power. Well, why should he? Nasim had always been master here, in spite of what outsiders thought. Sinan might have been the King of Assassins, feared by kings and warriors alike, but Nasim had been the one who had guided his footsteps. Everyone here at the fortress knew and groveled at his feet.

And they'd continue to grovel. He would not let this monstrous thing happen to him.

Balkir took a hurried step back as he saw Nasim's expression. "Perhaps I was mistaken. I beg your forgiveness for intrud—"

"No, stay. I have a task for you."

Balkir drew a relieved breath. "Another attack on the Frankish ships? Gladly. I brought you much gold from my last journey. I will bring you even more this—"

"Be silent. I wish you to return to Scotland, where you left Kadar Ben Arnaud and the foreigners. You are to tell him nothing of what has transpired here. Do not mention me. Tell him only that Sinan is claiming his price. Bring him to me."

Balkir's eyes widened. "Sinan? But Sinan is—"

"Do you question me?"

"No, never." Balkir moistened his lips. "But what if he refuses?"

Balkir was terrified, Nasim realized, and not of failing him. Nasim had forgotten that Balkir was at the fortress at the time Kadar underwent his training; Balkir knew how adept Kadar was in all the dark arts.

More adept than any man Nasim had ever known, and Kadar was only a boy of ten and four when he came to the mountain. How proud Sinan had been of him. What plans he had made for the two of them. He had never realized Nasim had plans of his own for Kadar.

All wasted when Kadar had left the dark path and rejected Sinan to live with the foreigners. What a fool the Old Man had been to let him go.

But it was not too late. What Sinan had lost, Nasim could reclaim.

If Kadar did not die as the others had died.

Well, if he died, he died. Kadar was only a man; it was the power that was important.

"He won't refuse," Nasim said. "He gave Sinan his word in exchange for the lives of the foreigners."

"What if he does?"

"You *are* questioning me," Nasim said with dangerous softness.

Balkir turned pale. "No, master. Of course he won't refuse. Not if you say he won't. I only—"

"Be gone." Nasim waved his hand. "Set sail at once."

Balkir nodded jerkily and backed away from him. "I will bring him. Whether or not he wishes to come I will force—"

The words cut off abruptly as Nasim turned his back on him. The man was only trying to gain respect in his eyes. He would have no more chance against Kadar if he tried to use force than he would against Nasim, and he probably knew it.

But he wouldn't have to use force. Kadar would

come. Not only because of his promise but because he would know what would result if he didn't. Sinan had spared the lives of Lord Ware, his woman, Thea, and the child Selene and given them all a new life in Scotland. Nasim had permitted the foolishness because he had wanted to keep Kadar safe until it was time to use him.

But no one would be more aware than Kadar that the safety Sinan had given could always be taken away.

Kadar had shown a baffling softness toward his friend Lord Ware and a stranger bond with the child Selene. Such emotions were common on the bright path, but Nasim had taught Kadar better. It seemed fitting that he be caught in his master's noose because he'd ignored his teachings.

The fortress gate was opening and Balkir rode through it. He kicked his horse into a dead run down the mountain. He would be in Hafir in a few days and set sail as soon as he could stock his ship, the *Dark Star*.

Nasim turned back to the setting sun. It had descended almost below the horizon now; darkness was closing in. But it would return tomorrow, blasting all before it with its power.

And so would Nasim.

His gaze shifted north toward the sea. Kadar was across that sea in that cold land of Scotland, playing at being one of them, the fools, the bright ones. But it would be just a matter of months before he would be here. Nasim had waited five years. He could wait a little longer. Yet an odd eagerness was beginning to replace his rage and desperation. He wanted him here *now*.

He felt the power rising within him, and he closed his eyes and sent the call forth.

*"Kadar."*

# Chapter One

"SHE'S BEING VERY FOOLISH." Thea frowned as she watched Selene across the great hall. "I don't like this, Ware."

"Neither does Kadar," Ware said cheerfully as he took a sip of his wine. "I'm rather enjoying it. It's interesting to see our cool Kadar disconcerted."

"Will it also be interesting if Kadar decides to slaughter that poor man at whom she's smiling?" Thea asked tartly. "Or Lord Kenneth, who she partnered in the last country dance?"

"Yes." He smiled teasingly at her. "It's been far too peaceful here for the last few years. I could use a little diversion."

"Blood and war are not diversions except to warriors like you." Her frown deepened. "And I thought you very happy here at Montdhu. You did not complain."

He lifted her hand and kissed the palm. "How would I dare with such a termagant of a wife."

"Don't tease. Have you been unhappy?"

"Only when you robbed me of craftsmen for my castle so that you could have them build a ship for your silk trade."

"I needed that ship. What good is it to produce fine silks if you can't sell them? It wasn't sensible to—" She shook her head. "You know I was right, and you have your castle now. It's as fine and strong as you could want. Everyone at the feast tonight has told you they have never seen a more secure fortress."

His smile faded. "And we might well have need of our fortress soon."

She frowned. "Have you heard news from the Holy Land?"

He shook his head. "But we walk a fine line, Thea. We've been lucky to have these years to prepare."

Ware was still looking over his shoulder, Thea thought sadly. Well, who could blame him? They had fled the wrath of the Knights Templar to come to this land, and if the Knights found out that Ware was not dead, as they thought, they would be unrelenting in their persecution. Ware and Thea had almost been captured before their journey started. It had been Kadar who had bargained with Sinan, the head of the assassins, to lend them a ship to take them to Scotland. But that was the past, and Thea would not have Ware moody tonight when he had so much to celebrate.

"We're not lucky, we're intelligent. And the Knights Templar are foolish beyond belief if they think you would betray them. It makes me angry every time I think of it. Now drink your wine and enjoy this evening. We've made a new life and everything is fine."

He lifted his cup. "Then why are you letting the fact that your sister is smiling prettily at Lord Douglas upset you?"

"Because Kadar hasn't taken his eyes off her all evening." Her gaze returned to her sister. Selene's pale-gold silk gown made her dark-red hair glow with hidden fires, and her green eyes shone with vitality—and recklessness. The little devil knew exactly what she was doing, Thea thought crossly. Selene was impulsive at times, but this was not such an occasion. Her every action tonight was meant to provoke Kadar. "And I didn't invite the entire countryside to see your splendid new castle so that she could expose them to mayhem."

"Tell her. Selene loves you. She won't want you unhappy."

"I will." She rose to her feet and strode down the hall toward the great hearth, before which Selene was holding court. Ware was right: Selene might be willful, but she had a tender heart. She would never intentionally hurt anyone she loved. All Thea had to do was confront her sister, express her distress, and the problem would be solved.

Maybe.

"Don't stop her, Thea."

She glanced over her shoulder to see Kadar behind

her. He had been leaning against the far pillar only seconds ago, but she was accustomed to the swift silence of his movements.

"Stop her?" She smiled. "I don't know what you mean."

"And don't lie to me either." Kadar's lips tightened. "I'm a little too bad-tempered tonight to deal in pretense." He took her arm and led her toward the nearest corner of the hall. "And you've never done it well. You're burdened with a pure and honest soul."

"And I suppose you're the devil himself."

He smiled. "Only a disciple."

"Nonsense."

"Well, perhaps only half devil. I've never been able to convince you of my sinful character. You never wanted to see that side of me."

"You're kind and generous and our very dear friend."

"Oh, yes, which proves what good judgment you have."

"And arrogant, stubborn, and with no sense of humility."

He inclined his head. "But I've the virtue of patience, my lady, which should outweigh all my other vices."

"Stop mocking." She turned to face him. "You're angry with Selene."

"Am I?"

"You know you are. You've been watching her all evening."

"And you've been watching me." One side of his

lips lifted in a half smile. "I was wondering whether you'd decide to attack me or Selene."

"I have no intention of attacking anyone." She stared directly into his eyes. "Do you?"

"Not at the moment. I've just told you how patient I am."

Relief surged through her. "She doesn't mean anything. She's just amusing herself."

"She means something." He glanced back toward the hearth. "She means to torment and hurt me and drive me to the edge." His tone was without expression. "She does it very well, doesn't she?"

"It's your fault. Why don't you offer for her? You know Ware and I have wanted the two of you to wed for this past year. Selene is ten and seven. It's past time she had a husband."

"I'm flattered you'd consider a humble bastard like myself worthy of her."

"You are not flattered. You know your own worth."

"Of course, but the world would say it was a poor match. Selene is a lady of a fine house now."

"Only because you helped us escape from the Holy Land and start again. Selene was a slave in the House of Nicholas and only a child when you bought her freedom as a favor to me. She was destined to spend her life embroidering his splendid silks and being given to his customers for their pleasure. You saved her, Kadar. Do you think she would ever look at another man if you let her come close to you?"

"Don't interfere, Thea."

"I *will* interfere. You know better. She's worshipped you since she was a child of eleven."

"Worship? She's never worshipped me. She knows me too well." He smiled. "You may not believe in my devilish qualities, but she does. She's always known what I am. Just as I've always known what she is."

"She's a hardworking, honest, loving woman who needs a husband."

"She's more than that. She's extraordinary, the light in my darkness. And she's still not ready for me."

"Ready? Most women her age have children already."

"Most women haven't suffered as she suffered. It scarred her. I can wait until she heals."

"But can she?" Thea glanced toward the hearth again. Oh, God, Selene was no longer there.

"It's all right. She and Lord Douglas just left the hall and went out into the courtyard."

How had he known that? Sometimes it seemed Kadar had eyes in the back of his head.

"Kadar, don't—"

He bowed. "If you'll excuse me, I'll go and bring her back."

"Kadar, I *won't* have violence this night."

"Don't worry, I won't shed blood on the fine new rushes you put down on the floor." He moved toward the courtyard. "But the stones of the courtyard wash up quite nicely."

"Kadar!"

"Don't follow me, Thea." His voice was soft but inflexible. "Stay out of it. This is what she wants, what she's tried to goad me to all evening. Don't you realize that?"

Where was Kadar? Selene wondered impatiently. She had been out here a good five minutes and he still hadn't appeared. She didn't know how long she could keep Lord Douglas from taking her back to the hall. He was a boring, stodgy young man and had been shocked when she'd suggested going out to the courtyard. "It's a fine night. I do feel much better now that I've had a breath of air."

Lord Douglas looked uneasy. "Then perhaps we should go back inside. Lord Ware would not like us being out here alone. It's not fitting."

"In a moment." Where *was* he? She had felt his gaze on her all evening. He would have seen—

"The Saracen was watching us," Lord Douglas said. "I'm sure he will tell Lord Ware."

"Saracen?" Her gaze flew to his face. "What Saracen?"

"Kadar Ben Arnaud. Isn't he a Saracen? That's what they call him."

"Who are 'they'?"

He shrugged. "Everyone."

"Kadar's mother was Armenian, his father a Frank."

He nodded. "A Saracen."

She should be amused that he had put Kadar, who could never be labeled, in a tight little niche. She was not amused. She fiercely resented the faint patronizing note in his voice. "Why not call him a Frank like his father? Why a Saracen?"

"He just seems . . . He's not like us."

No more than a panther was like a sheep or a

glittering diamond like a moss-covered rock, she thought furiously. "Kadar belongs here. My sister and her husband regard him as a brother."

"Surely not." He looked faintly shocked. "Though I'm sure he's good at what he does. These Saracens are supposed to be fine seamen, and he does your silk trading, doesn't he?"

She wanted to slap him. "Kadar does more than captain our ship. He's a part of Montdhu. We're proud and fortunate to have him here."

"I didn't mean to make you—"

She lost track of what he was saying.

Kadar was coming.

She had known he would follow her, but Selene still smothered a leap of excitement as she caught sight of him in the doorway. He was moving slowly, deliberately, almost leisurely down the stairs. This was not good. That wasn't the response she wanted from him. She took a step closer to Lord Douglas and swayed. "I believe I still feel a little faint."

He instinctively put a hand on her shoulder to steady her. "Perhaps I should call the lady Thea."

"No, just stay—"

"Good evening, Lord Douglas." Kadar was coming toward them. "I believe it's a little cool out here for Selene. Why don't you go fetch her cloak?"

"We were just going in," Lord Douglas said quickly. "Lady Selene felt a little faint and we—"

"Faint?" Kadar's brows lifted as he paused beside them. "She appears quite robust to me."

*He's not like us,* Douglas had said.

No, he wasn't like any of these men who had come

to honor Ware tonight. He was like no one Selene had ever met. Now, standing next to heavyset, red-faced Lord Douglas, the differences were glaringly apparent. Kadar's dark eyes dominated a bronze, comely face that could reflect both humor and intelligence. He was tall, his powerful body deceptively lean, with a grace and confidence the other man lacked. But the differences were not only on the surface. Kadar was as deep and unfathomable as the night sky, and it was no wonder these simple fools could not understand how exceptional he was.

"She was ill," Lord Douglas repeated.

"But I'm sure she feels better now." Kadar paused. "So you may remove your hand from her shoulder."

Selene felt a surge of fierce satisfaction. This was better. Kadar's tone was soft, but so was the growl of a tiger before it pounced.

Evidently Lord Douglas didn't miss the threat. He snatched his hand away as if burned. "She was afraid she would—"

"Selene is afraid of nothing." He smiled at Selene. "Though she should be."

Oh, yes, this was the Kadar she wanted to rouse. But he was wrong: She was afraid of him in this moment. She hid it as she smiled back at him. "I see nothing to fear. Lord Douglas can protect me."

"Oh, I don't think so. Because he's going to go and fetch your cloak, aren't you, Lord Douglas?"

Lord Douglas was nervously glancing from one to the other. "Perhaps we should all return—"

"I need a word with the lady Selene. I'm sure you'll understand."

Douglas drew a deep breath and then straightened his shoulders. "I feel it my duty to stay until she feels well enough to go back to the hall."

She hadn't counted on this. She had thought he would scurry away when Kadar showed his claws. Was he a fool that he couldn't see the danger Kadar represented? She shivered. "I do feel chilled. Would you please fetch my cloak, Douglas?"

He hesitated and then, to her immense relief, took the out she'd given him. He bowed. "As you wish."

She watched him hurry across the courtyard.

"You're usually better at reading people." Kadar's gaze was also on Lord Douglas. "He was braver than you thought."

"Yes." She didn't try subterfuge. It never worked with Kadar. He knew her too well. "Brave or blind. He may be the one lacking in judgment." She turned to face him, the excitement building. "What would you have done if I hadn't sent him away?"

"What do you think?"

"I'm asking you."

"Killed him," he said casually. "I was very irritated with our young lord. I was considering a knife to the belly. He would have died slowly and painfully."

"Why were you irritated?"

He smiled. "You know why."

"Tell me."

"He touched you. I'm sure it was by your design, but he still touched you. How did it feel to have his hand on you?"

She had barely been aware of that touch. She had been too focused on its effect on Kadar. "Exciting."

He chuckled. "You lie."

"Well, it could have been—under other circumstances. I'm weary of living life like one of the nuns at the abbey. You have no right to complain. Do you think I don't hear of the women you bed? You've not left a willing wench in the Highlands untouched, and heaven knows what you do on your journeys to Spain and Italy."

"Heaven knows."

"It's not funny. And it's not fair."

"Life is unfair."

"Well, I won't have it. I'm weary of being the only woman in Scotland you won't bed."

"So you tried to stir me to action with the sword of jealousy. As I remember, you threatened some such ploy before. Very clever." He tilted his head. "But dangerous."

"That was years ago. I was still a child."

"You're still a child in some ways."

"I'm *not*. Though you treat me as one." She drew a deep breath and attacked. "I want you to wed me."

His smile faded. "I know you do."

"I . . . care about you."

"I know."

"And you feel something for me. I also *know* that, Kadar."

"Oh, yes."

"Then wed me." She tried to smile. "You could hardly do better. Thea and I share the profits from the silk trade we started here at Montdhu. I'm a fine match."

"For any man." He shook his head. "Not now, Selene."

"Why not? I told you, I'm not a child any longer. I don't remember ever feeling like a child."

"That's part of our problem."

Disappointment surged through her. But it was what she had expected. She launched her second foray. "Then bed me. Now. Tonight."

He went still. She could see the tightening of his lips, the slight flare of his nostrils. She took a step closer. She had struck home. "I want you to do it."

"Do you?"

"I won't go on this way." She drew a deep breath. "Touch me."

He didn't move, but she could feel the tension of his body.

"You never touch me."

"There's good reason," he said thickly.

She moved closer, took his hand, and put it on her shoulder. It was heavy and warm through the silk of her gown. She felt a thrill of fear mixed with an odd, hot tingle. "I watched men and women couple in the House of Nicholas when I was a child. A moment of pleasure and then it was over. I know it will mean nothing to you."

"Then why do you want it?"

Because she wanted to be close to him. She had wanted that closeness since she had met him all those years ago, and now she saw a way to gain it. "Why do any of your lemans wish it?"

"But you're not like anyone else."

"Ware and Thea need not know. I could meet you in the hills and—"

"You think I wouldn't bed you because of my friendship with Ware and Thea?" He shook his head. "You don't know me as well as I thought. If I decided it was right for us, nothing in this world would stop me."

Hope leaped high within her. "It is right. You'll see."

"Ah, how I wish it was."

"Then stop wishing and *do* something." She took his other hand and plopped it on her shoulder. "Now."

He chuckled. "You lack a certain subtlety. Should I drag you down on these stones?"

"If you like." She was losing him, she realized in despair. Lust was fading, and amusement and tenderness were taking its place. She was probably doing this all wrong. She slid one of his hands down to cover her breast. "Anything you like."

His smile disappeared. "Selene..." His hand tightened on her breast and he squeezed gently, sensuously.

She lost her breath and felt a twisting in the pit of her stomach. Her eyes widened in shock.

"You didn't expect that?" He squeezed again, watching her expression. "What a delight it will be to teach you pleasure."

She swayed toward him. "Then stop talking and do it...."

He bent and brushed his lips in the hollow of her throat. She shuddered as a wave of heat went through her.

"But not now," he whispered. "You're not ready. Go back to the hall, Selene."

She felt as if he'd doused her with cold water. Shock turned to anger. She shoved him away. "Ready? I'm tired of that word. If it's not now, then it will be never. I won't wait on your convenience. I'll go away. I'll marry Lord Douglas or Kenneth or—" She turned on her heel. "I hate you, Kadar."

"No, you don't."

No, she didn't. She wished she could hate him, but the bond of years was too strong. Her eyes were glittering with tears as she looked at him over her shoulder. "Wait and see. I'll learn to hate you."

He smiled sadly. "But that would break my heart."

"Nothing could break your heart."

"You could. That's why I have to have patience."

"May heaven curse your patience."

"Actually, heaven applauds it. It's not often a sinner embraces such a virtue."

"It makes no sense. Why?"

"Trust. You don't trust me. I find I have a great hunger for your trust."

"I do trust you."

He shook his head. "You don't trust anyone. Except perhaps Thea. You make a pretense of trust to the rest of us."

"You're wrong."

"I'm right. You learned hard lessons in the House of Nicholas. One of them was lack of trust." He smiled and said gently, "But I deserve your trust. I've devoted a number of agonizing years to earning it. After the life I've lived, it stuns me that I would care this much about your complete faith in me. But I want every part of you, Selene. I won't accept less."

She glared at him. "And I'm supposed to wait until you decide I deserve you?"

"You're supposed to let time teach you what a fine bedrock of a man I am." His voice lowered to silky menace. "But I'll tell you what you're not to do. You're not to smile at any of those poor lads inside. It annoys me exceedingly. And if you let one of them touch you again, I won't be as lenient as I was to Lord Douglas."

"You'll not give me orders. I'll do what I wish." She whirled and ran up the steps and into the hall.

She stopped behind a pillar as waves of pain washed over her. Damn him. She had tried so hard and it had all come to nothing. Why wouldn't he—

"Selene?" Thea was beside her. "Are you well?"

No, she wasn't well. She was angry and frustrated and felt as if everything inside her was hurting. She tried to smile. "Of course I'm well. Why would you think otherwise?"

"It could be the tears that are running down your cheeks," Thea said dryly.

"Nonsense. I never cry." But she was weeping now, she realized. That stubborn idiot had done this to her. "I must have something in my eye."

Thea nodded. "Well, come to my chamber and I'll help you get it out." She pushed Selene gently toward the stone stairs leading to the bedchambers. "You can't go back into the feast like this."

She didn't want to face anyone. She wanted to go to bed and pound her pillow with her fist and forget Kadar and his stupid idiocies. But that would be a victory for Kadar. She'd do exactly what he had ordered her not to do. She'd go with Thea and wash her eyes and pinch her cheeks rosy and then come down and let Kadar know she cared nothing for what he said.

Well, perhaps she would not speak sweetly to any of the men in the hall. There was no point in it, and it wasn't fair to them now that Kadar had issued a warning. But she would dance and laugh and let him see she didn't care a whit for his—sweet Mary, why couldn't she stop hurting?

Thea opened her door. "Sit down on the stool." She went to the bowl on the washstand and dampened a cloth. "This shouldn't take long. Which eye is it?"

Selene dropped down on the stool. "We both know I have nothing in my eye."

"I wasn't sure you were ready to admit it yet." Thea moved the damp cloth gently over Selene's cheeks. "You shouldn't blame Kadar. You made him very angry."

"No, I must never blame Kadar," she said bitterly. "Kadar is perfect in your eyes. I'm the one who causes you disturbance."

"Kadar isn't perfect, but I'd trust him with everything I own."

Trust again. "Then you trust a fool. He won't take what's offered him and yet he expects me to wait while he samples every wench in Scotland."

Thea chuckled. "Perhaps not every wench. He does spend a good deal of time at sea."

"Probably to get away from me."

"It's a possibility. I must ask him if he's using our silk trade as an excuse. It seems a good deal of trouble for him to undertake to avoid one young girl. Though it's true you can be a great deal of bother on occasion."

"You're laughing at me."

Thea caressed her cheek. "Never."

"It hurts, Thea." She leaned her head on her sister's breast. "I never wanted this. I used to think you and Ware were foolish, you know. It seemed very dangerous to care so deeply about someone. What if they left you or what if they died, like Mama died?"

"It's always dangerous to care. One must just have faith."

Faith, trust. Why did everyone throw those words at her? "Kadar says I have no trust. Isn't that stupid?"

Thea was silent.

Selene lifted her head. "Thea?"

"I didn't realize he could see that. But then, Kadar is more perceptive than most people. I can see how your not trusting him would matter to Kadar. He does not give affection lightly, and his feelings for you are very strong. He would want all and resent you holding anything back." She stroked Selene's hair from her face. "It's not your fault that you're so wary. Everyone you've ever loved has gone away from you."

"Not you."

"Even me. When I ran away from the House of Nicholas and left you there. I knew that would hurt you terribly."

"But you came back."

"But you weren't sure I would, were you?"

"Of course I was." Then she shook her head. They had never lied to each other. "No, but I hoped . . ."

"You see?"

"That was a long time ago. I'm older now."

"And you love Kadar?"

"I do . . . care about him."

Thea shook her head. "You're too frightened to even say the words. I think Kadar may be a very wise man."

"What are a few words?" She flared, stung. "I think you must be as stupid as Kadar."

"Do you?"

She was instantly remorseful. Thea was everything that was loyal and loving. "No, I'm the stupid one. Forgive me. You should slap me."

Thea smiled. "Not while you're feeling this unhappy. Though I admit to wanting to give you a thorough tongue-lashing earlier."

Selene stared at her in surprise. "Why?"

"I wanted no bloodshed tonight."

"I would never have let it come to that." But she had been too absorbed in her plan to prod Kadar to notice Thea had been worried, she thought guiltily. "You know I would do nothing to hurt you."

Thea shrugged. "I know. Sometimes you don't think."

"It's true. I'm a terrible, terrible person. I was selfish." She jumped to her feet. "Come. We'll go back downstairs and I'll be very, very good. Kadar will think it's because of him, but you'll know. And tomorrow you stay late in bed and then spend the day playing with my godson. I'll tend the guests and then make the round of the cottages to check the weaving myself."

"You *must* be contrite." Thea smiled in amusement as she moved toward the door. "We'll see."

But she would probably be up at dawn as usual, Selene thought. Perhaps she would mention to Ware how weary Thea looked. It would need only a word for him to become passionately concerned. When Thea had come down with the fever last year after giving birth to Niall, Ware had nearly fallen apart. Selene had never seen a man so besotted with his wife.

But would he remain enamored when Thea was no longer young and lovely? Nicholas had often displayed a passion for the youngest and comeliest women slaves, but the older women received little of his attention. And the men Nicholas allowed to use his women chose only the ones blooming with youth and beauty. She knew Thea believed that Ware would love her forever, but how could she be so sure that—

Trust. Shock jolted through her. Ware was her friend, and yet she feared he would destroy her sister with his fickleness. If she distrusted Ware, was Kadar right about her lack of trust in him? She had always thought she knew herself, but she had deliberately blinded herself to—

"Selene?" Thea was at the door, gazing at her inquiringly.

"Coming." She moved quickly across the room. She would think of this more later. There was the rest of the evening to get through now, and she must help Thea all she could to make up for her lapse.

Trust . . .

# Chapter Two

MY GOD, he wanted her.

Kadar's hand tightened on his goblet, his gaze following Selene as she moved about the hall.

She was being meek and polite as an angel sent from heaven. Talking to the old ladies sitting at the side of the room, trailing behind Thea, and helping with the servants.

Not once had she looked at him since she returned to the room with Thea, but he knew she was as aware of him as he was of her.

The awareness was always there. It had been there from the beginning. Since the first time he saw her in Nicholas's house, her thin back scarred from that bastard's whip, he felt a bond he had never felt before for anyone.

Why was he still here? The little devil was not going to look at him, and she had evidently decided not to further provoke him.

Tonight.

He had no confidence she would give up entirely. She was as stubborn and determined as Thea and far more single-minded. It was probably best if he left Montdhu for a while. Perhaps when he returned she would be able to give him what he wanted.

Or more likely he would toss this damnable caution aside and forget everything but taking her to bed. Why not do it now? It shouldn't be so important to him. Nothing was perfect. His life had been full of compromises. He had grown up on the streets of Damascus, the bastard son of a Frank who had taken his Armenian mother and left her alone and with child. He had indulged in every kind of wickedness and dark pleasure, from the whorehouses of Damascus to the band of assassins led by Sinan, the Old Man of the Mountain. He knew all about filth and death and the few precious moments that made life worthwhile.

Then Selene had come into his life, only a child but touching, bonding with him, stubbornly holding back the darkness. It was a gift beyond anything he had ever hoped to possess. He should accept what Selene could give and be content. But, dammit, he wanted this one thing in their lives to be without blemish.

She had paused beneath a torch; her hair shimmered in its flickering light. She would never be the beauty Thea was, but her spirit lit this smoky hall like a thousand torches. He wanted to warm his hands before that fire, hold her, teach her...

God, he was thickening, hardening as he looked at her.

He couldn't stand this. He would cross the hall and hold out his hand to her, take her from these people and make—

He muttered a curse and strode out of the hall.

The fresh air did nothing to cool him where he needed cooling. He would probably not sleep this night. It would serve him well. He had always thought martyrs deserved their fate, and he was being disgustingly noble.

"Lord Kadar?"

He turned to see young Haroun, Ware's page, hurrying toward him. "What is it?"

"A ship has docked in the harbor."

He stiffened. "Our harbor?"

"No, the harbor at Dalkeith, where we first landed when we came to this land. Robert sighted it and rode to give us word."

It had come. They had always feared the Knights Templar would discover Ware was not dead and pursue him. "Only one ship?"

Haroun nodded.

One ship was not bad. The castle was well fortified and Ware had kept his men battle-ready. "Did Robert say who captained the ship?"

"Ali Balkir." Haroun moistened his lips. "It is the *Dark Star*, Lord Kadar. The ship that brought us here."

Sinan.

Kadar felt the familiar chill grip him. There had

been times when he had almost forgotten Sinan. No, that wasn't true. He had buried the memory, but the Old Man was like an underground river, ever present, an eternal danger. Ruler of a band of assassins whose skill and power had intimidated even the great Saladin, Sinan could never be dismissed so lightly.

"The captain sent a message. He wishes you to come and meet with him."

It was what he had expected. He nodded. "I'll go at once. Have my horse saddled."

"Do you wish me to come with you?"

The boy was afraid. Who could blame him? Balkir was an arm of Sinan, and the entire Christian world feared the Old Man of the Mountain. "No, I'll go alone."

Haroun was clearly relieved. "I'll go tell Lord Ware. Perhaps he'll want to accompany you."

"No."

"But I must. He will want to know about the ship."

"The *Dark Star* is no threat to him. Why should he be troubled when he has guests? I'll tell him myself— later. Tell Robert he's to return to the harbor at once."

"You're sure there is no danger?"

"Lord Ware is in no danger, and neither is Montdhu," Kadar repeated.

Haroun gave him a troubled glance but turned and ran back toward the stables.

Ware would be in a fury when he found out that Kadar had kept the news from him. Perhaps Kadar would tell him later. He would make a decision after seeing Balkir. It could be safe. Maybe he wasn't here for the reason Kadar suspected.

*Kadar!*

His head lifted and his gaze went toward the south, where the *Dark Star* lay at harbor. Imagination. He could not have heard the Old Man call him from halfway across the world. It was clearly impossible.

But not for the man who always stood in Sinan's shadow. Nasim, the master, the trainer of assassins, the man who was only waiting for the chance to become as powerful as Sinan. Kadar had seen many mysterious happenings that boggled the mind connected with Nasim.

A chill went through him at the thought. Nonsense. Nasim was only a phantom from the past. Sinan had not even mentioned him on that last trip to Maysef. It was Sinan who had sent the *Dark Star,* and Kadar had always been able to deal with him.

Kadar had spoken the truth when he had told Haroun there was no threat to Montdhu. Sinan had no interest in Ware or Thea or Selene as anything but tools. Kadar could keep them all safe.

All he had to do was answer the summons.

It was no use trying to sleep.

Selene swung her feet to the floor, wrapped a cover about her naked body, and moved across the room to the window. The stones were cool beneath her feet. It had grown chilly now that midnight had come and gone.

She gazed out into the darkness. Kadar was out there somewhere. He had left far before the evening had come to an end. She hadn't seen him go, but she had sensed the loss. It was always as if a flame had gone out when he left a room, everything drained of life. Where had he gone? To the stables to dice with Haroun and the other men? Maybe to the *Last Hope*. He had a chamber here at the castle, but he often spent the night on board his ship.

Was there a woman with him? He never brought his lemans to the castle, but the ship . . .

Rage seared through her and she quickly blocked the thought. No use to torture herself with imaginings. She had found out the reason Kadar held her at bay, and she had found out something about herself as well.

So what if she was wary and lacking in trust? What did he expect? She and Thea had been born slaves in Nicholas's House of Silk in Constantinople. They had spent most of their childhood in the house of women, laboring from dawn to dusk at the looms. The only trust they had learned at Nicholas's was to trust that the lash would fall if they failed in their tasks or tried to escape captivity. Why could Kadar not accept that in her? She couldn't give what she didn't have.

But if she didn't give him what he wanted, she might lose him. He might tire of waiting and go to some other—

She was doing it again. Trust. Why could she not trust that he would not leave her?

Because it would mean lowering her guard and letting herself become vulnerable. Yielding that part of her that she had fiercely protected all her life.

How could she be more vulnerable than she was to

Kadar right now? She could think of nothing else but the stupid man.

Her eyes were stinging again. She would *not* cry. She was not one to weep and moan when she could take action to find a solution.

But, dear God, the solution to this problem was agonizingly hard. She was not sure if she even knew how to go about it.


"You understand the message?" Ali Balkir asked.

Kadar nodded. "It's what I expected."

"You promised Sinan you'd come and do whatever task he set you. He's summoning you now. You will obey, of course."

"Will I?" Kadar smiled. "I'll have to think about it."

Panic tore through Balkir. It was what he had feared when Nasim had given him this mission. As a boy, Kadar had walked his own path, and he had even defied Nasim by leaving him. "You've got to come."

Kadar's smile faded. "I said I'll think about it."

"Don't be a fool. It's Sinan who sends for you."

"I'll let you know my decision in three days."

"We leave tomorrow. Sinan wants you at once."

"Then he'll have to wait." Kadar moved toward the gangplank. "And have your men stay on board the ship. I want no raping or violence here at Montdhu."

"Then you'd best make the right decision."

Kadar glanced at him over his shoulder and said softly, "I have no liking for threats, Balkir."

Balkir suppressed a shiver as he met Kadar's gaze. The overwhelming menace was almost as strong as what he felt when he had confronted Nasim. "It is Sinan's threat, not mine. You must come with me."

"Three days." He turned and went down the gang-plank.

Balkir's hand tightened on the rail as he watched him leave. By Allah, he had known there would be trouble. What would he do if Kadar decided not to obey the command? Terror iced through him. He had been given a mission, and one did not fail a mission given by Nasim.

Yet if he attacked the castle, he would risk injuring Kadar, and Nasim would regard that as a failure also. He would have to find another means to assure Kadar's compliance.

"Murad," he called over his shoulder. "Follow him. Make sure he goes nowhere but Montdhu. I want to know whom he sees, what he does. Don't let him out of your sight."

Murad scurried across the deck and ran down the gangplank.


"Why didn't you tell me last night, Kadar?" Ware demanded harshly. "It's only one ship. We can mount an attack."

"And, if they survive, then they'll mount their own attack and damage your fine new castle," Kadar said lightly. "Stop thinking like a warrior, Ware. No battle is necessary here."

"I am a warrior." Ware scowled. "And you're an idiot if you think I'll permit you to go and do that bastard's bidding."

"I made a promise."

"Promises to assassins should not be kept."

Kadar chuckled. "Speaks a man who never breaks his word."

"I've never given my word to a devil like Sinan."

"We all have our own devils. Mine just happens to be a true demon. Or so his men claim."

"You should know. You were once his man."

"I've known worse demons."

"Well, I haven't." Ware stood up. "I'll call the men to arms. We'll go to—"

"No, Ware," he said quietly. "I told you, no battle. I've told Balkir I'd give him my decision in three days. I won't have you interfere. If you attack the *Dark Star,* you'll make my decision for me. Even if you defeat Balkir, I'll find another way to get to Sinan."

"Damn you," Ware said in frustration. "Why won't you let me help? You made that promise to Sinan to guarantee he'd free us."

"Why would you think that?" Kadar teased. "I freed myself. I just took you along because you amused me. You know how I hate to be bored."

"Stop joking."

"Laughter is what makes life bearable. I've never been able to teach you that." He turned to leave. "You'll not tell Thea or Selene about this. There's no need to worry them."

"And how am I to keep them from finding out? They travel all over the glen, visiting the cottages."

"You'll find a way. You wouldn't want me to be forced into making a premature choice." He closed the door behind him and moved down the steps to the courtyard. The choice was already made, and he was sure Ware suspected what it would be. That was the reason he had told him the decision was to be made in three days. He didn't trust Ware not to explode into action as the deadline approached.

The clever thing would have been to say nothing and set sail with Balkir last night. He might have done it if the captain hadn't been so damn demanding.

He was lying to himself. He wanted these three days. He was always the stranger, living on the outside, but for the first time in his life he had begun to feel at home. Montdhu had drawn him in and made him part of it. He wanted to spend time with Thea and Ware. He wanted to walk the hills and talk to people who had become friends.

He wanted to be with Selene.

No, that would be a mistake. He should stay away from Selene. Sinan's summons had filled him with frustration and anger. His instinct was to claw and cling to what he had here. He was feeling too desperate, and desperate men sometimes destroyed what they wanted to protect.

Yes, he would watch her from a distance, but he must stay away from Selene.


"Kadar Ben Arnaud has made no attempt to leave Montdhu," Murad told Balkir. "He's done nothing of note for the past two days. He wanders about the countryside. He dices at the inn in the town. He visits his ship, the *Last Hope*."

"Is he readying the ship to set sail?"

Murad shook his head.

Balkir frowned. "Nothing else?"

"I cannot watch him while he's within the walls of the castle. Lord Ware's guards let no one in but townspeople having business with the household. I can only report what he's done outside those walls."

And that was to act as if the *Dark Star* did not exist, Balkir thought. Not a good sign.

"Has he talked to anyone at length?"

"Not outside the castle. He's at his ship again tonight. Shall I go back and set watch?"

Balkir's frustration was growing. "Of course. What else can we do?" He made a sudden decision. "Wait, I'll go with you."

"Is he here?" Selene strode up the gangplank of the *Last Hope*.

Kadar's first mate, Patrick, nodded. "In the cabin, Lady Selene. May I take a message?"

Relief poured through her. She hadn't been sure she would find him on the ship. "I'll tell him myself." She moved quickly toward the door leading to the cabin. She knew her way well. She remembered the first time she had come on board the *Last Hope*. She had been ten and three and Kadar had just come back from a voyage. She had been frantically eager to see him but had carefully hidden it. She had always been afraid to let Kadar know how he dominated her thoughts. Not that it did any good. Kadar always seemed to sense what she was feeling even when no one else did.

She paused at the door. What if he had a woman

with him? Well, what if he did? She had not come this far to go back to the castle. He would have to send the wench away.

She threw open the door. No woman, she saw with relief. Kadar sat across the room at his desk, a journal open before him.

She slammed the door behind her. "Why have you been ignoring me?"

He leaned back in the chair. "You shouldn't be here."

"I tried to speak to you twice at supper tonight and you acted as if you scarce knew me."

He looked away from her. "Does Ware know you're here at this time of night?"

"No one knows. But what if he did? No one would believe anything amiss. Not of you."

He stood up. "I'll take you back to the castle."

"No." She moistened her lips. "Not yet. I have something to say to you."

"You can tell me tomorrow. I'll come back to the castle before the noon hour and you can—"

"No." She shook her head. "Why are you being like this? We both know that I'm not like those other women in this land. I care nothing for what these Scots deem proper. Do you think I don't know that they'd shun me like a leper if they knew about the House of Nicholas? The lords and ladies in their great castles treat me with kindness only because Ware is a warrior and a strong ally."

"Not entirely." He smiled teasingly. "I've heard them say you have bonny bright hair and a sweet smile."

A little of the tension seemed to be leaving him, and she must take advantage of any weakness. "I need to talk to you." She moved forward until she stood before him. "You've never refused me before."

His smile disappeared. "There's always a first time."

"Well, you can't start now. I won't have it." Her hands clenched nervously. "This is too important."

"That's why I have to refuse you."

"It makes no sense."

"Go back to the castle, Selene."

She laid her head on his chest. "Don't do this."

His muscles became rigid.

"This is so hard for me," she whispered. "You've got to let me tell you."

"Oh, God."

His heart was pounding hard beneath her ear. "You want me to trust you? I'll try. No, I *do* trust you." She rubbed her face against his chest, struggling to get the next words out. "I...care for you, Kadar. I've always cared for you. I think I always will."

"Not now, Selene," he said hoarsely.

"It has to be now. I don't know if I'll have the courage again." She was shaking, she realized. "When I was a little girl, everyone always left me—Mama, Thea—and I saw how men always left Nicholas's women after...It...frightened me."

"I know."

"It was safer to be alone or not to expect anything."

"Selene, you have to leave." He stood rigid, not touching her. "Now."

"And then you came. You became...my friend. I didn't want it, but I couldn't seem to—It frightened me more than anything else. Because I didn't know how I could stand it if you went away too. And the years passed and I—"

"Come on." He grabbed her wrist and dragged her toward the door.

"No, I don't want—"

He was ignoring her. He pulled her along the deck, past a bewildered Patrick, and down the gangplank.

"Kadar, stop. You've got to listen to—"

"I've heard enough. Too much."

He was pulling her up the hill leading to the castle. She stumbled on a thick thatch of heather. "Let *go* of me."

"When I can turn you over to Ware."

"I won't be turned over to anyone." It was all for nothing, she realized in despair. She had let down the barriers, sacrificed her pride and independence, and it meant nothing to him. She doubted if he'd even heard her words. She struggled to free herself. "Let go of my arm. You needn't worry. I'll go back to the castle. I don't want to stay with you now."

He stopped on the path and turned to face her. "I have to—Oh, for God's sake, don't *weep*."

"I'm not weeping. I would never cry for a selfish, stupid clod of a man who cannot—"

"Selene..." He pulled her into his arms and rocked her back and forth. "Please...I cannot bear this. You tear me apart."

Oh, God, she loved to be close to him like this. No, not like this. She put her palms on his chest and tried to shove him away. "Don't you *dare* pity me."

"Pity?" He smiled. "I wouldn't dare. It's myself I

pity." His hand gently stroked the hair at her temple. "I've been doing my best to—It's the wrong time, Selene."

"Right time. Wrong time. You have no right to decide what's the wrong time for me."

"No one else has a better right. You belong to me. You always have."

"I belong to no one but myself."

"Then will you let me belong to you?" He smiled. "I'll be very fine property, meek, obliging, always ready to—"

"Stop it." She could barely see him through the tears. "Just let me go."

"I'm afraid it's too late. I don't think I can." He pushed the cloak from her shoulders. "I want it too much. Lord, I want it."

"Want what?" Then she realized what he meant, and she went still. "You wish to couple with me?"

He bent forward and his tongue touched her lips. "Tell me no. It will be hard, but I can stop if you tell me no."

Her lips tingled beneath his tongue, and she could feel the heat of his body reach out to her. Panic tore through her. Tell him no. She had always revealed too much of herself to him. The yielding of her body was another surrender.

Trust him. He's different. He won't leave you.

But what if he did?

She stepped back away from him.

He went still. "No?" His breath expelled. "Very well, if you—"

"Hush." All the years, all the bright ribbons of togetherness could not be denied. She closed her eyes, reached down, and pulled her gown over her head. "At the House of Nicholas the women came naked to the men they had to pleasure. Is that what you want?"

She heard the sharp intake of his breath. "Yes, that's what I want."

She opened her eyes to see his gaze on her body. "I don't know—I have strong feelings, but I'm not sure...I watched the women couple with the customers at the House of Silk and it seemed...You will not hurt me?"

"Hurt you? God, you're still not ready. I should wait until—" He took a step closer, his teeth clenched. "But I can't. May God forgive me, I *have* to have this."

He put his hand on her breast.

She arched upward as a wave of heat shot through her. She lost her breath. "That's how it starts?"

"Sometimes." He pulled her down on the ground. "It changes." He was rapidly discarding his clothing as his lips closed on her nipple. "But it's always good." His tongue teased while he sucked strongly.

Good? She didn't feel good. She was hot and tingling and filled with a strange, frantic need. She couldn't get close enough to him. She could smell the crushed heather beneath her and the scent of Kadar over her. Familiar, so familiar. Nothing to fear. Kadar wouldn't hurt her.

He did hurt her. But it was only for a moment and then he was deep inside her. He paused, his chest rising and falling, looking down at her. "Do you know how long I've wanted to be here, like this?" He flexed slowly and she caught her breath. "You're so *tight*. I'll try to go easy." His features were taut with strain as his hips began to move carefully. "Just don't move."

She had to move. She was too full, stretched, and yet she needed more. She lunged upward.

He gasped, his hands grasping her shoulders. "No."

"I need—"

*"Don't move."*

She paid no attention. Her hips moved to take what she needed.

His teeth bit into his lower lip. "All right. Have it your way. I should have known it would be like this." He plunged deep. He drew back. Plunged again. Fast. Hard. Harder.

She couldn't breathe.

Rhythm. Fire. Friction. Fullness.

She wanted to scream but no sound came.

Her hands reached out and clasped his shoulders.

Kadar. Part of her. Heat. Need.

Always.

Let it be always.

"Stay..." she gasped. "Don't leave me."

"Never." His teeth were drawn from his lips. "So good. I may stay in you forever."

No, he didn't understand, and she couldn't explain. Not now. Something was happening. Something...

"Now." He looked down at her, his face twisted with agony. "Please...I can't wait any longer."

She cried out as he thrust with powerful force. His back arched and his eyes closed.

Release.

He collapsed on top of her.

Her arms closed tightly around him.

Kadar . . . Kadar . . .

Hers.

He moved to the side and looked down at her. "I cheated you." He bent down and kissed her lingeringly. "Forgive me. I needed you too much. I couldn't wait."

She looked at him in bewilderment. "Cheated? But I found it very pleasant." It was an understatement. It was true she still felt restless and oddly unfinished, but . . . "Should there be something else?"

"Oh, yes." He grimaced. "Dammit, I wanted it to be perfect for you. All those years I pictured how it would be and I—"

"Stop complaining. I'm content." She huddled close to him. She knew him so well, yet Kadar's naked body felt strange against her own. Smooth in places, corded with muscle in others, the hair on his chest wiry and male against the softness of her breasts. Strange and stimulating. "Just stay with me."

"It's late. I have to get you back to the castle." He sat up and reached for her gown. "Put it on."

"I want to go back to the ship with you."

He shook his head.

"Why not?" Her smile faded as she gazed at him. "What's wrong?"

"Other than the fact I pulled you down in the dirt as if you were a whore from the streets?" He was throwing on his clothing, not looking at her. "It was a mistake. God, what a mistake."

"I didn't—What are you talking about? I wanted it."

"You didn't want it, dammit. How could you know whether you wanted it or not? You were a virgin."

"Well, I wanted to be close to you."

"So I took what I wanted because I knew you wouldn't refuse."

"Why are you talking in this foolish way?" Her hands clenched nervously. "You're confusing me. I came to you because you told—I had to show you that I trusted you."

"And I made you pay the price. Christ in heaven, don't you realize you could be carrying my child?"

Guilt? She smiled, relieved. "Is that all? That's nothing that can't be mended. Wed me, Kadar."

"I can't."

A chill went through her. "You don't wish to wed me?"

"I *can't*." His lips tightened. "I'm going away tomorrow."

She stared at him, stunned. "There were no plans for another voyage. Where?"

He was silent.

"*Tell* me."

He shook his head.

"When will you be back?"

"I'm not sure."

"I'll go with you."

"Not where I'm going."

"Anywhere."

He shook his head again. "You have to stay here."

Alone. He was leaving her. He was like all the others. Taking and then going away. "Very well." She slowly stood up and numbly pulled her gown over her head.

"Don't look like that." His hands fell on her shoulders. "Do you think I want to leave?"

"Men always do what they wish to do." She looked away from him. "They couple and then they go."

"For God's sake, I'm not like the men in Nicholas's house. You know that."

"I don't know anything. Except that you're going." She jerked away from him. "And that I'm a fool." Her eyes were suddenly blazing at him. "I'll not be one again. You need not run because you think I'll bother you. Coupling is nothing. Animals in the field do it and then wander away."

"It wasn't like that. You're not thinking, Selene."

No, she was only feeling, and the pain and anger were growing every second. "I would have done *anything.* I came to you and told you things that hurt me to say. I had no pride. I wanted to show you... Trust? You had no right to ask it of me." She snatched her cloak from the ground. "You had no right to ask anything of me."

She turned and started up the hill at a run.

"Wait." Kadar's footsteps behind her. "I'll go with you."

"Don't you come a step farther," she said over her shoulder. "Come close to me and I promise I'll knock you down this hill."

The wind tore her hair as she put on speed.

Go faster. Get away from the hurt.

Try to leave the pain behind.

Kadar's hands balled into fists at his sides as he watched Selene run up the hill.

He had hurt her. After all the years of care and patience, he had reached out and grabbed what he wanted. She had come to try to give him what he wanted of her. He had ignored that gift and taken her body instead. Then, in the next breath, he had destroyed that fledgling trust.

What was he supposed to do? Tell her about Sinan? Neither she nor Ware must know before he left on the *Dark Star*.

Damn, it had been hard not to tell her. Everything he wanted, she offered, and he'd thrown it back at her.

May God curse you, Sinan.

She was now lost in the shadows cast by the castle walls. He turned away and stared down the hill toward the harbor. He would board the *Dark Star* in the morning and tell Balkir to set sail at once. The sooner he reached Maysef, the sooner he could accomplish his mission and come home.

If he lived through it.

He would live. He wouldn't let Sinan win by claiming either his soul or his life. He would come back to Montdhu.

He would come back to Selene.


Kadar wasn't following any longer.

The drawbridge of the castle loomed ahead.

Selene could barely see anything in the dense shadows cast by the stone walls.

Soon she would be in her chamber, closing out the shadows, closing out Kadar.

Fool. She had been a fool. No more.

Build the wall again. Let no one in.

Safer that way. Let no one—

Agony seared through her left temple.

Darkness.

# Chapter Three

ALI BALKIR WAS WAITING on deck when Kadar walked up the gangplank of the *Last Hope*. "Good evening. What a fine ship you have. Almost as good as the *Dark Star*."

"Better," Kadar said curtly. He was raw and frustrated and in no mood to confront Balkir tonight. If the captain pushed him, he'd probably break the bastard's neck. "Go back to your ship. I told you I'd—"

"Give me your decision tomorrow," Balkir finished for him. "But Sinan gives neither of us a choice. I have orders and they must be fulfilled. We've waited too long already. I've decided we leave tonight."

"Indeed?"

Balkir started to take a step back and then stopped. "It would be most unwise of you to harm me. If I don't return to the *Dark Star*, the consequences will be most unpleasant. I've taken measures to assure your compliance."

Kadar stiffened. "What measures?"

Balkir's smile was smug. "It was necessary. The master must be obeyed."

"What measures?"

"The woman. Lord Ware's kin, the sister of his wife. We've taken her. At this moment she's on her way to the *Dark Star*."

"Selene?" Bluff. It had to be a bluff. "You lie."

"I do not lie. I had Murad take her as she was returning to the castle." He paused. "After we watched you coupling with her on the hillside."

Terror iced through him. No bluff.

"Ah, you're upset," Balkir said. "It is natural. She is of some importance to you."

It had been a mistake to let Balkir see that first response. It gave him a weapon. "She's only a woman. I forgot her the moment I left her body. Why would you think anything else?"

"I don't. As you say, a woman's body is nothing, a toy."

"Then release her."

"But this woman is of importance to your friend Lord Ware. He will be able to barter her to gain lands and found alliances through marriage." He tilted his head as if to consider. "Though her worth is considerably diminished since you've seen that she's no longer a pure damsel. Still, she is comely, and that may help."

Balkir was enjoying this, Kadar realized. The weasel

thought he had the upper hand. "She's of value to Ware. Not to me. Release her."

"I think she is of value to you. I believe you would not want to face your friend with her blood on your hands." He paused. "So you will come with me to the *Dark Star* and we will set sail at once."

"You've done this for no *reason*." His fists clenched at his sides. "Dammit, I was going to come with you anyway."

"Then you'll not mind coming now." He moved toward the gangplank. "Before my men get impatient. They've had no women since we left Hafir, and fair-skinned women have only one purpose in their eyes. I'm sure Murad will tell them how willingly she took you between her thighs tonight."

Kadar carefully controlled his rage. The time would come to kill Balkir, but this was not that time. "If I go, will you release her?"

"We will see." Balkir's smile was slyly triumphant. "I must think upon it. Come now. We must hurry."

Selene's eyes were closed, and a thin stream of blood trickled slowly from the wound on her temple.

"You bastard, you hurt her." Kadar looked away from Selene lying on the bunk to cast a lethal glance at Murad. "How bad is it?"

"I think she'll wake soon." Murad instinctively moved closer to Balkir for protection. "It was necessary to be quick. We were close to the castle gates."

"She'd better wake very soon, or the wound I put in *your* temple will pierce that ox of a brain." Kadar sat down on the bunk. "Bring me cold water and a soft clean cloth."

"I need Murad to help me put to sea," Balkir said. "He'll return as soon as he's no longer required for more-important duties."

"Water and cloth," Kadar repeated. "Now."

Balkir hesitated and then shrugged. "As you wish. A few more minutes will do no harm."

"Very wise." Kadar glanced at him. "I suppose that means you have no intention of releasing her?"

"I believe you knew that was a possibility. It seems the woman has more value than I thought for you. I'm sure Nas—Sinan would approve me giving him a weapon to guide you in the path he chooses."

Yes, Kadar had known there was every chance the whoreson would make full use of Selene. That realization didn't cool the rage searing through him. "This is between Sinan and me. She has nothing to do with it."

"As I said, a weapon." He turned to leave. "We put to sea at midnight. I must have Murad by that time. He may fetch and carry for you until then."

Murad cast Kadar a quick glance before he scurried after his captain.

Kadar's attention had returned to Selene, and he was barely aware they had gone. He gently stroked back the hair from Selene's forehead. God in heaven, she was pale. Why didn't she wake?

Selene slowly opened her eyes to see Kadar's face inches from her own.

Joy flooded through her.

Kadar.

"Thank God. You took your time about it." Kadar's voice was unsteady. "How do you feel?"

Pain. Joy. Bewilderment. Too many feelings to give an answer.

"Do you feel sick in your stomach?" He dipped a cloth into a bowl of water and carefully dabbed at her temple. "Do you see me clearly?"

"No. Yes." She frowned in confusion. Why was he asking these questions? She must be ill. She didn't remember—

Then she did remember. Kadar. The wrenching sorrow and the anger. The flight up the hill. Pain. Darkness.

"You...struck me?"

"Lord, no." His lips twisted. "I haven't reached those depths of depravity yet. Though I can see why you might think so."

"Who..." She glanced around her. A ship's cabin, but not the *Last Hope*. She became aware of a familiar rocking movement. Her gaze flew back to Kadar. "Are we at sea?"

"Not yet."

"What ship is this?"

"The *Dark Star*."

Her eyes widened. She whispered, "The Old Man of the Mountain. Sinan..."

He nodded. "He sent Balkir for me. I have no choice." He paused. "And neither do you now."

"There's always choice." She tried to sit up, and dizziness hit her like a hammer.

He pushed her back down. "You shouldn't move."

She wasn't sure she could. "You can't go to Sinan."

"I gave my word."

"To an assassin. You know how wicked he is."

"The vow remains. Sinan and I understand each other."

She knew they did, and the realization had always terrified her more than Sinan himself. She had seen how that dark life drew Kadar. "I won't *have* it. We're going back to the castle."

He shook his head. "It's too late. I'm going to Maysef and so are you. Balkir's decided you'll make a fine hostage." His hand closed on hers. "Don't be afraid. I promise, no harm will come to you."

Hostage. She was going back to Sinan's chill-ridden fortress in the mountains.

"Don't look like that. I didn't want this." Kadar's voice vibrated with intensity. "To have you involved is the last thing I intended."

"No," she said dully. "You just wanted to go away and close me out." She shut her eyes. Her head was pounding, her mind whirling. "I have to think."

"Just rest."

Her eyes flew open and she glared at him. "And let you make decisions for me? I will not. Your stupidity has gotten us into this quandary. No one asked you to give Sinan that promise. We would have found a means to free ourselves. Now we have to find a way to keep Thea and Ware safe at Montdhu."

"I told Ware that the *Dark Star* was here for me."

"But you didn't tell me." She tried to smother the

bitterness of the thought. There were other things to consider right now. "How soon before we sail?"

"Midnight. Perhaps a little less than an hour."

"And where are we moored?"

"Dalkeith."

"Our man, Robert, is at Dalkeith."

"And Haroun."

"He knew too? I wondered why Haroun wasn't at the castle for the last few days." She carefully raised herself on one elbow. "I need pen and parchment. I must send a note to Ware."

"Saying?"

"What do you think? That I go willingly to Maysef and they're not to follow. They'll believe me. Thea knows I would have followed you anywhere."

"Would have?"

She ignored his question. "You're not the only one at fault in this situation. I should never have been idiot enough to leave the castle and come to you tonight. I'll not have anyone else suffer for it. What are you waiting for? Do you wish Ware chasing after us and falling back into the hands of the Knights Templar? Ware and Thea are safe here. They have to stay safe. Get me pen and parchment."

He nodded slowly and moved to the desk tucked into one corner of the cabin. He riffled in the drawer and set out parchment and ink. "It still may not help."

"They have a child and responsibilities here at Montdhu, and they trust you." She slowly sat up in the bunk. "But, I must be the one to give Haroun the message." She straightened her hair, carefully covering the wound with a long strand. "Go tell Balkir to send for Haroun."

"I'll go myself. I doubt if he'd come for Balkir." He moved toward the door. "Stay and rest until I come back."

"How long will it take you?"

"They're camped on the hill facing the harbor. A quarter of an hour."

"Will Balkir let you go?"

"Oh, yes. He wants no trouble with Ware, and he thinks he's found a way to control me." He smiled grimly as he paused at the door. "He has you."

"I'll rest for a little while and then go on deck. Bring Haroun on board. I'll give him the note myself. He has to see everything is well." She gritted her teeth to ward off the pain as she swung her feet to the floor. She looked up to see Kadar still gazing at her. "Well, what are you doing just standing there? I don't need your help."

"My apologies. I was distracted." He inclined his head. "I was just thinking how proud I am of you."

He was gone before she could reply.

Get to the desk and write the note. Don't think how pleased she would have been at those words of praise from him only yesterday. Don't think of Kadar at all. Her efforts must be centered on keeping Ware and Thea out of this tangle.

"Don't try to escape," Balkir warned Selene. "You will say your piece to the man and then go back to your cabin."

"Do you think I want to see him hurt?" Selene clutched the rail to keep from swaying. Sweet Mary, her head throbbed. "It would help if you'd try to keep from looking as if you're about to throttle me."

"Here they come," Murad said.

Her gaze followed his to see Haroun frowning with concern as he scampered behind Kadar up the gangplank.

She forced a smile as she took a step forward. "Thank you for coming, Haroun. I know you'll see that this note gets safely to Lord Ware."

"You should not be here, Lady Selene," he whispered, shooting a frightened glance at Balkir. "Come back with me. Lady Thea won't like this."

"I'm sure Kadar explained everything to you. I must go with him. Don't worry, he'll take good care of me."

"She'll be safe." Kadar took her arm. He ignored her immediate stiffening as he added, "Tell Lord Ware he has my word on it."

Haroun nodded jerkily. "I know he values your word. But Lady Thea will not—"

"You'll have to hurry," Selene interrupted. "We sail soon." She handed him the note and brushed her lips across his cheek. "Go with God, Haroun."

He gave her one last agonized glance, then turned and ran down the gangplank.

Her breath expelled in a burst of relief. It was done.

"You did very well," Kadar murmured.

She shook off his grasp and stepped back. "Now, let's put to sea before Ware has a chance to ride here and try to change my mind."

"I captain this ship," Balkir said testily. "No woman tells me when to sail."

"You'd rather have to fight a battle? It doesn't surprise me. I've noticed you have the brain of a—"

"Hush." Kadar scooped her up in his arms and started down the deck toward the cabin.

"Put me down."

"When I have you safely behind a closed door. In case you haven't noticed, we're outnumbered, and I doubt if I could keep Balkir from strangling you if you persist in antagonizing him."

"He's an idiot."

"Granted. And he'll get his just deserts. But not now." He opened the cabin door and set her on her feet. "Go lie down while I help the 'idiot' get under way. I'll be back as soon as I can. We have to talk."

She shook her head.

He closed the door and leaned against it. "Stop treating me as if I were your enemy. Nothing's really changed. I'm the same man you've known all these years."

"Yes, you are." She crossed the cabin and sat down on the bunk. "Exactly the same."

"But now you wish nothing to do with me."

"You were going to leave me."

"I had to leave you."

"Without telling me? Without giving me a choice? You promised me once that if you ever went back to Sinan you would tell me. You lied."

"Yes." He grimaced. "I thought it was safer."

"And it was your decision. It's always a man's decision. If he wishes to take a woman's body, he does it.

If he wishes to desert her later, he does it." Her hands clenched at her sides. "Well, I won't sit meekly and let a man make my decisions. I won't let you have my body and then go away whenever you wish. I won't care. I'll *never* care again."

"The devil you won't. You can't change what's between us."

"I can. I will." She lay back against the pillow and closed her eyes. "I don't want to talk anymore."

"I almost wish I'd let Balkir strangle you," he said through his teeth.

"The usual solution to any man's problems."

"Selene, this is difficult enough. We need to— You're not listening."

"My head aches and I'm sick unto death of listening to you. Go away, Kadar."

He muttered something beneath his breath and then she heard the door slam.

She opened her eyes. Difficult? It was almost impossible to uproot all the years of feeling. Build the wall higher. She could do it.

She had only to keep him away.

It was a quarter of an hour later when the anchor was lifted and the ship eased away from the dock.

It was five minutes later when she heard the shouting on the deck.

Oh, God—Ware? No, he'd had no time to ride from the castle.

She jumped up and ran out on deck. She could see Kadar and Balkir in a crowd of sailors at the far rail. Angry sailors. Balkir was angry too. He lifted the club in his hand.

Kadar caught it and spoke rapidly to Balkir.

She ran toward them. "What is it? What's—" She stopped short as she saw the huddled figure in the middle of the crowd. "Haroun?"

The boy was sopping wet, his eyes wide with terror as he looked from Kadar to Balkir.

"What are you doing here?"

"He swam out and grabbed the anchor rope," Kadar said without looking at her. "Our captain wishes to club him and throw him back."

"No!"

"That's what I said."

"When a rat climbs on to a ship, you kill it before it can devour your rations," Balkir said. "He disobeyed you. He was supposed to deliver the note."

"I gave it to Robert to take," Haroun said. "I had to come. Lady Thea would have wanted me to take care of Lady Selene."

And he had come even though he was clearly terrified, Selene thought. He looked thoroughly miserable, not capable of caring for himself much less anyone else.

Balkir was struggling to release himself from Kadar's grasp. "Let me go."

"When you promise to let the boy live," Kadar said. "He may look like a rat, but I'm quite fond of him. See how lucky you are. Another hostage for Sinan."

"I don't need another—" He broke off as he met Kadar's stare. He moistened his lips. "Perhaps another hostage would do no harm."

Kadar released his arm and stood back. "I knew you'd be reasonable." He bent down and helped

Haroun to his feet. "Go with the lady Selene. I'm sure she can find you something to use to dry off." He shook his head. "You really are a great bother, Haroun."

"I'm sorry, Lord Kadar," he whispered.

"So am I. I wished you'd be less noble and more wise." He turned to Balkir. "I want to see your charts. I know these waters better than you do, and I intend to make sure Maysef, not the bottom of the sea, is my final destination."

"I've made the journey twice. I won't have you interfering in my—"

"It will do you no harm to show me the charts. Sinan ordered you to bring me to him. What if the ship sinks?" He nudged Balkir forward. "He's been said to be able to curse even the dead. Do you want him angry with you in the hereafter?"

Balkir frowned and then turned on his heel. "Follow me."

Kadar winked at Selene over his shoulder before sauntering after him.

Impudent rogue. She started to smile and then caught herself. So easy to fall back into the habit of years. "Come with me, Haroun." She led him down the deck toward her cabin.

"I'm sorry, Lady Selene." Haroun's sandals squished as he hurried after her. "I had to come."

"I know." She opened the door and ushered him into the cabin. She grabbed a toweling cloth on the washstand and handed it to him. "Dry your hair."

He began to rub his head. "The captain is a bad man. You should have waited and talked to Lord Ware."

"And you should have done as you were told." She grabbed the cover from the bunk. "Take off your clothes and wrap yourself in this."

He turned bright scarlet. "I cannot. It would not be fitting for a man to undress in your presence."

"It would not be fitting for me to have to tend you if you became ill from your foolishness. For heaven's sake, I've seen naked men before. Besides, you're scarce more than a boy."

"I'm older than you," he said indignantly.

Why, he must be, she realized in surprise. She always thought of Haroun as the boy she had first met those many years ago, before they had come to Scotland. He had been the survivor of a massacre by the Knights Templar, and Ware and Thea had taken him into their entourage. How eager and young he had seemed then. But young boys grew up, and she had hurt his pride. Thea would know what to say to ease that sting. Thea always knew what to say. Well, Thea wasn't here, and Selene must do her best in her own way. "You're right, it's not fitting, but this is an emergency. I'll turn my back." She faced the door. "But be quick. I wish to sit down. I'm not feeling well."

She heard the rustle of clothing behind her.

"You can turn around now."

Haroun was wrapped from ears to toes in the gray blanket.

"Sit down." She gathered his wet garments from the floor and spread them on the chair.

"You should not be waiting on me."

She smiled. "And you should not have swum out and clung to that anchor line. But, since you did, we must forget what is fitting and try to help each other to stay alive."

"You did not tell Lord Ware the truth in your note, did you?"

"No. I'm a hostage and so are you." She sat down on the bed. "But we don't want Lord Ware to know, do we? You know what danger he would face if he came after us."

He nodded. "That's why I told Robert nothing was amiss when I gave him the note."

"Good boy—man." Dear heaven, she was weary. She wanted only to lay her head down and go to sleep. "But while you're on board this ship, you must do nothing to anger Balkir's men. Stay out of their way."

"I will try."

Of course he would try. He seemed terrified of everyone connected with Sinan.

"I'm not usually a ... coward," he said, as if he had read her thoughts. "Lord Ware has trained me to be a warrior. He says I'm a good soldier. It's only ... all my life I've heard of the Old Man of the Mountain. His people are not as others. They are ... demons. One cannot fight demons."

"Don't be ridiculous. Kadar was once one of Sinan's people. Is he a demon?"

He shook his head. "But Lord Kadar is different. He walks alone."

"How many times have I seen you dicing together? He's your friend."

"Yes." He looked confused. "But he's ... different."

She gave up. Kadar was different. One had only to be with him for a short while to realize that beneath that light, charming facade lay impenetrable depths. "But you trust him?"

Haroun brightened. "Oh, yes."

"Then trust him to see that nothing happens to you at Maysef."

"I not only worry about myself. Great harm can befall a woman. I know you belong to Lord Kadar, but still the danger is—"

"I do *not* belong to Kadar."

"But everyone knows that you—" He saw her expression and added hurriedly, "But it seems you—"

"Everything is not always as it seems. I belong to no one but myself."

"But a woman must belong to someone. It is—" He sensed the storm approaching and changed the subject. "It does not matter. I will care for you."

She would probably be the one to have to care for him, but he meant well, so she resisted the impulse to tell him that. "Thank you, Haroun. If I'm in need of help, I will certainly—"

She stopped as the door opened and Kadar came into the cabin.

His gaze raked Haroun from head to foot. "Well, you look a pitiful sight."

"Lady Selene made me take off my clothes. You are not angry that I am with her like this? I told her it wasn't fitting."

"I'm not angry." He smiled. "She's hard to refuse, isn't she?"

He nodded, relieved. "And she has most strange ideas about...Even though she says she does not belong to you, I hope you will aid me in caring for her on this journey."

"Oh, is that what she says?" Kadar asked silkily. "I do hope you didn't make the mistake of believing her?"

"No, everyone knows—" He cast a glance at Selene. "I mean, everyone thinks that—"

"Enough." Selene was holding on to her temper by a thin thread. "What of Balkir? Are you sure Haroun's out of danger now?"

"As long as he doesn't make himself obtrusive."

"He can stay in this cabin with me."

"No!" Haroun's eyes were wide with horror.

Kadar shook his head. "That will make his position more tenuous. If the sailors think he could be getting favors they're being denied, they may throw him overboard. But there are only two cabins on board this ship, and one is occupied by Balkir." His gaze shifted to Haroun. "Suppose we sleep outside on deck in front of Lady Selene's cabin? Then anyone who tries to pass will have to go through us."

Haroun nodded vigorously. "Much wiser."

Of course he thought Kadar's plan was wiser than Selene's. They were both men. "Oh, go away, both of you." She lay down and closed her eyes. "I hope Balkir drowns you both."

"But then you would lack any protection at all. I realize you think us both unworthy at present, but we are good for something." Kadar clapped Haroun on the shoulder. "Come along. We'll try to find you something to wear besides that blanket. She may need it if the night grows cold." He opened the door. "I'll return in the morning, Selene."

She didn't answer and heard the door close behind them.

Go to sleep. Don't think of Kadar or this ship cleaving through the water on its way to Sinan.

Impossible. Now that she was alone and the need to act was gone, she could think of nothing else. She was shaking, she realized. Weakness. She was glad Kadar was no longer here to see it. She would be all right soon. She would sleep and grow stronger, and tomorrow she would be able to face Kadar with coolness and control.

Tomorrow . . .

# Chapter Four

THE NEXT MORNING, after a cursory knock, Kadar walked into the cabin. His arms were overflowing with garments. "Good day." He crossed the cabin and deposited his burden on the bunk. "I thought you'd need something to wear since Balkir gave you no opportunity to pack."

She wrinkled her nose as she picked up a mantle. "It stinks."

"I had to bargain with the sailors, and you may have noticed they're not overly clean. I'd hoped Balkir might have some female garments in the hold, since he also deals in piracy, but unfortunately there were none." He smiled. "But you're not unaccustomed to men's garments. Do you remember when I brought you from Constantinople? You insisted on riding your own horse and dressing like a young boy."

"I remember." It had been a great adventure, her first taste of freedom, and she had made the most of it. "But they didn't stink."

"Ah, a little seawater. I'll have Haroun fetch you a tub."

"How is he?"

"Not complaining about *his* stinking clothes, you ungrateful wench."

"What did you use to bargain for the clothes?"

"Another hour of life. It's a commodity of great value." His smile faded. "You didn't sleep well."

She should have realized he would recognize the signs. He knew her too well. "Of course I did."

He shook his head. "I almost came to you last night."

She stiffened.

"I assure you, I had other things on my mind than ravishment. Though we must talk about that as well."

"We don't have to talk about it. It's over."

He gestured impatiently. "It's not over. It's scarcely begun. It's just not the time to show you the way of it." He sighed. "As usual, you've distracted me. That's not why I was going to come to your cabin."

"You had no reason to come to me. I didn't need you."

"You did need me. We need each other. It's always been that way and it always will be." He reached out and gently touched her hair. "Reject me in every other way, but take comfort from me. I give it with my whole heart, and it hurts me to have you refuse."

She felt the familiar melting and steeled herself against it. "I don't want your comfort. I don't want anything from you."

He stared at her for a long moment. "And you care nothing that you hurt me." His lips tightened. "I know I made a mistake. I reached out and snatched when I should have been patient. But, by God, I've been patient for years. I'm no monk. You were there and willing, and I knew I was leaving and might not see you—for a long time."

"You were leaving," she repeated. "You knew you were going and still you took what I offered. Do I care that you took my body? It doesn't matter at all compared to you lying to me. If you truly cared for me, you would have found a way to take me with you wherever you went. I would never have left you. You preached of trust and then you didn't even tell me about Sinan."

"There's no use talking to you. You're not listening to me. Very well, then hug your anger close. Thrust me away. But when we reach Maysef, obey me. It may save all our lives." He started toward the door. "And while you're on this ship, stay in the cabin. If you want air, tell me and I'll escort you. Don't go among the sailors by yourself."

"I'm not a fool. I know men care for only one thing from a woman."

"Some men. If that's all I'd wanted from you, I would have bedded you years ago." He opened the door. "I'll send Haroun with food to break your fast."

The door closed behind him with a decisive force that was almost a slam. He was angry. Well, that was good. Anger would distance him. The faint unease she was feeling was just a lingering thread from that time when every breath he drew was important to her.

That time was no more.

"You summoned me?" Kadar asked.

"I'm going mad cooped up here." Selene glared at him. "I have nothing to do. Every hour of my day was filled at Montdhu. We've been four weeks on this ship. *When* will we arrive at Hafir?"

"Another two weeks perhaps. Haroun isn't proving entertaining? I sent you a chess set I borrowed from the good captain."

"He does his best. One cannot play chess every hour of the day." She scowled. "Besides, I win all the time."

"Poor Haroun. There are not many players your equal. I'd offer my services, but you made it clear you want none of my company." He arched a brow. "Unless you've changed your mind?"

"I've not changed my mind. But you play a fine game of chess. Why should I cheat myself? It's all your fault that I must endure this long, boring trip."

"And it's my duty to make it less boring." He bowed. "I recognize my responsibility. I'm at your service. Shall I get out the board?"

"No." She stood up. "I want to go on deck. I think I'm going to suffocate if I stay one more minute in this cabin."

"You could have called on me before this. I was waiting." He smiled. "Waiting for you seems to have become my life's vocation." He opened the door for her. "The sun is bright today. You should not stay out long."

She wanted the brightness. She drew the fresh salt air deep into her lungs and gazed contentedly at the sun's rays glancing off the blue of the sea. "I don't want to ever go in."

He took his burnoose from his head and plopped it on hers. "At least cover your head. That red hair is like a beacon, and you're attracting enough attention."

For the first time she noticed the glances she was receiving from the sailors. A little of her joy faded.

Kadar swiftly drew her to the rail and put himself between her and everyone else. "Look at the seagulls."

"How close are we to land?"

"You can see it on the horizon." He pointed. "That's Italy."

"Where the Pope lives."

"In Rome, yes."

"You went there last year to sell our silks."

He nodded. "Hard bargainers. I prefer dealing with the Spanish."

"I wanted to go with you. I wanted to see Rome and Naples. I wanted to see *everything*. You wouldn't take me."

"Perhaps I should have let you come." He grimaced. "As it happened, it all came down to the same thing anyway." His voice lowered. "If I had, I guarantee you wouldn't have been bored."

She felt the heat sting her cheeks. "You speak of coupling? I found it not so much. And one cannot couple for weeks at a time."

"One can but try," he murmured. "I think I know

enough variations to keep us entertained for that length of time. Did I tell you that as a boy in Damascus I once worked in a house of pleasure?"

Her eyes widened. "No, you did not."

"I probably thought it unfitting for your virgin ears. But you're no longer a virgin, are you? So I can tell you of Jebra, who spent more time on her knees than she did her back. Or of the tight kiss that can bring more pleasure than—"

"I'm not interested in this."

"Of course you are. You have a great zest for life, and you're curious as a cat about everything around you. But so far you've only stood back and watched." He smiled. "As I did at the house of pleasure for the first few months. Then I decided if there was a skill to be learned, I should apprentice myself wholeheartedly to the task. I found there were many paths both bright and dark to explore."

Bright *and* dark?

"Ah, that intrigues you." His gaze focused intently on her face. "If you like, I could lead you a little way on the dark path. Not too deep, or one can become—"

"No." She pulled her gaze away and drew a steadying breath. "I told you I didn't want to hear this."

"But I feel it my duty to distract you. Skimming the dark waters holds a fascination for most people. Don't worry, I'd hold you afloat. I'd never let you be pulled down."

"Bright path, dark path. It sounds like Sinan."

"Oh, no. It was all dark when I was with Sinan. He believed only in the dark pleasures. Far darker than any I practiced in Jebra's house."

She searched desperately for a way to shift the subject. "What task has Sinan set for you?"

"I don't know. I only promised to come when he needed me."

"You don't know? You agreed blindly?"

He shrugged. "I had to find a way to get him to let us go. It can be no worse than other things I've done in my life."

"It could be more dangerous."

"It probably is. Sinan always gets his price in any bargain."

And his price might very well be Kadar's blood. She stared blindly out at the sea. "You're such a fool."

"The better to keep you entertained." He was silent for a moment. "There's something you should know. Sinan will try to use you."

"He doesn't need me to make you do his bidding. You're all too willing."

"He'll still use you, if I can't prevent it. It's his nature to bend everyone to his will, and I don't bend. It's a battle that's waged between us for years. It's better if he believes you mean nothing to me." His lips twisted. "If I can fool him. It may not be possible. I've only known one man more clever."

"Who?" she asked curiously.

He shrugged. "Nasim. He was..." He searched for the right word. "Linked to Sinan."

She frowned. "I've never heard you speak of him."

"Because he doesn't matter. That was a long time ago." He switched back to the previous subject. "I think Sinan realized what you were to me all those years ago. He'll be pleased with Balkir for delivering you into his hands."

"He won't use me. I won't permit it."

"I hope you're right. I suppose it's foolish to ask you not to interfere?"

"Why should I interfere? You're the one who was idiot enough to promise to do his will. I wish only that Haroun and I are freed so that we may return to Montdhu. Be sure that is part of any bargain you make."

"I'll try. I can only promise that you'll both survive." He took her elbow. "Have you had enough air? I think we'd better go back to your cabin. That sailor aft has been eyeing you and edging closer for the past few moments. I don't want to be forced to toss him overboard."

She hadn't been aware of anything but their conversation, but Kadar had noticed. Kadar always knew everything that was going on around him. Sinan wasn't the only one who was uncanny. "I suppose I'm ready."

"Astonishing," Kadar murmured as he guided her back to the cabin. "Knowing how displeased you are with me, I thought surely you'd want to see me put to the trouble of ridding us of him."

"Sinan will give you enough trouble when we reach Maysef. He needs no help from me."


Sinan . . .

After Kadar had taken Selene back to her cabin, he returned to the rail to stare out at the sea. Selene's last remark had stirred the uneasiness that had been growing in him during these weeks on board the *Dark Star.*

Something was not as it should be. When he had spoken to the sailors casually of Sinan, they had frozen and then made excuses to bolt away from him.

And Balkir's slip of the tongue on the night of their departure. He had scarcely noticed it at the time, but it had evidently stuck in his memory.

*Nas—Sinan.*

Nasim?

The familiar chill swept over him at the unwelcome possibility.

But possibilities must be faced before they became realities that caught you by surprise.

He turned on his heel and strode to where Balkir stood at the front of the ship.


"There's something you should know," Kadar murmured as he helped Selene down the gangplank at Hafir. "It wasn't Sinan who sent the *Dark Star.*"

"What?" she asked, startled. "But it had to—"

"Sinan is dead. He died years ago."

Relief poured through her. She hadn't known until this moment how frightened she'd been of facing that evil old man again. Joy followed on the heels of relief as she realized that the threat that had dangled over Kadar's head all these years was gone. "Thank God."

"It may not be an occasion for rejoicing. Nasim sent Balkir to bring me here."

"Nasim?" He had mentioned Nasim, she recalled. "The man you said was linked to Sinan?"

He nodded. "Sheikh Jabbar Al Nasim."

"What do you mean, *linked*?"

"When one of Sinan's followers was deemed ready to walk the dark path, Sinan sent him to Nasim."

"Why?"

"Training."

"But I thought Sinan trained you."

"He did. Nasim's teaching was...different. Some called him a sorcerer. Sinan was able to go only so far. It's not easy to take the final step on the dark path or lead someone else to take it."

She didn't like this. It seemed impossible that anyone could be more threatening than Sinan, but Kadar's tone was making her uneasy. "He wasn't at Maysef when we were there."

"He has his own camp a day's journey away. He seldom came to Maysef except during the training or when he wanted something from Sinan." He paused. "And he always got what he wanted, Selene. I never saw Sinan yield to anyone but Nasim."

"And does he now lead Sinan's followers?"

He shook his head. "He was never interested in that kind of glory. He only wanted the power. According to Balkir, Nasim just comes and goes as he always did, watching the power struggles among Sinan's followers. He always stood apart."

"Then why does Balkir obey him?"

"He trained most of Sinan's assassins, and it's difficult to shrug off...I suppose the fear is still there. It's hard to describe the influence he wielded. He held absolute control over us." He stopped beside a small mare whose reins were held by one of Balkir's sailors.

"Don't be frightened. It will be all right. I just wanted to warn you."

Don't be frightened? He had just told her that this man was even more evil than Sinan, and he expected her to be calm about it? "What does he want of you?"

He shrugged. "I don't know. Balkir said he was only told to bring me and not to let me know Sinan was dead."

"I don't like it."

"Neither do I," Kadar said soberly. "Not at all."

The fortress of Maysef was everything Selene remembered it to be: the castle strong, stark, forbidding; the white-robed followers moving ghostlike about the courtyard and dim halls. She hadn't realized her memory of that first encounter was so clear and vivid.

"Wait here." Balkir dismounted from his horse. "I must go and make my report to the master. I will send for you if he wishes to see you."

"But Kadar never likes to wait." A man in a billowing black cloak stood on the top step, looking down at them. "So I came to greet him."

Kadar inclined his head. "Good day, Nasim."

"It is a good day now. I've been waiting a long time."

Selene suppressed a shudder as she saw Nasim's fierce gaze fasten on Kadar like the talons of an eagle. Why, she was afraid of this man. She hadn't been afraid of Sinan, though she supposed she should have been. But this man . . . The menace and power that surrounded him were nearly visible. Nasim was clearly an old man. His face was deeply lined and his dark hair, tied back in a queue, was white at the temples. But his eyes glittered with an almost feverish vitality that defied age.

Kadar didn't seem afraid. He said lightly, "It's the least you could do after I've come such a long distance at your request."

"Command."

"Request," Kadar repeated with a smile. "I no longer obey commands, Nasim."

"Brave words. It's deeds that count. You don't seem surprised that it's I who summoned you." His glance shifted to Balkir.

The captain flinched and said hurriedly, "He guessed, but not until we were almost here. I didn't tell him. He already knew when he came to me and—"

"You have the brains of an ox." Nasim's gaze shifted to Selene. "Who is this?"

"The lady Selene," Balkir said. "It was necessary that I—"

"You have bold eyes," Nasim said. "Too bold for a woman."

"Lower your eyes," Balkir muttered.

She would *not* lower her eyes.

"Why is she here, Balkir?" Nasim didn't wait for an answer. "Your choice, Kadar?"

"No, a mistake on the part of the captain," Kadar said. "She'll only be in the way."

"He couples with her," Balkir said quickly. "I saw him."

"And did you see anything but conflict between us other than that one unimportant act?"

"I thought she might prove useful." Balkir's desperate gaze was fixed on Nasim. "But if it displeases you, I will dispose of her."

"Why do that?" Kadar asked. "Send her back to Montdhu with the boy. It will pacify Lord Ware and prevent the possibility of him coming after her."

"Boy?"

Balkir jerked his head in the direction of Haroun behind him. "He's Lord Ware's servant. Shall I dispose of them, Lord Nasim?"

Nasim's glance moved from Selene to Kadar and then back again. "I think not. One never knows when dross may turn into gold. Find them chambers." He turned to Kadar. "Come with me. We will talk."

Kadar nodded. "The sooner, the better." He deliberately avoided looking at Selene as he dismounted and climbed the steps. "Get them food, Balkir. It's been hours since they broke their fast. We don't want them sent back to Lord Ware in poor condition."

"If we send them back." Nasim entered the castle with Kadar following closely behind.

"Come. Quickly," Balkir tossed over his shoulder to Selene. "You heard the master."

Selene slipped from the saddle.

Haroun immediately sidled next to her. He was trembling, his gaze fixed fearfully on the castle. "Don't worry, I'll protect you."

"I know you will." She didn't know any such thing. She hadn't expected to be this shaken. "But the danger is not great. I think this Nasim is bluffing."

"You do?" Haroun asked uncertainly.

She didn't believe that cold devil ever bluffed, but

there was no use alarming Haroun. She followed Balkir up the steps. "Of course he was. You saw that Kadar was not afraid of him."

"But Lord Kadar is—They seem . . . alike."

She whirled on him. "They are *not* alike," she said fiercely. "They are nothing alike."

He took a step back. "I beg pardon, Lady Selene. I meant no—"

"It's all right." She tried to steady her voice. She shouldn't have exploded like that. Haroun's words had provoked a response that had come out of nowhere.

She was lying. She had merely blinded herself. She hadn't wanted to see what Haroun had seen. She had hoped that time and distance would bring about a change that had not happened. As she had watched Kadar and Nasim, the tethers that bound them together had been almost visible. The bond between the band of assassins and Kadar was still there.

"I didn't mean that Lord Kadar—I spoke without thinking," Haroun said.

"I know." She walked quickly up the stairs. Haroun's remark had been spurred by pure instinct, and sometimes instinct was more revealing than thought.

And far more frightening.

"You may sit in my presence, Kadar." Nasim gestured to a cushioned divan. "Your journey must have wearied you."

Kadar shook his head. "I'm not tired."

"No, you're young and strong," Nasim said impassively. "Your years in that cold land didn't weaken you."

"Did you expect them to?"

"One cannot tell what will happen when one walks the bright path. Strength sometimes becomes dissipated. The dark path always keeps its force."

"Does it?"

"Do you doubt my words?" Nasim lashed out. "Then you're a fool. Shall I show you my—" He drew a deep breath. "You always manage to anger me. But I will forgive you since I rejoice that you are here."

"And why am I here?"

"Because this is where you belong."

"Not any longer. Sinan is dead, and that severs my last tie."

Nasim shook his head. "I claim the service you promised him."

Kadar was not surprised. "By what right?"

Nasim's smile was cold. "By the only right that we both recognize. Power."

Kadar shook his head.

"I could have had Balkir attack the castle at Montdhu. I held my hand, but I can still send him back. Don't be hasty in refusing me. My temper is short these days."

Kadar could sense the raw turmoil just beneath the surface, and it surprised him. The Nasim he remembered had always been ice cold and controlled. "And what task do you have for me?"

"I wish you to fetch me a treasure beyond price."

"What treasure?"

Nasim shook his head. "I will tell you more when it's time for you to start your journey. I sent a messenger to verify that the treasure still exists in the same place. When Fadil returns, you will set out and bring it to me."

Kadar frowned. "When do you expect him to return?"

"A week...perhaps two." He shrugged. "If Fadil lives. He may not."

"And you wish me to wait here?"

"Ah, you're so anxious to be on your way. I'm the one who should be impatient." Nasim lifted a brow. "There are other tasks you can do for me. I'm sure we will find something interesting for you to do while you're here. I already have a few ideas."

"What ideas?"

"I leave that to your imagination. You have a superb imagination, Kadar. Use it." He waved a dismissing hand. "I'll summon you when I decide it's time that you do my bidding."

"I've not said I'll do your bidding, Nasim."

"That is true." He smiled. "The child Selene has become a woman, hasn't she? I remember Sinan telling me about her when she was here before."

Kadar affected indifference. "I wouldn't think he would bother to confide something so unimportant."

"You know Sinan told me everything. I decided what was unimportant. How was she at coupling, Kadar?"

He stiffened. "Ordinary."

"She is too bold to be ordinary." Nasim turned his back and walked over to the window. "You may go."

Kadar stared at his back for a moment longer. By God, he didn't want to go and leave this conversation unresolved. He knew Nasim had deliberately dropped Selene into the conversation hoping to destroy his composure. He had succeeded.

"Sinan told me he wanted to sample her when she was a child and you stopped him," Nasim said.

"She was ordinary then. She's ordinary now. Beneath his notice." He paused. "And beneath your notice."

"We will see. I will think upon it." Nasim's tone held a note of finality.

Kadar had heard that tone many times before. There was no use trying to speak to him any more right now. He turned on his heel and left the chamber.

"What does he want of you?" Selene asked as soon as Kadar walked into her bedchamber.

"He didn't tell me. I only know it involves a journey to bring him a great treasure, a treasure beyond price. He's waiting for a messenger. He said it may be a week or two before he gets word."

"A treasure beyond price," Selene repeated. "What would that devil consider beyond price?"

Kadar shrugged. "I have no idea, but whatever it is, he wants it badly."

"And we have to stay here?"

He nodded.

Her hands clenched into fists. "Is there nothing we can do?"

"Escape?" He shook his head. "I must do the task he sets me, or everything I won from him will be lost."

"And you hate to lose."

"So do you. Particularly when it affects the people you love." He crossed to the window and looked down at the courtyard below. "I must stay with you in this chamber. It's not safe for you to be alone."

She stiffened.

"Don't fight me on this. We've shared a chamber before and for the same reason." His tone was abstracted. "I'll make a pallet on the floor."

"It's necessary?"

"Without question."

"Then, of course, I'll permit it."

"I won't inflict my presence on you overmuch. Nasim will allow me the freedom of the fortress and the countryside."

"But not me or Haroun." It was a statement.

"Haroun can be allowed limited freedom. It's not safe for you to leave the chamber."

But Kadar would be wandering among these assassins and would often be in Nasim's presence. The thought chilled her. She said lightly, "You need not think I will permit you to abandon me. I will not suffer boredom here any more than I would on the *Dark Star.* You must entertain me."

He smiled faintly. "Oh, must I?"

"Yes, and I need something else to wear. I'm weary of these rough garments. Fetch me cloth and needle and thread. And I may wish you to help me with them."

"You want *me* to sew?"

"Are you too proud?"

"Pride? I've set myself to humbler tasks, but I find it unusual you would require my aid."

She shrugged. "You are here. You might as well help."

"Anything else?"

"Not now. Perhaps later."

"I'll journey forth immediately on the quest." He turned and headed for the door. "Bolt the door and open it only to me."

She leaned her forehead against the wood of the door after she had bolted it behind him. Everything was going amiss. She had meant to keep Kadar at a distance, but she had been forced to draw him closer. Well, it was only for the short time she was here.

She would *not* let that evil man have Kadar.

# Chapter Five

"SWEET MARY," Kadar swore softly as he stabbed the needle viciously through the soft muslin. "You will not be able to wear this gown. It's stained with the blood of a thousand pinpricks."

"It's brown." Selene bent to stir the fire in the hearth before settling back on her stool. "The blood will hardly show at all."

He scowled at her. "I have no liking for this task. Why must we sew in the evening as well? I might survive if I could see what I was doing."

"The fire gives adequate light. We've only completed one gown. I need another."

His gaze suddenly lifted from the cloth. "Do you? I think not."

"Why else would I go to this bother? Do you think

I like hearing you curse and moan over a little pin-prick?"

"A *little* pinprick? My fingers are—" He paused. "Very clever. You almost distracted me." He set aside the cloth and linked his arms around his knees. "You don't need another gown. You wish to keep me with you."

"Nonsense. Your vanity is out of all bounds."

He looked at her, waiting.

"Why should I wish to keep you with me? You curse and moan and I must show you stitches that a babe would learn in the cradle."

"You're trying to annoy me." He smiled. "But I would never be so ungallant as to show anger to my savior."

"Savior? I don't know what you mean."

"We've never talked about it, but you know. You've always been my savior." His gaze shifted to the flames. "It's so easy to walk the dark path. Easy and exciting. And once you've tried it, you always want to go back. It's like the first scent of hashish. You want more."

"But you didn't want more. You left here."

"Because I didn't want to be like Nasim. I could see myself being drawn deeper and deeper.... Life has never treated me with any particular kindness, and I *liked* the idea of the power Sinan and Nasim wielded."

"Nasim is evil."

"Yes, but then, so am I. Most men have a wicked streak."

"You're not evil. You may be witless and unfair, but you're not like him."

"Part of me is. But I can control it, if I have reason

to fight him." His gaze shifted from the fire to stare directly into her eyes. "You give me reason, Selene."

His dark hair shimmered in the firelight, and his eyes...

Dear God, she was melting. She wanted to reach out and touch him.

She would not be drawn like this. She would not be hurt again.

She tore her gaze away. "Then find another reason. I won't be responsible for your virtue or lack of it."

"You can't help yourself." He smiled. "Why else am I here suffering grievous wounds? You don't trust me enough to let me out of your sight."

"I can help myself. I just choose to—Haroun and I have no one else in this horrible place. It's only sensible to—Don't laugh at me." She threw the gown at his head.

"Ouch." He pulled the gown from around his face and gingerly touched the scratch on his cheek. "You could have removed the pins."

"Go away. Go to that hideous old man and walk your dark path. What do I care? I don't want to see you—"

He was heading for the door. Panic raced through her.

"Wait." She struggled for words. "You cannot leave with this gown half finished. I won't—"

"Shh." He smiled at her, his warm, beautiful smile. "I'm not going to Nasim. I'm going to take a walk in the courtyard. I'll return before the hour has gone."

She tried to hide her relief. "It's nothing to me where you go."

"My God, you're stubborn." He sighed. "Sometimes I wish you were not quite as strong as you are. It would make my lot much easier."

She didn't feel strong. She was shaken. He had never spoken to her of his past and his struggles before. Seeing beyond that cool, mocking facade made him seem infinitely closer. She didn't want him closer. "If you're going for a walk, do it." She snatched up the gown again and began to stitch. "Don't come back tonight. I won't have you waking me up."

The night was clear and cool, and a full moon cast a silver luminescence on the gray stones of the courtyard. It was the kind of night Kadar had hated when he had been in training here. It was difficult to move with the deadly invisibility Nasim required on such an evening, and failure was met with swift and brutal punishment. But he had learned; moonlight merely meant adjustments, distractions, and a—

"So she released you from woman's duties?"

Kadar turned to see Nasim coming toward him. "I released myself." He wasn't surprised Nasim knew what transpired behind a closed chamber door. Nasim made it his business to be aware of everything that happened. "I felt in need of air."

"Why do you let her dishonor you in this way?"

"To learn a new skill is never a dishonor. It may be useful later."

"You wish to make more gowns for women?" Nasim asked contemptuously as he fell into step with him.

"No, but sewing a gown requires the same skill as stitching a wound." He glanced at Nasim. "What do you want?"

"Perhaps I also need air."

"Then you would go to the battlements, as you usually do. I'd wager you saw me down here and decided to join me. Why?"

"I feel you're wasting my time," he said bluntly. "You're here to do me service and you spend your time with that woman, stitching."

"We'll discuss service when your messenger arrives. Have you heard from him?"

"No, but we'll discuss service now. I want your promise."

Kadar shook his head.

"You'll give me the service you promised Sinan, and for the same reason." Nasim smiled maliciously. "If you don't, you'll find your friends in Scotland most uncomfortable. I'll have to decide whether to raze their castle myself or send the Knights Templar to do it for me. Do you doubt I'd do either?"

"No."

"Then give me your word."

"You always told me lies were the weapon of a clever man."

"But it's one lesson you never learned. You don't break your word, and I want that chain on you. Give me your word or I'll send Balkir and a force to Montdhu at dawn."

The bastard meant it. He had no choice. "Very well, you have my promise to do *one* task for you."

"I thought you'd agree." He smiled. "And I've

thought of a useful and amusing way for you to serve me while we wait."

"I promised only one service."

"Oh, I believe you'll accommodate me in this." He gazed up at the sky. "It's a full moon tonight, a good sign. The soothsayers say a full moon brings fertile earth and good crops."

"You don't care about good crops. You make tribute."

"True. But I've become very interested in fertility of late. It comes as a surprise to me." His gaze remained on the night sky. "Sinan wished you to follow him as master here, you know. We discussed it often. I approved his plan. It would be stimulating to control you as I did Sinan. It would only take a word from me and you'd slide into your place as head of the assassins."

"It holds no interest for me. It's too limiting."

"You lie. But you're stubborn. You could yet go your own way."

"You may count on it."

"I count on nothing that doesn't please me. Still, I must take precautions. Men do die."

"No one should know that better than you."

Nasim chuckled. "Yes, I've made a study of death. A master should be able to pass such knowledge on to one worthy. I've found no such acolyte but you, Kadar." His smile faded. "So I've decided you shall provide me with another."

"And how am I to do that?" he asked warily.

"The woman." Nasim frowned. "Though she's displeased me by yoking you to needle and thread. It's an insult to me."

"It has nothing to do with you. There's no connection."

"Everything you do is connected to me. Because I choose it to be so." He paused. "That's why you will bring the woman to the tower every night for the next two weeks."

Kadar went still. "I told you that she was ordinary, beneath you."

"She must be very ordinary, since you sleep on the floor instead of in her bed."

"She doesn't interest me."

"She interests me. She's bold, and it's always exciting to break the bold ones." He smiled. "But I fear you must develop interest in her. It's you who will couple with her."

"Why?"

"I want a child by her. Your child."

Kadar inhaled sharply. "What madness is this?"

"I cannot sire children. I've tried several bitches, but nothing has come of it." He lifted his chin. "It has nothing to do with my manhood. I've decided that, when a man is given special powers to wield, Allah sometimes does not see fit to let him perform as other men. But that doesn't mean I can't have what I want. If I cannot have you to mold, I'll take a substitute."

"I've no desire to get her with child."

"Ah, yes, she has no interest for you. Still, it will happen."

Nasim had made up his mind, Kadar realized with frustration, and it was never any use to argue with him when he had made a decision. He would have to try to work around it. "If you wish me to sire a babe, send a whore to the tower room. At least she would have the skill to amuse me."

"Our whores are lacking in spirit. The foreign woman has the boldness I want."

"You detest her boldness."

"In a woman, not in a child she would birth."

He tried another tactic. "It could be a female child. What would you do then?"

"Kill it. I have no use for bitches. But you would not father females, Kadar. We are too much alike."

"I don't *want* this woman."

"You will. Remember the tower room, Kadar?"

Kadar's gaze went to the tower. Yes, he remembered it. The sweet smell of hashish, naked bodies on silk cushions, the ultimate in acts of debauchery. He felt himself hardening, thickening at the memory.

"You see?" Nasim smiled maliciously. "It will happen."

That was what he feared. "And what will happen if I refuse?"

"Then she will still bear a child, but it will be by one of my men who is far less worthy. In fact, I may have to set a different man between her thighs every night and let fate decide who will father it. Do you think your Lord Ware would take her back after a month of such treatment?"

"What if she's not fertile? Am I to delay going on your mission to couple with a mere woman?"

Nasim's smile disappeared. "Nothing will be permitted to delay you. When the message comes, you will go. I've waited too long already." He turned and stalked across the courtyard. "The tower. Tomorrow, at nightfall."

Kadar watched him until he disappeared into the castle. God's blood, Nasim couldn't have chosen to put him in a worse quandary. Selene was striving to distance herself from him, and he was to go to her and say they must couple until a child was conceived? She would throw more than a gown at him.

Dammit, and just when he had begun to see slight signs of softening in her.

But there was no hint of softness in him at the moment; he was rock hard, and a dark excitement was beginning to build. It was exactly the response Nasim wanted. But he wished he could be as sure of Nasim's motives as he was of his manipulations. Did he really want an acolyte of Kadar's blood, or did he want to pull Kadar deeper into the dark morass? In the past, sexual excess had been offered as a stimulus and a reward, and Kadar had reveled in it. Nasim would remember that fact as he remembered everything else. It was a potent weapon he would not hesitate to wield.

Kadar's gaze lifted again to the tower.

*The tower. Tomorrow, at nightfall.*


"I'll not do it." Selene jumped to her feet, stung. "I won't be a slave and do that man's bidding. I'll never be a slave again."

"I've told you the consequences of refusing. You'll admit I'm the least offensive of the alternatives."

Kadar grimaced. "Or maybe you won't. But I swear this is not by my design."

She knew it was not. Kadar might attempt seduction, but he would never force her to his bed. The realization did nothing to abate her anger. "He expects me to bear your child and then hand it over to him? Is he mad to believe I'd do such a thing?"

"He would take it—if it was a boy. If it was a girl, he would kill it."

Shock surged through her. "You're so calm. You accept this."

He shook his head. "I'm calm because I would never accept it. It will not happen. No child of mine will ever be subject to Nasim's will."

A little of her anger ebbed away. "Then how will we prevent it?"

"I don't have the answer yet. We may not have to prevent it. Two weeks isn't a long time. Many women do not get with child immediately."

"It took Thea years." Another wave of anger hit her. "It makes no *sense*. He's an old man. He may not even live to raise a child."

"The child may not really be his aim."

"What do you mean?"

He shrugged. "He knows the tower will bring back memories of the old life. He knows that I don't treat you as other women. If he forces me to treat you in that manner in that chamber, it will be a victory for him. He may think it will draw me farther along the dark path."

"Dear God, he's a devil," she whispered.

"Yes."

"And I'm to be the pawn in this battle between you." Her eyes blazed at him. "I *won't* be a pawn. I won't do this."

"Very well. Then at nightfall tomorrow, we won't go to the tower."

"And what will happen?"

"He'll send a man to get you and I'll kill him. He'll send two and I'll kill them too." He added quietly, "But I cannot fight all of them, Selene. Eventually they will kill me."

"Nasim wouldn't let that happen."

"Perhaps they'd not mean to kill me, but I'm very good. They'd have to kill me to take you against your will."

He meant it. "No, you should let them take me. Coupling is nothing. It would bring them no victory."

"Perhaps not." He added simply, "But I could not bear it."

And he would die trying to prevent it, she realized in agony. "Is there no way to stop this? What if we go to the tower room and do nothing?"

He shook his head. "There's a peephole in the chamber next door that allows Nasim to observe when he wishes."

"How do you know?"

"I've watched too. Many times. Sometimes watching is exciting."

Heat stung her cheeks as she envisioned Kadar's gaze on naked, writhing—"You're as depraved as that wicked old man," she said tartly.

"In this, I may have been more depraved. That's why he wants to lure me back to the sport."

"Sport? With women as prey?"

He swore softly, "What do you wish me to say? Yes, I was hunter and women were prey. But I've never treated you as prey."

"But Nasim hopes you will."

"Of course, and I won't lie to you. I don't know how I'll use you if you agree to Nasim's demand. It's too easy to lose control in the tower room."

"And satisfy that hideous man?"

"And satisfy myself. I probably wouldn't be aware of Nasim or anyone else." He fell to his knees and curled up on his pallet on the floor. "There's no value in talking any more. I've given you your choice. Think about it and give me your decision in the morning."

Choice? What choice? Kadar's death or letting him have her body. She slipped into bed, pulled her gown over her head, and tossed it on the floor. Not only letting him have her body but having that loathsome old man watching them...

Her gaze went to Kadar on the hearth. His eyes were closed, but he was not asleep. She always knew when slumber took him from her.

*Took him from her.*

The thought had come out of nowhere. No one could take what was not hers, and she had rejected him. Thinking of Kadar in that manner was merely habit. They were not joined. She belonged only to herself, and so did he.

But if she went to the tower room, they would be joined in body if not in spirit. He would enter her as he did on that last night at Montdhu. He would touch her and ignite that odd, searing excitement.

But that excitement had not lasted long, and when he had left her body she was still Selene. The world had not changed because they had coupled.

But the world could change if Kadar was killed because she would not couple with him. If it meant so little, why was she refusing?

Because she feared getting closer to him in any manner, feared that the bond she had broken would mend itself. Well, then she would have to reinforce the barriers she had raised, because she could not face the alternative.

"Kadar."

"Yes."

"I will go with you to the tower room."

She saw his muscles stiffen, but he made no response.

"But it must stop as soon as we see a way out."

"What if you decide you don't want it to stop?"

"I won't do that."

He turned his back to her. "Tell me that after a week in the tower room."

The smell was sweet, musky, vaguely familiar, and coming from the tower room. Selene paused before she reached the top step. "What is that scent?"

"Hashish. Do you know what it is?"

"It smells...familiar."

"It should. Nicholas offered me hashish when I was at the House of Silk. He smoked it on occasion. It's said to relax and heighten sensation."

"Did you take it?"

"No, I was there to buy you. I had to keep my wits, and I knew what hashish could do to a man." He stopped before the heavy oak door. "Nasim keeps it burning in a copper brazier here. You cannot help but breathe it in. It's not as potent as smoking it from a pipe, but it will affect you."

"How?"

"It relaxes, increases sensuality, makes everything more vivid." He looked down at her. "Are you ready to go in?"

"No." Her hand was shaking as she reached past him and opened the door. "But I won't be any better later." She walked into the chamber. "If it must be done, let's do it and get it over."

The chamber was round and surprisingly luxurious compared to the austerity of the rest of the castle. Only two candles lit the dimness of the room, but she could see richly patterned rugs warming the coldness of the stone floor; a tapestry portraying a lion hunt in the desert occupied the wall across from the door, and two divans heaped with silk pillows were set facing each other in the center of the room. "It doesn't look like a room that belongs in this castle." Her gaze was drawn to the far corner and the large copper brazier Kadar had mentioned. "I think I'm getting used to it. I don't smell it anymore."

"I do." He reached out and unfastened her cloak. It slipped from her shoulders to the floor. "Undress."

She stood unmoving. "Is he watching us?"

He was swiftly disrobing. "Probably."

"From where?"

"The tapestry. The lion's eyes."

She wheeled to face the tapestry. In the dimness she couldn't discern anything but an outline of the lion. "Are you sure he's there?"

"No, but I'm sure he'll be there sometime tonight."

Nasim was there, watching. Now she could see a moist glittering where the lion's eye should be. The helplessness she felt suddenly changed to fury. She would not let him win this victory. "I don't care. Do you hear me, Nasim? I'm not doing this because you force me. This is by *my* will." She pulled her gown over her head and kicked off her sandals. "I feel no shame. The shame is yours. Watch all you please, you foul old man."

"Selene." Kadar was behind her. His hands fell on her naked shoulders. Warm, hard hands that sent a shock through her.

She whirled and buried her head in his chest. The dark triangle of hair felt springy against her cheek. "I hate this," she whispered. "He makes me so angry I want to punch a stick through that tapestry right into his eye."

"Ignore him." He lifted her head and looked into her eyes. "Or show him that he truly has no power over this."

"Of course he does. I was lying."

"Then make it truth." His head lowered slowly until he was only an inch away. His tongue touched her lower lip. "Help me and I promise you'll forget he's watching."

Her lip felt strange under the warm moistness of his tongue; heavy, swollen. Her breasts, pressed against him, were beginning to feel the same heaviness. "What do you want me to do?"

"Be at ease. Relax." He pulled her closer, his hands sliding around to knead her back. "It will be easier if you—"

"You're not relaxed." She could feel his arousal pressing against her, hard, demanding.

"I don't have to be. You'll recall, it's vitally necessary that I'm not."

His hands slipped down to cup her buttocks. "I'm going to lift you. Put your limbs about my hips."

"Why—" She instinctively clasped him with her legs as he sank deep within her. Her eyes closed and she lost her breath. The sensation was tight, stretched, hot. "What a peculiar—" He was walking. She grabbed hold of him. "Where are—"

"Here." He pressed her back against the tapestry. "Nasim can't see here. Only straight ahead."

Nasim. She should be grateful he couldn't see, but she couldn't seem to think. She was only aware of Kadar inside her and the soft tapestry against her buttocks.

And then she was aware of nothing but sensation, as Kadar began to lunge in and out of her with frantic force.

*Need. More. Move.*

She was making soft, frantic cries deep in her throat as the fever grew.

He reached between them, his thumb seeking, finding.

Her teeth bit into his shoulder to stifle a scream as his thumb pressed, teased, rotated. "Ah, you like it?"

She couldn't answer. The muscles of her belly were tensing and releasing with every movement, and the tension was mounting, growing.

"Kadar, it's—"

"I know." His hand left her and he was driving harder, faster. "Let it go," he said through his teeth.

"I'm trying, but I don't know if—"

Release. More fiery and climactic than anything that had gone before. She clutched him tighter. Tears streamed down her face.

"Good," he gasped. "Oh, God." He plunged to the quick.

She was vaguely aware of him shuddering, flexing within her, as she desperately held on to him.

His chest was laboring as he fought for breath. "Are you all right? Did I—hurt you?"

She didn't know if she was all right or not. She felt as if she had been through a storm that had uprooted everything she knew and tossed it to the winds.

"Selene?"

"Not hurt. I'm—It was—"

"Hush. It will be fine soon." He left her body and shifted his hold. He was carrying her toward the divan.

Softness beneath her. Kadar beside her, cradling her.

"Before it was pleasant," she whispered. "That was not—pleasant. It felt—I was not myself. I didn't know it would be like that."

"No, *pleasant* isn't the word. Much too tame." He brushed his lips across hers. "But I think your pleasure was as intense as mine."

Yes, it had been pleasure, she realized. The sensation had been so intense that it had been hard to identify. "Will it be like that again? Is that what you feel all the time?"

"The pleasure is deeper with you." He cupped her breast. "But it will be like that again every time."

"Then I can see why you rutted with every woman in Scotland."

He chuckled. "I'm glad for your understanding." He bent and ran his tongue over her nipple. "But I fear you've spoiled me for other women."

Her breast was swelling beneath his touch and she could feel a tingling between her thighs. "Are we going to—"

"Soon. But the urgency is gone." His fingers were delving between her thighs. "I thought we'd play a little first."

"Play?" At Nicholas's there was no play. The coupling she had watched was quick, brutal, and then the man left the house of women as if his partner no longer existed. "What are you going to—"

She arched upward with a cry as his fingers entered her and began to move. "You see?" Kadar whispered. "Play, Selene."


"You're very good at this," Selene said drowsily as she cuddled closer. "I believe I approve of your apprenticeship at that house in Damascus."

"I'm glad." He brushed the top of her head with his lips. "At least one episode in my iniquitous past meets with your approval."

"But just because I liked it doesn't mean anything has changed. It merely makes this...tolerable."

"Very tolerable."

"Are you laughing at me?"

"I wouldn't presume."

A sudden thought struck her. Nasim. She had completely forgotten him. She glanced beyond Kadar's shoulder at the tapestry. "Is he still there?"

"No, not for hours."

She was indifferent, she realized in surprise. Kadar was right; by not allowing Nasim to matter, they had won a victory.

"How do you know?"

"I always feel when he's near."

That terrible dark bonding between them. "When we were coupling?"

"No, not then." He chuckled. "I feel nothing but you."

"That's good." She relaxed against him again. "Should we go now?"

"Not until dawn. Are you not comfortable?"

Too comfortable. She was enveloped in a lazy haze of contentment. Strange to remember how nervous and fearful she had been when they opened that door those many hours ago. "Is it that hashish that makes me feel so happy?"

"Partly." His arm tightened around her. "Only partly."

He meant it was also because they were together. She shook her head. "It doesn't change—"

"Hush." Two fingers touched her lips. "Rest now. I

wish to show you one more road to pleasure before we leave here."

"Another? I didn't dream there were so many."

"Did I forget to tell you of the whore from India who claimed that there were over a hundred ways of pleasure?"

"I think she lied. It's not possible." She yawned. "And I'm too tired."

"Then sleep." His voice was a deep, soothing murmur in her ear. "I'll wake you at dawn."

She nodded, nestling her cheek against his shoulder.

"Or before." He whispered, "For she did not lie, Selene."

# Chapter Six

"YOU LOOK...ROBUST." Haroun tilted his head, studying her.

"Do I?" Selene moved her bishop.

"You have fine color. I cannot see how this foul place can so agree with you."

The "fine" color deepened. "It does not agree with me. I hate it."

"So do I."

She glanced up from the chessboard. "Has it been very hard for you these last weeks?"

"Not hard. You are kind, and Lord Kadar lets me go riding with him every day." He bit his lower lip. "But it's an evil place. I wish we could go home to Montdhu."

Poor Haroun. Why had she not noticed his distress and been more sympathetic?

Foolish question. She had been aware of little going on around her. It was as if during the day she existed in a silken cocoon, sewing, spending time with Haroun, and... waiting.

Waiting for the moment when Kadar would hold out his hand and they would walk up the curving stairs.

When she would shed her gown and go into his arms.

When he would show her another way to pleasure.

"Lady Selene," Haroun prompted, gazing at her in puzzlement. Oh, God, she must look as weak-kneed and meltingly soft as she felt. She hurriedly lowered her gaze to the chessboard.

"Your move."

"I already moved."

"Oh, I see you did." What was wrong with her? She felt as if she were seeing, feeling everything through a veil.

Everything but Kadar.


Kadar was holding out his hand.

"We should talk," she said.

"Later. It's almost nightfall."

Nightfall. The tower. Pleasure.

Instinctively she rose to her feet.

He took her hand. "Come."

He was smiling, but she could feel the tension in his body. It was as strong as the tension that gripped her own. Her breasts were swelling and the tingling between her thighs was beginning, although he had done nothing but touch her hand. Sometimes no touch at all was needed. He would look at her and she would be swept away in a storm of sensuality and anticipation.

This was not good. She must force herself to think as well as feel. "I don't see you anymore during the day. Where do you go?"

"Anywhere." They began to climb the steps. "Away from you."

"Why?"

"I find I cannot draw the line at the tower. I can think of little else except coupling. You have to have some rest."

She lost her breath. "I do not think this...healthy. I've never—Is it Nasim or the hashish?"

He shook his head. "It is the two of us. I always knew it would be this way."

"It's madness," she whispered. She added haltingly, "I can think of little else either. Body should not rule the mind. It must stop."

"Tomorrow." He opened the door of the tower room. "We'll talk about it tomorrow."

Hashish.

Silk.

Mellow candlelight falling on the divan where they took pleasure.

"Yes." She slowly moved into the chamber. "To-morrow."

He smiled. "After all, it's only pleasure. What harm can—My God."

Her gaze followed his to the divan. "What is it?"

"Nasim."

A slender whip with leather thongs lay on the soft cushions.

Kadar walked slowly toward the divan.

"Why is it here?" she whispered.

He didn't answer. He reached down and picked up the whip.

"Kadar."

"Get out of here," he said through clenched teeth.

"Why? What do you mean?"

He whirled toward the tapestry. "By God, *no*, Nasim."

He hurled the whip at the tapestry.

The next moment he had grabbed her arm and pushed her toward the door. "Out."

The door slammed behind them and he half-pulled, half-pushed her down the curving staircase. He was cursing softly, venomously.

"What's happening?"

He paid no attention to her.

She stopped at the foot of the steps. "I'll not go another step. Tell me."

He drew a deep breath, struggling for control. "We weren't proving amusing enough to Nasim. He wanted me to use the whip on you."

"He wanted to punish me?"

"He didn't—It's a form of coupling."

"What?"

"Sometimes pain increases the intensity."

She stared at him, shocked. "For you?"

"I've never liked it. Even with a woman who did."

"I cannot believe anyone would like it. As a child I felt the whip often and—"

"I know. Just believe me. Some women do like it."
He pushed her toward the door to her chamber. "Lock
the door. I'm going to talk to Nasim."

She remembered the rage with which he had
hurled the whip. "He'll be angry with you."

"Yes." He gave her a nudge. "Go on."

An angry Nasim would be formidable, and Kadar
would bear the brunt of his displeasure. "I'll let you
do it."

"What?"

She tried to smile. "It won't be the first time I've
been beaten. It is nothing. I've enjoyed everything
else you've done to me; perhaps this will not be so—"

"No." He took a step closer and cupped her face in
his hands. He looked down at her with a tenderness
that took her breath away. He kissed her forehead.
"Absolutely not." He dusted a kiss on the tip of her
nose. "Never."

Before she could respond, he turned and walked
away.

"You treated me with disrespect," Nasim snapped as
soon as Kadar walked into the hall. "I should have
your throat cut from ear to ear."

"But then you'd have no one to accomplish your
task."

"I wanted to see how she'd respond to the whip."

"And I had no desire to use it on her."

"I *want* it."

"No." He held Nasim's gaze. "I've done everything
else you've asked. I won't do this."

For a moment Kadar thought Nasim would persevere, but then Nasim shifted his glance and shrugged. "It is of no importance. I just thought it would be amusing. You've done everything else to her."

"I don't find it amusing."

"But you find her amusing," Nasim said. "She is... remarkable. You lied when you said she was of no interest."

"Every woman is of interest in the tower room."

"Hashish? I think not." He smiled. "Do you think you've gotten her with child?"

"How should I know? It's been only a fortnight, and she tells me it's not time for her flux." Kadar changed the subject. "And no word from your messenger Fadil?"

"Not yet."

"Will he come by sea?"

"Yes." He arched a brow. "You're so eager to start your journey?"

"A man grows bored without a challenge."

"Particularly you, Kadar. You always needed to find new ways to negotiate old paths. However, this challenge may prove too much for you."

"But it will be worth it." He smiled. "A treasure beyond price."

Nasim frowned. "My treasure. Don't forget. *My* treasure."

"I'm sure you'll find a way to remind me." He turned to leave. "In the meantime, I'll not return to the tower room. My mind must be clear and I need rest for the journey."

"It's true you've been very strenuously occupied."

Nasim chuckled. "Very well, I admit you've done everything possible to assure that she is with child. You may rest until we see if your seed has taken hold."

"Many thanks," Kadar said with irony.

"Impudence." Nasim gestured a dismissal. "I'm astonished I permit it from you."

Kadar started to leave.

"But I still think the whip would prove interesting. If she's not with child, we will try it the next time you go to the tower."

Kadar didn't bother to argue. Nasim always had to win, but Kadar had bought a delay. By the time the issue emerged again, the messenger might have arrived.

Now he must consider what action to take when that occurred.


"What happened?" Selene asked as soon as she unlocked and threw open the door.

"Nothing of importance." Kadar came into the chamber. "We no longer have to go to the tower. At least, not for a while."

Shock and another emotion less identifiable surged through her. "Why not?"

He smiled crookedly. "I pleaded weariness. He doesn't want me to be overtired when I start my journey."

"Has the messenger arrived?"

"Not yet." He pulled his mantle over his head and walked naked to the pallet. "Nasim said we will wait until we see if you're with child. If you're not, we must return to the tower room."

"I see." She moved slowly across the room toward the bed. It was the first time since they had started going to the tower that she had thought of the possibility of a child. The pleasure of the act itself had overwhelmed all else. "What if I am?"

"We must hope you aren't. The tower room is the lesser danger."

"We may not know for a while. My flux is often late." She took off her gown, blew out the candle, and climbed into bed.

A child...

She lay staring into the darkness. She had thought only of the danger of refusal, not of the babe itself. A child born of Kadar and her. Perhaps a boy like Thea's babe, Niall. Gurgling laughter, soft, and silken smooth as—

A baby Nasim would either take or kill.

Panic soared through her. A child born in this dark place and taken from her. Nasim would—

"For God's sake, stop shaking." Kadar was sitting on the bed beside her.

How had he known she was shaking from across the room? But Kadar always knew. She reached out and clutched his hands. "I won't let him take my baby," she said fiercely. "He can't have it."

"We don't know that you—"

"I don't care. I'll kill him before I let him—"

"Shh." He lifted the covers and slipped into bed beside her. "It will never happen." He gathered her into his arms. "I promise you he'll never touch any child of ours."

A little of her terror eased. "It's just...I never

thought of it before. The possibility seemed so far away...." And now it was too close. A week or two and she would know if—

"Will you stop trembling?" he said gruffly. "You're tearing me apart. I've never seen you this frightened."

"It's not for me. It's the babe. We had no right. A babe is helpless and cannot—"

"But we're not helpless. If necessary, we can protect him." He held her closer. "Now forget this and go to sleep."

Yes, he was right. They could protect their child. Kadar and she could do anything together. She relaxed against him even as she said, "You shouldn't be in my bed. You said Nasim would know..."

"Nasim may go to hell."

"He would be at home there." She was silent for a moment, thinking. "I'll not stay here without you."

"I never intended to leave you or Haroun here."

"Then what will we do?"

"Would it be too much to ask you to stop worrying and leave the matter to me?"

"Yes. I can't stop worrying." She paused. "But you know Nasim better than I do. I will listen to your suggestions."

"Thank you."

"You're welcome." She yawned. "Now I'm going to sleep. It seems I haven't had a good slumber in—"

"Weeks?" Kadar chuckled. "I wonder why?"

She didn't want to think of the reason why, nor of the sensual, passionate Kadar of the tower room. Right now she felt comfortable and treasured and safe.

"You know why. Please have the courtesy to stop talking about it."

He brushed his lips across the top of her head. "Yes, my lady. Anything you command. Whatever you wish."

Not very likely, she thought drowsily, but she was too tired to refute him. She would tell him tomorrow that never in their acquaintance had she had everything entirely as she...

She slept so soundly she didn't hear the thundering at the door a few hours later.

She lifted her head drowsily as Kadar slipped from the bed. "What is it?"

Kadar didn't answer as he moved across the room and threw open the door.

Nasim strode into the chamber.

Selene hurriedly sat, jerking the cover up to cover her breasts.

A futile effort. She might as well have been invisible for all the attention Nasim paid her.

"My messenger has come." The old man set the candle on the nightstand, his dark eyes glittering with excitement. "By Allah, I was sure he'd be sent back to me in pieces, but he came riding in only an hour ago. You must set out at once."

"May I clothe my nakedness first?" Kadar asked dryly as he pulled his tunic over his head. "And who is chopping up your messengers?"

"Tarik. He guards the treasure. A clever, dangerous

man." He smiled grimly as he watched Kadar slip on his shoes. "And he does not like my people."

"How many have you sent?"

"Five over the past twelve years. My most clever and talented of assassins. This is the only man who has ever returned." He frowned. "I have to wonder why he was permitted to come back unscathed."

"Perhaps this Tarik is no longer as formidable as he was once. Men weaken as years pass."

"Tarik would not weaken. You'll still find him most formidable."

"If he let your messenger return, it could be he found him more than he could deal with. Send Fadil back to get your treasure."

"Fadil is good, but he's no match for Tarik. I would be a match for him. No one else." He paused. "Except you."

"Then you'd better break your silence and tell me where I'm going to find this treasure." Kadar was at the washbasin, splashing water in his face. "And how you think I'm going to accomplish this."

"That's your problem." For the first time since he'd entered the chamber, he glanced at Selene. "Women have big ears and busy tongues."

"You're right. Dress and wait in the hall, Selene."

"Wait." Nasim smiled. "You're too eager to rid us of her presence."

"I want to protect your secrets."

"You want to protect her. If she knows, she will never be permitted to leave."

"Unless the treasure is delivered to you. Then there is no secret as to its location. But if we send her—"

"She stays. You're too eager to have her go," Nasim said flatly. "The treasure is being held at the castle of Sienbara in Tuscany."

"Italy."

"Yes, not a far journey." He added maliciously, "But you will find it interesting."

"How well guarded is the castle?"

"Guarded well against an army, but a man like you can go where armies cannot. You will slip in like a ghost and pluck my treasure from Tarik."

"If he doesn't make me a true ghost before I do it. Where is this treasure kept?"

"It's hidden in Tarik's chamber. It's contained in a large gold box with a bejeweled cross on the lid. You'll recognize it at once."

"A cross? Is this a holy relic?"

"What do you care?"

"I care if this Tarik will be able to call on the Church to protect the treasure."

"He won't call on the Church. He stands alone."

"Except for an army guarding his fortress. How do I get there?"

"Ali Balkir will take you on the *Dark Star*. He'll stay with you and bring you back when you have the treasure."

"And to assure that I will return."

Nasim nodded. "Though I have little need of such assurance while I keep the woman and the boy as hostages."

"No."

Nasim stiffened, his eyes narrowing. "What are you saying?"

"I'm saying that the boy and the woman go with me."

"And I'm saying they stay."

"Then you'll wait a long time for your treasure."

"You'd break your word?"

"You know me better than that. But I may take another twelve years to finish your task, and you appear very impatient."

Nasim muttered a curse. "You cannot have your way in this."

"Why not? You're sending Balkir with me. Tell him to kill the woman and the boy if I try to cheat you."

Nasim glanced at Selene. "What if she's with child? I *want* that child."

"Which do you want more? The treasure or a child who may or may not be a reality?"

"Both."

"You can't have both. Choose." He stared directly into Nasim's eyes. "Or I swear you will wait a long, long time for any treasure I bring you."

"I could settle the argument by throwing them both off the battlements now."

"And rob yourself of hostages? Besides, that would anger me. You've never seen me angry, Nasim. You don't know which way it would make me jump."

Nasim was silent a moment. Then he shrugged. "As you say, I'll have Balkir there to butcher them if you seek to betray me."

"But that's the only area in which Balkir will not be under my orders. You'll see that he obeys me in everything else."

"He won't like it."

"What difference did that ever make to you? It will clearly be difficult enough to steal this box without having to worry about a captain who may sail off and leave me stranded."

Nasim shrugged. "Very well, he'll have orders to obey you as he would me." He turned and moved toward the door. "I'll go have the horses saddled. Come down to the courtyard at once. I wish to give you more details on the location of Tarik's chamber."

Selene watched the door close behind him before she said, "You handled that very well." She swung her legs to the floor. "Though I was ready to kick him to make him stop treating me as if I weren't in the room."

"Now, that would have caught his attention. I'm glad you refrained." He rummaged in the saddle baskets and tossed her the sailor's garments she had worn when she arrived. "I was walking a fine line as it was."

"I'm not an idiot. I knew that the only thing of importance was getting us out of here. We'll worry about escaping Balkir later." She scrambled into her clothes and ran her fingers through her hair. She would have liked to braid it for the journey, but it was better to leave at once. She didn't want to give Nasim time to change his mind. She headed for the door. "You gather our things while I go wake Haroun."

"Balkir is in a rage." Selene watched the captain stride about the ship barking orders. "I almost wish Nasim had told somebody else to go with us."

"I don't." Kadar leaned his elbows on the rail and

gazed out at the sea. "If he hadn't given the task to Balkir, I would have asked for him."

She turned to look at him in surprise. "Why?"

He changed the subject. "I doubt if I'll have an opportunity to set you and Haroun free before we reach Tuscany. Balkir's terrified of offending Nasim, and he'll be on guard. But a chance may occur when the action begins."

He meant when he had to find a way into Tarik's fortress. "Nasim is mad. How can one man hope to do what an army cannot?"

"We'll have to see. It may be possible." He smiled mockingly. "I've told you before: I'm very, very good, Selene."

"You'll be very, very dead."

"And then will you weep for me?"

She shook her head.

"You wept for me once."

"I was a child and a fool."

"A child perhaps, never a fool."

She looked down at the water. "Don't do this, Kadar."

"I must. If I give him the box, he'll leave Montdhu alone. Besides, I gave him my word."

"A promise to that demon means nothing."

"It does if I made it. I'll bring him his golden box."

She whirled on him, anger flaring. "And you'll send me away and then go back to him."

He lifted his brows. "But you said you wanted to leave me."

"Stop smiling. I do want to go. Do you think the

tower chamber meant anything to me? Pleasure for the moment. That was all. Now it's over."

"I assume that means you'll no longer allow me in your bed?"

"I told you that I would couple with you only while it was necessary."

"So you did."

"And it's no longer necessary."

"Not to save lives, but perhaps to save souls."

"Coupling will save your soul? I think not."

"Coupling is a form of closeness, and closeness saves souls. Perhaps even your soul, Selene."

"You're talking nonsense. My soul has nothing to do with you."

"It has everything to do with me. Just as my soul has everything to do with you." His smile faded. "There's a fate that guides all of us. We were meant to be together. I've known it almost since the first time I saw you. Sometimes fate goes awry, but not this time. You can fight it all you please, but we'll still come together in the end."

He believed what he was saying, and his intensity sent a ripple of uneasiness through her. Even if his talk was foolishness, she did not like the idea of being herded willy-nilly along a path decreed by any force but her own. She turned away. "Believe what you like, but it won't be in my bed that we'll come together."

# Chapter Seven

THE *DARK STAR* DOCKED at the small port of Lantano a little over a week later.

"It didn't take as long as I thought." Selene gazed out at the gently curving coastline. "Didn't you tell me Tuscany was far to the north?"

"This port is halfway between Rome and Tuscany. We'll have to find horses and supplies to purchase. We go overland from here." Kadar took her elbow and urged her toward the gangplank. "There's no port near Sienbara."

"That will make it harder to escape with the treasure. There's sure to be a pursuit."

"Perhaps."

"You know there will be." Her gaze narrowed on Kadar's face. "What are you thinking?"

He smiled. "Only that someone has to lead a pursuit."

She shivered as she realized what he meant. "You'll kill this Tarik?"

"It would be the safest thing to do."

"No."

"He evidently had no compunction at slaughtering Nasim's men."

"That's different. They were trying to steal from him. Just as you're trying to do."

"How do you know he didn't steal this treasure first?"

"It doesn't matter what he stole or didn't steal. I won't have your soul tainted by committing murder." Her tone became fierce. "Do you hear me? I want your promise."

"And what would you do if I refuse to give it?"

"You won't refuse. You know I'm right."

"But that's no reason for me to hold my hand. Shall I tell you how seldom in my life rightness has had anything to do with what I've done?"

"You're not like that any longer. Give me your promise."

He held her gaze for a long moment. "Why does it matter to you?" he asked softly.

She glanced hurriedly away from him. "Why do you think? If you kill, you'll be doing what Nasim wants you to do. I won't give him that victory."

He chuckled. "That's not the only reason. Will you never tire of trying to—"

"Think what you like. I've told you my reason.

Now give me your promise or I'll be the one who goes to the castle to steal that treasure."

"By God, you'd do it." All trace of humor had vanished from his tone. "You're to stay away from that castle. Do you understand?"

"Your promise."

He muttered a curse. "Very well, I won't kill him unless I find it absolutely necessary. That's all you'll get from me."

It was all she could expect. She had no desire to tie Kadar's hands if it meant robbing him of defense. Besides, she wasn't at all sure she wouldn't take action herself under those circumstances. Best not to pursue the subject. "How long will it take to get to Sienbara?"

"If the road is good, a week of hard riding."

Her pace quickened. "Then let's find those horses. I wish this over."

Selene shivered. "It looks very strong."

Sienbara Castle was perched on one of the highest hills in the Tuscany countryside. Though small, its stone walls and moat were as impressive as any she'd seen. Even the windows were well situated. She had watched Ware build his castle and knew the value of correctly positioned windows for the loosing of arrows.

Kadar's gaze was on the castle. "You're frightened. Why? It's less formidable than Nasim's fortress."

It was true. Maysef had been a ghost fortress surrounded by stark mountains. Sienbara was merely a small, well-guarded castle surrounded by lovely rolling countryside. She didn't know why she was feeling this disturbance. Her uneasiness had erupted like a dormant volcano the moment she caught sight of Sienbara.

Kadar met her gaze. "I feel it too," he said quietly.

"Do we make camp here? It's growing dark," Balkir demanded as he rode up to join them. He cast a contemptuous glance at the castle. "It is nothing. Nasim should have sent me alone. He didn't need you."

Evidently Balkir felt none of the unease she and Kadar shared, Selene realized. She glanced at Haroun. The boy looked tired but not frightened. No one but Kadar and she seemed to sense this impending—

Kadar nodded. "Tell the men we'll camp here for the night." He slipped from the saddle before helping Selene from her horse. "But keep a sharp watch."


Selene moved restlessly on her blanket. She was tired, bone weary from the long journey, but she could not sleep. Why didn't Kadar come back to the camp? After they had eaten, he left without a word and climbed the slope overlooking Sienbara.

He was still there. She had left her tent flap open and she could see him silhouetted against the moonlit sky.

What was he thinking?

Well, she would never know unless she asked him, she thought impatiently.

She tossed her blanket aside and left the tent. A moment later she was climbing the slope.

"I was expecting you." His gaze didn't leave the castle as she came to stand next to him. "It took you long enough."

"I can't sleep. What are you doing?"

"Listening."

"Listening?"

"Don't you hear it calling?"

She tilted her head. It was a still night, and yet, did she hear...? "I hear nothing. You're mad."

"Perhaps." He smiled down at her. "Or perhaps you're afraid to hear it."

"There's nothing to hear but the wind blowing through the cypress."

"Nasim taught me there's always more to hear than one would think. Places call, people call. One must only open one's mind to hear them."

His head lifted, his gaze returning to the castle, and she could sense his excitement. It was as strange as this place, and it frightened her. "It's only the wind. Come back to camp and go to sleep."

"In a moment."

"Now."

"What a nagging wench you are." He turned and started down the slope. "There's nothing to fear. You should embrace new experiences."

"Like trying to find a way into an enemy castle to get that foolish box?" She fell into step with him. "When will you go?"

"Tomorrow night. Midnight. I'll scale the south wall."

"Alone?"

"I'm safer alone. Nasim was right in that."

"Then he should have come himself."

"I think he was afraid."

"What?"

"I've never known him to fear anything, but I think he was afraid to come here. Interesting, is it not?"

More chilling than interesting. "So he sent you to face this Tarik."

"Tarik…" He glanced over his shoulder at the castle. "Nasim told me little about him. That's odd in itself. He usually made sure I knew everything about a situation."

"You know that Tarik usually sends back Nasim's men in pieces. You've made no attempt to hide our presence here. What if he finds out there are strangers about?"

"He already knows."

She stared at him in astonishment.

"We've been watched since early this morning. It has to be Tarik."

"And you're still going to the castle tomorrow night?"

He nodded.

"Dear God, you're truly a madman." She tried to steady her voice. "Why?"

"He's waiting for me."

"Then let him wait."

"But that would be no challenge at all."

"*Damn* your challenge."

He went on as if he hadn't heard her. "I'll tell Balkir and his men to wait for me near the south wall. He should leave only a token guard on you and Haroun. It may be the best opportunity for you to escape. Run to the woods and hide. I'll find you."

She was supposed to leave while he was in Tarik's castle? "No."

"It will be better for me not to have to worry about you."

"I want you to worry about me. You should worry. It's your fault we're here. Maybe if you worry enough you won't be so eager to take challenges from men who—" She broke off and drew a deep breath. "I'll wait to leave until you come back."

If he came back.

"I'll come back," he said, as if he'd read her mind. "There's something waiting here, but I don't think it's—" He shrugged. "But I could be wrong. Death has many masks to fool a man."

Her hands clenched into fists. "Don't you *dare* die. I won't have it."

"I'll try to oblige you." They had stopped beside her tent. "There's something I have to ask you."

"Then ask it."

"Are you with child?"

"Would it stop you from going if I was?"

"No, but I'll need to make plans and find a priest to wed us. I must take care of my child."

He would make plans to keep her and the babe safe, but he would still go his own way, as he'd done that night at Montdhu. She would not have it. "I will not wed you. I'm not with child."

"You're certain?"

She was not at all certain. It was time for her flux, but she was often late and she had missed her time before. It could be true. "Of course I'm certain."

His lips twisted. "I know I should be relieved, but I

find I'm disappointed. I've been thinking of you with child of late, how you'd look, how you'd feel..." He pushed her into the tent and lifted her blanket. "Enough of this. Now lie down and go to sleep—if you can."

"Of course I can." She dropped to her knees on her pallet and jerked the blanket from his hands. "You don't think I lie here worrying about you? I was just restless tonight."

"You might ask yourself why. Was it concern, or did you hear what I—"

"Neither. It was caused by a bellyache from the rabbit stew I had for supper." She snuggled down and closed her eyes.

His low laugh was full of amusement.

But when she opened her eyes a few minutes later, he was not laughing. He was kneeling by his blanket a few yards away from her tent. His head was lifted to the night sky.

Listening.

Kadar pulled himself up the final few yards and over the wall.

No guard.

Too easy.

He froze in place, his gaze raking the courtyard below. Soldiers were at the gate and on the far battlement, but not here.

Why?

It didn't matter. He couldn't stop now. The excitement was growing with every breath. He moved silently along the battlement, opened the oak door, and started down the long, twisting stairs.

No torch brightened the thick blackness, but he was accustomed to darkness. His hand tightened on the hilt of his dagger.

*Where are you, Tarik? Around the next curve? Waiting at the bottom of the steps?*

He was almost disappointed when he reached the foot of the stairs and encountered no one. He moved quickly down the hall.

*Second door on the left, Nasim had said.*

He stopped short.

*The door was standing open.*

"Come in. Come in." The man's deep voice issuing from the room was impatient. "I need to close this door. There's a dreadful draft."

Kadar moved warily forward.

"Hurry."

"Tarik?"

"Of course. And have the courtesy to take your hand off that dagger. I'm not armed."

Kadar was still to one side of the open door. How had Tarik known his hand was on the dagger hilt?

"You're here to steal, Kadar. It's only logical that you have a weapon, and you always prefer a dagger. Now come in. You know you can never resist satisfying your curiosity once it's aroused."

He was right. Kadar drew his dagger, took a step forward, and stood in the open doorway.

"My, my, you are a lethal-appearing specimen." Tarik was lounging in a cushioned chair across the chamber. "After you finish ogling me, please shut the door."

Kadar had trained himself never to make assumptions, but he must have made them about Tarik, for he was surprised. This was not the fierce warrior capable of bringing fear to Nasim. He was lean, perhaps near his fortieth year, garbed in a purple tunic. The low-burning fire in the hearth lit his coal-black hair with a matte glow. It was his face that was compelling. A broad, high forehead, a long beak of a nose, and mocking dark eyes dominated that golden-skinned visage. It was not a comely face, but the alertness and intelligence of expression made it riveting.

"Enough?" Tarik asked. "We've both taken the other's measure. Now we can be at ease."

"Can we?"

"How cautious you are. I have no soldiers behind the door ready to leap on you. They would have been waiting on the south wall if I'd wanted you intercepted."

"I thought it was too easy. How did you know I'd choose the south wall?"

"It's the one I would have chosen." He smiled. "And you're a very clever man, Kadar."

"How do you know my name?" His eyes narrowed as a thought occurred to him. "Nasim?"

"You think Nasim betrayed you?" He shook his head. "I can see your reasoning. Nasim is both treacherous and convoluted, but I assure you he sent me no messages."

"Then how did you know me and my mission?"

"I have my own people at Maysef."

Kadar stared at him skeptically.

"Ah, you think because Nasim's followers are such fanatics that I could not inveigle my people among them. It was difficult but not impossible."

"Why would you do that?"

"Because Nasim is clever and persistent. I knew he would eventually find someone he considered capable of taking the box from me. He chose well in you. I've followed your progress with interest from the time you were a boy. You're truly unique."

"You're too kind," Kadar said ironically.

"I'm not kind at all—unless moved. And it takes a great deal to move me these days." Tarik gestured to the chair opposite him. "Well, are you going to put up that dagger and come in and make yourself comfortable?"

"What would you do if I didn't?"

"I would take it away from you."

"Indeed?"

"Without harm to you, of course. You're too valuable to damage. Even Nasim realized that truth."

"You think you could do it?"

"I didn't mean to arouse your competitive instincts." He sighed. "Yes, I could do it. You're very good, but I'm older and I've had more experience."

"Older is not always better."

"In this case it is. But I have no intention of humiliating you. Though I believe you're one of the few men who could accept and learn from it. You always have before."

He spoke with such absolute certainty that Kadar was intrigued. What the devil. The situation was too interesting not to explore. He thrust his dagger back in its scabbard and kicked the door shut with his foot.

"Good."

Kadar strode across the room and dropped into the chair Tarik had indicated. "Why didn't you fortify the south wall?"

"That wouldn't have been hospitable."

"Why?" he persisted.

"Because I wanted you here," Tarik said simply. "I've been waiting for a long time for Nasim to lose patience and send you to me."

"You wanted me to steal your treasure?"

"No." Tarik smiled. "I wanted to steal you from Nasim."

Kadar went still. "I'm no slave. Nasim doesn't own me."

"He owns a small part of you. You try to shrug off the bondage, but it's very strong. Why else are you here?"

"You evidently know why I'm here."

"Ah, yes, my treasure. Did Nasim tell you what it is?"

"A golden box with a cross on it."

"And in the box?"

Kadar shrugged. "I don't care."

"Because you're not a greedy man. But you're a curious one. Curiosity guides your life. I think you'd like to know what treasure made Nasim sacrifice all those men."

"Perhaps."

"You know you would." Tarik chuckled. "That's

what I find most appealing about you. Your thirst for knowledge. It's a good and wondrous gift."

"Why did you want me here?" Kadar's lips curled sardonically. "Do you also have a task for me? A treasure to be stolen? A man killed?"

"Oh, yes, I have a task. A far more difficult and terrible task than the one Nasim set you."

"So terrible you can't stop smiling."

"One must always smile or weep. Smiling is better."

"What task?"

"I'm not sure yet. I think you're the one I've been seeking, but I must be certain." He sipped his wine. "So you will stay here with me for a while."

"You're taking me prisoner?"

"Not unless it's necessary. I wish you to come voluntarily." He leaned forward, his eyes twinkling. "Consider. You'll be in a position to win my confidence, lull my suspicions, and then snatch my treasure from beneath my nose."

"And what if I choose to accomplish the same aim in my own way?"

"I fear it won't be permitted. I've taken precautions." He stood up. "And now I know you will wish to depart and get back to Lady Selene. She will no doubt be concerned."

Kadar stiffened. "What do you know of Selene?"

"I know she must be unusual to be of such concern to you. You will, of course, bring her with you. I'll welcome her to Sienbara. Captain Balkir and his men will stay outside the gates. He acts rashly on occasion, and I wish this period to be serene and without trouble.

There are decisions to be made, and battles are so unsettling."

"I believe that might be described as an understatement," Kadar said dryly.

"It depends on the battle. Balkir would cause me little trouble. May I expect you back after dawn?"

"Why should I come back at all? Why not go back to Nasim and tell him I failed?"

"Because you didn't fail. You say I made it easy for you to gain entrance. Didn't you also make it easy for me? You're very clever. Why didn't you concoct a more complicated plan? Why just come over the wall?"

"Sometimes the uncomplicated plans are better."

"For Balkir, possibly. Not for you."

"Are you saying I wanted you to capture me?"

"All I'm saying is that we're all guided in mysterious and wonderful ways." He grimaced. "And, then again, sometimes not at all wonderful. At times, hideously unpleasant. But we both know you didn't fail and that there's no danger of you giving up and telling Nasim that."

Kadar was silent a moment, remembering his excitement and eagerness as he climbed that wall tonight. That excitement was still present. "I'll consider returning."

"Shall I throw in a few small tidbits to sweeten the pot? Consider that it will be much easier for Lady Selene and the boy to escape if you separate them from Balkir. Consider also that I will promise to take the box from hiding and let you view it. Isn't that tempting?"

It was tempting. "And you'll also let me view the contents of the box?"

"Ah, you strike a hard bargain. No, I'm afraid I must be more cautious than that." He thought for a moment. "But I will show you the object that made Nasim redouble his efforts to obtain my treasure. Agreed?"

"As I said, I'll consider it."

"Good. I'd have been disappointed if you'd given up so easily. Think upon it. Weigh the threat against the advantages."

"I shall." Kadar started for the door.

Tarik called after him, "And go out through the front gate. No one will stop you. I'd hate to have you fall and break your head when everything is proceeding so splendidly."

"I don't like it," Selene said. "How do we know it's not a trap?"

"He could have had me tonight. He didn't have to let me go."

"It's all most peculiar. What manner of man is this?"

Kadar smiled. "Most peculiar."

"But not like Nasim?"

"Not at all like Nasim. He's hard to describe."

She studied him. "God in heaven, I think you actually like him."

"It's too early to make judgments, but I respect him."

"And he intrigues you," Selene said shrewdly.

"You've always liked puzzles. Did it occur to you that he set up this situation to give you something to unravel?"

"It occurred to me."

"But you still want to return to the castle."

"The puzzle exists." He paused. "But you don't have to go with me. There's a possibility Tarik might use you as a hostage the way Nasim tried to do. I could ask him to wait a few days and we could try to arrange an escape for you and Haroun."

She shook her head.

Kadar's smile widened. "I didn't think so. You also have a strong streak of curiosity."

"Nonsense."

"No, you only try to smother it because curiosity can lead you down dangerous paths and away from safe havens."

Her gaze went to the castle. "Like the one leading you there."

"Perhaps."

"Then don't go."

"But there's a puzzle to be solved and a challenge to be met," he said lightly.

"And a fool to be slaughtered. Don't take the chance."

His smile faded. "When I was a boy, I used to cling to safety as you do. Then I learned that death and poverty still seek you out, whether you're hiding behind strong walls or sleeping in the middle of a battleground. You might as well live life to the fullest every minute of the day."

"I'm hardly hiding behind strong walls," she said dryly.

"No, but only because you were forced outside. You wouldn't have taken the step on your own. Those years at Montdhu have made you cautious about leaving safety behind." His lips tightened. "And who could blame you once you found a secure niche? Nicholas made sure your childhood was hell on earth."

Was it true? Selene wondered with sudden uncertainty. Had her years at the House of Nicholas made her afraid to risk any disruption of peace? Well, it didn't matter if it was true or not. She had been happy at Montdhu, and it was only sensible to cling to what made you happy. "No one but a madman like you would want to sleep in the middle of a battleground. I've no desire to do anything but go back to Montdhu, where I belong." She looked away from him. "But Tarik's words about separating us from Balkir have substance. It may be easier to escape once we're within the castle."

"Unless Tarik becomes the threat instead of Balkir."

"But you don't believe Tarik is a threat." She added sarcastically, "He's only a puzzle."

"He may be a threat once the puzzle is solved. I want you to think about this and—"

"We're going." She stared at him in exasperation. "First you tell me there's no safety in the world, and then you mouth warnings and argue with me."

He shrugged. "I never said I was reasonable."

"Then why should I pay any attention to you?" She turned away. "I'll go tell Haroun."

At dawn Balkir rode with them to the castle gates.

He turned to Kadar as the gates slowly swung open. "I will be here waiting." His tone was savage. "If you don't come out with Nasim's treasure within a week, I'll launch an attack. Don't think you'll be able to fool me."

"Never," Kadar said. "But you might consider that it may be more than a week, and Nasim would not be pleased if you rush in and spoil my chances."

Balkir's baleful glance shifted to Selene. "She should stay here with me. I have my orders."

"I told you, Tarik wants her to accompany me. What do you fear? As you said, it's a small, puny castle, unworthy of our efforts. You'll be camped right outside the gates. You can take it at will." He kicked his horse into a trot. "Good day, Balkir."

Selene heard the captain mutter a curse as she followed Kadar through the gates.

Haroun edged his horse closer to her as he saw the guards standing on the battlements. "Is this wise?"

"I think so. We'll have to see."

"Welcome, Lady Selene." A tall man was walking—no, limping—toward her. Kadar had not mentioned Tarik was crippled. "I'm delighted you saw fit to join us. I am Tarik."

She nodded warily. "Lord Tarik."

"Only Tarik." He smiled. "It's true I am lord of this castle, but I've never been able to accustom myself to being addressed so. I grew up as scum of the streets, and one never forgets."

A little of her wariness eased at his frankness. "You grew up in Tuscany?"

"No, much farther east." He turned to Haroun. "I hear you're a brave man and an excellent swimmer. I have use for such a soldier. Perhaps I can persuade you to join my guard?"

Haroun shook his head. "I must stay with the lady Selene."

"Lady Selene could not be safer." Tarik gestured and a soldier ran forward. "This is Adolfo. Suppose you go and let him show you how well my men are treated."

Haroun hesitated. "I cannot."

"Loyalty. That's good." Tarik smiled. "But haven't you missed the life you lived at Montdhu, a soldier among soldiers?"

Haroun frowned uncertainly. "Yes."

"Go on," Kadar said. "I'll summon you if there's any question of her needing you."

"Lady Selene?"

She saw eagerness as well as excitement in Haroun's expression. The boy wanted to go. He had been miserably unhappy dancing attendance on her for the last weeks. She nodded. "I'll call on you if there's need."

He smiled with relief and quickly followed Adolfo across the courtyard.

"He'll be content now," Tarik said.

She turned to see Tarik's gaze on her face. "A soldier is always a soldier. He's been ill at ease in the role you gave him."

And she was ill at ease that he seemed to know so much about all of them. "Your spy in Nasim's fortress told you that?"

"No, I have eyes to see."

Those eyes saw too much, she thought as she gazed at him. One glance and he'd been able to say the exact words to rob her of antagonism; another look and he'd identified Haroun's problem and set about solving it.

"Now, just what are you thinking?" Tarik asked softly.

"I'm thinking you're a very clever man." She paused before adding deliberately, "And that we'd better examine every word you speak carefully."

Kadar smothered a laugh.

Tarik blinked with surprise before recovering immediately. "Oh, yes, I'm a devious man." He stepped forward and helped her from her horse. "But I only lie when necessary. It's not necessary now. At present I'm no threat to your friend Haroun or to Kadar. My earnest hope is that we will all enjoy an interesting and rewarding visit."

Kadar dismounted. "Balkir will prove troublesome if the visit lasts more than a week."

"We'll deal with Balkir when it becomes necessary," Tarik said. "Come. You must rest. I will show you to your chambers. I'm sure you did not have a peaceful night." He moved across the courtyard. "But now that you're reassured of my excellent intentions..."

The chamber Selene was given was as comfortable as the one she occupied at Montdhu. Cream-colored silks draped the bed, and tapestry cushions and wall hangings were scattered about the room. The sunlight streaming through the narrow window burnished a brass pitcher studded with lapis lazuli on the wash-stand.

"You are pleased?" Tarik asked.

She nodded. "It's lovely. That's a fine tapestry."

"Yes." He gazed up at the tapestry. "My wife brought it to me as part of her dowry."

"Your wife?"

"My second wife, Rosa. She's dead now." He turned abruptly away. "Come, Kadar. Your chamber is just next door. I understand you and Lady Selene no longer occupy the same bed. Pity."

He seemed to know everything about them. But Selene's annoyance was tempered with sympathy at the pain she had glimpsed in his face when he spoke of his wife. He might be clever and more perceptive than she liked, but he was also human.

"I'll send servants with hot water and a tub for bathing in a few hours. Everyone in my household bathes every day here." He grimaced. "I've never become accustomed to this foul custom of leaving one's body uncleansed for days on end. Where I spent my youth, water was looked upon as a blessing, not a curse. I cannot abide filth. I can accept almost everything else, but such sacrifices are too much to bear."

"We have no liking for filth either." Kadar paused. "Where did you spend your youth?"

Tarik didn't answer. "I'll send a servant to bring you food to break your fast. But I hope you'll see fit to join me later for a more substantial meal." He quickly ushered Kadar from the room.

Selene slowly unfastened her cloak and dropped it on the stool by the window. It was true she had not slept well last night, but she doubted if she would be able to nap now. Her mind was too full of questions. She could see why Kadar had been intrigued with the puzzle Tarik presented.

A very unusual man.

# Chapter Eight

"YOU DID NOT EAT WELL," Tarik said disapprovingly. "You don't like my food?"

"I'm not hungry," Selene said.

"I could send for something else."

"The food is excellent. I've just had little appetite of late."

"It's good to eat heartily at midday. It gives you strength to—"

Kadar interrupted, "If she doesn't wish to eat, don't urge her."

"Ah, you're quick to jump to her defense even in this small thing." Tarik smiled. "I meant no harm. I've no intention of forcing food upon the lady. I merely wish you both to enjoy it here."

"We're not here to enjoy ourselves. You promised to show me the box."

"And so I shall." He rose to his feet. "This very minute. Come with me to my chamber." He turned to Selene. "Would you also like to see it? It's an object of great beauty, and you must be curious."

"I'm seldom curious." She avoided Kadar's amused glance as she stood up. "But I have nothing better to do."

Tarik's chamber was as stark and simple as the room he had given her was soft and textured. A gauze-draped pallet instead of a bed. No tapestry to keep out the night chill. A table and two unadorned wooden chairs. The only ornate object in the room was the chest set against the wall. It appeared very old but lovingly cared for. The intricately carved scene on the dark-teak lid was a small boat drifting down a river past three long-legged birds wading among graceful cattails.

"Beautiful, isn't it?" Tarik lifted the lid. "It was carved by a young slave of the court."

Kadar pounced. "What court?"

Tarik only smiled. "But this wooden chest is far less impressive than the object it shelters. I'm sure you'll agree."

Kadar's eyes widened in surprise, as he only saw a small wooden statue resting on a bed of purple silk. "I'm afraid I don't agree."

Neither did Selene. She had been expecting splendor, and the nine-inch wooden statue had nothing splendid about it. The crudely carved figure was that of a robed woman but with the head of a jackal. She said, "Your statue is interesting but no treasure beyond price."

"It is to me." Tarik lovingly stroked the statue. "Tell me, Kadar, do you see no beauty in it either?" When Kadar didn't answer, he glanced at him. "What is it?"

Kadar was staring at the statue with narrowed eyes. "Nothing. It just looks...familiar."

"You've seen something like it before?"

"No, I don't—" He shrugged. "Perhaps, but I can't recall where." His gaze shifted to Tarik's face. "Is this a ploy to deceive us? I didn't come here for a statue. Where is the box?"

"You hurt me." Tarik sighed. "Oh, well, perhaps you'll prefer this." With a flourish, he removed the purple silk on which the statue had rested.

Selene inhaled sharply.

"My God," Kadar whispered.

The shimmering gold box was perhaps two feet by one foot and it, too, was intricately carved. Not with a gentle country scene, as the chest was, but with odd, sharp symbols. Lapis lazuli stones formed a scrolled needlelike cross that covered the entire length of the box.

Selene reached out and gently touched the cross. "It's truly wonderful..."

"Yes."

"No wonder Nasim wants it," Kadar said.

Tarik shrugged. "He'd crush the coffer beneath his horses' hooves if it meant he could have what's inside."

Selene shook her head. "I can't believe that. Even if he cares nothing for beauty, it must have great value."

"He'd destroy it." Tarik carefully draped the silk back over the box, placed the statue on top of it, and closed the chest. "Without a second thought."

"The cross must have some meaning," Kadar probed. "Though Nasim assured me the content was not a religious relic and I'd have no trouble with the Knights Templar."

Tarik raised his brows. "And you believed him?"

"Not entirely. Is it a holy relic?"

"Some might consider it so."

"And you keep it here in your chamber, unguarded?"

"My men are loyal. It would be no easy task to wrest it from me." He shrugged. "And perhaps, in my heart, I wish it to be stolen away from me. Sometimes the burden becomes too great."

Kadar smiled. "Then let me oblige you."

"Maybe I will." He turned toward the door. "We shall see. Would you like to inspect my guardroom and see how well I've quartered your friend Haroun?"

"Why not?"

Tarik glanced at Selene. "I'd ask you to accompany us, but my soldiers are rough and not accustomed to ladies."

"I've no desire to go with you." Selene moved toward the door. "I'll return to my chamber."

"And be bored." Kadar shuddered. "For which we will pay dearly later, Tarik."

Tarik chuckled. "Will it help if I send her fine silks to embroider?"

"Maybe."

"I understand she plays a fine game of chess. Perhaps I could have the honor of a game after we sup tonight."

"Not if you continue to speak as if I'm not in the room," Selene said bluntly.

Tarik chuckled and bowed deeply. "My apologies, sweet lady. Will you do me the courtesy of forgiving this lowly serf and amusing me this evening?"

"I don't play for amusement. I play to win."

"Fair warning." His smile faded and he suddenly looked very weary. "I haven't hungered for victory for a long, long time. It must be pleasant to care that much for small things."

"Women are only permitted pleasure in small things."

"Most women. But what you're not permitted, you take. Is that not true?"

"Yes." Kadar grinned. "You read her well, Tarik."

"She's a good deal like my wife."

"Rosa?" Selene asked, remembering that moment in her chamber.

"No, my first wife, Layla. Rosa was a gentle soul and took only what she was given."

"A pleasant change?" Selene asked.

"Not necessarily. I loved them both very much."

Again Selene was aware of a great sadness in him. She impulsively reached out and touched his arm in comfort. "I'm sorry for your loss. I know how you must feel."

"You have a good heart." His gaze searched her face. "But you cannot know. You've not known great loss yourself. That is to come."

"I have had a loss. My mother died when I was a child."

He shook his head and gently removed her hand from his arm. "It is to come."

A multitude of emotions surged through Selene as she watched them walk away. She liked him. She had not expected this response to such a complex man. Tarik could be humorous one moment, gentle and wise the next, but he was also an enigma. It was dangerous to be drawn to him.

"Checkmate." Selene looked up from the board in triumph. "That last move was not at all clever, Tarik."

Tarik groaned and leaned back in his chair. "Not only a thrashing but verbal abuse." He glanced at Kadar, who was seated on the hearth a few yards away. "Save me, Kadar."

"You say that every time, but still you play her." Kadar smiled and his gaze shifted back to the fire. "She's right, the last move was stupid."

"I was distracted," Tarik defended. "After all, I'm a man of many concerns."

Selene made a derogatory noise.

"That sounded suspiciously like a snort." Tarik frowned. "And not at all respectful of a man of my years."

"Excuses. How old are you? Forty?"

He flinched. "Do I look forty?"

She relented. "Well, perhaps a *little* less than forty."

"You're too kind," he said ironically. "I'm a man in

my full prime. It's dealing with young rascals like you
and Kadar that has aged me."

"Another game?"

"Not now." He stood up and limped toward the
table across the room. "I need a goblet of wine."

Selene grinned. "Coward."

"Abuse again..." he murmured.

"It's a constant threat with Selene," Kadar said.

There was no threat in this chamber tonight, Selene thought lazily. There was only peace and laughter and ease. It was strange how comfortable they had
become in Tarik's presence during the past eight days.
Even at Montdhu she had never felt more content,
and she could see Kadar felt the same way. He spent
most of his days with Tarik, and in the evening it had
become the custom for them all to gather in the hall
for chess.

But Kadar had been very quiet tonight, she realized
suddenly. She had played him first, and when Tarik
had taken his place, he seated himself on the hearth
and watched them with none of his usual banter. "Are
you well?" she asked. "You've scarcely spoken."

"I was just thinking."

"Ah, a dangerous practice in a man like you," Tarik
said as he poured wine from the pitcher into his goblet. "I believe you need another goblet of wine too."

"No." Kadar met Tarik's gaze. "I believe I need to
see the object that made Nasim send me here."

Tarik stopped pouring in midmotion. "I was wondering when you'd retrieve that particular promise."
He set the pitcher down. "But I was enjoying your

company so much that I'd almost forgotten I'd given it."

"I don't think you did. But you made it easy for us to forget."

"You believe I've been lulling you into a false sense of security? You're wrong; you *are* secure here. Every day that passes convinces me that endangering you is the last thing in the world I'd want."

"The object," Kadar prompted.

"Tomorrow morning."

"Tonight."

"You're very stubborn." Tarik sighed. "Very well, tonight." He set his goblet down and picked up a candelabra. "Follow me, it's in the chamber at the end of the corridor."

The room to which Tarik took them was small and sparsely furnished. A long oak table and two chairs occupied the center of the room. On the table was a wooden pedestal on which a brown leather-bound manuscript rested.

Tarik gestured. "There it is."

"That's no treasure," Selene said.

"But it's what led Nasim to seek the treasure," Tarik said. "And a manuscript's value is in the eyes of the beholder."

Selene felt a surge of excitement. "An entire chamber for one manuscript?"

"Don't read importance into that. If I could obtain more volumes, I would do so. I have a passion for words. What a rare delight they are in this rough world."

Kadar was already seating himself at the table and

carefully opening the volume. "I'll need light. Leave the candles, Tarik."

"The light would be much better if you'd wait for morning."

"Leave the candles."

Tarik set the candelabra on the table. "You'll go blind. The script is none too good. It was done by a scribe, not a monk from the abbey." He turned to Selene. "Will you, at least, be sensible and go to your bed?"

"Presently." She sat down in the chair across the table from Kadar. "I'll stay awhile."

Tarik's gaze went from one to the other, and a faint smile curved his lips. "I should have known to argue would be of no avail. A sip is never enough when you have a great thirst, and you both have a voracious thirst for life."

"And so do you," Selene said.

"I once did. But I've drunk deep enough to quench my thirst." He moved toward the door. "Well, I'm going to my bed. Don't wake me. I won't answer any questions until morning."

As the door closed behind him, Kadar's gaze eagerly fastened on the parchment.

Selene settled back in her chair, watching his face, waiting.

She was being carried up the stairs.

Selene opened drowsy eyes to see Kadar's face above her. His expression held excitement and tension.

Were they going to the tower chamber?

No, this was different. No scent of hashish . . .

"Kadar, where—"

"Shh, you fell asleep at the table." He was taking her to her chamber, laying her on the bed.

She had fallen asleep at a table? What a strange— the manuscript!

"What did it say?" She sat bolt upright in bed, wide awake. "What was in it?"

He sat down on the bed beside her. "Nothing to become excited about. I think the manuscript must be a jest of Tarik's."

"A jest?"

"It's a troubadour's tale. *Le Conte du Graal* by Chrétien de Troyes. It's the story of a king and a wandering knight named Perceval."

"And it does not mention the box?" she asked, disappointed.

"No."

She could barely see him in the moonlit dimness, but there was something in his tone. He was not telling her everything. "Or what's in it?"

"I don't think so." He paused. "Unless it's the grail."

"Grail?"

"A goblet used by Christ at the Last Supper. A cup with special powers sought by the knights of King Arthur's court."

"Dear God," she whispered.

"A troubadour's tale. Though sometimes it does not read like a tale, and Chrétien de Troyes tells of another document from which he took his story."

"But it could be this grail that's in the box in Tarik's chamber?"

"Or what Nasim thinks is the true grail. He worships power. He would do anything to obtain a magical grail that would give the possessor Godlike powers."

"He's an evil, evil man. I cannot believe God would give him any more power than he has already."

"But it's not what you believe but what Nasim believes. To him, God is Allah, and Allah has always smiled on him."

"It could not be. It has to be a troubadour's tale, as you say."

"Well, we cannot wake Tarik and ask him. He made it clear we'll have to wait until morning." He rose to his feet. "Go to sleep."

Go to sleep when her mind was filled with coffers of gold and magical grails? "Will you?"

"Perhaps." He leaned down, brushed a kiss on her forehead, and whispered, "I know a remedy that would make us both sleep deeply."

She did not answer.

"No?" He sighed and then moved toward the door. "Then I fear our minds will get no more rest than our bodies this night."

*She was coming toward him, moving gracefully, rhythmically, her bare feet seeming to scarcely skim the stone floor.*

*Tarik waited.*

*She was almost there.*

*His heart was beating hard, he was sweating with anticipation.*

*She stopped before him. He could see the shimmering*

*beauty of her dark eyes illuminating the impassive jackal face.*

*He took an eager step forward, reaching out to her.*

*She shook her head.*

*Agony shot through him. He could feel the pain twisting, tearing.*

*Why?*

*He could not see her mouth move but knew the word it formed.*

*Fool.*

*She was walking forward, past him.*

*No!*

*He had to follow her.*

*He couldn't move. He was chained.*

*He watched, helpless, as she disappeared over the horizon.*

*Emptiness. Loneliness.*

*Come back.*

*But she would never come back.*

Tears were running down Tarik's cheeks when he opened his eyes.

He hadn't had the dream in a long time, but he had known it would return. It always came back when his soul was in conflict. At other times he could block it, but not when the longing for freedom became this overpowering.

And was that longing so terrible? He had made his decision. Why was he hesitating when he had worked and planned for so long? Did he not deserve to be set free?

She would say he did.

She had called him a fool.

He turned over on his side and looked up at the tapestry Rosa had made for him.

Rosa had never called him a fool. Rosa had been kind and gentle and without a thorn. She had wanted only what was best for him. There had been neither torment nor crisis of conscience when she was by his side. He should be dreaming of Rosa.

But he never dreamed of Rosa.

When he dreamed, it was always of his love, his passion, his nemesis. The woman who moved with the exquisite grace of a dancer and who stared at him with scorn from that jackal's face.

Selene and Kadar were sitting, waiting, when Tarik strode into the great hall the next morning.

"It's almost noon," Kadar said.

Tarik raised his brows. "Is this a sin? Selene made much of the fact of my advancing years. I decided a crippled old man needed his rest."

"Or perhaps decided to torment us for pushing you to show us the manuscript," Selene suggested.

"Were you in torment?" He smiled slyly as he dropped down in a chair and stretched out his legs before him. "What a pity."

"Why does Nasim think you have the grail?" Kadar asked.

"Questions before I've even broken my fast?"

"Why?" Kadar repeated.

"There have been rumors about my pretty golden

box for some time. You're aware that Nasim knows everything that goes on in all of Christendom. When we met many years ago, he was curious about the treasure. Later, when he obtained a copy of *Le Conte du Graal*, he became convinced my golden coffer contained the grail."

"Why?"

Tarik shrugged. "Perhaps because he wants it so desperately. He's studied the ways of power all his life and thought this was a true path."

"God would not give that monster power," Selene said flatly.

"If the grail is of God's making."

"What do you mean?"

"You read de Troyes's claim that he took the tale from another document? The ancient Celts have many legends concerning the grail. There is always a king who guards the treasure, there is always a wandering knight, but the rest of the stories differ. Some of them say the treasure is not a vessel at all but a precious stone loosed from the crown of Lucifer during his struggle with God. Don't you think that tale would appeal to Nasim?"

"Yes." Kadar stared directly into Tarik's eyes. "Is it a grail in your box?"

Tarik smiled. "What do you think?"

"You're not going to tell us," Selene said in frustration. "Why show us the manuscript, then?"

"I promised I'd show you what persuaded Nasim to involve you in his machinations. I promised nothing else. Wouldn't I be a fool to give you a description of the treasure Kadar intends to steal? Perhaps it would make him even more eager to take it from me."

"Nonsense. He doesn't want it for himself. He promised Nasim, and he regards any promise as sacred."

"And you do not?"

"Not if it's made to a man who would break any promise himself if it suited him."

"Ah, but women are so much more practical than we men when it comes to honor. We seem to be blinded by our own code." He looked at Kadar. "But what if it was the grail and it would give Nasim greater power? Would you still give it to him?"

Kadar slowly nodded.

Tarik chuckled. "I thought as much. It's an obstacle that I must overcome if I'm to win you. I'd far rather set Selene to the task, but, unfortunately, she isn't ready yet."

"What is this task?" Kadar asked.

Tarik shook his head. "Not yet. We're coming closer each day, but I must be sure."

"And I cannot linger here forever. More than a week has passed. This afternoon I'm going outside the fortress to speak to Balkir before he decides to storm the gates."

"Very wise. He's a very impetuous man. By all means, go and reassure him that you're doing everything you can to wrest my treasure from me." He paused. "I will, of course, keep Selene and Haroun safe until you return."

Selene stiffened. "Prisoners?"

"What an ugly word. Guests. Kadar would not wish you with Balkir. I'm the better choice."

"Yes," Kadar said. "And who knows, Selene? He may decide you're more ready than he thinks and give his great task to you instead."

"I've chosen you. She does not have your experience and searching mind. That will come in time, but I'm too weary to wait."

"And because I'm a woman."

Tarik shook his head. "I'm not so foolish. I know the worth of women. The cleverest human being I've ever encountered was my first wife."

"And she had this 'searching mind'?" Selene asked.

"More than I," he said sadly. "She shone like the sun."

"Well, I've no desire to shine like the sun. I merely wish to be free to go my way and do as I please."

"So did she. Soon." Tarik turned away. "I'll go and tell the guards at the gate that you're to be permitted to leave, Kadar. Do try to return by dark. I look forward to our evenings together. Selene, will you join me in the courtyard to bid him farewell?"

"Perhaps."

Tarik smiled over his shoulder at her. "Difficult. But the interesting women always are. I believe you'll be there."

"Why?"

"Because life is uncertain and your heart is greater than your stubbornness. You'll not let Kadar go back to Balkir without a last good-bye."

She met Tarik's gaze and then looked away. "You don't know me as well as you think."

Tarik smiled as he saw Selene approaching. "You could not resist."

She didn't look at him but at Kadar going through the gates. "Only because I had nothing better to do. It's not as if he goes into danger. Balkir knows better than to harm Kadar. Nasim would kill him."

"And so would you." Tarik's gaze followed hers. "You love him. Why do you fight it so?"

"I *will* not love him. He lied to me. He was going to leave me. He cared nothing for his promise. And you know nothing about me. You cannot know how I feel."

"I know that sometimes the excuses we seize not to do things are not what really move us."

"It's not an excuse."

"I believe it is. Your instinct is not to run but to fight. So why are you not fighting for Kadar? Fear?"

"Why should I be afraid?"

He shrugged. "I don't know. You may fear to love him too much. You have an idea what he is and perhaps you sense what he may become. Your instincts are correct. He is in great danger."

She felt a stirring of panic. "Don't be foolish. Kadar is too clever. Nasim will not have him."

"Not Nasim. Me."

She gazed at him in surprise. "You? You will not hurt him. I'm not blind. You like Kadar."

"We have a great bond. That will not prevent me from doing him the greatest damage any human can do to another." His lips twisted. "The temptation is too great."

"Why are you telling me this?" she whispered.

"Because muddled thinking causes waste and

unhappiness. I speak as one who knows. I would not have lost Layla if I'd been able to see truth instead of my own pain. Even now I'm still not sure . . . I like you, Selene. I don't want you to make the same mistake."

"What difference does it make what I feel or do if you intend to destroy Kadar anyway?"

"Love always makes a difference. We have to grab it and hold on until the last moment."

Last moment. A chill iced through her at the words. He was talking about Kadar's last moment. "I'm going to tell him what you've said about hurting him."

"I don't doubt it, but he won't be surprised. Kadar and I understand each other." He paused. "And he also understands that sometimes destiny forces us all to do what we have to do just to survive." He smiled sadly. "I often see myself in Kadar."

"He's *not* like you. He would not kill you for any reason." She whirled on him. "We will leave here. I won't let you do it."

"He won't go. He may send you, but he won't go himself. He hears the call."

Her chill increased as she remembered that night before Kadar had come to the castle. "What call?"

"Curiosity. Fate. Who knows what calls a man? But he hears it."

"It's not true."

"Ah, I believe you know it is." His gaze went to Kadar, who was now nearing Balkir's tent. "If you would permit yourself, you would hear it too."

"I'll never permit myself to indulge in such foolishness."

"Never is a long time, Selene."

# Chapter Nine

"BY GOD, you've been there over a week already. How much longer will it take?" Balkir demanded.

"I have no idea," Kadar said.

"Then I want the woman returned to me."

"Tarik prefers her to remain at the castle. I doubt if he would release her."

"Why not?" Balkir's fists clenched in frustration. "What is this about?"

Kadar smiled. "It's about getting Nasim's treasure for him. Why else are we here?"

"I'm sure Nasim would not like this. I sent a messenger to tell him what you were doing the moment you entered the gates."

Kadar's smile vanished. "And has he replied?"

"Not yet. But he will. He'll tell me to storm this castle and take the treasure as you could not."

"He's wiser than that. He'll tell you to wait and obey my instructions." Kadar turned to go. "If I don't return with the treasure in another week's time, I'll come out and inform you of my progress."

"I'll not wait forever." Balkir's voice lowered menacingly. "I won't face Nasim's anger because of your dawdling. I think you seek to betray him."

"Nonsense. I'll be in touch with you." Kadar left the tent and strode toward his horse. As he mounted, he saw Balkir standing beneath the awning at the opening of the tent, balefully watching him. Ordinarily, Kadar would not have been overly concerned, but he could sense a change in Balkir's attitude. He was growing more belligerent, and his fear of Nasim's wrath was growing.

Frightened men were always dangerous.

"He's sent a message to Nasim?" Tarik frowned as he moved his pawn. "That's not good."

"But to be expected." Kadar studied the chessboard. "You couldn't keep us here indefinitely with no action being taken."

"Am I keeping you here?" Tarik smiled. "I believe you would stay regardless of anything I said or did now."

He was right, Kadar thought. With each passing day he felt as if he were being drawn deeper into the web Tarik was spinning about them. Strange, he had fought Nasim's power but he was not battling Tarik.

Maybe because he knew he could tear the delicate web aside and break free at any time. His glance went to Selene standing at the windows across the hall. "I noticed a change in Balkir. I want her away from here. Find a way to get her away from the castle without Balkir seeing her and send her back to Montdhu."

"She wouldn't go."

"If you want me to stay, then you have to send her safely from here. You'll discover a way."

Tarik leaned back in his chair and gazed at him. "I'm not sure I wish to do that. What if my plans for you come to naught and I must look elsewhere? It would be a great inconvenience to retrieve Selene from Montdhu."

Kadar's head lifted with sudden menace. "I'll not have you using her."

"How quickly you rise to her defense. It's truly touching."

"I'm weary of your games and your sarcasm. Let's be done with it. Tell me what you would have me do and I will answer yes or no."

"You grow impatient."

"And you speak in riddles and secrets. Is it the grail in your coffer?"

"Do you fear God will strike you dead if you steal a holy relic?"

"Answer me."

Tarik was silent.

"Then tell me how you came to have the box."

"My, how persistent you are." He raised his voice. "Selene, come. Kadar has persuaded me to reveal my secrets. I would not leave you out."

"Don't involve her any further," Kadar said in a low voice. "I told you I wanted her away from here."

Tarik smiled and held out his hand to Selene, who was coming toward them. "Kadar is being unfair. He wishes to exclude you from our discussion."

Selene seated herself on a stool by the fire. "It does not surprise me."

"Where did you get the coffer?" Kadar asked again.

"It was given to me by a young prince. He said it was a gift, but I knew he sought to bribe me to give him the treasure. I took the gift and gave him nothing. I thought it a good lesson for him." He grimaced. "No, that's not true. I took it because I was a poor man and the gold and jewels of the box dazzled me."

"You said you were born of scum of the streets. What did scum have to do with princes?"

"Any man becomes valuable to royalty if he possesses something they want."

"And what court did this prince grace?"

Tarik shook his head. "You never cease trying to trap me, do you?"

Kadar tried another question. "How did the prince learn of the treasure?"

"Layla told him. She was afraid and wanted to protect us."

"By giving the treasure away?"

"You don't understand."

"How can we understand when you don't tell us anything of worth?" Selene asked.

"Ah, you wish me to tell you something of importance." Tarik lazily leaned his head back. "Let me think... What does Nasim regard as important?"

"Power," Kadar said.

"And he believes my treasure will bring it to him." He paused. "It's true, it will."

Kadar went still. "How?"

Tarik ignored the question. "Power is a beacon. It attracts you, doesn't it, Kadar? What if I told you that you could have enormous power but you would lose everything that meant anything to you? That you would wield it alone?"

"More riddles." But Kadar was aware that Tarik's laziness was only a pose; the other man's gaze was fixed watchfully on his face. "What man would want power that much?"

"Nasim." Tarik pushed back his chair and stood up. "But apparently not you. I thought not, but there was always hope. It seems I must still make the choice."

"What choice?" Selene asked.

"Good, evil. I've come too close to you. I find myself wavering." His lips tightened. "But I'm a selfish man. No doubt self-love will triumph in the end." He turned and walked out of the hall.

Excitement gripped Kadar as his gaze followed him.

"What did he mean?" Selene asked.

"I'm not sure." But he was beginning to catch a glimmering on the horizon. Impossible. It could not mean...No, impossible.

"He frightens me more than Nasim does," Selene said. "He wants to destroy you."

Kadar shook his head.

"Don't be foolish," Selene said fiercely. "You heard him. We must leave here. And don't tell me you have to keep your promise to Nasim. I weary of such madness."

"Then I won't tell you." She was frightened, and he wanted to pull her into his arms and comfort her. He knew she would not permit it. Instead, he gently touched her cheek with his forefinger. "I'd hate to risk your displeasure."

"Don't jest." She moved her face to avoid his touch. "Will you come with me?"

"Soon."

"Why not now, tonight?"

"Why are you so eager to go? There's no more threat tonight than there was a week ago."

"Yes, there is. He ... It's changing. He was—but now he's—Something's going to happen."

He could feel it too. But to him the realization brought anticipation, not fear. "I've discussed with Tarik getting you out of the fortress and back to Montdhu. As soon as it's safe, I'll—"

"But you won't go." Her hands clenched into fists at her sides. "Thickheaded ox. Idiot. Buffoon. I want to strike you."

She whirled and ran out of the hall.

He was tempted to follow and comfort her, but if he did, there would be more arguments. He would let her regain her composure and try to talk to her in the morning.

He picked up his pawn from the board and fingered it thoughtfully. Are we just the pieces on a chessboard to you, Tarik?

Maybe in the beginning, but that had changed. Kadar's instincts told him that Tarik had become more involved than he wanted. Now that Tarik realized that truth, he would take action.

But what action?

*Something was going to happen.*


He was a fool.

Selene's fist crashed down on the stone window embrasure. She wished it was Kadar's stubborn head or his eyes that refused to see.

She leaned her cheek against the wall as she gazed blindly out at the courtyard below.

Why would he not listen to her? He saw the danger of Nasim, but he appeared oblivious to any threat from Tarik. Kadar didn't seem to be aware of the dark tempest she could sense gathering around him.

They should leave this place. Balkir was no threat at all compared to Tarik.

And she was hiding in her chamber bruising her hand against a stone wall when she should be doing something about it.

Think.

What would force Kadar to leave?

It was difficult to reason. She was too frightened by that whirling storm she could sense coming nearer by the minute.

*Something was going to happen.*


Fear was causing her stomach to clench, but she was breathless with excitement.

It was the same feeling she'd experienced when

she'd run away from the House of Nicholas those many years ago, Selene thought.

She drew her cloak closer about her. Breathe deep. Don't show any emotion.

The guard of the south wall was standing at the head of the rope ladder a few feet above her. He was a young man but not obtuse. She could see he was wary of anyone invading his watch in the middle of the night.

She hoped not too wary. She had waved to disarm him before coming up the ladder. She smiled now as she accepted his hand and he pulled her up the last few feet. "I thank you."

"You should not be here, Lady Selene."

"I know." She sighed. "I could not sleep."

He gazed at her suspiciously.

"Lord Kadar visited Captain Balkir's camp today. He said the captain threatened to storm the castle." She shivered. "He frightened me."

The young soldier's demeanor softened a trifle. "You shouldn't worry. His force is not large enough to prevail against us."

"I'm not sure. Captain Balkir is a fierce, cruel man. I woke up a short time ago from a dream in which he was creeping closer and closer to this wall. I tried to go back to sleep, but I lay there shaking." She nibbled at her lower lip as she gazed out into the darkness. "I thought if I could see for myself that he was nowhere near, I'd be able to rest. Is that his encampment over there?"

The soldier nodded. "And there's been no sign of movement all night."

"Are you sure? What if he's managed to slip his men out of the encampment? What if he and his men are down at the bottom of the wall right now, just waiting to loose their arrows?"

He smiled indulgently. "There is no one here."

"What if there is?"

"I will show you." He took a step closer to the balustrade and leaned over so that he could see the ground directly below. "No sign of anyone. You see? No one at—"

He grunted as Selene struck him with the brass pitcher she had hidden beneath her cloak.

She caught him as he fell so that he wouldn't tumble to the courtyard below.

"I'm sorry," she whispered. She hoped she had done no more than stun him. He had seemed a pleasant young man.

An instant later he gave a low groan. A mixed blessing. Now she must worry about him regaining his senses before she could get down the wall.

She quickly untied the rope she had wound around her waist and tied it to an abutment.

The guard moaned again.

She slipped over the side and began crawling carefully down the wall.

"There you are." Tarik threw open the door of the library and limped into the chamber. His dark hair was mussed but he was fully dressed. "I've been looking all over the castle for you. What are you doing here in the middle of the night?"

Kadar closed the cover of de Troyes's manuscript. "I remembered something and I wanted to reread a few passages."

Tarik's gaze narrowed. "Why?"

Kadar countered, "Why are you so concerned about my whereabouts that you come looking for me in the dead of night?"

"I thought you might have gone too."

Kadar stiffened. "Gone?"

"Selene saw fit to knock out the guard on the south wall and leave the fortress."

"Lord in heaven." Kadar muttered a curse at his own stupidity. He had known she was upset. He should have followed her. "Haroun?"

Tarik shook his head. "She went alone."

"And you came looking for me."

"I didn't think she'd be able to persuade you to leave, but I thought you might have followed and tried to find her."

"I will," he said grimly.

"No need. When the guard regained his senses, he saw Balkir's encampment astir. The captain must have intercepted her as she was trying to escape."

"She wasn't trying to escape."

"What?"

"If she had been trying to escape, she would have taken Haroun. She feels responsible for him."

"Then why did she crawl down that wall?"

"I wouldn't go with her. She knew I'd follow if she placed herself in Balkir's hands."

Tarik pursed his lips in a soundless whistle. "Clever."

"I want to *strangle* her. By God, I'd wager she

marched into Balkir's camp and woke them up so that they'd take her prisoner."

"That picture doesn't lack a certain humor."

"To me it does." Kadar headed for the door. "I'm the one who has to get her back."

"Wait."

Kadar gave him a cold glance over his shoulder. "I won't let her stay in Balkir's hands, Tarik."

"I didn't think you would. I merely wondered if you wanted me to send an escort with you."

"If Balkir thought there was any chance he'd lose her, he'd cut her throat. I'll go alone."

"He'll kill her? Did she realize the danger?"

"She knew it. This was no wild impulse. She knew exactly what she was doing."

"Then she'll try to keep you from coming back," he said softly.

"I'm going, Tarik. Don't try to stop me."

"It would not be to my advantage for you to go now."

Kadar stiffened at the silken threat in the other man's tone. He gazed directly into his eyes. "I won't leave her there. You'll have to kill me to keep me from going."

"No, I wouldn't. There are many ways to—" Tarik stopped and the menace left his expression. He said wearily, "But it appears I lack the will to use them." He waved his hand. "Go on. Bring her back. We'll let fortune decide. Maybe I'll be lucky. God knows, fate owes me a good turn."

"I thought you'd come." Balkir smiled smugly at Kadar. "Though I have no idea why you'd be so foolish. After all, she's only a woman."

"And a troublesome one at that," Kadar agreed. "I don't know why I'm bothering to retrieve her. We had a small disagreement and she decided to punish me by fleeing."

"Then you won't mind my holding her?"

"I wouldn't mind, but Tarik wishes her back. Where is she?"

"In her tent." He paused before he added, "Where she will stay until you return with the treasure."

"I told you that you must be patient until—"

"I'm done with patience. Bring me the treasure or I'll kill the woman."

"Nasim would not approve of such impetuous behavior. He would punish you for—"

"On the contrary, I do approve."

Kadar whirled to face the tent entrance.

Nasim moved forward. "Hello, Kadar. I, too, am done with patience."

"I didn't realize you were here."

"I arrived only an hour ago. Just before dawn. I didn't like the message that I received from Balkir. It stank of treason."

"I told you I'd bring you the box. I will do so."

"If Tarik doesn't tempt you away from me. You've found him very persuasive, haven't you?"

"I'll bring you the box."

He shook his head. "I no longer trust you."

"You never did. You trust no one."

"Certainly no one tainted by that devil Tarik." He

smiled. "So we will keep the woman until you bring the box. I will give you until dawn tomorrow. By the way, is she with child?"

"No."

"Pity. I'll have to remedy that when I take her back to Maysef."

Don't show the rage. Control. "Tarik wants her to return to the castle. It will be easier for me to steal the box if we keep him content."

"Content? Is he coupling with her too?"

"No, but while she's at the castle he feels he has a hold on me."

"He does," Nasim said. "So she will stay here."

He would not be swayed, Kadar realized with frustration. He'd had a small chance to persuade Balkir to release Selene, but never Nasim. "May I see her?"

"Of course. You may even couple with her." Nasim smiled. "As a gesture of good faith. I wish to keep you content as well."

Kadar turned to leave.

"Has Tarik told you what's in the box?" Nasim asked.

He glanced at him over his shoulder. "No."

"Not even a hint?"

It would be unwise to lie. Nasim might have a man in Tarik's castle. "He showed me the manuscript by de Troyes."

"Ah, and what did you make of it?"

"A foolish troubadour's fable. Surely you cannot believe it."

"There's some truth in most fables." His gaze bored into Kadar's. "And you're too clever not to sift through the chaff to the gold beneath."

"You do believe it."

"Enough to risk a great deal to get it. After I have it, I'll put it to the test and know soon enough."

"Put it to the test?"

Nasim waved his hand. "Go to the woman. I want you back with Tarik by nightfall and the treasure in my hands by tomorrow morning. Being this close is making me eager to have an end to this."

Kadar could see that for himself. Nasim's black eyes were glittering, and there was a faint flush on his cheeks. He had never seen Nasim in such a fever of excitement. It did not bode well.

But often signs that appeared adverse could be turned to advantage if you could only find the means. Though, God knows, he could see no way out of this coil now.

"What do we do?" Selene demanded the moment Kadar entered her tent. "I saw Nasim arrive. We're in great danger, aren't we?"

"Yes, I believe we are. It appears he's grown weary of waiting."

"Can you do nothing with him?"

"Not this time."

And she had brought him here into Nasim's hands, she thought in agony. She squared her shoulders. "Well, say something."

"What?"

"I know it's my fault. I wanted you away from Tarik. I thought you'd be safer here. I knew Balkir would be no real danger to you."

"You didn't know Nasim would be coming."

"But it's still my fault."

"Yes, it is." He smiled. "When Tarik first told me you'd fled, I wanted to strangle you."

But he wasn't angry now. He was worried and that made her feel worse. "You were being foolish. You wouldn't listen to me."

"I'll listen now if you can tell me how we'll get out of this. I'm to return to the castle by nightfall, and I must deliver the box to Nasim by dawn."

"And I'm to stay here?"

He nodded. "Nasim is no fool. He knows I'll come back for you."

"Tarik will kill you if you try to steal the box."

"And Nasim will kill both of us if I don't."

"Then we must escape and get away from both of them."

"So simple." He shook his head. "If we escape, we return to Tarik."

"No!"

"Better to ally ourselves with Tarik than be hunted over the countryside by both him and Nasim."

"But Tarik will—"

"Kill me? No, I've been doing some thinking. I don't believe that's what he has in mind."

"I told you what he said."

"He gave you a warning he knew you'd repeat to me. When I left the castle, he said that fortune would decide."

"Decide what?"

"I'm not sure. I'm beginning to have an idea, but I intend to make certain when we return."

"I can't persuade you not to go back to him?"

"It's the wisest way."

"It's not wise. It's the way of your curiosity."

He shook his head. "I might risk my own neck but never yours, Selene."

She knew that, but it didn't make his choice easier to accept. "Very well, we'll go back." She scowled. "But I don't promise to stay there."

He smiled. "You'll have a harder time going over the wall next time. I'm sure Tarik gave that guard you struck on the head a severe punishment."

"I hope not. He seemed decent enough." She changed the subject. "How are we to escape? The tent is guarded."

"I'll have to think about it."

"I've already thought of a way." She looked away from him. "You should leave me and go back to the castle. Then later tonight I'll escape by myself. You can wait for me by the north gate and let me in."

He shook his head.

"It's the best plan. You know it is. If you try to take me, we may both be killed."

"We go together."

"Don't be stubborn. Do you think I need to rely on you for help? I got myself into this predicament, it's up to me to get myself out."

"Together." He smiled. "Always together. Haven't you learned that yet?"

She felt the tears sting her eyes. "I could not bear it if you were hurt for my sake," she whispered.

"You could bear it. You could bear anything."

She smiled shakily. "Of course I could. And I don't

know why I should be concerned about you anyway. Everything that's happened is all your fault."

"And I thought you were blaming yourself. I'm glad you've recovered your senses."

"It's my fault we're in danger right now, but we'd still be safely at Montdhu if you—"

"Hush." He was chuckling as he shook his head. "Very well, everything is my fault. I admit it."

"Well, almost everything." She moved toward the tent entrance and gazed out at the walls of the fortress. "And if you can think of no other plan, then we will go with mine. Do you understand?"

"I understand I'm growing weary of ultimatums. I like yours no more than I did Nasim's."

Despair surged through her. "Please," she whispered.

"Come here."

She glanced over her shoulder. He had dropped down on the pallet and was holding his hand out to her. "Why?"

"Because I'm worried and a little discouraged and I need comfort. Will you give it to me?"

She could feel her resistance melting. What other man would admit weakness and need to a woman? She moved slowly toward him. "You wouldn't have to worry if you'd leave and then let me—"

"Shh." He pulled her down on the pallet. "Don't talk. Just let me hold you."

"We should be making plans."

"We have several hours, and my mind doesn't seem to be working properly at the moment."

She drew him protectively closer. "It will be all right. I'll think of something."

"Will you?" He kissed her temple. "That would be a great relief to me."

She had not lain with him since the last night at Maysef, and there was a warm sweetness to the moment. Surely it would do no harm to just lie here and comfort him.

And take comfort herself.


The sun rays streaming into the tent were lengthening, Kadar noticed. They had little time left. He should wake Selene.

She had dozed off over an hour ago, but he had been lying here thinking, weighing his alternatives. Not that there were many choices open to them. He could see only one that had even a possibility of success.

"It's late." Selene's eyes were open, her expression panicked.

"It's all right. There's no hurry." He sat up. "I've decided your plan is best after all."

She sat up straight. "You have?"

"Why are you so surprised? You assured me that it was our best choice."

"But you aren't always sensible."

"I can accept the premise but not all the details. I'll go back to the castle at nightfall. Near midnight, when the camp is asleep, I'll return for you."

The mere idea made her panic. "No, you'll get yourself killed."

"If I hadn't learned how to infiltrate a camp, Nasim

would have banished me very early in my training. Be ready."

"Don't come. I won't be here. I'll leave before you arrive."

He smiled. "But then I'll surely be killed, for I'll have to blunder around the camp looking for you." He bent down and brushed a kiss on her nose. "Be ready."


He should have been here by now, Selene agonized.

He had said near midnight.

Had they caught him?

No, she would have heard something.

Why? It took no noise to slip a dagger between a man's ribs.

Selene drew a deep breath. Stop it. Imagining the worst would do no good.

She flexed her hunched shoulders and scooted closer to the entrance of the tent. Through the slit in the cloth, she could see the two guards standing a few yards away. How could one man take out two guards without rousing the camp?

One of the guards lifted his head as if listening. He said something to the other guard and then strode around the right side of the tent.

What had he heard?

Then she heard it. A soft trilling sound that might have been a bird.

It was not.

She heard the sound of a falling body through the thin material of the tent.

One guard left, but it would be difficult for Kadar to surprise him now that he had taken out the other man.

She jumped up and threw open the flap. The guard whirled to face her.

"I need to see Nasim," she said. "I have something to tell him."

The guard shook his head. "Tomorrow."

"Now." She moved out of the tent and to the left, still facing him. "He will punish you if you don't wake him."

The guard half-turned, following her. "He is more likely to punish me if I—"

Kadar was on him. His hand covered the guard's mouth as his blade entered his heart. The man dropped to the ground.

Kadar motioned silently and Selene flew to his side. He pushed her ahead of him around the right side of the tent.

Selene almost tripped over the body of the first guard Kadar had lured away. Then Kadar took her hand and was pulling her through the labyrinth of tents.

A few minutes later they reached the edge of the camp. Selene drew a deep breath. Too soon to be safe, but at least they had gotten this far without being discovered. Now they had only the run to the castle and—

"I thought you'd come back for her."

They whirled to see Balkir standing beneath a tree a few yards away. The moonlight gleamed on the blade of the sword in his hand. "I've been waiting for you. Nasim was wrong to trust you. He should have let me fetch his treasure. I would never betray him."

Kadar's hand closed on Selene's elbow. "Run," he whispered in her ear. "I'll follow."

She shook her head. She would not leave him to face Balkir alone.

"Stop whispering. You've lost. Nasim believes you to be so clever, but I'm the one who'll give him what he wants." Balkir stepped forward, hatred twisting his features. "And I'll take away what you want."

He lunged forward, the sword pointed at Selene's breast.

Die. She was going to—

Kadar leaped in front of her, knocking her to the ground.

The sword entered his chest.

"No!"

Balkir wrenched out the sword and Kadar fell to the ground. Selene watched the blood gush from the wound. She fell to her knees beside him. "Oh, sweet Jesus, please..."

Kadar's eyes were open. "Run..."

"No." Tears were running down her face. "Be silent. You're hurt..."

"Run." His eyes closed and he slumped sideways.

Dead?

Agony tore through her. She cradled him in her arms, rocking back and forth.

"Get away from him," Balkir said.

She scarcely heard him.

He took a threatening step forward. "I said, move away from that—"

"By Allah, what have you done, Balkir?" Nasim was striding toward them from the direction of the tents.

Balkir cringed. "They were trying to escape. You said we would kill the woman if he betrayed us."

"You clumsy fool, I didn't say to kill Kadar."

"He stepped in front of my sword."

Nasim knelt beside Kadar.

Selene drew Kadar closer. "Don't you touch him," she said fiercely.

He ignored her as he examined the wound caused by the sword thrust. "He's not dead yet, but it's a death wound." He glared menacingly at Balkir. "He won't last the night."

"He stepped in front of my sword," Balkir repeated.

"Leave us alone," Selene said. "He won't die. I won't let him."

"No one can save him. It's a death wound," Nasim said. "Tarik and I will both be cheated of him." He suddenly went still. "Or perhaps not." He turned to Balkir. "Prepare a stretcher and put him on it. Be gentle. I'll not have your clumsiness kill him too quickly. We'll send him back to Tarik."

Balkir scurried away.

Nasim turned back to Selene. "Go with him. Tarik can heal him if he chooses. Persuade him to use his powers." He turned and stalked after Balkir with not another glance at Kadar.

Tarik could heal him. She grasped desperately at the straw Nasim had extended. Kadar didn't have to die. Tarik could help him.

Dear God, Kadar was so still. It seemed impossible he wasn't dead already.

Selene's grasp tightened around him as she rocked back and forth.

*Live, Kadar.*

*Live until I can get you to Tarik.*

# Chapter Ten

TARIK MET THEM as they entered the gates.

"Great gods." Tarik's face twisted with pain as he looked down at Kadar lying on the stretcher in the courtyard. "What happened?"

"He saved me," Selene said. "He's *not* going to die because he saved me. Do you hear me? He's not going to die at all."

Tarik bent down to examine the wound. "Bring that torch closer," he said to the soldier a few steps behind him.

The light of the torch flickered over Kadar's pale face. Tarik gently pushed aside the linens covering the wound. He closed his eyes for an instant as he saw the gaping hole. "A death wound."

The same words Nasim had uttered. "It's not a

death wound," Selene glared up at him. "Stop saying that."

Tarik gently touched her hair. "Child, he's dying."

She shook off his touch. "Then do something. Or tell me what to do. Nasim said you could heal him. Do it."

He stiffened. "Nasim said that?"

"He said you had the power to heal."

"Damn him."

"If you have any power, you have to heal Kadar."

"I'm no sorcerer." He scowled. "Nasim doesn't care about Kadar. It's a test, and I won't let him maneuver me into this position."

"Don't *tell* me that." Her eyes blazed in her white face. "Kadar isn't a battleground for you and Nasim to test your strengths. He's a man, a far better man than either one of you. I don't care if you use sorcery or prayer. It doesn't matter as long as you heal him."

His expression became shuttered. "It does matter. More than you know."

He wasn't going to help, Selene realized in panic. He was going to let Kadar die. She closed her eyes as waves of pain flowed over her. "Please," she whispered. "I'll do anything you say for the rest of my life. Do you want a slave? I'll be a slave. Just save him."

"Selene..."

When she opened her eyes, she could barely see him through the veil of tears. "Answer me. Can you save him?"

He was silent a moment before he said, "Possibly. I have some medicinal skills."

"Then use them."

"He's too ill to consent to my helping him."

"What difference does that make? I'll consent. I'll be responsible."

"Responsibility can be a terrible burden. One must think carefully about—"

"Stop talking." She tried to steady her voice. "He's lying here dying. He may slip away at any moment."

He stood there looking at her. Then he turned on his heel. "Take him to his chamber and get him to bed. I'll join you very soon."

Hope flared within her. She scrambled to her feet but kept tight hold of Kadar's hand as the soldiers lifted the stretcher.

"Hold on. It's going to be all right," she whispered. "Do you hear me, Kadar? We've got a chance now."

She was kneeling by Kadar's bed when Tarik came into the room, carrying a black leather pouch. "Where have you been? It's been almost an hour."

"You're fortunate I'm here at all. I'm not convinced I'm doing the right thing in interfering." He opened the pouch and set two small bottles on the bedside table. "Perhaps God meant Kadar to die this night."

"No."

"He may still die. It may be too late to save him." He pointed at the tiny blue bottle. "Make him swallow every drop of the contents of this vial. Then wait an hour and give him the contents of the white vial. It will settle his stomach." He drew the strings of the pouch. "As I said, he may still die. The medicine is very strong and he's barely holding on."

"When will I know?"

"If he's still alive at dawn, he has a good chance."
He turned and left the chamber.

Dawn. Daybreak must be at least four hours away.
Tarik didn't expect Kadar to live for that dawning.

He *would* live.

She pulled the stopper on the tiny blue bottle. So
small a vial to hold all her hopes. Her hand was shaking as she lifted it to Kadar's lips.

She parted his lips and poured a tiny portion into
his mouth, then stroked his throat until he swallowed. She followed the procedure three times until
the bottle was empty.

She set the empty vial on the table. One more hour
and she would give him the potion to soothe his
stomach.

If he lived that long.

She knelt again on the floor by his bed and laid her
cheek on his hand. "Help me, Kadar," she whispered.
"We've been together so long. I don't think I can live
if you die."

He did not stir. He was so still he gave the appearance of death even now.

She shivered and then blocked that cruel thought.
She must not think of death but of life. Tarik's medicine would heal him.

If only Kadar could hold on until dawn.


Dawn came and passed. Noon came and passed.

Kadar lived but remained in that deathlike stupor.

Evening was drawing near when Tarik returned to the chamber.

"He still lives?" He came over to the bed and examined the wound. "No fester. It may be starting to heal."

"He won't wake up. I need more medicine to give him."

Tarik shook his head. "It's too strong. A deep sleep is not uncommon in these instances. He will wake when he's ready."

"But he will live?"

Tarik nodded. "Without question."

Joy and relief surged through her with dizzying force. "Thank God."

"Perhaps." He turned to leave. "I'll send Haroun to help you. You'll need his assistance when Kadar wakes. I'll return tomorrow to check his wound." He glanced at her over his shoulder. "And get some sleep. You look worse than he does."

"I'll sleep when he wakes."

"That could be days." When she didn't reply, he shrugged and smiled faintly. "Do what you will. I suppose a few days without sleep won't harm you."

She forced a smile. "If it does, you can give me some of your fine medicine."

His smile disappeared. "No, I won't interfere again. Harm yourself and you'll have to do your own healing."

She looked at the empty vial on the table. "Was it a sorcerer's brew?"

"I thought you didn't care, if it saved Kadar."

"I don't. I just wanted to know."

"It's no sorcerer's brew. I have no magic powers. As a young man, I worked in a house where such medicines were used on occasion."

"But you said Nasim sent you Kadar as a test. He clearly believes you have magical powers."

"Does he?"

"You know he does."

"I know he questions everything and everyone. Do you believe in magic, Selene?"

"I don't know. I've seen strange things." She straightened her shoulders. "It doesn't matter. If magic will cure Kadar, it can't be bad."

He chuckled. "Always practical and clear-seeing. You'd use the devil himself if it suited you."

"Why not?" She turned back to Kadar. "I'll need a strengthening broth to feed him. Will you see to it?"

"I'm dismissed?" She could hear the amusement in his tone. "Yes, I'll see to it, Selene."


Kadar woke near dawn of the next day. One moment he was sleeping deeply and the next he was staring up at her, wide-awake.

"What's wrong? You look terrible. Are you ill?" he whispered.

"No, you are." She tried to subdue the joy soaring through her. He was *alive*. He was with her again. "Don't you remember?"

He thought for a moment. "Balkir."

She nodded.

"How long ago?"

"This is the second dawn." She shuddered. "It was a terrible wound. Everyone thought you'd die, but Tarik saved you."

"How?"

"He had a medicinal potion that cured you."

"And how did I come to be back here?"

"Nasim sent us back. He said he knew Tarik could save you."

"Interesting. What else did—"

"Be silent. You must save your strength."

"I don't feel weak. I'm growing stronger every minute."

"Oh, no, you're not at all weak. That's why you've slept like the dead for all this time."

"If I'm ill, you should have the mercy to refrain from stinging me with your serpent's tongue. It might send me into a decline."

Did he speak truth? Dear God in heaven, she had not meant to—

"Don't look like that. I was jesting."

"A poor jest," she said unsteadily.

He reached out and gently touched the delicate skin beneath her eye. "Shadows. You're wizened and gaunt as an old woman. It would make anyone sick to gaze at that face."

"Ungrateful oaf."

"Go away and rest. I need someone both more pleasant to behold and more appreciative of my humor to tend me."

She rose to her feet. "Then I'll no longer waste my time on you. I'll send Haroun to care for your needs."

"For the next day and night. After that you may be recovered enough that I can tolerate you."

"And am I to tolerate your abuse? You're a foolish man, and I should never have suffered and labored to keep your carcass alive. I didn't ask you to step in front of Balkir's sword."

"I could do nothing else." His eyes closed. "But at the moment I'm feeling a few twinges of regret. This hole in my chest must be as big as a turret."

She instantly frowned in concern. "Are you in pain?"

"Perhaps." He opened one eye and smiled slyly. "Or perhaps I see no other way to hold my own with you. You cannot attack a man in such woeful straits."

"I could." She moved toward the door. "And I will, if you don't behave yourself."

"I'll try."

His voice was a mere wisp, and she glanced back at him with renewed panic. He looked so pale and weak. He had come so close to death, and that specter might still be hovering. "Balkir almost killed you. We were both wrong about him."

"I knew he could be dangerous if backed into a corner."

"And yet you wanted him to come with us. You said you would have asked for him."

"I wanted him close."

"Why?"

"He had to pay for what he did at Montdhu." He didn't open his eyes. "He hurt you...."

———

Tarik was standing over him when Kadar woke again.

"So you survived," Tarik said. "I wasn't sure you would."

"You appear to be disappointed."

"I'm not disappointed. I just don't like to interfere when death comes calling."

"Then you shouldn't have helped me to live."

Tarik grimaced. "I had no choice. Selene would have cut my throat if I hadn't found a way to keep you alive. She can be very savage."

"And that's the only reason you saved me?"

"Perhaps. Perhaps not. I choose not to examine my motives in the matter. How do you feel?"

"Well enough."

"Pain?"

"Yes. Can you give me a potion to rid me of it?"

"No, you must bear it. I've no potion to prevent the pain of healing. Besides, I've done too much already. Nasim will probably hear that you still live and assume I've delved into sorcerers' tricks to bring that about."

"And have you?"

"You too?" He sighed. "I'm no sorcerer, and we must try to convince Nasim of that truth. Now he'll be more certain than ever that my treasure gives power, and I've no desire to battle him at present."

"He'll go away if you give him the golden box." Kadar paused. "And the grail with it."

Tarik smiled. "But then you'd have no reason to stay, and I'd be desolate if I could no longer have the pleasure of your company. No, I think we must think of another ploy to rid ourselves of Nasim."

"We? I came here on Nasim's mission."

"But don't you think a sword through the chest frees you of any promise to him? That act would sway even someone as stubborn as you." He turned to go. "Think upon it. I'll return tomorrow to check your progress. I think you'll heal quickly, but one never knows with a chest wound."

Within a week Kadar was well enough to sit up in bed. Another few days and he was taking a few halting steps around the chamber. By the second week he was prowling like a tiger and proving the impossible.

"Sit *down*," Selene said. "I've never seen such a foolish man. What if your wound breaks open?"

"It's healing well. I don't believe there is any danger." He paused and then said tentatively, "I think I'll go down to the courtyard today."

"You most certainly will not." She pushed him down in the chair. "I've not worked to get you well to have you spoil everything by being impatient."

"Is he proving troublesome?" Tarik stood in the doorway. "I suppose I could toss him over the battlements to Nasim."

"Are you sure Nasim is still here?" Kadar asked.

"Oh, yes, I understand he's still waiting like a hungry cobra scenting a saucer of milk." He strolled forward. "I've always feared cobras. When I was a boy, it was not uncommon to wake and see a snake slithering about the floor of the hut where I lived. I learned to leave nothing about to attract them."

"You didn't learn that lesson well."

Tarik chuckled. "You speak of my treasure? One must always weigh threat against value. Someday I may decide that the threat is greater than the prize, but that time is not yet. Besides, the treasure may not be the only saucer of milk Nasim is hungering after. I believe he's curious."

"About why Kadar is still alive?" Selene asked.

"Exactly." He pushed aside the bandage and looked at the wound. "Not pretty, but I don't think you need worry about him any longer, Selene. Let him go his own way."

She felt a sense of loss that she quickly hid. "Good. I've no desire to put up with any more of his nonsense. He's been a great bother to me."

Kadar smiled knowingly. "Have I?"

She ignored him and addressed Tarik. "Will Nasim attack?"

Tarik shrugged. "Who knows what Nasim will do? He has not attacked yet. Maybe he's waiting and watching for the right moment."

"And you're content to stay here and let him do it?"

"What else do you suggest?"

"I don't care what you do. Just let us go. Kadar is still weak, and we have nothing to do with what is between you and Nasim. I escaped here once before and I could have avoided Balkir's men. We can go over the wall again."

"What an admirable single-mindedness you possess," Tarik said. "You ignore everything but what you wish to protect. I'm afraid it's not that simple." His gaze shifted to Kadar. "Is it?"

Kadar met his gaze. "Her plan is not so bad."

They were closing her out, Selene realized with helpless frustration. The look they were exchanging was one layered with understanding and some other emotion she couldn't define.

"Then will you go?" Tarik asked.

"I haven't finished what I came here for."

"You almost died. Balkir nearly carved out your heart," Selene said harshly. "Do you want to stay here and let it happen again?"

"It won't happen again," Tarik said. "I went to a great deal of trouble to keep him alive, and I don't like to see any effort wasted. Now I consider it my duty to watch over Kadar."

"You can't know it won't happen again."

"I know that he has a better chance under my guardianship than under yours." He added bluntly, "We both know that his wound would never have occurred if you'd not left the castle."

She felt as if he had struck her.

"Tarik," Kadar said warningly.

"I've no wish to hurt her, but I'll not lie."

"It was my choice to go back for her."

"Stop defending me." Selene swallowed to ease her tight throat. "He's right. It was my fault. But that doesn't mean—" Their faces were blurring before her. She couldn't stay in this chamber without breaking down and weeping like a desolate child. "I have to go. I need—I forgot—"

She was running from the chamber and down the hall.

She had reached the staircase when she felt a hand on her shoulder.

"Stop," Tarik said. "I can't run down those stairs after you without taking a tumble. Won't you take pity on a crippled old man?"

She didn't look at him. "No, you don't need my pity. Even crippled, you can keep Kadar safer than I did. You were right. It was my fault that—"

"Enough. I feel quite guilty. We both know I used those harsh words only to win my own way."

"True words."

"True but cruel. Now turn around and let me see if my words are easing you."

She slowly turned to face him. "Is that why you came after me?"

"Partly. I've grown very fond of you. I don't like to see you in pain."

His words had the ring of truth, and his expression was more gentle than she'd ever seen it. "But you did it deliberately anyway."

"Not willingly. I would never hurt you willingly, Selene."

His tone held a note of sadness and finality that made her suddenly wary. "You said easing me was only part of the reason you came after me."

He nodded.

"Tell me."

"I want you to leave the castle. I'll provide you with a guard, gold, and a way of departing here that's much safer than the means you chose before. There's a tunnel beneath the dungeon that ends in the woods a few miles from here. You and Haroun should reach Scotland before the winter storms."

"I and Haroun," she repeated slowly. "Not Kadar."

"Kadar stays here."

"I won't go without him."

"He'll be quite safe. After you're safely away, I'll take him out the same way."

"Then why not let him come with me?"

He shook his head.

"Why?"

"You made me a promise. You vowed you'd do anything I said, if I saved Kadar's life. I saved him. Now I'm asking you to keep your word."

"I'm not Kadar, who obeys promises blindly. Do you think I'll let you get Kadar killed by using him to do some foolish task for you?"

"You'd prefer to get him killed protecting you?"

Pain sliced through her. "That's not fair. It wouldn't happen again."

"I wish I could believe you. I cannot. He won't be safe until you're safely back at Montdhu."

"I told you, nothing would have happened to him if everything had gone as I planned. I didn't know Nasim would come to—"

"True, but circumstances seldom can be manipulated. Things go wrong, and every man has a weakness. You're Kadar's."

"I'm not anyone's 'weakness,'" she said, bristling. "Certainly not Kadar's."

"He almost died for you. And he would do it again. Nasim knows that as well as I do. I have to take you out of the mix. I can't afford to have him either threatened or distracted right now." He paused. "I'm speaking the truth. And you know it. You're a danger to him. Admit it, Selene."

She didn't want to admit it. She wanted to argue with him, to tell him—what? He was right. She had almost caused Kadar's death. Nasim had used her before and would try to use her again.

She could feel the tears sting her eyes and hurriedly looked away. "When do you want me to go?"

"Tonight. The sooner, the better."

"No. Kadar isn't well. He still needs me."

Tarik shook his head.

She lifted her head and forced a smile. "Very well, I'll go. It's not as if I wasn't planning on leaving him anyway. It was only a matter of time." Her voice was uneven and she steadied it. "And you needn't stare at me as if I was the one who was wounded. I'm fine. This is exactly what I wanted to do."

"Is it?"

"Of course it is." She turned away. "I'll be ready to go after I give Kadar his supper tonight." She looked back at him and added fiercely, "But if you're lying, if you cause anything to happen to him, I'll come back and cut your heart out."

"Nothing will happen to him," he said gently. "I promise, Selene. I want to keep him well and alive as much as you do."

She believed him. He meant what he said. But that didn't mean he would succeed in protecting Kadar. "When will you take him away from here?"

"Tomorrow night. Once you're safely away."

"And you have a place to hide him from Nasim until he's well?"

"I know such a place," he said. "I know it's hard for you to let him go, but it's for the—"

"It's not hard. It's just not sensible for me to work so hard to keep him alive and then have you place him in danger again." She moved down the hall. "I'm going back to him now. Make your preparations."

"I will." His words followed her: "One more thing. No words of love. It must not be a sweet good-bye. He must not follow you."

"I do not love—" She couldn't finish. She did love Kadar. She had always loved him and, God help her, she probably always would. Too much had happened for her to deny it any longer. She had protected herself against the fear that he would someday leave her, and look where it had led her. "It makes no difference if I love him or not. I'm doing this because it's best for him. It changes nothing."

"It can change everything. But it must not, in this case. You're better apart."

Apart. Separate. She felt a surge of loneliness. "I agree, but not because you say it." She could feel his gaze on her back as she walked quickly down the corridor.

Kadar turned away from the window when she came into the chamber. He gazed at her searchingly. "Are you well?"

"Why shouldn't I be well? Do you think a few sharp words can hurt me?" She turned back the coverlet on the bed. "It's time for your nap. You've been up too long already today."

"Tarik shouldn't have said that. It was my decision. The fault was mine."

"Of course it was. I wasn't thinking clearly. I realized it immediately once I thought about it." She gestured to the bed. "Now come over here and lie down. Tarik may think you well, but I don't believe it."

He hesitated, then crossed the room and sat down on the edge of the bed. "I truly don't need rest. It seems I've done nothing else of late."

She pushed him down and pulled up the cover. "Be silent and close your eyes."

"I won't go to sleep."

"Close your eyes."

"Then I won't be able to see you. You wouldn't deprive me of my only pleasure?"

He was smiling coaxingly and she could not resist him. She didn't know when she'd see that smile again. Perhaps never. She sat down on the stool beside the bed. "Do what you like. I've told you what's good for you."

"*You* are good for me." He winked. "And, if you'd slip into this bed beside me, I'd show you how you could cure all my ills."

She was tempted. Not for the passion that she knew would come but to be near him one more time. What was she thinking? It would only make the agony of parting more intense. Just sitting here by him, she was painfully aware of every nuance of his voice, his every expression.

"No?" He sighed. "I thought Tarik's words might have inspired enough guilt to make you waver. It seems a long time since the tower."

"You told me I had no guilt."

"But when have you ever listened to me?"

"When you speak wisdom instead of foolishness."

"Ah, you admit I'm not completely foolish."

"Not completely." She heard the first hint of unevenness in her voice and knew she must cut the conversation short. "Only when you chatter when you should be sleeping. I will no longer indulge your idiocy."

"There's something wrong." He was studying her face. "God, you look tired. Rest. Don't come to me tomorrow."

She nodded slowly. She wanted to keep on looking at him, but she shifted her gaze. He always saw too much. He mustn't see more than the expected weariness.

He mustn't see the pain.


"Hold the torch higher." Selene held on to the wall as she carefully negotiated her way down the stone steps. "It's black as pitch down here, and these stairs are slippery. Do you want me to tumble down them?"

"Stop complaining. I'm the cripple, not you." Tarik held the torch a little higher. "We haven't much farther to go. The door to the tunnel is just beyond the next flight of steps."

"And you're sure Haroun will be waiting for me in the woods?"

"I told you, I sent him and my man Antonio out earlier this evening so they could fetch the horses from the village." He stopped at the bottom of the stairs and turned to face her. "Stop questioning me, Selene. You know this is no trap."

"How do I know?"

He smiled. "Because you trust me."

"And is that why I ran away?" she asked sarcastically.

"No, you ran away because I was foolish enough to think that I could alter fate by frightening you into action."

Her eyes widened. "You're saying you wanted me to go to Balkir's camp?"

He shrugged. "Perhaps. I'm human. I've wavered to and fro since you and Kadar came into my life. My motives can sometimes be twisted by emotion." He swung open the heavy iron door. "It didn't alter the situation. Fate seldom allows diversion from her chosen path."

She tensed as she stared into the darkness.

"You'll be safe. There's nothing in that tunnel but a few rats." Tarik handed her the torch. "In a week you'll be in Genoa, boarding a ship for Scotland. I've given Antonio a note to the captain of my ship. He'll set sail at once."

"What about Kadar?"

"We'll go to Rome and be lost in the crowds there."

"That's your fine hiding place?"

He shook his head. "Merely the first stop."

"You've got to keep him—" She broke off as she met his eyes. What was she thinking? He was an enigma. She had never been entirely sure of Tarik's thoughts, even in his most approachable moments.

But there was no use talking now. Her decision was made, and it had all been said before. "I don't know why I should trust you, but I do. Don't you *dare* betray us."

She strode into the darkness of the tunnel.

# Chapter Eleven

"YOU'RE LOOKING ABYSMALLY BORED this after-noon." Tarik strode into Kadar's room. "What are you doing back in bed? Aren't you well?"

Kadar shrugged. "Fine. Selene needs rest. I told her to stay away today, but she may come anyway. If she sees me in bed, I'll be able to convince her I don't need her hovering over me."

Tarik didn't speak for a moment. "Good thinking." He changed the subject. "I came to tell you we're going to have a visitor. Nasim sent word that he wishes to see you."

"And you're permitting it?"

"I feel a certain malicious pleasure in satisfying his curiosity. Besides, I have a reason to keep his mind occupied."

"What reason?"

"Nasim should be riding through the gates any minute." He turned toward the door. "Why don't you come down and meet him in the great hall?"

Kadar made a face. "Selene would not be pleased if I left my chamber. She would make me pay."

"I don't think that will be a problem. I haven't seen her today."

Then she must have stayed in bed as he'd told her, Kadar thought with sudden anxiety. She must be even more weary than he thought. After Nasim had gone, he would stop by her chamber to see if—

"Well, are you coming?"

"Yes." He threw the cover aside and sat up. "Go greet him. I'll be down shortly."

Nasim and Tarik were just coming through the front door when Kadar reached the bottom of the stairs.

Nasim's disgusted gaze raked Kadar's face. "You look weak as a puling babe."

"And a good day to you, Nasim," Kadar said.

"I thought you said he was doing well, Tarik."

"As well as anyone could expect considering his wound," Tarik said. "Contrary to your belief, I cannot perform miracles."

"Can't you?" Nasim's gaze narrowed on Tarik's face. "I've never seen a man survive a wound that severe. That was a miracle."

"Kadar is very strong."

"No man is that strong. It was sorcery. It was the grail that gave you the power."

Tarik gazed at him guilelessly. "What grail?"

Nasim turned to Kadar. "Since you're well, you'll do as I ordered."

Kadar raised his brows. "You don't believe the sword Balkir thrust into me ended my obligation?"

"That was not by my will." He gestured toward Tarik. "You will fight *his* magic and return to me."

"He is no sorcerer."

"No?" Nasim smiled grimly. "Ask him the circumstances of our first meeting."

"As I remember, it was not an unusual encounter." Tarik pretended to think. "Did I pull lightning from the sky?"

"By Allah, you will not laugh at me." Nasim glared at him. "I will have your magic, Tarik. And then I will have your head."

"Indeed?"

Nasim whirled on his heel. "I've seen what I came to see. You will do my bidding, Kadar, or you will suffer for—" He stopped suddenly as he reached the door. "Where is the woman?"

Kadar stiffened.

Nasim turned back to face him. "Where is she?"

"Why do you ask? You believe a woman has no place in the affairs of men."

"But she is a very interfering woman and you permit it. I find it strange that she's not here."

Tarik said quickly, "She was weary from nursing Kadar, and we didn't tell her of your arrival."

Nasim studied him for a moment in silence. "I still find it strange."

Tarik gazed after him with a frown as he left the

hall. "Unfortunate. I hoped he wouldn't notice her absence."

"Why?"

"He's a clever man. It may start him thinking."

"Stop talking in circles." Kadar took a step toward him. "Why are you so worried about him commenting on Selene?"

"Because she's no longer here."

Kadar froze. "What?"

"I sent her and Haroun away last night. They should be well on their way to board a ship that will return them to Scotland."

"Where is the ship docked?"

Tarik shook his head. "I'll not have you following her this time, Kadar."

"You won't have me—" Kadar tried to smother the white-hot rage searing through him. "*Damn* you, where is she?"

"Safer than she was here," Tarik said. "She has Haroun and my best man, Antonio, to guard her. Antonio has instructions to join us in Rome to tell us that she's safely away, as soon as she boards the ship."

"Rome?"

"This place isn't safe for either of us any longer. We can't count on Nasim sitting quietly outside the gates forever."

Kadar was cursing.

"Why are you so upset? You once asked me to send her away."

"It was different then. You shouldn't have done it. Not with Nasim waiting outside the gates to pounce on her. Not without telling me."

"I didn't abduct her. It was her choice to go. She knew it was best." He met Kadar's gaze. "And so do you. She's safer at Montdhu. You heard Nasim. As long as she was within his reach, he would try to use her against you."

"You had no *right*. She's mine."

"Think."

Kadar didn't want to think. He wanted to strangle Tarik. "I would have gotten her safely away. I would have taken her to—"

"And had Nasim following you. That would have put her in even more jeopardy. My way is better. It will keep you both alive." He shook his head as he saw Kadar's expression. "You're too angry to reason now. I'll come to see you when you've had a chance to grow calmer."

"I'm not going to get calmer about this," he said savagely. "We're not game pieces for you to move at will."

"If you were, my lot would be much easier," he sighed. "You're both very difficult people. Selene trusted me. Cannot you do the same?"

Kadar didn't answer.

"I've made plans for us to leave the castle tonight after midnight. Come to my chamber, and please be ready."

Kadar uttered an obscenity.

Tarik shrugged and started up the stairs. "Later."

Kadar's hands clenched at his sides as he watched him go. He felt helpless and enraged and terrified.

Selene.

He had always known where she was, always been

able to reach out and protect her since they had come together when she was a child. Now she was alone, on her own. It didn't matter that Tarik had done what Kadar would probably have done in his place. He had no right. He should have told him. He should have let Kadar go with her and put her on the ship himself.

And Nasim would have followed.

Tarik still had no right. Kadar would not let—

He was letting anger shatter his control and keep him from thinking. That was dangerous. If he had learned nothing over the years, it was that only the stupid allowed rage to control their emotions.

Selene was out there and he was helpless to protect her.

He drew a deep breath. Tarik had urged him to think. He would think.

But he doubted if Tarik would care for the results of his pondering.

It was almost midnight when Kadar strode into Tarik's chamber.

Tarik was sitting quietly in a chair by the fire, reminding Kadar of the first night he had come to the castle.

"Ah, I presume this means you are to go with me?" Tarik asked.

"Perhaps. When I have answers." He moved toward the carved chest across the room. "I'm weary of your secrets. Unlock the chest. I want to see the grail."

Tarik shook his head.

Kadar turned and stared into his eyes. "I'm not asking you. Unlock the chest or I'll smash it open."

Tarik shook his head again. "You're not one who smashes. That would lack both subtlety and finesse."

"I don't feel in the least subtle." He paused. "And I would take great pleasure in smashing either you or your chest at the moment. Take your choice."

"I don't like either one. Suppose I choose to argue instead," Tarik said. "I believe you need an incentive. Naturally I'm taking the chest with me. Suppose I agree to open it when we reach Rome?"

"Now."

He studied him. "I suspected that you'd be angry but not that you'd lack reason. It convinces me that I was right in sending Selene away. She's truly your Achilles' heel."

"Unlock the chest."

"You're not ready."

"Unlock it."

"In Rome." He hurriedly held up a hand as Kadar took another step toward the chest. "Wait."

Kadar stopped. "I want answers. Give me answers and I'll wait until we reach Rome to see the grail."

Tarik sighed. "Very well. Ask your questions."

"Is it truly the grail in the box?"

"In a manner of speaking."

"I'm tired of your forked tongue. Answer me."

"I did." Tarik met his gaze. "I think you've already reached some conclusions of your own and merely want me to confirm them. Isn't that true?"

"Perhaps."

Tarik chuckled. "It is true. Was it the manuscript?"

Kadar was silent.

"Tell me. What secrets did I reveal by showing you my wonderful book?" He leaned forward. "Am I the magician Nasim believes me to be?"

"No." He paused. "You're no magician."

"Oh, dear, don't tell Nasim. He would be very disappointed."

"I wouldn't think of telling him. Not after you've gone to all the trouble of trying to fool him."

"Have I done that? In what manner?"

"I believe you wrote the manuscript yourself."

Tarik's smile faded. "Interesting. And what led you to such a belief?"

"In every Celtic legend mentioned in the manuscript, there is a fisher king who is custodian of the grail. He's always crippled. The coincidence is too blatant. You wrote the manuscript yourself."

"Why would I do that?"

"How do I know? Maybe to lead Nasim to believe that the custodian must be crippled and so make you the obvious choice. Perhaps it's part of the games you and Nasim play. Perhaps surrounding yourself with mystic powers is your way of protecting your treasure."

"Wouldn't it be more logical to assume Nasim is right about my powers? Or don't you believe in magic?"

"In my life I've seen many things I cannot explain, but this I know. You're not a magician, Tarik. Though you may be clever enough to fool Nasim into believing you are."

"I'd have to wish to fool him very much indeed to

spend years creating that weighty manuscript. You think me that patient?"

Kadar slowly nodded. "I think you can be anything that you wish to be."

"I wish that were true." Tarik sighed wistfully. "Life would be so much easier."

"Did you write the manuscript?"

"I did not."

"Did you have it written?"

Tarik smiled. "It could be that I had a little to do with its creation. I've told you how I worship books."

Kadar pounced. "Then you admit it?"

"My only admission is that you're entirely correct in assuming that I'm no magician." He stood up and limped toward the door. "Now pick up the chest and follow me. It's time we left."

"I didn't say I'd go with you."

"Of course you'll go with me. There was never any question of that. The only way you'll know Selene is safe is to accompany me to Rome to receive the message from Antonio. Besides, you wouldn't want to stay here. You'll be lonely. I've given orders that within four days Sienbara is to be abandoned. My men will use the tunnel and fade into the countryside. I'll leave no sacrifices for Nasim to vent his anger upon." He turned at the door. "Wait here. I have to go down and fetch the manuscript. It's only a matter of time until Nasim discovers that we're gone. I can't chance him going into a fury and destroying it."

"You act as if the manuscript is more important than the chest."

"You find that unusual?"

"Not if there's no de Troyes and you created the manuscript."

Tarik smiled. "That would be a singularly good reason. But another would be that, to me, the written word is more priceless than any treasure. You can try to decide which is the most likely on our way to Rome."

"I'll not promise to stay with you in Rome. When Antonio comes with the message, I'll have a few words with him." He paused. "And if I find you've lied to me about putting her on a ship to Scotland, you won't live another day."

"I haven't lied. I made all the arrangements." He shrugged. "But men's arrangements are often altered by destiny. One must always take that into account."

"Not where Selene is concerned. This Antonio had better be able to care for her."

"I thought long and hard before I chose Antonio for the task." Tarik moved down the hall. "He can be trusted to do what's necessary."


GENOA


"I don't trust him," Haroun whispered, his gaze on Antonio riding a few yards ahead of them. "And I don't think this is the way to the waterfront."

Neither did Selene. She had caught glimpses of the sea from outside Genoa and, since they entered the gates, it seemed they were moving away from it. But she might be wrong, and Haroun's first judgment was the most important. "Why don't you trust him?"

"I don't know. He keeps too much to himself. He's

too quiet. When he was in the guardroom, he would not...He was not like the other soldiers."

"That's no condemnation. All men are different. Tell me something of substance."

"I don't trust him." Haroun scowled. "And we should not be here. Lord Kadar would not like it that you ran away without telling him."

It was not the first time he had made his feelings known on that score, and her temper was raw. The journey had been long and one she had not wanted to make. Haroun's criticism was only an additional abrasive. "I don't care what Lord Kadar likes," she said through clenched teeth. "How many times must I tell you that I don't belong to him or any man? I make the decisions that concern me."

Haroun immediately backed down. "I did not mean—It's just that Antonio is not—"

"Antonio led us safely here. If he was betraying us to Nasim, he would have done it before we left Tuscany. And Lord Tarik sent Antonio with us. Do you suspect him also?"

Haroun shook his head. "Lord Tarik is an honorable man. But Antonio could be in the pay of Nasim. Perhaps he paid him to bring us here, where he could gather us in like fish in a net."

"And perhaps you've decided you like serving Lord Tarik and don't wish to go home to Lord Ware?"

"No." Haroun's eyes widened in horror. "It's not so, Lady Selene. Lord Ware is my master. It's true I've enjoyed serving under Lord Tarik, but I would never—"

"I know you wouldn't," Selene cut him short. The rawness of her own pain was making her unfair.

Haroun was genuinely worried, and it was never wise to ignore instinct. She just wished her mind was clearer so that she could make a judgment. She had felt as if she were wading through a fog since she left Sienbara. "And we will watch Antonio carefully until we meet the captain of Lord Tarik's ship."

Haroun nodded with satisfaction. "We must be ready to—"

"We're here." Antonio was riding back toward them, smiling broadly. It was the first smile she had seen on his face since they started the journey. He waved at a small building just ahead. "I thought it best to bring you to an inn, where you could have a clean bed and water to wash away the dust of the road before we go to the ship. I'll wager you'll have enough of seawater before your journey is over."

She heard Haroun mutter a curse as he dismounted. "I'll go in and see if the quarters are fitting for you."

And that there was no trap waiting inside. She could not allow him to do it. "No, I'll go by myself."

"It's clean enough," Antonio said as he turned his horse. "I've stayed there many times. But see for yourself. I'll go fetch the captain."

She watched him ride leisurely away. If he had set a trap, he showed no sign of guilt. Perhaps there was no trap. It could be that Haroun's suspicions were groundless. She slipped from the saddle. "Wait here."

"No, I'll go in and—"

"Wait here," she repeated. "That's an order, Haroun." She strode into the inn before he could protest.

The hall was small and filled with crudely crafted wooden tables. The scent of herbs and meat drifted to her from the large open fireplace across the room.

The rushes on the floor were fresh, the wood of the tables clean. She had seen many inns like this before. The plump, balding man coming toward her was smiling cheerfully. "Ah, welcome, I'm Mario. How may I serve you?"

She could see nothing threatening here. It was certainly too small to hide any force sent by Nasim. A little of her tension left her. "A chamber, a bath, and hot meals for me and my man in the stable yard."

"At once." He led her toward the stairs. "I have only one small chamber. You're fortunate it's unoccupied. Your man will have to sleep in the common room or the stable."

One chamber. Again, little room for any hidden men. "I'll need it for only one night, perhaps less. The bath is the most important." They had reached the room at the top of the stairs and Mario was throwing open the door. "I will need fresh soap and—"

There was someone standing at the window across the chamber.

Tall.

Billowing black cloak. Dark hair drawn back in a queue.

*Nasim.*

She whirled back toward the stairs.

"No." Mario's hand was grasping her shoulder. His tone was no longer jovial.

She kneed him in the groin.

He squealed, but his grasp didn't loosen.

Her hand tightened on the dagger beneath her cloak.

She had no chance to draw it.

"Bitch." Mario jerked her back into the room and cuffed her hard on the back of the neck.

Pain.

She was falling.

She mustn't faint. Fight off the dizziness. Nasim would bend over her. She must be ready to plunge the knife into his chest.

Footsteps on the wooden floor. She kept her eyes tightly closed.

He was coming toward her.

"Idiot. I told you not to hurt her."

"I had to do it. She tried to unman me."

"I'd do it myself if I didn't know your brains are all in your gonads."

That low voice was not Nasim's. Selene's eyes flew open.

A woman!

"So Mario didn't do as much damage as I feared." The woman's gaze was on Selene's face. "You're pale, but that could be fear."

"I'm not afraid of you."

"You ran away."

"I thought you were someone else. Nasim."

"I'm not flattered you thought I was a man. But I can be much more dangerous than Nasim." She turned to Mario. "Go get the boy Haroun and give him food. Tell him she's bathing and will talk to him later."

Mario scampered from the chamber.

"Who are you?" Selene asked. "Are you one of Nasim's followers?"

"I follow no one." The woman moved toward the basin across the room. "Sit up and remove your hand from that dagger. I've no desire to harm you until I find out what I need to know."

Selene's hand stayed on the dagger hilt as she rose to a sitting position. She sat watching as the woman dipped a cloth in the water in the basin. She was perhaps near her thirtieth year, as tall as most men, broad shouldered, and the black cloak she wore half hid, half revealed the lean grace of her body. Her face was not beautiful. Her nose was a trifle too large and her jaw too firm and broad, but her mouth was full and beautifully shaped and her large, dark eyes truly magnificent. "I'll tell you nothing."

"Don't be so hasty. You have no idea what I want to know." She was coming back toward Selene and stopped a few feet away. She tossed the damp cloth into her lap. "Wash your face and then press the cloth to the back of your neck. I'd do it for you, but I don't believe you'd appreciate my service, and I'm not good at that sort of thing anyway." She sat down in a chair and stretched out her long legs in front of her. "We will talk as soon as you finish."

Selene didn't touch the cloth. "We will talk now."

"I said we will—" The woman studied Selene's expression and then slowly nodded. "Very good."

Even seated, the woman possessed power and presence, and Selene instinctively moved to a position of less subservience. She scrambled to her feet so that she was the one looking down.

The woman again nodded approvingly. "Even better."

"Who are you?"

"My name is Tabia."

"And you have no link with Nasim?"

"I did not say that. I said I didn't follow him."

"And did he hire you to bring me here?"

Tabia shook her head. "Nasim has nothing to do with this, and you would realize that fact if you were thinking. Nasim has the arrogance and stupidity of most men where women are concerned. He would not think us clever enough to lay a decent trap." She made a face. "And he would be right in most cases. We have let men dull our wits and lie to us for so long that we women have become a pitiful lot. Do you not agree?"

"No. I'm not pitiful. I will never be pitiful."

For the first time, a faint smile touched Tabia's lips. "I believe you speak the truth. That is refreshing. I cannot tell you how weary I am of whimpering—"

"Why am I here?"

"Because Tarik sent you to me."

Selene stiffened. "Tarik betrayed me?"

She shook her head. "Tarik doesn't have the subtlety necessary for lies and betrayal."

"He does know how to lie. He told me he would send me back to my home in Scotland. That's why I'm here in Genoa."

"And I'm certain he sent a message with Antonio to the captain of his ship giving him instructions to do just that."

"Then he didn't send me to you. You don't make sense."

"Tarik is a man in conflict. Sometimes he wants things all ways. He has excellent instincts, and I think he knew Antonio was in my employ. We'll discover how good they are tonight." She stood up. "I'll call Mario and tell him to bring us wine and a meal."

"I will not eat with you."

"Because you think me your enemy?"

Selene looked at her in astonishment. "You struck me on the neck. You lured me here. It's a reasonable assumption."

"But reason seldom tells the whole tale. I'm not your enemy. It may be that I'm your best friend. We will have to see after you answer my questions."

Selene shook her head.

"One must trust one's feelings. Look at me. You don't really think I mean you harm?"

Tabia's glance was bold, direct, and seemingly without guile. What of that? Selene thought impatiently. It would be foolish to trust her.

Tabia smiled. "I'm sure Tarik left you frustrated and confused. It's a habit of his. You'll find I'm much more open. Aren't you curious as to what plans he has for Kadar?"

Selene froze. "What do you know of Kadar?"

"I make it my business to know as much about Tarik's doings as I can." She frowned. "But I don't know why he chose Antonio to bring you here. I have to know everything that went on at Sienbara."

"Then ask Antonio."

"He cannot tell me what went on behind closed

doors. I'll bargain with you. You tell me what I need to know, and tomorrow morning you and the boy will be free." She met Selene's gaze. "Knowing Tarik, I doubt if what transpired has any import that you would believe dangerous to you or Kadar."

"Then why do you have to know?"

She shrugged. "It's part of the game Tarik and I play. I don't understand this move and it troubles me."

Anger soared through Selene. First Tarik had dared to use them, and now this woman was trying to do the same. "I won't be part of your game."

Tabia raised her brows. "Not even to save your Kadar?"

Selene drew a deep breath, trying to disguise that the words had struck home. "I don't know that you can or want to save him or that he is in danger at all."

"Oh, he is in danger. Don't you wish to know from what direction?"

"You promise to tell me?"

"I promise," Tabia said. "You'll find I'm not nearly as secretive as Tarik."

Selene's nails dug into her palms as she clenched her hands. The woman was right: What had occurred at Sienbara presented no obvious threat. She could avoid mention of the box and the manuscript that—

"For instance, I'd wager he showed you the golden coffer but refused to let you look inside. I'd never be so rude."

Selene's eyes widened. "You know about the box?"

Tabia glanced away from her. "Does he still keep it with that ugly wooden statue?"

"Yes."

"Sentimental idiot." Tabia whirled and headed for the door. "I'll call for food."

"I didn't say I'd changed my mind."

"You know you have."

"Evidently I can tell you little you don't already know." Selene paused. "But I'll still hold you to your promise."

"Yes, yes." Tabia waved an impatient hand. "I know all that. Do you think I'm a fool?"

No, the woman was intelligent, manipulative, with a reckless disregard for anyone's will but her own. "I wished to make it quite clear."

"And what could you do if I decided not to honor our bargain?"

"Find a way to hurt you."

Tabia blinked. "Indeed? Interesting." She threw open the door and shouted, "Food, Mario. And the best wine in the house."

# Chapter Twelve

"THAT'S ALL?" Tabia leaned back in her chair. "You've told me everything?"

"Yes. I told you that you probably knew all that I did."

"Not quite all." Tabia wiped her hands on her napkin before tossing it aside and reaching for her goblet. "And have your Kadar's wounds healed sufficiently for him to travel?"

"He's not my Kadar." Selene sipped her wine. "He almost died. He should not travel."

"But he could?"

Selene nodded.

"Then I'd wager Tarik has him halfway to Rome by now."

"I didn't mention Rome."

"I noticed that omission. But Tarik has a house there, and it's a reasonable place to hide Kadar while he trains."

"Trains?"

"Yes." Tabia's abstracted gaze was fixed on Selene's face. "This is the first time Tarik has sent me anyone. He must have a fondness for you. Has he bedded you?"

Selene's eyes widened in shock. "No."

"I didn't really think he would. You're too bold for his current taste. He likes his women meek and honey sweet. You have nothing sweet about you." She grimaced. "That's good. I sicken at the taste of honey. I enjoy a sharp bite but not smoothness. More wine?"

"No."

"One more goblet. It will help you sleep." She got up and strode to the table by the door, where Mario had set a fresh pitcher. She carried the pitcher to the table and poured the wine into Selene's goblet. "You'll need it."

"You're certain now that Tarik purposely sent me to you?"

"There's no question in my mind. Though he'd probably deny it."

"Why would he do that?"

"He wants me to do what he cannot."

Selene tensed. "And what is that?"

Tabia chuckled. "By the gods, you think I mean to kill you."

"It occurred to me."

Tabia's smile faded. "I don't kill. I would not even kill that monster Nasim. Death is a horror to me."

Selene believed her. Every word she had spoken

had rung with passion. "He wanted to keep me far away from Kadar. Perhaps he doesn't know that you feel as you do."

"Oh, he knows." She dropped back onto her chair. "We know each other very well. Finish your wine and I'll tell you how well."

Selene slowly sipped her wine. "I don't care about your dealings with Tarik."

"Even when the dealings concern you and Kadar? Of course you do."

"Very well, what is Tarik to you?"

"He is my husband."

Selene stared at her, stunned. "His wife is dead. He told me so."

"Rosa? She was never his wife. How could she be when I was still alive when he wed her?" She looked away. "I'm his only wife."

"Layla..."

Her gaze swung back to Selene. "He told you about me?"

"He told me of Layla, his first wife. He said I was like her."

Her lips twisted. "I assure you that was no compliment. We are not on the best of terms."

Selene's mind was whirling. "You said your name was Tabia."

"A small, necessary lie."

"Why is a lie necessary?"

"You were confused enough. I saw no need to increase the muddle. Tarik and I parted long ago."

"But you still send spies to Sienbara."

"Because we have a joint interest. Not for any personal reason."

"The treasure?"

"Tarik is a dreamer. One cannot always trust dreamers to do what is best. The coffer is too valuable to be left in his hands alone."

"Then it does contain a grail?"

Layla nodded. "There is a grail. But there is no magic connected with it, as Nasim thinks."

"It's the grail of the Last Supper?"

Layla shrugged. "I do not think so. Perhaps. The grail is very old and was in the Holy Land at one time."

"At one time?"

"It came into Tarik's and my hands in Alexandria." She drank deep of the wine in her goblet. "Do you know Alexandria?"

"It's in Egypt. When I was at the House of Nicholas, we had patrons from there come to buy the silk."

"Ah, yes, I remember now." She smiled as she saw Selene stiffen. "You don't like the fact that I know your roots. I told you that I had to know everything about everyone connected to Tarik."

"The connection was not by our will."

"But it exists." She brushed the argument aside. "Besides, you should be proud of rising above that prison where you grew up. It was a battle well fought."

"Kadar got me away from Nicholas's house."

"So I was told. But you would have found a way to free yourself given time." She grimaced. "However, it's true, you were fortunate. I was not able to release myself from my prison until I reached womanhood."

"Your prison?"

"I grew up in the House of Death."

Selene's eyes widened.

"But, of course, you don't know what that is. I was born in a small village north of Alexandria. When I was eight, I was chosen by the priests to be brought to the House of Death at Alexandria. I never saw my parents again."

"House of Death?"

"The house where the dead are taken to be prepared for burial. The place where their bodies are wrapped to preserve them for eternity and their souls are guided by the priests to the land of eternal joy." Layla's tone was laden with irony. "And I was selected by the gods to help them cross over. Don't you think it's a fitting task for a girl of eight years?"

"Gods? There is only one God."

"Here in Christendom. In Egypt many still believe in the old gods. It's such a comforting religion. One need not be good if one is rich or powerful. And it's possible to take all of your most precious worldly goods with you. Providing you can keep the robbers from finding out the location of your tomb. Thieves have been known to strip the linen from the corpse to see if any jewels were left on the body."

Selene shivered. "I've never heard of such a thing."

"Thieves are thieves. Whether they steal from the dead or the living. In my opinion, it's less horrible to steal from the dead. The living need their possessions."

"From what you say, according to your religion, so do the dead."

"It's no longer my religion. Perhaps it never was. I

began to doubt from the moment I stepped over the threshold of the House of Death. I could not *bear* to be used in that fashion."

"What did they have you do?"

"I was the symbol of Akuba. I wore the mask of the jackal and stood over the body when the priests chanted and purified the body." She paused. "And then I stood and watched while they removed the organs."

Selene's stomach lurched. "Dear God."

"Don't look so horrified. I grew accustomed to it. Soon I didn't even smell the decay of flesh and the scent of incense. Children can become used to anything."

Selene's gaze searched her face. "I think you lie."

Layla lifted her goblet in a mocking toast. "Wise child. I hated it every minute of my waking days and dreamed of it every night. I wanted only to be free. I tried to run away once and they brought me back. I was beaten until I couldn't stand. They told me the next time it would be death. I knew about death. I decided not to risk it until I was sure I wouldn't be caught. So I stayed in the House of Death until my twenty-sixth year. I listened, I learned, I sought a way to free myself. I found it."

"How?"

"I heard stories of a young man called Selket, who had labored in the House of Death before I came there. He had been killed by the priests."

"Why?"

"He'd found a special treasure among the belongings of one of the dead and wouldn't share it with them. They tortured him to death, but he died without revealing where he'd hidden it. Selket was clever. He made sure that even after his death they couldn't find it."

"What treasure? The grail?"

She nodded. "And if the priests wanted it, I knew I didn't want them to have it. I would have buried it or burned it rather than let them have anything they wanted. The priests gave up the search after a few years. I did not. I saw the treasure as my salvation. For years I searched and dug and questioned. I had to be very careful not to let the priests know what I was doing. In time they began to think me cowed and submissive to their every whim. I was even permitted to go alone about the city. Then I found a clue. Two weeks before his death, Selket had visited his uncle, who was a scribe in the halls of the Great Library."

"Library?"

"A place where thousands of scrolls and documents were kept. Scholars and scribes came from all over the world to work and visit the library. I learned Selket's uncle was dead, but there might still be something to point the way. He was a scribe—perhaps he'd written something on one of the scrolls. But the library was not a place a woman could go without suspicion, and there were thousands and thousands of scrolls. I had to find someone to help me. I watched and studied the people who worked in the library and finally chose a scribe who seemed more approachable than some. He had lived within the walls of the library most of his life, and his work was his only passion." She smiled. "His name was Tarik."

"Tarik was a scribe?" It was not really such a surprising thought when she remembered the expression on his face when he had shown them the manuscript. "Go on."

Layla shook her head. "I believe I've told you enough for the moment. Far more than Tarik would like. He always counseled caution. Besides, you're almost ready to swoon from weariness. It's time to go to sleep."

"No, I want to hear—"

Layla was on her feet and heading for the door.

"Wait. Don't you go one more step until you tell me what plans Tarik has for Kadar."

"Oh, he wishes him to guard the grail." The answer was offhand.

"That is all?"

"I assure you it's more than enough to cause him many problems." She opened the door. "We'll have to share the bed. Finish your wine and get to bed while I go down and make sure your Haroun has been fed and provided with bedding."

"I can do—"

Selene stopped as the door slammed behind Layla. It was clear the woman would brook no arguments. Well, perhaps she was right. Selene was tired and her head was buzzing from the events and revelations of the day.

But she didn't want to go to bed. She wanted to hear more. She had been touched and horrified by Layla's story. Her own time at Nicholas's had been terrible, but to live in a House of Death . . . She could see why the woman seemed hard and self-willed. It was a wonder Layla had managed to survive and keep from going mad in such a place.

She was making excuses to pardon Layla, Selene realized with astonishment. The woman was volatile, reckless, and probably as hard as stone. Selene should be wary of being in the same room with her, and tonight they were going to occupy the same bed. Why wasn't she more cautious?

Because she sensed that Layla had a streak of vulnerability beneath that hard surface.

Perhaps she and Layla possessed similar qualities. Selene, too, disliked anyone seeing too deep and wanted things her own way. Well, one of those things was making sure Kadar was safe, and she couldn't do that unless she knew where the danger lay. Tomorrow she would make sure that Layla told her more.

She finished her wine and set the goblet on the table before stripping off her clothing and climbing into bed.

Where was Kadar now?

Aching loneliness washed over her. It was unreasonable to feel this pain. Was she going to be this idiotic all the days of her life?

Oh, Lord, she was afraid she was.


Selene was deeply asleep, sprawled over the bed like a weary child.

Layla shook her head ruefully as she gazed down at her. She couldn't possibly get in the bed without waking her, and she wasn't willing to do that. Selene needed sleep this night.

Oh, well, Layla had slept in chairs many times before. She dropped into the chair in front of the fire. She grimaced as she reached for her goblet. This chair had no cushions and was more uncomfortable than most.

Stop whining. She would probably not have slept much anyway.

Her gaze wandered from the fire back to Selene. So much pain. So much passion. She could see why Tarik had been torn. He must have become very involved with Kadar and Selene during these last weeks.

Don't worry, Tarik. I won't fail you.

Poor Tarik. Was it weariness or discouragement that was pushing him toward her? It didn't matter.

She didn't care about anything. As long as he came back to her.

Her eyes closed tightly as waves of memory washed over her.

*He was leaving.*

*"But I love you." Layla's hands tightened frantically on his arms.*

*"I know you do." Tarik's lips were thin with pain. "It doesn't matter."*

*"How can you say that? It does matter. Stay."*

*"You're too strong. You'd always convince me you were right and I was wrong."*

*"I am right."*

*Tarik shook his head and pulled away from her. "I can't do it any longer."*

*It was killing her. Couldn't he see that she couldn't live without him? "Then don't do it. Just stay with me."*

*"And watch you do it? It's the same thing."*

*"It wasn't your fault."*

*He opened the door. She wasn't going to be able to stop him, she realized in despair.*

*"Then go. Live with your damnable guilt. Eat with it, sleep with it."*

*"I don't want to hurt you."*

*"You're not hurting me." She raised her chin. "I'll forget you. Why do I need a fool like you?"*

*He closed the door behind him.*

*Tarik!*

She should not have let the memory return. The agony was too intense. It was as if she were living it over again. How many times during the past years had she smothered the thought of that scene and closed that part of her?

But now it might be all right to remember. There were signs he was yielding at last.

He had sent her Selene.

She was dreadfully ill, Selene realized even before she opened her eyes.

She barely made it to the basin across the room before she started to throw up.

"What's wrong?"

Someone was behind her. Layla.

"Answer me."

Dear God, couldn't the stupid woman see she couldn't answer her?

Layla was beside her, her arm bracing Selene's shoulders while she heaved. "It's all right—I think."

"It's not all right. I'm dying." Her stomach was empty but she was still miserable. She staggered back to the bed and crawled beneath the covers. "Go away."

"You're not dying." Layla was standing by the bed. "I won't have it."

She opened her eyes to see Layla frowning down at her. "Go away."

"You're not being reasonable. If you're truly ill, I'm the only one here who can help you. Now be silent while I decide what course to take."

Selene was too sick to argue. She shut her eyes, trying to fight off the new surge of nausea that was overwhelming her.

Cold water was running down her face and onto the covers.

She gasped, and her eyes flew open to see Layla wielding a sopping-wet cloth with vigorous authority. "You're drowning me."

Layla scowled. "Well, it was all I could think of to do. I told you I wasn't good at this sort of thing."

"You're right."

"And you're not supposed to be ill. I hadn't planned—Why are you?"

It wasn't enough that she was sick, but this heartless woman expected her to make apologies for it. "It's probably from being in the same chamber with you," she said through her teeth.

"I don't think so. Do you hurt anywhere?"

"No." She huddled beneath the covers. "I don't want to talk."

"We must find out the problem. Did the beef from supper disagree with you?"

"Get that cloth away from my face or I'll throw it at you."

"Very well. It doesn't seem to be doing much good anyway. I've always suspected bathing brows is much overrated."

"I'm going to try to go back to sleep. Leave me alone."

"I suppose that would be all right." Layla dropped down in the chair. "But I'll wake you if the sleep appears too deep."

Probably with another ice-water dousing. "If you do, I may throttle you."

"Ungrateful wretch." But the gentleness with which she straightened Selene's covers belied the roughness of her tone. "Rest. I won't let anything hurt you."

The nausea was gone when Selene opened her eyes again.

"Better?" Layla asked. "Can you eat?"

She was still too befogged from sleep to think. "I don't know."

"You should try. It's afternoon. You've slept half the day away."

She *was* hungry, she realized with amazement. All trace of illness had vanished and she felt wonderfully well. It was as if that sickness of the morning had never been.

Morning sickness.

Mother of God.

"You're ill again," Layla sighed. "Do you need the basin?"

"No," she whispered. "I feel fine."

"You've turned pale." She frowned. "Talk to me or, by God, I swear I'll bathe your face again."

"I'm with child."

"What?"

Selene felt as stunned as Layla looked. "My flux is very late, and this sickness is like the one my sister went through during her early months."

"You're sure?"

She was sure. How strange and wonderful that she was this certain Kadar's child was growing within her. "I didn't want to believe it. I refused to think about it."

"You don't want this child?"

"Of course I want it." The answer came with an instant fierceness that surprised her.

Layla held up her hand. "Don't attack me. It's a reasonable question. You said you didn't want to believe it, and neither you nor your bastard would have an easy time of it in this world."

"I know that." But she didn't want to be reasonable. She was feeling soft and mellow as warm honey. She had never dreamed it would be like this. Where had all the fear and panic gone? A child was inconvenient, even a danger. None of that seemed to matter. "Do you think that I'd let my child be called a bastard?"

"How will you prevent it?"

"I'll wed Kadar." She sat up and swung her feet to the floor. "It's not as if he would not wed me to protect our child."

"And then?"

"I'll return to Montdhu as I intended." She went to the basin and rinsed out her mouth. Sweet Mary, it tasted foul. "Call Mario. I need a bath and a meal before we start out."

"And where are we going?"

"To Rome. You're going to take me to Tarik's house."

"Am I?"

"Or I'll go looking for it myself." Selene looked at Layla over her shoulder. "I'll certainly not stay here, and I don't believe you'll let me go alone, if you think Tarik sent me to you."

"Very wise. I would not." She frowned. "Though things are not going as I would have hoped. I never counted on the child."

"Neither did I." But it was here, and the knowledge gave her a buoyant feeling she had never experienced before. The exuberance might not last, fear and depression might soon intrude, but now she would ride the crest. "We must make the best of it."

Layla smiled faintly as her gaze rested on Selene's radiant face. "Yes, we can try to do that." She turned away. "Very well, but we'll take Haroun and Antonio."

"I don't want Antonio."

"Because he's my man? You'll take him anyway.

Don't worry, I'll have him stay out of sight as much as possible. But I won't start this journey without a guard to stand watch." She glanced over her shoulder. "Nasim is no fool. He will be moving."

SIENBARA

"Genoa," Balkir said. "Tarik has a ship there. We've questioned everyone in the castle and village. It has to be Genoa."

"It's too obvious." Nasim frowned. "Too easy. Tarik is a deceptive man."

"Should I return and try again?"

"Fool. What if it is Genoa? Should we let them sail halfway to Scotland before we're able to overtake them?"

"But you said that—"

"We try Genoa." He frowned. "The woman may have departed here before Tarik and Kadar. It could be that they sought to confuse me by going in different directions. Now, that's a ploy worthy of Kadar and Tarik."

"Then we leave Sienbara at once?"

He nodded curtly as he mounted his horse. "At once."

"Not again," Layla sighed as she fell to her knees on the ground beside Selene. "This is the third time since we started our journey. When does this morning illness end? It's most distasteful."

"I can't help it." She threw up again. "And you're without wits, woman, to think that I can. I'd wager you threw up many times in the House of Death."

"Only once. The beating I received for showing emotion made me hesitate to give in to weakness again."

"Well, I'm not sorry for you." But she was, and it only made her angrier. "Go back to your pallet and leave me alone."

"You'd only keep me awake with your retching here in the bushes." She made a face. "And it annoys me to have Haroun look at me with those big reproachful eyes. You've not seen fit to tell him of your affliction, and he thinks me a cruel and unnatural woman to ignore you."

"I don't care. He's right. You are a cruel and unnatural woman."

"Here." Layla thrust a damp cloth into her hand. "Bathe your own forehead, since you're not happy with my tending."

"Tending?"

"I'm trying. Don't I twiddle my thumbs, letting you sleep the morning away after you wake me at dawn with this nonsense?"

"It's not nonsense. Many women have this affliction when they're with child. And I never asked you to—"

"Shh, I know." She gently brushed the hair back from Selene's temple. "It's a wonder that women have more than one child if this is the way of it."

"Don't be foolish. How would they keep from it?"

"There are ways."

The illness was subsiding at last. She sat back on her heels and drew a deep breath. "You've never had a child?"

Layla shook her head. "And probably just as well. As you see, I'm not overgentle."

Selene sensed a hint of pain beneath the carelessness of Layla's words and said impulsively, "I think you'd be a very good mother."

Layla's eyes widened in surprise.

"You would," Selene insisted. "You're clever and strong and protective."

"That would make me a good father, not a good mother," Layla said dryly.

"Well, who is to say there must be softness. Besides, I believe you could be...gentle."

"You near choked on that word." Layla took the wet cloth and dabbed awkwardly at Selene's lips. "And you clearly must be dizzy from your sickness. It's time you went back to your pallet."

"I'm not dizzy." But she was weak as the babe she was carrying, she realized as she struggled to her feet. "I don't have to sleep all morning. Just a small nap. I know we should not linger."

Layla nodded as she stood up. "No, there are too many people at Sienbara who knew Tarik had a ship in Genoa. Nasim would have little trouble finding someone who would tell him about it, and Genoa is a small place."

"But we're no longer in Genoa."

"But Mario is still there, and he has a tongue as loose as his wits."

"You think he would tell him our direction?"

"With a little persuasion." She shrugged. "Or maybe not so little."

"Then we should leave at once."

"And have you fall off your horse and break something? Then we would truly have a problem. A few hours will make no difference. We'll make it up by stopping later for the night."

Selene was not so sure it wouldn't make a difference. "Just a small nap."

"We will see." She grasped Selene's arm and gently pushed her toward the fire. "Leave it to me. I feel the need of a nap myself after witnessing the disgusting spectacle you made of yourself."

"I did not ask—" Protests to Layla were like rain beating against a stone wall. Besides, she was beginning to learn she should pay more attention to Layla's actions than anything she said. Her words might be harsh and completely lacking in sympathy, but during the last days she had been constantly at her side, unobtrusively watching, helping. Perhaps Layla could be no other way after the life she had lived. Selene could understand the need to build walls. She had erected high ones of her own. "I . . . thank you for trying to help me."

Layla looked at her in surprise. "Then I'm no longer cruel and unnatural?"

"Yes, but I've decided you cannot help it and should be forgiven." She smiled faintly. "But I give warning I may not feel the same when you rant at me tomorrow morning."

"Then you should try to control this sickness. It annoys me."

"Tell that to the babe." She had reached her pallet and sank to her knees. "I seem to have no control of it. My sister's illness went away after the fourth month."

"It should not be so. It's not fair that women must suffer like this. If I were with child, I'd find a cure that would prevent this idiotic—"

"I'm sure you would." Selene nestled beneath her blankets and closed her eyes. "By all means, seek out a preventive. But quietly." She yawned. "Very quietly. I need more sleep."

"Oh, very well." She heard Layla nestling into her own blankets across the fire. "But you should not give in to this. It insults our bodies to have to undergo this trial. We should find a way for women not to have to suffer to give birth."

"Fine, you find a way. I need to nap."

"So it goes away in four months. What if you have another child? Would you have to go through this again? It would not be—"

"Layla."

Layla sighed and then fell silent.

Selene was almost asleep when Layla murmured, "We will try herbs. I know a great deal about herbs."

# Chapter Thirteen

"VERY PLEASANT, TARIK." Kadar's gaze raked the columned stone structure on the hill. Trees bordered the road leading to the impressive cream-colored edifice. To the north of the house Kadar saw the glimmer of a formal pool surrounded by statuary. "A veritable palace. But I'd not choose a place with no fortifications. It's not safe. Nasim's men could overrun it in less than a heartbeat."

"It would take longer than that. I have guards watching all the roads, so we'd be warned long in advance." Tarik kicked his horse into a trot. "And Nasim cannot attack what he doesn't know exists."

"He knew about Sienbara."

"Because I wanted him to know. I had to throw some bit of knowledge to him to make sure he didn't look deeper." He smiled. "I believe you'll be comfortable here. This villa once belonged to the leman of Pope Giulano. He gifted her with it when she gave birth to his son. I understand Aurelia was a magnificent beauty, and she certainly had remarkable taste. I bought the villa from her son. A most intriguing man. I'll tell you about him once we've settled."

"I'm not interested in this Pope's son and I'm not concerned about comfort." He jerked his head at the coffer tied to the horse ahead. "You know what interests me."

"Won't you even let me get within the safety of my walls before you attack me?"

"No. You promised when we reached Rome you'd show me."

Tarik sighed. "Very well, tonight after we sup." He held up his hand as Kadar opened his mouth to protest. "Don't argue. It's the only victory you'll wrest from me."

Kadar knew Tarik well enough to realize that he had dug in his heels and would not be swayed. It was only a few hours. He didn't know why he'd even attempted to coerce him. He was not usually this impatient.

He did know. He was brimming with frustration and worry about Selene. He could do nothing about that situation but wait, and so he was reaching out to control everything else within his grasp.

"We'll hear soon." Tarik's gaze was on his face. "Antonio will be here within a few days to tell us she's safely on her way to Montdhu."

After supper, Tarik sent the servants to bed and limped to the corner where he'd set the wooden chest. "Light another candle. If you must see the grail, then you might as well view it clearly."

Kadar lit another candle from the one on the table. "At last."

"Sarcasm isn't necessary. I had to be sure of you."

"And now you are? I hate to disappoint you, but I'll not be manipulated by you any more than I will be by Nasim."

"It's been taken out of both of our hands." He set the chest on the table and unlocked it. "Fate sometimes does that. Haven't you noticed?"

"I've noticed you have a tendency to dabble with fate."

"Actually, I've suffered a great deal because I try to keep from dabbling." He lifted the lid of the chest, removed the statue, and set it aside. "It's only of late that I've grown weary and given in to temptation." He plucked off the purple silk cloth and opened the golden coffer. "Here is your grail. Beautiful, isn't it?"

Tarik's tone was almost casual—too casual. Kadar's eyes narrowed on Tarik's face, and then he took a step closer and looked down into the box. The candlelight shimmered on the gold object cradled in a nest of velvet.

"It *is* a grail."

Tarik smiled. "I told you. Now are you not ashamed you were suspicious?"

"No. Considering that forked tongue of yours, I'd

be ashamed if I wasn't suspicious. May I take it out of the box?"

"Of course."

Kadar carefully lifted the grail and held it under the candlelight. The workmanship was magnificent. Every inch of the gold of the grail was intricately carved with pictorial symbols. Kadar's finger gently touched one of the pictures. "What is this?"

"It's the language of my birth. Much more clear and civilized than the script of the Greeks and Romans."

"I've seen it before."

"I thought as much, when you said the statue was familiar." He glanced at the statue on the table. "It was to be expected that you'd recognize it. You're better traveled than most men, and you have a curious mind."

"Egypt."

"Yes."

He looked down at the cup again. "What does it say?"

"It's a story about a young man and a quest. You'd enjoy it."

"Then tell it to me."

"You want stories? How strange." He smiled. "Nasim would not be interested in stories, only in the power of the cup. Don't you feel the magic of the grail? Can't you feel the force of it coursing through you as you hold it in your hands?"

"No."

Tarik laughed. "Nasim would feel it. He believes in the grail."

"Then he's a fool. There's no magic here."

"You'll not be able to convince him. You can never convince men like Nasim they cannot have what they need. And sometimes it's best not to try."

"Tell me what's written on the cup."

"Impatience again. It's a long tale, but I'll tell you what is written here." He tilted the cup so that Kadar could see the inscription engraved on the inside of the rim. "It says, *Protect*. That's what I've been doing. But I'm tired now. I deserve to rest. It's time someone else took over the task."

"Me?"

Tarik nodded.

"You chose the wrong man. I've no desire to protect your grail. It means nothing to me."

"But it will. Sit down." He sat down himself and stretched out his crippled foot. "Take your time. You wanted to see the grail, now examine it at your leisure."

Kadar seated himself and slowly turned to the grail. "There's something else on the other side of the cup."

"*Eshe*."

Kadar looked at him inquiringly.

"I believe you've digested enough for now. I've always found it's best to go very slowly when the tale is so long and involved."

"I want to hear it now."

Tarik shook his head. "Hold it, become accustomed to it. Then I'll put it back in the coffer until I think the time is right."

Kadar's grasp clenched on the cup. "I've no liking

for this teasing. What game is this you're playing with me, Tarik?"

"One where I make the rules." Tarik leaned back in his chair. "Enough talk of the grail. Now relax and I'll tell you about the man who sold me this fine villa."

Selene spat out the leaf. "I'll eat no more. Do you hear me? It tastes terrible."

"Maybe you've had enough of it." Layla tucked the last of the leaves into the pouch at her waist and kicked her horse into a trot. "We'll see tomorrow."

"We've tried rosemary, thyme, the leaves of the bush with that red berry. When will we stop?"

"When you're no longer ill."

"It's bad enough to be ill, but it's worse to have to eat these foul plants you keep stuffing in me."

"Stop complaining. This is a worthwhile thing we do. Not only for you but for other women."

"We? I'm the one who's suffering."

"I would do it, if I were with child."

The exasperating thing was that Selene knew she spoke the truth. Layla was utterly relentless and completely convinced what she was doing was right. It was difficult to refuse someone with that extreme dedication. She could only hope that either her illness would naturally pass or Layla would find something she thought had allayed it. "If you give me one more nasty-tasting leaf to eat, I may not survive to bear—" She could see Layla was not listening.

Her expression was abstracted, her brow knitted in

thought. "If it doesn't work, tomorrow we will try basil."

Selene wanted to knock the obstinate woman off her horse. She muttered an imprecation and spurred ahead to where Haroun and Antonio were riding.

Haroun fell back to ride beside her. "What is wrong?"

"Nothing," she said curtly. "Why should anything be wrong?"

"You seem . . . disturbed. And you were ill again this morning." He moistened his lips. "It is not a good thing to be ill every day. I've been worried."

"It's not good, but there's nothing to be worried about."

"Is it the fever?"

She shook her head.

"We should stop and let you recover."

Why not tell him? She couldn't keep it secret for long when he would see her every day. "It may take many months for me to recover from this affliction. I'm with child, Haroun."

He smiled brilliantly. "I wondered . . . I remember Lady Thea was so taken. That's why we're going to seek out Lord Kadar?"

"Yes."

"It is wise. He is honorable, and you and the babe will be safe with him."

"I'm not going to put myself in his care. After we wed, I return to Montdhu."

He nodded vigorously. "Until it's safe for him to come to you. This land is not the place for you to be. Don't worry, I will care for you in his place."

"I don't need you to—" She couldn't finish. Haroun was so happy and earnest. If his attitude was annoying, it was also sweet. She was most moved. "I thank you for your concern. I'll try not to be a burden." Good God, that last sentence almost turned her stomach again. "I know I will be safe with you, Haroun."

He flushed, and his smile became even more radiant. "You will. I promise. I'll take care of you. You'll be safe, Lady Selene."

"The boy is hovering around you like a bee at a honeycomb," Layla said in a low voice as she watched Haroun make up Selene's pallet that night. "You told him?"

Selene nodded. "He had to know sometime. He was concerned."

"We should have told him before. He seems a good enough lad."

High praise from Layla. Selene smiled. "Very good."

"But his fussing is going to annoy you."

"Probably." But not as it would have once, she realized. It was as if the knowledge of the child had softened and dulled all the sharp edges. She seemed to think more clearly, react less impulsively.

"You're feeling well tonight." Layla was studying her.

She smiled. "You didn't force any herbs on me this evening."

"Tomorrow. It's not always good to mix." She shook her head. "No, it's something else."

Hope. The thought came out of nowhere. How

odd. Hope had always been a rarity in her life. She had been too often disappointed. You took action to achieve your needs; you didn't hope for them. Yet it was hope stirring within her now. It had been growing day by day on their journey. The child?

"I feel . . ." She couldn't explain what she didn't understand herself. "I feel as if everything is going to be all right."

"Perhaps it will."

She made a face. "Or perhaps this contentment is God's way of protecting babes."

"It's possible. It's certainly brought a change in you. You've not even mentioned Tarik or the grail since you found you were with child."

It had not seemed important. Only getting to Kadar and the reality of the child was of any significance. "Kadar says when I fix my mind on something, I can't see anything else. I suppose he's right."

"He appears to know you very well."

"Yes." All those hours and days and years together. "How long before we arrive in Rome?"

"Three days."

In three days she would see Kadar again. Three days and he would know about the child. Not that it would change things, but she would see his face and it would be—

"Sweet Mary, are you ill again?"

Her startled gaze flew to Layla's face. "Why would you think that?"

"You have a most asinine and befuddled expression."

Selene frowned. "I do not. I was merely—" She

stopped as she realized Layla was smiling. "Your humor is unkind."

"Humor is humor. Kind or unkind, it's our salvation. Become accustomed to my roughness. I can be no other way." She looked into the fire. "Will you stay with him?"

"No."

"Why not? A blind woman could see you have a fondness for him."

"Yes."

"But you're fighting it."

"No, I'm done with fighting it. But that doesn't mean I should stay with him. It probably means I should not." She paused. "I thought he was the one person on this earth who would never lie to me. But he did."

"Treachery?"

"Not exactly."

"We all lie to each other on occasion. To be kind, to be cruel." She paused. "Just as we lie to ourselves."

Selene stiffened. "You're saying I lie to myself?"

"Possibly. You said Tarik told you that you were like me. There's a part of each of us in the center of our being that remains alone and inviolate. It's hard for me to let anyone get close to that center, even a loved one. You may be the same." She lifted her gaze. "If you have reason, leave this Kadar, but don't lie to yourself to protect that aloneness. Loneliness can be very bitter."

"I never lie to myself," Selene said quickly. "And, besides, Tarik said if I stayed with Kadar I'd be a danger to him."

"Tarik had his own reasons to want you away from him."

"But I believe this to be true."

"There are other solutions to danger than running away." She rolled up in her blanket and closed her eyes. "Think about it."

"I don't need to think about it. I've made my decision and I'll not—"

"Go to sleep." Layla yawned. "I weary of talking to you, and I need my rest. No doubt you'll wake me early with that hideous retching."

She had closed her out, Selene realized with frustration. She turned and strode to her own pallet.

"You look troubled. Do you not feel well?" Haroun asked from his own pallet a few yards away.

She smiled with an effort as she lay down. "I'm only tired."

"We should not force the pace. You need your rest."

"That's what I'm trying to do." She rolled over on her side and closed her eyes. "I'm fine. It will only be another three days."

But she wasn't sure she would be able to survive Haroun's hovering for those three days without exploding. She should never have told him about the babe.

"Do you need another blanket?"

"No, I'm quite warm."

"I could stir the fire."

She said slowly and carefully, pausing between each word, "I don't need anything, Haroun."

She didn't know which was worse: Layla, with her relentless determination to use her to better the lot of all women, or Haroun, who wanted to smother her beneath this blanket of cosseting. She'd be glad to get to Rome.

And Kadar.

Even if she could not stay with him, it would do no harm to imagine his joy when he learned of the child. He had grown up alone in the streets, and a babe, someone of his own, would mean as much to him as to Selene.

Too much? Would it hurt him when she left with the babe? Dear God, she never wanted to hurt Kadar.

One step at a time. She would face the consequences later. Now she must only get to Rome and make sure the babe was protected by holy vows from the cruelties of the world.

"Lady Selene!"

Haroun.

His hand was on her shoulder, roughly shaking her.

"You must wake. We must leave. Nasim—"

*Nasim.*

She was instantly awake and saw Haroun's anxious face above her.

"Antonio says there are riders coming down the road." He pulled her to her feet. "He thinks he recognized Nasim."

It was still dark. Only a thread of pale moonlight filtered through the cloud cover. How could Antonio be sure of—

They couldn't take the chance. "How far?"

"I don't know. Minutes—" He turned away and ran

toward the horses and began saddling her mare. Layla had finished saddling her own horse and was leading it toward Selene. "Get on my horse and get out of here," Layla said curtly. "Hurry."

"No, I'll wait for—"

"No time. We'll be right behind you. Would you risk the child?"

*I want* that child.

Terror tore through her. If Nasim learned she was with child, he would take a boy child, kill a girl. She could not put the babe in danger. She stopped arguing and mounted Layla's horse. "Where will we meet?"

Layla pointed to a dense wood in the distance. "It should be easy to hide among the trees." She struck the horse on the hindquarters and sent it careering off at a dead run.

Wind stung her cheeks.

Her clothes pressed close to her body.

She glanced over her shoulder.

No one was coming. Where were Layla and—

Mustn't panic. It had been only a few minutes.

Relief poured through her as she caught sight of Layla, Haroun, and Antonio tearing out of the glade.

She could see no one pursuing them. Perhaps it was all a mistake. Perhaps it was not Nasim.

And perhaps it was.

She put spurs to the horse.

The wood was just ahead.

Then it was here, around her. Darkness. Shadows. The thick canopy of branches overhead. Safety.

"Off the horse." Layla reined in beside her and

jumped down. "Give your horse a slap to set him running and hide in the underbrush. He's coming."

"Nasim?" Her gaze flew to the road. Riders thundered toward the wood, and in the lead were Balkir
and Nasim.

She slipped from the saddle and gave her horse a
sharp slap. The horse plunged forward into the brush.

Antonio and Haroun had reined in, and Antonio
jumped off his horse. Haroun still sat his horse, looking behind him.

"For God's sake, hurry, Haroun," Selene called frantically as she plunged into the shrubbery.

"They're too close." His face was tight with fear.
"They'll find you. I have to—"

He kicked his horse into a run.

Her eyes widened in horror. "Haroun!"

Layla covered Selene's mouth as she jerked her
down on the ground.

The riders were upon them.

Dust. Thunder. The crash of branches.

Selene could see the hooves fly by only feet from
where they lay.

"There! Ahead!" Balkir's voice. "The boy!"

Earth churned as the riders passed the shrubbery
where they were hidden.

Layla's hand slid away from Selene's mouth.

"They'll kill him." Her agonized gaze searched the
darkness where the riders had disappeared. "They'll
catch him."

"We can't stay here." Layla stood up and jerked her
to her feet. "They'll be back. We have to find a hiding
place." She turned to Antonio. "Go on ahead. Head

south. Find a cave. Even a tree we can climb. Anything out of sight."

Antonio nodded and faded into the bushes.

"Come on." Layla took her arm. "We have to get away from here."

"We have to help Haroun. They'll kill him."

"We can't help him. He has to help himself. He may escape. Anyway, we couldn't catch up with them on foot. Even if we did, we couldn't stop them. We're outnumbered."

"We have to try. You know they'll kill him if they catch him."

"Of course they'll kill him." Layla's voice was lash-sharp. "Don't be stupid. They'll kill us all if given an opportunity. Or maybe they won't kill you but will use you and the child to get to Kadar and Tarik. Do you want to give us all up to Nasim to try to save a man who can't be saved?"

"He tried to save us."

"Yes, and he knew exactly what he was doing. Are you going to let his sacrifice be wasted? Use your reason."

Selene didn't want to reason. She tried to pull away from Layla's grasp.

"The child," Layla said. "Think of the child. You have no right to risk killing it."

The child.

Haroun.

No one had a right to choose who was to live or die.

She closed her eyes as waves of pain washed over her.

"Come," Layla said. Her hand gripping Selene's

elbow was gentle but determined. "It's the right thing to do."

Layla always seemed to think she knew what was right to do, Selene thought dully. How comforting that must be. God knows, she did not.

She let Layla lead her in the opposite direction from that taken by Haroun and Nasim.

A few hours later Antonio located a small cave in the side of a hill.

They spent the next hour masking the entrance of the cave with branches. Antonio stationed himself close to the opening. Then their only recourse was to wait and watch.

And worry about Haroun.

"Stop fretting." Layla's gaze was on Selene's face. "This isn't good for you."

"Don't be asinine. How can I stop?" Selene wearily leaned her cheek against the cool stone of the cave wall. "We should have gone after him."

"Then blame me. I made the decision."

"No, I did it. I'm the one at fault. I didn't have to go with you."

"That's true. But then I would have hit you on the head and had Antonio carry you. Either way I wouldn't have let you go after Haroun."

"It wasn't your choice."

"Nevertheless, I made it." Her lips twisted. "It was easier for me. I wanted the babe and you to live, and I've only a small affection for Haroun. Besides, I'm accustomed to making decisions of that nature."

She was speaking of life and death, Selene realized with a shiver. "Have you ever killed?"

"Not intentionally. I told you I could not bear it. Still, things happen." She shrugged. "And I will not hide from it. I'm not like Tarik."

Selene didn't know what Layla meant, but she was too stunned and numb to probe. All she could think about was the expression on Haroun's face in the moment before he had spurred away from them deep into the forest.

"He was terrified of Nasim," she whispered. "Haroun wasn't a brave man."

"You're wrong; to face your fears is very brave."

"It was the babe. He promised he'd take care of me. I shouldn't have told him about the babe."

"And you think he wouldn't have done it anyway?"

"Perhaps." She closed her eyes. "I don't know. He risked his life to come after me at Montdhu."

"Then the babe had nothing to do with it. Now stop thinking. Try to sleep."

Sleep? If she hadn't been so numb, she would have laughed aloud. "How long before we can go looking for him?"

"A day, perhaps two. Maybe longer. When we're sure Nasim has given up the search and left the forest."

"He won't give up."

"He will if he thinks we managed to elude him and are no longer here. That's why we must make no move."

"How will we know when he leaves?"

"Antonio's very good in the woods, but I won't let him go out until we think it's safe."

"Of course not." The last thing she wanted was to put another innocent person in danger. Her burden of guilt was already too great.

She closed her eyes. Let nothing happen to him. Please let Haroun be safe.

Twice the next day, riders came within yards of the cave. Once two of them dismounted and walked into the nearby bushes to relieve themselves.

But they did not discover the entrance.

On the third day Layla sent Antonio out to reconnoiter.

He shook his head when he returned a few hours later. "They're still here. But they're camped on the edge of the forest to the west. They may be getting ready to leave."

"Haroun?" Selene asked. "Is he a prisoner?"

"I didn't see him in the camp."

Fear shuddered through her.

"Don't think the worst," Layla said. "That may be good news. He could be hiding in the forest. Now sit down and have some of these fine berries Antonio brought us."

"I'm not hungry."

"Eat anyway. You've barely eaten anything for the past few days. You have to think of the babe."

She had thought of the babe and let Haroun ride into danger. She had chosen the child, and Kadar and Haroun might suffer for—

"Eat," Layla repeated.

If she had chosen, then she must at least make sure

something good came out of this. If Haroun died, it must not be for nothing. The child must live.

She reached out, took a berry, and began to eat.


The next day Antonio ventured out again. When he returned, he reported that Nasim and his men had left the forest.

They waited until nightfall to make sure he did not return and then began their search for Haroun.

They found him on the second day, tossed in a gully like a scrap of garbage.

He had been chopped to pieces.

"Don't look." Layla stepped in front of Selene, blocking the way. "Antonio and I will take care of him."

"Get out of my way." Selene thrust her aside and fell to her knees beside Haroun. No face. No face. It wasn't even Haroun anymore. "Oh, God."

Layla's hand fell on her shoulder. "I'm sorry."

"They didn't have to do this to him," Selene whispered. "To kill is bad enough. That monster didn't have to do this."

"Selene, we have to bury him," Layla said gently. "It's been too long already."

"Yes," she said dully.

"Antonio and I will do it. You go back to the cave and wait until—"

"No, I'll do it."

"It's too much. You—"

She jumped to her feet and whirled on Layla. "I said *I'll* do it," she said fiercely. "You didn't know him. You didn't care about him. He deserves to have someone—" Her voice broke and she had to stop until she was able to go on. "You and Antonio go dig the grave. I'll prepare him."

"It's not wise. It would be easier for—"

"I don't care. I don't want it easy. He wasn't allowed to have it easy." She turned back to Haroun. "Go away."

A moment later she heard the sound of Layla's and Antonio's departure.

She needed a shroud. She took off her cloak and laid it on the ground. "We have to do this together, Haroun," she whispered. "You've always helped me. Now let me help you."

They laid Haroun to rest at sunset.

For a long time Selene stood looking down at the pile of earth. It didn't seem right that any man's life should end like this. There should be . . . more.

"Are you ready to go?" Layla asked.

"Not yet."

*Haroun laughing as he diced with Kadar in the stable at Montdhu.*

*Haroun wet and shivering after he'd been pulled up with the anchor on the* Dark Star.

*Haroun smiling brilliantly, hovering over her after he'd learned of the child.*

Pain rippled through her as she remembered how annoyed she'd been at that cosseting.

"Selene!"

Layla sounded alarmed, Selene realized finally. Something must be wrong.

Of course something was wrong. Darkness was all around them. Haroun was dead. Haroun had been chopped—

"Catch her, Antonio."

It was too late. She fell to the ground beside Haroun's grave.

# Chapter Fourteen

LAYLA WAS BATHING HER FOREHEAD when Selene opened her eyes.

"It's about time." Layla threw the soft cloth aside. "I was beginning to believe you would never wake. Do you realize I'm becoming deplorably adept at this boring task?"

They were in the cave, Selene realized. "How long..."

"You fainted three days ago."

"Three—" She shook her head. "It's not possible. No faint lasts that long."

Layla glanced away from her. "There were other problems."

She stiffened. "What other problems?"

"There was...blood."

"What?"

Layla's gaze returned to her face. "I think you've lost the child."

"No!"

"I understand it sometimes happens. The shock of Haroun's death, the strain of the last days—"

"No."

"Do you think it was easy to tell you this?" Layla said roughly. "I wanted you to have this child. But it's happened and it's best you face it now."

She didn't want to face it. She wanted to go back to sleep and return to oblivion.

"Don't you dare." Layla reached out and grasped her shoulders. "Open your eyes. You stay awake. So God isn't fair. You just have to go on."

"All for nothing," Selene whispered. "Haroun died for—"

"Haroun died because Nasim butchered him. The fault wasn't yours. And nothing you did caused your child to die. If you want to blame anyone, blame Nasim. He was responsible for both deaths."

Selene didn't want to think of blame right now. She wanted to go back to the time when the baby beneath her heart was still alive.

"You should be ready to travel in a few days," Layla said. "Do I take you back to Genoa to board Tarik's ship or do we continue to Rome?"

"I don't know." She rolled over on her side and curled up in a ball facing the wall of the cave. "I... can't seem... to think clearly."

"Don't you go back to sleep."

"I don't feel as if I'll ever sleep again." She stared

straight ahead. Empty. She felt empty and cold and lonely. Strange that she'd feel lonely for a babe she'd never held in her arms.

"I hear it sometimes helps to weep," Layla said awkwardly. "You might try it."

"I don't want to weep." What she was feeling was too deep for tears, the agony too intense to allow her release. "It's all wrong. Haroun...my baby...It shouldn't have happened."

"I know." Layla's hand gently stroked her hair. "I know, Selene."

Layla didn't know. She couldn't experience this pain. She couldn't know the emptiness.

She couldn't feel the anger.


Selene didn't speak for the next two days. She would not eat and Layla doubted if she slept. When Layla tried to talk to her, Selene shook her head and turned away. Neither gentleness nor roughness ignited any response. It was as if she were cocooned in a web of pain that would allow nothing to unravel it.

Layla woke in the middle of the third night. Her gaze flew to Selene's pallet.

Empty.

She muttered a curse and threw back her blanket. Idiot. She should never have nodded off. It was her duty to protect Selene. Who knew where she'd wandered—

Selene was standing in the entrance of the cave, staring out into the darkness.

Layla heaved a sigh of relief before getting up and moving to stand beside her. "You should go back to your pallet. You need your rest."

"Soon."

It was the first word she had spoken in days, but Layla's relief was short-lived. Selene's tone was quiet, contained, with no hint of her former passion and agony. It was not natural, and it made Layla distinctly uneasy. "You need to sleep. You've not slept for a long time."

"No, I had to think."

"Brooding does no good at times like this."

"I wasn't brooding. I was trying to make sense of this."

"And did you?"

Selene turned to look at her, and Layla stiffened with shock. In the moonlight her face reminded Layla of one she'd seen engraved on a cameo—smooth, hard, without expression. "No, but I decided what I must do."

"And what is that?"

"Leave for Rome tomorrow."

"It's dangerous. Antonio said Nasim's tracks were going in that direction. He's probably hoping to over-take us, but he may double back."

"We'll be careful."

"You need to rest. A few more days will make no difference."

"You're wrong." She moved toward her pallet. "I know exactly what I need, and rest isn't it."

———

The next day they started out on foot toward Rome. They weren't able to find a village in which to purchase horses until the second day. Even then, they had to proceed cautiously and send Antonio ahead several times to make sure they didn't cross Nasim's path. Consequently, they didn't arrive at Tarik's villa until more than a week later.

Layla reined in at the bottom of the hill. "Go on ahead. Antonio and I will come a little later. Tarik and I haven't seen each other for a long time. It's best that there be no one present when we meet." Her lips twisted. "And your Kadar will not be pleased that Antonio betrayed you. You need the chance to tell him that he meant no harm before Kadar cuts his throat."

"Very well." Selene supposed she should have thought of the repercussions herself, but she seemed to be only feeling, not thinking. That must stop. She must reflect calmly, coolly, block everything else out but what had to be done. "I'll tell Tarik you're waiting here."

Tarik and Kadar were coming down the steps when Selene rode into the courtyard.

"Thank God." Kadar ran forward. His smile illuminated his face as he lifted her out of the saddle. "I was nearly crazed when Antonio didn't come. I was about to set out for Genoa. Are you well?"

"No." She turned to Tarik. "We weren't challenged as we approached. Are we safe here?"

"Yes, we weren't sure it was you, but we knew three riders were coming. If you'd appeared threatening, we'd have been ready."

"How did you know?"

"A guard stationed on a hill ten miles from the villa brought the message."

"What do you mean, no?" Kadar's hands grasped her shoulders. "What's wrong? Why didn't you board the ship at Genoa?"

She felt a stirring of warmth within her at his touch. Strange, she hadn't thought she could feel anything anymore. Strange and dangerous. Emotion could weaken her and get in the way. She stepped back away from him and glanced at Tarik. "I don't want to talk anymore. We've been riding for days and I need rest and a bath."

Tarik nodded. "But there were two other riders. Where are they?"

"At the bottom of the hill. Layla said she wished to meet with you alone."

He stiffened. "Layla?"

"Your wife." He looked genuinely astonished, Selene thought. Maybe Layla was wrong about Tarik sending Selene to her. "You didn't know Antonio was in her pay?"

"Of course I didn't." He paused. "She didn't—hurt you?"

Selene shook her head. "She wasn't gentle, but we came to an understanding."

"No, she's seldom gentle." His expression was a mixture of eagerness and dread as he gazed down the hill. "Perhaps I'd better go and see..." He moved quickly across the courtyard.

"What is this about?" Kadar said.

"Later. Will you show me where I'm to sleep?"

"Selene—what is—" He broke off and took her

arm and started up the stairs. "All right. We won't talk now."

She again felt that stirring and moved away from him. "Don't touch me."

"For God's sake, I'm not trying to—" His gaze was narrowed on her face. "I've never seen you like this. You're cold as stone. What's happened to you?"

"I don't want to have to say it twice. I'll talk to you and Tarik and Layla this evening."

"You're shutting me out," he said through his teeth. "I don't like being grouped with Tarik and this Layla. I won't *have* it."

"This evening," she repeated as she stopped inside the door. "Now will you show me where I'm to sleep?"

He stared at her for a long moment and then gestured to a young boy hovering nearby. "Show her to a chamber, Benito. One that's close to mine. See that water is brought for a bath."

Benito nodded eagerly and set off down the long marble hallway.

"Wait," he said as she started to follow the boy. "You'll need clothing. I'll send someone down the hill to tell Haroun to bring up your packs."

"There are no packs to bring. I'll make do with what I'm wearing." She didn't look back at him. "And no one can tell Haroun anything. He's dead."

He was coming.

Layla instinctively braced herself as she saw Tarik walking down the hill. He looked the same as that day when he'd left her. Well, what had she expected? Of course he looked the same. She could hardly expect him to pine away. He had done everything he could to show her he no longer needed her, even taking another wife.

But he *did* need her. Just as she needed him.

She forced a smile and started toward him.

He didn't return her smile. "What are you doing here?"

"Selene wanted to come."

"If I'd wanted her here, I'd have brought her with us. She was to go to Scotland."

"And you chose Antonio to take her." She met his gaze. "I think you lie. I believe you had no intention of sending her to safety. I think you knew Antonio would bring her to me."

"I had no idea Antonio was in your pay."

For a moment she was shaken by the flatness of the assertion. "You knew. I'd wager you know every man hired by me or Nasim in your household."

"You'd lose. I didn't know about Antonio. Why should I think you'd have spies in my camp?"

Because I love you. Because you know I'd never let you go. She moistened her lips. "Eshe. Why else?"

"You sent me the coffer. You don't trust me to care for it?"

She had sent it to him because she wanted to forge a link that would bring him back to her. "You have a tendency to be foolish. I had to be sure. When you sent me Selene, I hoped you were seeing clearer."

He went still. "And why do you think I sent you Selene?"

"Eshe. To do what you could not."

He inhaled sharply. "Good God in heaven, what have you done?"

Pain shot through her. "Don't talk to me in that way. I'm not a monster." She lifted her chin and stared at him defiantly. "I've done nothing. Do you think I'd rush to please you? I just thought—"

"Then why did you bring Selene here?"

"She's suffered a great loss, and I thought it best to humor her. She was not—"

"What loss? What happened to Haroun?" Kadar was striding down the hill toward them. "How did he die?"

"You're Kadar." It was a statement. He was young enough to be Selene's lover and was clearly a man of considerable stature, as was necessary to be Tarik's choice. "I'm Layla."

"I don't care who you are." His tone vibrated with anger and frustration. "I want to know what happened to Haroun and what's wrong with Selene."

"There's no need for harshness," Tarik said. "Layla didn't harm Haroun."

He was defending her. Layla felt a rush of warmth. How pitiful she had become to feel so much pleasure from such a little thing. "How do you know? You seem to think me capable of anything."

"How did Haroun die?" Kadar repeated.

"Nasim killed him." She briefly related their flight into the woods and the discovery of Haroun's body.

"God's blood," Kadar murmured. "Haroun . . ."

"He seemed a good lad and very devoted to Selene."

"Yes, he was."

"Particularly toward the last." Should she tell him?

Why not? She didn't know whether Selene intended to tell him about the child, but she had not been able to reach Selene in the past days. Perhaps Kadar could do it. "After he learned Selene was with child."

Kadar's eyes widened in shock. "What?"

"That's why she was coming to see you. She thought you'd give your name to protect the child."

A slow smile lit his face, and in that instant she could see why Selene was drawn to him. "Of course I—"

"Wait." As usual, she had been clumsy. "She lost the child after we found Haroun."

His smile vanished. "Dear God," he whispered.

"It was a terrible blow to her. Together with Haroun's death, it was—She seemed to change overnight."

"You don't have to tell me that." His fists clenched at his sides. "I've never seen her like this. She's not the same."

"Don't be stupid. Of course she's not the same. Some women *need* children to complete them. To lose a babe tears the heart from your body. Do you expect her not to show—"

"Gently." Tarik's hand fell on her arm. "We all know Selene is in pain. Now we have to find a way to help her."

"If she'll let us," Layla said. "It's as if she's built a wall around herself to keep everyone out."

"She'll let us," Kadar said. "Because we'll do everything we can to make sure she does." A muscle jerked in his taut cheek. "Do you hear me? I won't have her hurting like this."

"Time and patience will help heal the wound," Tarik said.

"Selene has never understood patience, and I can't see her learning now."

"You're the one who appears to be without patience."

"She's *hurting*. I won't stand for it. I'm going to fix it." He glared at Tarik. "And you're going to help. Whatever it takes, whatever she wants, you're going to give her."

"If it's within my power."

"That's not good enough. You're going to give it to her." His glance went from Tarik to Layla and back again. "I don't care what's between you. I don't care about the grail. I'm tired of having you and Nasim interfering with our lives. It's not going to happen anymore."

"Kadar, I'm not arguing about—"

"She wants to talk to all of us after supper tonight." He turned and started to stalk back up the hill. "You're going to listen and, by God, if you say one word to upset her, I'll make you pay."

"Why didn't you tell me?" Kadar asked.

Selene whirled to see him standing in the doorway of her chamber. His face was pale, his eyes glittering, and she instinctively stiffened. "What are you doing here?"

"Didn't I have the right to know?" He moved forward and slammed the door. "It was my child, for God's sake."

"I was going to tell you."

"When? This evening? A joint announcement to Tarik and me? You didn't think I deserved to hear it alone?" His hands fell on her shoulders. "You let Tarik's wife, a stranger, be the one to tell me."

She looked away from him. "I didn't want to talk about it."

His face softened. "Selene." His hands gently kneaded her shoulders. "We have to talk about it. We shared the pleasure that created the child, now let me share the pain. I can help you."

She could feel herself softening, bending toward him like a tree in a strong breeze. He would understand. He had wanted the child.

She mustn't soften. She had to remain strong and rock hard. "Do you want me to weep and moan? My babe is dead. Haroun is dead. Weeping won't bring them back."

"I don't want you to weep. I want you to let me share. You're not being fair to me."

She backed away from him. "I want you to leave me now. I'll see you this evening."

"The devil I'll leave you." He took a step forward. "You can't shove me into the background and lump me with Tarik and Layla. We've been comrades and lovers. For God's sake, we've conceived a child. We've shared too much."

"That doesn't matter."

"It does matter. Nothing matters more than—" He drew a deep breath. "This is wrong. I lost control. I didn't mean to argue with you. I meant to be all that was gentle and understanding."

"Then understand that I want you to go."

"I'm leaving." He moved toward the door. "And for now I'll obediently fade into the background where you want me. But it won't last, Selene. I won't let it last."

He did not slam the door, but the closing was crisp and decisive.

He was gone. She crossed her arms across her chest to still their trembling. She had thought she was frozen, but she was coming alive again. She had desperately wanted to reach out and take the comfort he offered. She should have known Kadar would be capable of getting past any barrier and jarring her.

But she hadn't yielded, and he had left her.

Triumph.

It didn't feel like triumph. It felt bitter and uncertain and very, very lonely.


Kadar's hands clenched into fists as he walked blindly down the hall.

She was in pain and he couldn't help her.

By God, he couldn't *bear* it.

She had shut him away from her. It had happened before, but he always knew that given time and patience he could break through. But this was not the same. He had never seen her like this. She seemed years older, and the walls she had thrown up were iron hard.

Stop feeling and start thinking. There was always something to be done. There had to be some way to approach her that she would accept.

But they knew each other too well. She would be on guard against any familiar ploy. Whatever path he chose would have to be one they had never walked before.

That evening Selene was about to leave her chamber when Kadar knocked on the door.

"I trust you have no objection to me escorting you?" Kadar asked silkily. "I may not be of importance to you in any other way, but I do have my uses."

She moved past him and down the hall. "This isn't necessary."

"But you don't know the villa." He fell into step with her. "You might become lost."

"I doubt it. It's not even as large as Sienbara."

"Then indulge me because it brings me pleasure. That gown is quite becoming. I've always liked you in white. Where did you get it?"

"Tarik. I suppose it's one of the servant's. They all wear white."

"Very considerate. I should have thought of it myself, but I was a trifle preoccupied."

She glanced at him warily. There was none of the barely repressed frustration and despair that had characterized him earlier. His tone was lazy, his demeanor faintly mocking, but she was aware of some other emotion that she couldn't define, and it made her uneasy. She wasn't accustomed to not knowing what Kadar was thinking.

He smiled. "I suggested Tarik and Layla wait for us

on the terrace. The evening is too fine to stay inside. Did you notice the sunset?"

"No."

"One should always pay attention to beauty. There's no way of predicting when it will leave us." He gently nudged her toward a columned doorway to her left. "You might consider that."

She strode ahead of him out onto the terrace.

Layla and Tarik were standing at the balustrade and turned as Selene approached.

"Ah, you look more rested. I hope you were made comfortable." Tarik glanced at Kadar and smiled slyly. "I hate to think of my fate if you were displeased. It seems Kadar is a trifle upset with us."

"Oh, I've recovered my temper. You needn't worry." Kadar dropped into a chair at the wooden table beneath the vine-covered arbor. "As long as you heed the thrust of our discussion." He looked at Selene. "Here we are. Gathered at your command, meekly awaiting your words. What do you wish of us?"

Ignore the mockery. Say what had to be said. "I want Nasim dead."

Kadar's expression didn't change. "I thought that might be it."

"I'm going to need help. I'd do it myself, but he has too much power, too many men."

"I'd judge your assessment is correct. I can think of no one who would go up against him without help. Some would say it's impossible. He's seldom alone. He can call on the assassins at any time."

"Are you saying you won't help me?"

"No, I'm saying it would be difficult and possibly

lethal." His tone was detached. "And you have no training that would make such a foray successful."

"But you have. You could show me."

"Do you wish to invest as many years as I have on learning the dark path?" He shook his head. "I don't think so. It wouldn't suit your temperament, Selene."

"It would suit me to see him dead. I'll do whatever I have to do toward that end."

"You believe you will, but thought and execution are not the same. It takes a certain savagery that you don't possess."

"Then I'll acquire it. I've had many lessons lately. All I'll have to do is remember Haroun." Her voice was suddenly fierce. "Did Layla tell you how Nasim hacked him to pieces? He tried to save us, and that monster—"

"She told me," he interrupted. "But emotion ebbs and flows, and it tends to get in the way of reaching goals. That memory will hinder, not help you."

He was so cool and objective, not like the Kadar she knew at all. She didn't know what she had expected, but it wasn't this remoteness. Kadar had never distanced himself from her. "I cannot help it. The emotion is there. It will always be there." She added deliberately, "I suppose I cannot expect you to feel anything for the child that died because of Nasim. He wasn't real to you."

Some emotion flickered in his expression, but it was gone in an instant. He lifted his brows. "Was that jab supposed to bring blood? You'd best aim your arrows at the real enemy. One of the first things I learned was that one must concentrate on the important things and ignore the rest."

"The important thing is that Nasim killed, and I won't have him go unpunished. It's not fair. What happened was all wrong. He shouldn't be permitted to destroy and ride away. I won't let him do—" She broke off and tried to temper the passion in her voice. "I won't run and hide from him any longer. It has to end."

"Be patient. Time has a way of vanquishing the most vicious foes," Tarik said gently. "The risk is too great, Selene."

She whirled on him. "Don't tell me about patience. You're almost as bad as Nasim. Since the very beginning you've all played your games and moved Kadar and me about as if we had no importance."

Tarik sighed. "It's precisely because you do have importance that you were drawn into our machinations. I was so weary. I thought I had the right to—I never wanted either of you to be hurt."

"Well, we *were* hurt. Kadar was nearly killed. Haroun was murdered. I lost a child."

"Stop attacking him," Layla said. "You don't understand. He blundered, but he meant you no real harm. It was Nasim who did this."

"It's true. I don't understand. You've both made sure that we didn't understand." She met Tarik's gaze. "But that's going to change. I'm not going to wander blindly in the dark any longer. Nasim wants the grail. It's a weapon I can use to trap him. I need to know why he wants it. I want to know everything about it."

"I'm sorry, I can't tell you."

"Don't you say that. I deserve to know."

"Tell her," Layla said suddenly.

"Be silent, Layla."

"I won't be silent. She's right and you're wrong."

"You've always thought me wrong when I'm merely being responsible."

"You're not God; you can only do your best. Should that stop you from taking any action at all? And what of Kadar? Would you leave him with no knowledge of what has happened?"

"I was going to tell him. I was going slowly."

"Why? He doesn't impress me as being oversensitive. Not one man in a hundred would respond as Chion did."

"I resent that judgment. I have a very sensitive soul." Kadar paused. "But I admit my curiosity is greater than my delicacy of feeling. It would please me if you'd stop this bickering and give Selene the information she desires."

"Tell her, Tarik," Layla repeated. "Or I will."

Tarik was silent for a long moment. "It's a mistake."

"Then make a mistake. It will be good for you."

He shrugged. "It's on your shoulders."

Layla smiled. "I can bear it."

Tarik turned to Selene. "Ask your questions."

"Why does Nasim want the grail?"

"He thinks it will bring him power."

"But he's mistaken."

"No, it could bring him power but not the way he thinks."

"What do you mean?"

"The grail has an inscription," Kadar said. "What is it? The location of a great treasure?"

"Yes." Tarik's lips twisted. "Or of hell."

"It has nothing to do with hell," Layla said fiercely. "It's a great gift."

Tarik shook his head.

"It is," Layla insisted. "If you would only let yourself see that there are possibilities that—" She drew a deep breath. "It's not a map, it's directions for—No, I'm doing this wrong. You must start at the beginning, Tarik."

"You give me little opportunity." He shrugged. "The beginning for me was when you came to the Great Library." He looked at Kadar. "I told you of the library and what it meant to me. When Layla came and told me that she wished me to search the scrolls to find a document dictated by Selket, I regarded it merely as a challenge. She didn't tell me what the scroll contained."

"Scroll? What of the grail?"

"The grail came later. It took me many weeks to locate the scroll. I had to search in my free time. When darkness fell, I would let Layla into the library and we would comb through the Greek scrolls. At first I wasn't sure it was the correct one, but at the beginning we saw a word that couldn't be mistaken. It was then that Layla told me what the scroll contained. I didn't believe it. I laughed at her. She took the scroll and tried to gather all the herbs listed on it. It wasn't easy. Some of them we had never heard of, and the primary ingredient was a rare herb grown on the banks of the Nile. Finally we thought we had all we needed and rented a small hut near the marketplace and began to put the mixture together. For me, it was merely an adventure. An exercise in learning." He paused. "But Layla believed. She became obsessed with it. She ran great risks each time she came to the hut. The priests were becoming suspicious, and I tried to persuade her to come away with me to the country, where we might be safe. She wouldn't do it. She had to finish the work."

Layla shrugged. "And when we finished, we didn't know what to do with it. How could we test it? How would we know whether Eshe was truth or myth?"

"Eshe?" Selene asked.

"The word engraved on the cup," Kadar murmured.

Tarik nodded. "And the word I recognized on the scroll."

"What does it mean?"

"Life," he said simply. "Selket named his mixture Eshe because that's what it was—a way to cheat death. He thought he'd found a way to extend life far beyond the ordinary span." He smiled. "You're both staring at me the way I looked at Layla when she told me what the scroll contained. You don't believe me." He shrugged. "I knew that would be your response. You're intelligent, and that's the intelligent reaction."

"It smacks of sorcery, and I've never believed in magical elixirs," Kadar said. "Men have always sought a way to avoid death and it has always come to naught. I see no reason why this should be any different."

"And you, Selene?"

She shook her head impatiently. "Even if I did

believe it, it wouldn't make any difference. The only thing that matters is if Nasim believes it and if we can use it to trap him."

"Life and death," Tarik said. "I've presented you with a fascinating possibility. Aren't you even tempted to dwell on life instead of death?"

He didn't understand, Selene realized. Until Nasim was punished, she could think of nothing else.

"You speak of this Eshe," Kadar said. "What does that have to do with the grail?"

"Papyrus is frail and easily destroyed. Gold is the most permanent of metals. Layla and I had the information on the scroll engraved on the cup."

"And Nasim heard rumors about the grail and thought it a magic chalice," Kadar said.

"Nasim's no longer in his first youth, and his power is waning," Tarik said. "Unlike you, he does believe in sorcery. Such a tale would appeal to him."

"Then he'd do anything to get it?" Selene asked.

"I believe he demonstrated that at Sienbara," Tarik said.

"I have to be sure."

"It's not possible, Selene," Layla said gently. "I realize how you feel, but we can't use the grail to bait Nasim. We'll give you gold, soldiers, anything else you wish. But we can't risk losing the grail."

"You don't know how I feel. And we *will* use it."

Layla's expression hardened. "No. Do you think I've fought and worked for Eshe to let it—"

"I believe it's time to say good night." Kadar quickly rose to his feet and grasped Selene's elbow.

"We can discuss this tomorrow. Shall we all meet here two hours after sunrise?"

"I want to discuss it now," Selene said.

"No, you don't. We all need to think about the problem and the solutions. I'll take you to your chamber." He half-pushed, half-guided Selene toward the door. "Tomorrow."

Before she realized it, she was in the hall. She jerked her arm from Kadar's grasp. "It has to be settled tonight."

"It would be settled. Tarik and Layla would dig in their heels and refuse you. Is that what you want?"

"Of course it's not what I want." But it was what would happen, she realized. Despair and anger had led her to push too hard, and neither Tarik nor Layla responded well to coercion. No matter how desperately she needed to put a plan into place, she would have to wait and approach the situation from another angle. "I'll talk to them tomorrow." She started down the hall.

"You're being very reasonable," he murmured as he fell into step with her. "It doesn't bode well."

"I don't feel reasonable." She didn't look at him. "Are you going to help me?"

"I haven't decided. It's a very dangerous course you've chosen."

Shock rippled through her. Tarik and Layla's help had never been certain, but she had never doubted she could count on Kadar, whether he approved or not. "It's the right thing to do."

"As I said, I haven't decided. I'll have to think upon it."

They had reached her door and she whirled to face him. "You're different tonight."

He smiled. "Am I? Perhaps you're just seeing me clearer. I don't believe anyone else would see a difference."

No, but he had never been with her as he had with the rest of the world. He had shown everyone else that mockery, the darkness, the deadliness just beneath the surface. He had never turned that face to her.

Until tonight.

"Why are you like this?"

"You think I should be gentle with you? You don't want my gentleness. You want the same thing from me the rest of the world wants. A man to be killed, a task to be done." He bowed. "So I must treat you as I do everyone else and weigh the advantages and the consequences of giving you what you want." He opened her door. "I bid you good night. Sleep well, Selene."

"I didn't mean to—" She stopped. What could she say? She did need him, and she planned to use him, as he had said. No wonder she had distanced him. "I mean you no harm. I don't want you to kill Nasim. I only want you to show me how to do it."

He didn't answer. He was walking away.

Don't think of the hurt you must have dealt to turn him into this stranger. Think of Haroun. Think of Nasim.

Think of the act to be done.

# Chapter Fifteen

"THEY DON'T BELIEVE US," Layla said.

"We didn't expect them to." Tarik moved over to the balustrade to gaze into the garden. "It's a wild tale."

"Yes." She stood beside him. "I'm not sure Kadar was a good choice. He likes his way too much."

"And you do not?"

She grimaced. "I like it, but I seldom got it. Not with you."

"As I remember, I told you no only once."

But it had been the most important plea, when she had asked him to stay. "But there were always arguments." She braced herself. "Why did you wed her?"

"Rosa? She was kind. I was lonely."

"I was lonely too. I never took a husband to ease it."

"I don't wish to discuss Rosa."

"Neither do I. I only wondered." Her gaze traveled around the trees and flowers of the moonlit garden, the clear serenity of the rectangular pool. "This is pleasant. It reminds me a little of our house in Greece. Is that why you bought it?"

"No. I bought it because I was weary of living in walled fortresses."

"I never walled myself away from the world. You didn't have to do it either."

"You sent me the grail."

"But you created the chains yourself. When you treat a treasure as if it's not a treasure, you attract less curiosity. I would have rubbed some mud on it, tossed it in my saddlebag, and forgotten about it."

"No, you wouldn't. It guides your life."

"It guides both our lives. That doesn't mean it has to be everything. We have to live our lives with joy."

His gaze rested on her face. "And have these years been joyful for you, Layla?"

She looked away from him. "There have been moments of joy."

"It must have been painful for you to learn that Selene was with child."

"Do you think me so petty? I was *glad* for her. I wanted her to have what I could not." She turned to face him. "And I also wanted to see Nasim dead for what he did. I tried to soothe and say all the fine, wise things, but I know how she feels."

"Layla." His hand reached and hovered near her shoulder.

She held her breath.

His hand fell away without touching her.

She mustn't let him see the pain. She smiled with an effort. "But, as usual, we must forget what we feel and protect the grail. It may be more difficult to guard it from Selene and Kadar than from Nasim." She must get away. She could stand no more tonight. "I think I will go to my bed. I'm journey weary."

Tarik nodded. "Good night."

She could feel his gaze on her back as she walked toward the door.

We're here together at last. Don't let me go.

Stop me. Talk truth to me.

Touch me.

He did none of those things.

He watched her walk away.

There was someone in the chamber.

Selene came wide awake, her gaze searching the darkness.

"Don't be frightened. It's only me," Kadar said.

He was sitting cross-legged on the floor beside her bed. She could see him only dimly in the pale moonlight streaming through the windows. The light glimmered on his dark hair but left his face in shadow. "I'm not frightened. What are you doing here?"

"Looking at you. I couldn't sleep. There was much to consider."

"You cannot see me in the dark."

"I can see you. I was trained well by Sinan and Nasim. Did you hear me when I crept into the room?"

He shook his head. "No one hears me. Nasim would be dead by now."

A ripple of shock went through her.

"What's wrong? That's what you want, isn't it?"

He had sensed her disturbance with that sixth sense that was always between them. "I want him dead. I don't want you to fall upon him in the depths of sleep."

"You want him to have an honorable death? There are no honorable or dishonorable deaths. There is just death."

"I don't want you—I'll do it."

"We will see."

"You've decided to help me?"

"Perhaps." His tone became mocking. "If the price is high enough. I'm an assassin without peer. You cannot expect to have me cheaply."

"Price?"

"I wanted your child. I didn't realize how much until Layla told me it was dead. I still want it." He paused. "That's my price, Selene. You must give me a child."

She lost her breath. "I would never give up a child."

"I didn't ask you to give the babe over to me. I know what it's like to grow up without a mother. You're part of the bargain." His voice was velvet soft. "It should be no great trial for you to accept me. Our bodies love each other, and once we return to Montdhu we will both be busy with our duties. Of course, we will have to exchange vows. I'll not leave my child unprotected when I go after Nasim."

"I cannot—I don't—"

"You don't want another child?"

She had not even considered it. The pain of loss was too fresh. She was confused and stunned by the thought. "Now?"

"It would not be now. I believe it takes nine months."

"I mean it—"

"It's my price, Selene. Give me this and I'll persuade Tarik and Layla to let us use the grail. I'll show you how to get Nasim, and I'll kill him myself if that's your will."

"It's not my will." She moistened her lips. "And I'm not sure—I know you, Kadar. I may not have to do anything for you to do this for me."

"Very clever. It's true I would have done almost anything for you. I still might. But you don't know, do you? And do you really know me?"

Not this Kadar. Not the Kadar who had shown up at her door this evening. "I don't like the power vows give to a man."

"I do. With a woman like you, a man needs any advantage he can claim. And, as I recall, at one time you asked me to wed you."

"That was a long time ago." It seemed a century since that last night at Montdhu. "I'm not that woman any longer."

"No, you're not. So I offer you a bargain."

"I'll...consider it."

"You have little time. It's necessary to strike fast and hard at a man like Tarik. Otherwise he'll have time to bolster his defenses."

"It's not only Tarik, it's Layla. They seemed very determined. Are you sure you can sway them?"

"I'll sway them." He added lightly, "Or, if not, I'll steal the grail for you."

"And then we'd be running from them as well as having to concoct a plan to trap Nasim. You must persuade them."

"And if I do?"

Her hands clenched on the cover. It could be a terrible mistake. She was not certain of anything any longer. Not Kadar. Not herself.

No, she was certain of one thing. Nasim must be punished.

"You'll have your price."

"Good."

Silence in the chamber. She grew uneasy when he did not move but still sat looking at her. "Well, go to your bed. We have nothing more to say."

"Soon. I'm enjoying this."

"I am not. Go away."

"You would, if you permitted yourself. The darkness makes everything more sensual, doesn't it? I've always loved the scent of you. I can hear every change of tempo of your breath. A bar of moonlight is lying across your body. I can see your breasts covered by the blanket, but your shoulders are naked and shimmering...." He suddenly chuckled. "Your breathing has quickened. Why?"

He knew why. He always knew everything about her body's responses. "I want you to leave."

"Do you?" He was suddenly kneeling on the floor by her bed. His features were still shadowed. "And I want to put my hand on that strip of moonlight." His hand came out of the darkness to lightly rest on the blanket covering her belly. The muscles of her abdomen clenched beneath the touch. "Look at us," he whispered.

She couldn't help but look. His touch was light, but the warmth seemed to burn her through the blanket. His hand gleamed pale against the brown wool. From the forearm he was in shadow, but his hand was bold and clear, strong, fingers spread wide and stiff.

She was having trouble breathing. "This is not my will."

"Shh, it's not unusual for a man of my profession to be given a small payment for a deposit." He was pushing the blanket aside.

She should move.

She couldn't move.

His cheek was against her belly, rubbing slowly back and forth. She could feel the slight male roughness against her softness.

"Here," he whispered. "Soon, Selene."

A child. He was talking about a babe.

His hand moved down to stroke, rub, pluck.

A shudder went through her.

His mouth was suddenly on her nipple and he was sucking, hard, fast.

His fingers plunged deep.

She gave a cry and arched upward.

"Yes." He gave her more, in, out, fast, deep. "Call out. Let me hear you."

Her fingernails dug into the sheet.

Faster. Harder.

"Come for me."

Darkness. Deepness. Searing heat.

She cried out as the tension climaxed.

He stopped, his forehead slowly bent to rest on her stomach. His breath was warm on her flesh, his chest laboring.

She was panting. Her heart was beating too fast. She felt as if it would leap from her breast.

He raised his head. His hand was leaving her, pulling the blanket up to cover her body. He stood up and stepped back from the bed. "I'll leave you now. Good night, Selene."

She felt a ripple of shock. "But you didn't—"

"Ah, no, and I'll suffer for it tonight. It's not my way to collect until the task is done. I needed to touch you, but I can wait for the rest."

"But you—what was this all about?"

"It's about you learning the pleasure is still there, waiting to be tapped. It's about bringing your body alive again. It's about preparing the way." He moved toward the door. "I'll need to speak to Tarik and Layla alone tomorrow. I'll come to see you later in the day."

Selene huddled beneath the blanket after the door closed behind him. She had to stop trembling.

*It's about bringing your body alive again.*

Dear God, her body was too alive. The blood coursed through her veins, and her skin was flushed and tingling. There was a familiar aching emptiness between her thighs.

The tower.

He had pleasured her, and still it was not enough. She wanted more.

She could have more. It was no surrender, no loss of herself. A bargain had been struck.

It could be like the tower.


Tarik and Layla were sitting on the bench when Kadar strode onto the terrace the next morning. They both looked at him warily.

"And where is Selene?" Tarik asked.

Kadar smiled. "I thought we could speak more freely without her. I'll tell her of our discussion later."

"I wouldn't think she'd thank you for going behind her back," Layla said dryly.

"Oh, we're in complete agreement. I had a long talk with her last night. She knew you were going to refuse her. I didn't want her to be further distressed."

"None of us does," Tarik said.

"But we can't do what she wishes," Layla said. "Find another way."

"I would, but she's right. The grail is the only bait that will draw Nasim." He smiled. "So that's the bait we have to use."

Tarik shook his head.

"Yes," Kadar said.

"Are you going to threaten us?" Tarik asked. "I believe you know that won't accomplish anything."

"It depends on the threat." Kadar moved over to the balustrade and looked up at the bright blue sky. "I've always loved the night. The stars, the shadows. But the morning is good too. Feel the freshness of the breeze? Since I came so close to death from Balkir's sword, I've learned to appreciate those small pleasures even more." He paused. "What was the potion that so miraculously cured me, Tarik?"

Tarik was silent.

"At the moment Selene is too numb to focus on anything but ways to use the grail to lure Nasim, but, as you were talking, things began to slide together for me. There was more than the grail in the coffer, wasn't there? Eshe?"

Tarik nodded.

"And you had Selene give it to me."

"It saved your life. I wasn't sure it would. You were almost gone."

Kadar's brows lifted. "You claim this Eshe can cure a sword wound?"

"No, I was surprised that it helped you. It only seems to increase the body's strength and repel disease." He gave Layla a sardonic smile. "But perhaps you should ask my wife. She has vastly more experience with Eshe than I do."

"Because you hide your head and won't deal with it," Layla said. "But, as far as I know, it does little good with wounds. He should have died." She shrugged. "It's difficult to judge. I've never given it to anyone in such dire straits. It would have been a waste."

"And you were too ill for me to give you a choice," Tarik said. "It was a great struggle for me."

"To keep me alive?" Kadar gazed directly into his eyes. "Or to extend my life span?"

He smiled. "You told me you don't believe that's possible."

"But you do."

"Oh, yes, I believe it. Would I have protected the grail all these years if I hadn't believed it?"

"But you're tired of protecting it. You wanted to shift the responsibility to someone else. You chose me."

"It was a very painful choice. Particularly after I got to know you."

"I thought I recalled signs of uncertainty and remorse."

"There's no reason Tarik should be remorseful," Layla said. "He saved your life and gave you a great gift."

"I don't think he regards it as a great gift. Do you, Tarik?"

He shook his head. "It's a terrible, terrible burden."

"Because you make it so," Layla said. "There's no reason for you to agonize. Just look at Kadar. He's nothing like Chion. He can withstand it."

"I hope so."

"Who is this Chion?" Kadar asked Tarik.

"My brother."

"And what happened to him?"

"I loved him. I wanted to share Eshe with him." His lips thinned with pain. "He went mad. He killed himself."

Kadar went still. "Not a cheerful prospect. I believe I'm beginning to be a trifle upset with you, Tarik. Does this potion often unbalance the recipient?"

"Chion was always delicate and nervous," Layla said. "It's never happened before or since."

"How do you know?" Tarik asked. "You're so generous with Eshe that I'm sure you don't keep track of all to whom you give it."

"I do keep track." She glared at him. "Yes, I'm generous, but I'm not irresponsible. There was never another Chion."

"One was enough." Tarik turned back to Kadar. "But I hoped it would have no adverse effect on you. I might never have given it to you at all, if you hadn't been hurt. It seemed as if destiny took the decision out of my hands."

"I'll take comfort from that, if I see madness approaching," Kadar said dryly.

"It won't happen," Layla said. "And you need not try to make Tarik feel guilt. He feels nothing else. You're the first person he gave Eshe to since Chion died."

"I'm honored," Kadar said. "Then I assume he's merely acted as protector for the grail?"

"Yes." Her lips curved in a bitter smile. "Since he would not help me in any other way. I thought it only fair that I send him the grail to keep safe."

"Safe?" Tarik repeated. "Do you know how often I've been tempted to melt it down and bury it?"

"But you couldn't do it. Because, deep in your soul, you know you're wrong."

Kadar looked from one to the other. He could almost feel the tension and emotion vibrating in the room. He had been so absorbed with his own frustration, he had not paid any attention to the strange alchemy existing between the two. A very tumultuous and diverse river appeared to be flowing beneath the surface, carrying currents of deception, restraint, passion, and loyalty. "Why is he wrong?"

"I'm not wrong," Tarik said. "It should stop here."

"Is that why you gave it to Kadar?"

"I gave it to him because I wanted to save—" He wearily shook his head. "No, that was an excuse. I gave it to him because I was selfish and I wanted to be free."

"At last," Layla said. "Now, when you admit you have the right to be selfish and not godlike, we will have made great strides."

"I don't agree," Kadar said. "I take umbrage at anyone being selfish with my well-being." It was time to take control. "I believe you owe me a debt, Tarik."

He could sense the sudden return of wariness in the room.

"He owes you nothing," Layla said. "It's you who owes him a debt."

Kadar ignored her, concentrating on Tarik. "You disrupted the course of my life, you risked my sanity." He recalled another thing Tarik mentioned that seemed important to him. "And you gave me no choice."

"He couldn't give you a choice," Layla said. "You would have died if he—"

"Be silent, Layla. I don't need you to defend me." Tarik's gaze was fastened on Kadar's face. "I admit to all that."

"Do you admit that you owe me a debt?"

"Perhaps." He shook his head. "But I cannot let you use the grail."

Kadar had hit a blank wall. He went in another direction. "I have value for you. You went to a great deal of trouble to choose me to act as guardian for your grail."

"So?"

"Selene needs Nasim dead. I have to give her what she needs. With the grail, it will be much safer. But with or without it, I have to give her Nasim. I'm very good, but it's clearly a near-impossible task. That means that my risks of being killed are entirely in your hands."

Layla's eyes widened. "Why, you bastard."

"In truth, that's exactly what I am. But it's also true that the guilt is Tarik's if he doesn't provide me with the weapon I need." He smiled at Layla. "And you've already told me how prone he is to suffer guilt."

"He's not prone to be made a fool."

"If he were a fool, I'd try to trick him. I'm merely telling him the truth." His gaze shifted to Tarik. "My death would not serve either your conscience or your well-being. Whom would you saddle with your grail? All your worrying and soul-searching would be for naught. Much better to let me have it."

"No," Layla said flatly.

"It's my decision, Layla." Tarik added wryly, "After all, you gave me the custody of it."

"The risk is too great."

"I promise you that I'll return it safely," Kadar said.

"Dead men don't keep promises."

"Tarik?"

"I'll consider it." He held up his hand to still Layla's protest. "He speaks the truth, Layla. He could die. Nasim could kill him."

"Either of us would die to save the grail from Nasim."

"But it would be our choice."

Kadar knew he had done all he could. He thought it would probably be enough. "You'll let me know tomorrow?"

Tarik nodded. "Tomorrow evening. I'll think about what you've said."

Kadar turned to leave.

"But now I want a promise from you."

Kadar glanced inquiringly over his shoulder.

"You say that Selene is too stunned to think of anything but Nasim, but what of you? Aren't you avoiding thinking about Eshe too? I can think of at least three questions you should have asked me that you didn't. Where is your curiosity, Kadar? You may not believe Eshe can do what Selket wished it to do, but what if it can? What if it's not a myth? What if everyone could live far beyond their sixtieth year? Promise me you'll think upon it." Tarik smiled grimly. "And think what you risk in losing the grail, if it's not a myth."

Kadar nodded slowly. "A fair trade."

But he didn't want to consider those possibilities, he realized as he left the terrace. Tarik was right: He had been trying to avoid thinking about anything but the ways and means of accomplishing what Selene needed. He knew the reason he had instantly rejected the promise of Eshe was that he had known the idea held a fascination for him. It piqued his curiosity, and that had always been the goad setting him into motion. The chance to learn, to probe, to become more than when he started.

But he must not be caught by that lure. His entire

attention must be devoted to helping Selene, not thinking of a clearly impossible—

But in helping Selene, he had made a promise to Tarik. That promise had virtually forced him to think of the possibility, the alluring myth.

Oh, yes.

He plunged eagerly into the wondrous territory of the impossible.


"It took you long enough. It's the middle of the afternoon." Selene threw open the door. "You could have persuaded God to make another world in this time."

"It might have taken a little bit longer than that." Kadar entered the chamber. "Though if I truly brought all my powers of persuasion to bear, it could—"

"What happened?"

"Tarik is going to consider it." He held up his hand. "I don't think there's a doubt that he'll do it."

"There's always doubt until he agrees. It couldn't have taken this long. Why didn't you come and tell me sooner?"

"I was busy."

"Doing what?"

"I took a long walk."

"A walk? And you let me wait for—" Her gaze narrowed on his face. It was almost without expression, and yet she was aware of something just beneath the surface. Excitement. It was the same excitement she had seen on his face the night before they had arrived at Sienbara. "What's happened?"

"Nothing."

"Then why do you look—"

"It has nothing to do with Nasim. And that's the only subject in which you're interested, isn't it?"

He was wrong. She was intensely interested in whatever had stirred that excitement. But it was clear he wasn't going to share it. She smothered her disappointment and nodded. "That's the only thing that's important right now."

He smiled. "You're sure?"

"Of course I'm sure. When will we know?"

"Tomorrow evening."

Her disappointment and frustration increased. "Perhaps I should talk to him."

"I know it annoys you to sit and do nothing, but that would be the wrong thing to do. Let him come to the decision himself."

"And we wait and twiddle our thumbs."

"No, we sup. We talk. I need you to tell me more of Layla. He fights it, but she wields great influence with Tarik. Perhaps a game of chess." He bowed. "If you'll do me the honor."

"I don't wish to play chess."

"Too bad. In your present distraught state I'd easily sweep you away. Then do you wish me to leave you?"

"Would you?" she asked, skeptical.

"No, I'm selfish. After this endeavor gets under way, I don't know how often I'll be able to enjoy your company. I intend to take full advantage of this lull."

"Then, since I have no choice, I suppose I'll have to put up with you."

"And you're relieved to have even my humble

company to while away the time." His eyes glimmered with mischief. "Admit it."

She was relieved. She didn't want to spend any more time alone and, for some reason, Kadar's hard edge seemed to have vanished. "Perhaps." She smiled. "Very well, I admit it."

"Ah, graciousness in a barren world." He took her arm and led her toward the door. "Come. I'll show you the garden."

"It's beautiful." Her finger gently touched the petals of a magnificent crimson rose growing on a bush beside the path. "I've never seen roses this late in the year. Scotland is not kind to roses."

"This is a gentler land. Could you become used to it?"

She shrugged. "I suppose one could become accustomed to anything, but I prefer Montdhu. This land is too easy. I don't see how the people here keep from becoming soft."

He chuckled. "Not all people require a challenge every day."

"Then they should." She gazed at the serene stillness of the crystal pool. "It's lovely, but I cannot imagine sitting here every day."

"I'm certain the woman for whom this villa was purchased was not of your nature. Tarik tells me the Pope bought the villa for his favorite mistress. She created this world to her own taste."

"Then she must have been a very docile and restrained woman."

"Not too restrained, or the Pope would not have thought her worth keeping." He paused. "Tarik says she gave him a son. It was the son who sold the villa to Tarik."

His tone was odd, and she asked, "So?"

"His name was Vaden."

Her eyes widened. "Vaden?" It was too bizarre. It could not be the same warrior who had been a Knight Templar with Ware. The enigmatic knight who had pursued and persecuted and, finally, saved them all. Yet she had heard that Vaden came from Rome and no one knew his background. "The son of the Pope?"

"It would explain why he was accepted into the Knights Templar."

"It can't be our Vaden. The coincidence is too great."

"The description Tarik gave me is very close." He gazed thoughtfully down into the mirrored waters of the pool. "And haven't you noticed some people seem tied together throughout their lives? Their paths weave in and out, come together and part, to form a pattern."

"Astonishing," she murmured, still dwelling on the coincidence. "Is he still in Rome?"

"I have no idea. Maybe. Tarik said he had formed a small army and was selling his sword to the warring factions in this land."

"Find out if he's here."

"Why?" His gaze shifted to her face. "Now what do you have in mind?"

"Vaden was a great warrior. He helped Ware once. Isn't it possible we could get him to help us?"

Kadar threw back his head and laughed. "I should have known."

"Why are you laughing? It's a possibility."

"I'm not laughing at your idea, just your single-mindedness. I bring you to look at roses and you think only of recruiting knights to ride under your banner."

"Find out."

He was still smiling. "I'll find out."

"Tomorrow."

"Tomorrow. Now will you put such thoughts out of your mind?"

"I cannot."

His smile faded. "I know. Try." His gaze shifted back to the pool again. "I'll give you something else to think about. What if their Eshe is the miracle they think it is?"

She shook her head.

"I know it's unlikely, but—"

"Not unlikely—impossible."

"In the Scriptures there are tales of long life."

"Men chosen by God. I doubt if God would choose heathens from Egypt to receive such a blessing."

"Who knows," Kadar murmured.

"Are you beginning to believe Tarik's tale?" she asked, surprised.

"I believe he believes it. And Tarik is no fool. I cannot speak for Layla. You know her better than I do."

"Even a clever woman can be blinded by what she wants to see."

"Very well. Then assume it's merely an interesting dream. It does no harm to imagine what it would be like." His brow furrowed. "I know few men who live much beyond forty years. Sixty is a great age. What if you could live beyond that? Would you want to do so?"

She thought about it. "The only one I know who is so old is Niall McKenzie. He's two and sixty. His joints ache, his vision is dimming, he sits before the fire and thinks only of his youth." She shook her head. "That is no life. Better to go out like the flame of a candle in the wind."

"But if you could remain strong? Think of all the things you could learn."

She could see why such a prospect was intriguing to Kadar. His curiosity about everything could never be satisfied. "That would be a joy." She was silent a moment. "Would there not be a point when you could learn no more, when everything seemed the same?"

"If that time ever came, it would only pose another challenge." He smiled. "And I doubt if you could ever learn everything in this world."

"Unless everyone grew old with you, it would be a lonely life." She shivered. "I would hate to see all the people I love die."

His smile vanished. "And, if everyone grew very old, there would be far too many people to be fed. Famine breeds war." His lips twisted. "And war would kill far more certainly than old age. Checkmate."

Kadar had thought of wars, and she had thought of Ware and Thea and all the people at Montdhu she cared about. It was too sad. She would think no more about it.

She shifted her shoulders as if to rid herself of the

burden. "If you have no more pleasant conversation than of war and famine, I will think better of spending the evening with you. I don't know why you wish to dwell on such impossibilities anyway."

He smiled. "It's my dark soul. I merely wished to hear your thoughts on the subject."

"You've heard them. Now take me back to the house. All this talk of famine has made me hungry."

# Chapter Sixteen

"YOU MAY USE THE GRAIL," Tarik said. "But Layla and I will go with you, and if we think the grail is in danger, don't expect us to let you keep it."

Kadar nodded.

"This is Tarik's decision. I hope you're satisfied. You played on his guilty feelings very well," Layla said. "It's not my will. I think it complete madness. I'll be watching you closely."

"I'm sure you will," Kadar said. "I'll be watching you too."

She looked at him inquiringly.

"I'd judge you to be a dangerous woman if thwarted."

She met his gaze. "More than you dream."

"And that in the past you probably played on Tarik's feelings yourself."

"Yes, I did. I'd have used anyone to break free of the priests and that house I hated," she admitted calmly. "But that was long ago."

"How long?"

She glanced at Tarik. "Ah, questions. He's been thinking as you bid him."

"I keep my promises," Kadar said. "You wanted me to ask questions. I'm asking them." He turned to Tarik. "You said that at first you didn't believe in Eshe. You do now?"

Tarik nodded.

"Why?"

"The only way to test it was to take it ourselves. One evening Layla and I had a celebration. We had honey cakes and wine and at the end of the evening we drank a toast." He shrugged. "And the next day there was nothing different. We didn't know what to expect, but there should have been *something*."

Layla smiled, reminiscing. "There was something. A headache from too much wine."

"True." Tarik returned her smile. "And the conviction that all of our work was for naught."

"Your conviction. I still believed."

Tarik nodded. "I wanted only to forget and go on with our lives. We made plans to run away from the city. I managed to smuggle Layla out of the city to my brother, Chion, in the country. I was going to follow the next week."

"But you didn't?"

"The priests had found out Layla was visiting me

the night before she left the city. They decided to try to persuade me to tell them where she'd gone."

"Persuade?"

"They tortured him," Layla whispered. "They broke all the bones in his foot, but he told them nothing."

"I was fortunate that was all they had time to do. The head librarian was my great friend and he had influence at court. He managed to talk Ptolemy into making the priests free me and then found a way for me to leave the city."

"He didn't walk for a year." Layla's tone was stilted. "And when he did, it was the way he does now. He was a fool. He should have told them where I was."

"We've talked of this before," Tarik said. "Stop blaming yourself. If I'd told them, they'd have killed me. I did it for myself."

She shook her head.

"And the priests didn't find you?"

"No," Tarik said. "When I was well, we left Egypt and went to Greece. My brother, Chion, went with us."

Kadar said, "The brother who went mad."

"It wasn't Tarik's fault," Layla said defensively.

"I didn't say it was. I wouldn't know. But I'm trying to find out. If you didn't go mad after taking the potion, why would Chion?"

"He didn't go mad at once. It was later."

"How much later?"

Tarik met his gaze. "Two hundred years."

Kadar went still. "Two hundred..."

"As Layla said, he was a gentle, simple man. He had seen too many loved ones die."

"Two hundred years." Kadar couldn't get past that

incredible statement. He shook his head. "It's not possible. I thought perhaps eighty. Though that, too, stretches the imagination."

They both looked at him, waiting.

He knew the question for which they were waiting. "How long ago did you take the potion?"

"Ptolemy the Fourteenth was in power. He died the year we left for Greece and his sister Cleopatra was given the throne by Julius Caesar. That was more than forty years before the birth of Christ."

"Before the birth of Christ?" Kadar gazed at them in wonder. "Do you think me mad too?"

"Incredulous, not mad."

"And how long do you claim to be able to live?"

Tarik shrugged. "I make no claims. How could I? We know nothing about this. I could die tomorrow."

"Or live forever?"

"Dear God, I hope not."

"And you haven't aged?"

Tarik shook his head. "Now you see why I feel guilty enough to let you use the grail. It's a great burden I've put on you."

"It's a great gift you've given him," Layla corrected.

"You can see that Layla and I have a different viewpoint regarding Eshe. After Chion died, I couldn't give the potion to anyone else. I didn't have the right."

"Who else has the right?" Layla demanded. "Were we to put it in a cave and let it be forgotten? As the years pass, surely there will come a time when it will be safe to bring it to light."

"And that time is not now?" Kadar asked.

"Some of the herbs are rare. We could make only a

small amount each year. Do you realize the uproar that would shake Christendom if everyone knew about it and we couldn't offer it to all?"

"Oh, yes." Kadar's lips twisted. "And you'd be fortunate not to be burned at the stake for sorcery—or blasphemy."

"I've been close to that point twice quite recently," Layla said. "Bad judgment. This is a terrible dark time, and not everyone can accept gifts. It frightens them."

"I wonder why?" Kadar asked dryly.

Tarik was looking at Layla. "You didn't tell me."

"Why should I think you'd care? You weren't there. You were living happily at Sienbara with your Rosa." Her lips tightened. "I'm surprised you weren't tempted to give Eshe to her."

"I might have been. I wasn't given the opportunity. She died from a fall from a horse."

Kadar barely heard them. "And, if I'm to believe you, I could live as long as you?"

"It's possible." Tarik glanced at Layla. "I yield to your greater experience."

"Almost certainly," Layla said.

Kadar felt as if he'd been bludgeoned. He'd been toying, playing with the idea on a minor scale. This was something entirely different.

"It's enough to daze anyone. That's why we've always gone slowly when telling anyone." Tarik's gaze was on Kadar's face. "I was lucky. There was no shock for me. The years came and went and let me accept it gradually."

Kadar tried to fight his way through the maze. "The manuscript..."

"I wandered a great deal after Layla and I parted. I settled for a while in Britain." He smiled. "It amused me when I heard of de Troyes's work. It didn't amuse me when Nasim fastened on it with such ferocity. We had encountered each other twice. Once when Nasim was a young man and the second time nine years ago. He had grown old, I had not."

"And he had heard rumors of your treasure."

"Yes." Tarik tilted his head and gazed quizzically at him. "Any other questions?"

"Just one. Selene. Did you give her the potion?"

Any hint of amusement vanished from Tarik's expression. "No, never. She's quite wonderful, but she wasn't like you. You'd been seasoned by a hundred fires. I felt it might possibly be safe to give it to you. Selene has a very tempestuous nature, and I couldn't foresee any of her responses. If you wish her to have it, you'll have to give it to her yourself. I won't take the responsibility."

"When are you going to take responsibility, Tarik?" Layla asked. "You cannot narrow your choices to one man. What if we die? What if he dies? Who will protect the grail? Who will make the decision when it's time to let the world know about Eshe?"

"You'd give Eshe to everyone on earth if you could. What of the sacrifice to them?" He turned to Kadar. "You'll be tempted to give Selene the potion. You love her and you'll want to keep her with you. But once it's given, there's no going back. Would you risk her going mad? Or all the bitterness and hurt she would know? What of the boredom and the weariness? What of the constant moving and uprooting to avoid people noticing she's still young and comely while they grow old? Not to mention the danger of torture and death from those who either fear her or want the secret for themselves."

"You paint an ugly picture," Kadar said.

"It can be ugly."

"So is life," Layla said. "It can also be joyful. Are we all to die in the womb because we fear to face the harshness?"

It was clearly an old and bitter battle between them, and Kadar had enough with which to deal without having to think of their conflicts. "The decision wouldn't be mine. I'm not like you, Tarik. I'd give her a choice."

Tarik flinched. "That was unfair. You weren't able to—"

"But you were planning to do it anyway. You manipulated Nasim to bring me to your doorstep and then—" He shook his head as he realized the subject he was arguing. "God in heaven, I'm talking as if I believe all this. It's the wildest tale I've ever heard, and there's no way of proving it true or false."

"You'll get your proof in a hundred years or so," Layla said. "Providing you don't do something foolish and get slaughtered in battle."

"A hundred years." He could take no more of this. He turned to leave. "I have to go tell Selene you've agreed to let us use the grail."

"But nothing else?"

"Why should I tell her something I don't believe myself?"

Tarik's smile was sad. "But you are beginning to believe it, aren't you?"

God help him, he was. He didn't believe in sorcery, and if Tarik and Layla had told him the grail was magical, he could have shrugged off the rest of the story. But the discovery of the potion through intense curiosity and hard work was a concept with which he could identify. From his own experience, he knew the miracles that could be wrought with those two weapons. "It doesn't matter whether I am or not. Since it can't be proved, I just have to live my life as if it's only a mad tale." He grimaced. "Which is probably the truth."

"But now you'll be more careful of the grail," Tarik said. "Because, in your heart, you know its value."

"I'll be careful because I gave you my promise and for no other reason. I cannot consider any of this idiocy right now. There are plans to be made."

"I'm surprised you haven't already made them." A hint of sarcasm deepened Tarik's tone. "You seemed very sure of me."

"I have a few thoughts on the subject." Kadar smiled. "But Selene also has an idea. She wishes me to involve an old acquaintance, who is probably going to cost you a great deal of gold. What do you know of Vaden's whereabouts?"

"This is a foul place." Selene stepped gingerly over one of the many scraps of garbage littering the alley. "And it smells of dung and—"

"Stop complaining. You wished to come." Kadar

grasped her elbow. "The inn is just ahead. Stay close to me. From what Tarik said, it's a low place frequented only by soldiers and whores." He pushed open the door. "Don't be surprised if you see things you don't want to see. In a place like this, no one bothers to seek privacy when they wish to rut."

"Then it's no different than the House of Nicholas."

But it was different. The place was as different from the pristine cleanliness of Nicholas's house as silk was from leather.

Dimness.

Noise.

Smoke.

The sour smell of sweat, wine, and ale assaulted Selene's nostrils as she followed Kadar into the room. Only a few candles lit the darkness. The room was crowded, the tables full, but she couldn't make out the faces of any of the men or women.

"I don't see him. Are you sure he should be here?"

"No. Tarik said he spent time here when he wasn't selling his lance to local lords. He might not be in Rome at all. Why are you so determined to have him?"

She wasn't sure herself. Perhaps it was the coincidence of having Vaden suddenly emerge from the veil of years. It seemed almost like a sign. "He helped us before. If he's selling his lance now, Tarik might as well buy him for us." She frowned. "It's too dark in here. We'll have to go farther into the room."

"I never actually saw Vaden. Would you recognize him?"

"He has fair hair." She had seen him only once, and

then his face had been blackened by smoke. "Like a lion. I'd recognize his hair."

No one seemed to pay them any attention as they moved about the room. They were too occupied in their own pleasures.

"Well, there's no fair hair in this room that I can see. The Romans are usually dark."

Selene dragged her gaze from the sight of a naked woman straddling the hips of a young soldier, making guttural sounds deep in her throat. She had thought she would not be shocked, but the sight brought back too many memories of the women she had known as a child. "Have you ever had a woman in a place like this?"

"When the hunger struck me and there was no other alternative."

"Did you pay them well?"

"Yes, as I told you, I spent time in a house of pleasure. I wouldn't cheat them."

"These women do not look—Do you suppose they're paid a fair sum?"

"No." His gaze narrowed on her face. "It's the way it is. It's a hard life. They have something to sell that's worth a meal, a place to sleep for the night. Nothing more. The women at the House of Nicholas were fortunate in comparison."

"They weren't more fortunate. They were slaves. At least these women have choice."

"Yes." An indefinable expression flickered over Kadar's face. "Choice is important."

She had the odd sense that he was no longer talking about the women of Nicholas's house.

But then the expression was gone and he was glancing away. "If you don't see him, we might as well leave. This place is upsetting—"

"There. What is that?" She had caught a glimpse of something in the dark corner across the room—shimmering, moving. She eagerly moved closer. "It might be..."

Lion-colored hair flowing over naked shoulders...

His shoulders were not the only portion of his body that was naked. His tunic lay on the rushes beside him, and he was crouched between the thighs of a woman as naked as he. He was moving quickly, stroking deeply, murmuring encouragement to the whore beneath him. She needed no encouragement. It was clear that she was entirely willing and in the throes of pleasure.

"Is it him?" Kadar asked.

"I can't see his face." The man's head was bent over the woman, long strands of tawny hair veiling his features. "I'll have to get closer."

"Not too close. He may resent any interference at this point."

"I think he'll be too occupied to notice."

"It's the woman who is occupied. He's a warrior and trained to notice an attack."

"I'm not attacking." She edged closer. "I just wish to see his—"

He lifted his head and tossed back his hair.

Vaden.

Even covered with smoke and soot there had been no doubt about the regularity of his features, but she had never realized how comely he was. Those deep-set sapphire-blue eyes were impossible not to recognize. It was his face that was a surprise; it should have belonged to an Adonis or, considering the tawny hair, perhaps an Apollo.

"Well?" Kadar asked.

"It's Vaden."

He must have heard his name. He froze, his gaze left the face of the woman.

Selene instinctively braced herself as she met Vaden's gaze. In the space of a heartbeat she felt weighed, judged, and dismissed.

Vaden returned to his coupling.

She was disconcerted. "What do we do now?"

"Well, we don't interrupt. He should be finished soon."

She hoped that was true. She felt very awkward standing here watching him couple.

And not only awkward.

"No one would notice," Kadar murmured in her ear. "We could find our own corner."

She shook her head.

But watching a man as beautiful as Vaden perform was causing the heat to flow through her. She had never understood the tapestry in the tower room, the excitement of watching others couple.

She did now.

Thank God, they were finishing. A moment later he was rising, pulling the whore to her feet.

He was laughing as he pulled on his tunic and searched in his money pouch. He patted the woman on her backside and pressed a coin into her hand. He turned to Selene and smiled. "I'm a little weary now, but give me time. It's a long night."

Kadar chuckled at the shocked expression on Selene's face. "What did you expect? I told you, only whores come here. She doesn't wish you to rut with her, Vaden. That's not why we're here." He took another step closer. "Do you remember me?"

The amusement left Vaden's face. "Kadar."

"I thought you'd recognize me. We never actually met, but I was with Ware during the many years you watched and stalked him." He pulled Selene forward. "You may not recall Selene. She was much younger when you encountered each other."

"I think he should remember," Selene said dryly. "Considering he pulled me from my horse and threatened to kill me."

Vaden smiled. "I do remember you. You're the sister of Ware's woman."

"His wife," she corrected. "They are wed."

Vaden shrugged. "I cannot remember everything." He dropped into a chair and reached for his wine goblet. "She shouldn't be here, Kadar."

"I know. She insisted on coming. Could I persuade you to leave this place with us?"

"No." He lifted his wine to his lips. "I like it here."

"It stinks," Selene said succinctly.

"True. You should leave before your delicate nose is further offended. But I'm a little drunk, and I make it a habit to never go out into dark alleys unless I have all my wits about me."

Selene dropped down in the chair across from him. "We want you to help us."

"I helped you once before." He smiled. "Don't expect more from me. I'm not a generous man."

"We're not asking for generosity," Selene said. "We want your sword. You'll be well paid."

"Ware?"

She shook her head. "Ware knows nothing about this. Tarik. You remember him?"

He sipped his wine. "How could I forget? I sold him my birthright. Is he enjoying it?"

"It's a beautiful villa."

"Yes." His gaze went to Kadar. "You're hovering over her the way you did Ware. Don't you weary of protecting those around you?"

"It's become custom."

"I always found it strange. Particularly after I found out of your association with the assassins."

"Ware told me you spent some time with Sinan. Did you ever meet Nasim?"

"He came twice to the fortress while I was there. Sinan seemed to lean on him." He smiled. "It was amusing watching them together. I never could decide who had the darker spirit."

"Nasim," Selene said.

"Possibly." He leaned back in his chair. "I gather it's Nasim you wish me to vanquish?"

"Yes."

"Then I hereby end this discussion."

"Not without help," Kadar said.

"You know the power of the assassins," Vaden said. "They never stop. If I killed Nasim, they'd be pursuing me for the rest of my life."

"You wouldn't be the one to strike the death blow."

"Then they'd pursue me for only half my life."

"Tarik would pay very well," Selene said. "What do you want?"

"I have what I want." He waved at the dim room. "Uplifting surroundings. Good company. Fine wine."

"What do you want?" Selene repeated.

"To live another year."

"If we promised to see that Nasim did not know—"

"He would know." His gaze fastened on her face. "You're very determined. Why me? There are other warriors. I grant you, not as magnificent as me. And not many who would face Nasim, but I could name you one or two."

"I want you."

His eyes gleamed. "I told you I was weary. But if you insist, I'll try to—"

"Stop it." She could feel the heat rise to her cheeks. "You're trying to discourage me. You'll not succeed that way."

"And the suggestion of intimacy is beginning to annoy me." Kadar smiled sardonically. "Selene feels your involvement was meant to be. In truth, your appearance at this particular time and place seems heaven-sent."

"I have nothing to do with heaven and no credentials from that quarter."

"I don't care. I *need* you," Selene said. "Ware trusted you. If you help us, I promise you won't be hurt by it."

Kadar pressed her shoulder. "Let's leave him to think about it. We'll be at the villa. When your head is clearer, perhaps you'll let us know your decision."

She reluctantly rose to her feet. She supposed Kadar

was right. They were making little progress with Vaden. "Help us. Nasim is a monster. He hurts everyone."

Vaden looked at her, his eyes blue and cool as a mountain lake. "Did he hurt you?"

"Yes," she whispered. "He hurt me."

He glanced down into his wine. "He hasn't hurt me."

She turned on her heel and strode toward the door.

Kadar caught up with her outside. "It's not entirely hopeless."

"I don't see how it could be any worse."

"I'm not certain. It's hard to judge what Vaden's thinking."

"He told us what he was thinking. No."

"That doesn't mean that will be his final decision. Even Ware was never quite sure of Vaden. We'll wait for a few days and then I'll approach him again."

"I don't know if I still want his help. He's an arrogant, self-indulgent, brutal—"

"And a greater warrior than even Ware. You want him."

She sighed. "Yes, I want him."


Vaden appeared at the villa two days later. He wore light armor that shone bright in the afternoon sunlight. He was clean, sober, and even more startlingly comely in daylight.

"Good heavens," Layla murmured as she saw him walking up the steps. "Magnificent. Who is this?"

"Vaden. And I'm sure he'd agree with you." Selene eagerly moved forward to greet him. "You came. Why?"

"Lady Selene." He bowed. "It was necessary. I ran out of wine."

"We have a plentiful supply here." Kadar strolled forward to stand beside Selene.

"Good. Then my journey won't be for nothing." His gaze traveled around the anteroom and rested on a bust of Pope Giulano. "I'd forgotten. I'm surprised you haven't gotten rid of that statue of His Holiness."

"Why? It's well executed," Tarik said. "Everything in the villa is extremely well done. Your mother had excellent taste."

"She had no taste of her own. She studied His Holiness's likes and whims and gave him what he wanted." His tone was without expression. "She was a mirror." He turned to Kadar. "The wine and then conversation. Shall we go out onto the terrace?" He didn't wait for an answer but strode out of the antechamber.

"It seems we shall," Tarik murmured. "Do you suppose I should remind him he's no longer master here?"

"I doubt if it would do any good." Selene hurried after Vaden, followed by Kadar, Layla, and Tarik.

"You paid too much, Tarik." Vaden was leaning on the balustrade, his back to the garden. "I would have taken much less to rid myself of this place."

"I know." Tarik seated himself on the bench. "But then guilt would have marred my enjoyment."

"It's the bane that rules his life," Layla said.

Vaden turned to her. "And you are?"

"Layla."

"Tarik's wife." Kadar poured a goblet of wine and

carried it to Vaden. "Your wine. Must we wait until you finish before we start?"

"Nothing should interfere with a fine goblet of wine." Vaden smiled. "But I suppose I could make an exception."

"You've decided to help us?" Selene asked.

"If you can meet my price."

"We'll meet it."

"Don't be so eager," Tarik said. "It's my money pouch you're depleting."

"But you're clearly a wealthy man," Vaden said. "Only the very rich can afford to suffer guilt."

"What's your price?"

"First tell me what my part is in this endeavor."

"What you always do: You and your force will attack when we deem it necessary," answered Selene.

"When *I* deem it necessary," Kadar said. "An army with too many heads tends to get them all chopped off."

"And that's why I'll make the decisions," Vaden said.

Kadar shook his head. "I know Nasim, and your part in this may be minor depending on how we can position him."

"My part is never minor." He met Kadar's gaze and then shrugged. "But we can decide details later."

It was a major victory, Selene thought, and one she hadn't expected Kadar to win. "First we have to find Nasim. We think he's somewhere near Rome."

"Pompeii," Vaden said. "The assassins never venture too near any city in Christendom. Fear is one of their weapons, and distance lends mystery. Nasim and his men have set up camp above the ruins."

"How do you know?" Selene asked.

"This is Rome. It's the place of my birth. I make it my business to know everything that happens here."

"Then you knew Nasim was here when we first spoke to you."

"I knew he was near, and I located him yesterday morning." Vaden's smile was angelically beautiful. "But I hadn't run out of wine yet."

She wanted to hit him. She drew a deep breath. "Nasim is searching for us. We have to strike before he finds out where we are."

"We could try to draw him here." Vaden glanced around the cool tiled beauty of the terrace. "In fact, I think that's a splendid idea. The villa would make a fine battleground. If Nasim rode his horses through here, we could rid Tarik of several of those abominable statues."

"That's not amusing," Tarik said. "You obviously not only intend to beggar me but to deprive me of my property."

"Well, we probably couldn't lure him here anyway," Vaden said. "We'll have to rely on attack."

"We can lure him. We have something he wants," Kadar said. "But we'll have to choose a better place than the villa."

Vaden's eyes narrowed. "What do you have that Nasim wants?"

"It's none of your concern," Layla said.

"Everything that affects my life and that of my

men is my concern." He paused. "Is it the golden coffer?"

Layla stiffened. "How did you know of—"

"Rumors." His gaze shifted to Tarik. "There were many interesting stories swirling about you when I sold you this villa. I was almost tempted to reach out and take the coffer myself."

"It was fortunate you didn't try."

"I wouldn't judge Nasim to be a man who'd be interested in a small treasure. What's in the coffer?"

"You know enough," Layla said.

"No, he's right," Selene said. "He risks his life. There's only a grail in the coffer."

He gave a low whistle. "A grail? I've heard tales of the Holy Grail."

"I assure you, there's nothing holy about this grail," Tarik said.

"Then why does Nasim want it?" Vaden shook his head. "Never mind, I don't want to know. It's probably some mystical nonsense I'd be better off not filling my head with." He finished his wine and set the goblet on the balustrade. "Since our business is concluded, I'll return to the city and send word to my men to gather. It will take two days." He started for the door. "Kadar, if you don't have a reasonable plan in that time, you'll have to step aside and leave it to me."

"I'll have a plan," Kadar said. "But you haven't told Tarik your price. Is it kind to leave him in suspense?"

Vaden glanced over his shoulder at Tarik. "I'd prefer to give you my price after Nasim is defeated. I promise not to take quite everything you own."

"A most unusual arrangement," Tarik said dryly. "What if I decide not to pay you?"

"You'll pay me." Vaden's smile was tiger bright. "Everyone pays me."

# Chapter Seventeen

"WELL, ARE YOU CONTENT?" Kadar asked as he escorted Selene back to her chamber a short time later.

"Yes." She grimaced. "Though I don't know why. He's a most unsettling man. I don't know what he's thinking."

"You don't need to know. All we have to worry about is Vaden's power in battle and his loyalty."

"I'd judge Vaden to be a man who hates to be held in check. How far will loyalty stretch?"

"There's no use discussing it. It's done. We'll just watch him."

She suddenly frowned. "He seemed uncomfortable talking about the grail."

"Ware told me Vaden was always a man who believed only what he could hold in his hands." He smiled. "Yet he traveled all the way to Scotland to deliver your sister's banner to her. I'd wager he was even more uncomfortable performing that task."

"But he did it." Her jaw firmed. "And he'll do this for us." She stopped in front of her door. "Will you have a plan in two days?"

"Yes, I'll have a plan." He paused. "But we have other things to do in those two days. I told Tarik that we'd need a priest for tomorrow evening."

"A priest? Why should—" She understood. Vows. "You still wish this?"

"We have an agreement. I persuaded Tarik to let us use the grail. Now I'm ready to help you trap Nasim. Why would you think I'd changed my mind about my reward?"

Because he had not shown her that other, darker side of him in the past days. He had been the old Kadar, and it was that other Kadar who had made the demand.

She moistened her lips. "It would be wiser to wait."

He smiled. "I'm not like Vaden. I believe in taking the bulk of my reward in advance. You can never tell what will happen to prevent you from enjoying the fruits of your labor."

"Nothing is going to happen to you. I won't let it."

"I bask in your assurances." He met her gaze. "But the vows will still take place tomorrow evening."

His tone had taken on that harder, cooler edge and so had his expression, she realized with shock. The familiar Kadar was gone again. How easily he had slipped into that darker side.

"If that's what you wish. I never intended to cheat you."

"I know." His smile banished the hardness. "It's just that vows are not what is most important to me." He lifted her hand and brushed it with his lips. "And what I hope will become important to you again. Rest well. I'll see you tomorrow."

She watched him until he disappeared around the turn of the hall.

Vows.

She would be wed tomorrow. The idea was strange. She had put the prospect completely out of her mind in the past days. She must do that again tonight.

Because she was feeling the beginning of a tingling excitement and anticipation that was blocking out everything else. Kadar had always loomed larger than anything or anyone around him, and he was now a distraction she couldn't afford.

She could block him out tonight, but what of tomorrow night? Vows had not been his only price.

The tower.

Don't think of the tower. Don't think of his body or the music it had made as it merged with her own.

Don't think at all.

"I've brought you something to wear tomorrow," Layla said when Selene opened the door. She motioned to the soft blue material draped over her arm. "It's not fitting that you wear a servant's gown for such an occasion."

"It's very kind of you, but I don't—"

"Of course you do." Layla entered the room and shut the door. "Weddings are very important." She tossed the material on the bed. "It's not really a gown. It's only a length of silk, but the color is pretty and it will feel good against your body. I'll come back tomorrow morning and show you how to drape it."

Selene frowned skeptically at the material. "Drape it?"

"The women of Egypt and India do it all the time. It's much more graceful than clumsy stitching." She smiled. "And much easier to remove."

"I believe I prefer stitching."

"Not for tomorrow." She was silent a moment. "I was surprised you'd decided to marry at this time. I've noticed Kadar can be very dominating. Is this by your will?"

"It's by my will."

"Because if it's not, tell me. You're not yourself, and I won't have him intimidate you."

"He's not intimidating me." She found herself smiling. "And I'm enough myself to prevent such bullying. I thank you for your concern."

"I have a liking for you." The words came awkwardly. "I want things to go well. You may resent me for trying to keep Tarik from letting you use the grail, but it's not because I don't understand your pain."

"I don't resent you." It was true, Selene realized. It was clear Layla's passion to protect the grail was as strong as her own passion to use any means to accomplish her end. "You've always been kind to me." She made a face. "Except for that first night. I've still not forgiven that blow."

"Mario's blow, not mine." Layla grinned. "If it had been mine, it would have been harder. I never strike unless I wish to disable. Have you supped?"

"Not yet."

"Good. I'll call for food. We will sup together."

"You don't wish to eat with Tarik?"

Layla looked away from her. "He's avoiding me." She started for the door. "Not that I care. It just seems a foolish move. I've no wish to make him uncomfortable."

Pain and loneliness. The impression was stark and raw in those few words. Selene had the impulse to reach out in comfort, but she knew Layla would deny she needed comfort. There was one thing Layla would accept, though. "I'd like to sup with you, Layla." Her gaze went to the fabric on the bed. "And I thank you for the draping."

Layla laughed. "It will truly be fine. You will see."

"Did you wear such a garment on your wedding day?"

Her smile faded. "No, we wed in secret. I wore the same white linen robes I wore every day. But I placed a lotus blossom in my hair. Tarik said I looked beautiful." She shrugged. "I knew he lied, but sometimes lies can be a great comfort."

"I'm sure you were beautiful."

"It didn't matter whether I was or not. I *felt* beautiful." She opened the door. "I'll return soon."

*Tarik kissed her breast before whispering, "Will you wed me, Layla?"*

She became still. "Marriage?" She raised herself on one arm and looked down at him. "You wish to wed me?"

He smiled. "Why are you so surprised? You know I love you."

"Yes."

"And you love me."

She was silent.

"Layla?"

She nestled her head into the hollow of his shoulder. "Why do you wish to marry? We couple; we have joy."

"Why do you not?"

She stared at the darkness beyond the window across the room. It was a hot, humid night, and she had left the woven shutters open. She smelled the scent of incense of palm oil she had burned to mask the stench of the streets. She knew those streets: the thieves who stole from the living and the dead, the beggars, the whores. She had forced herself to walk those byways and learn the wickedness that lay around every corner. But it was a world Tarik had never known behind the walls of the Great Library.

Until she had forced him to come out from behind those walls.

"Layla."

"I'm . . . not like you."

"Why should that matter?"

"I don't meditate and worship at the feet of those great philosophers whose words you copy down in your scrolls. Most of the time I don't think at all. I just do what seems best to do, what I want to do."

"You think a great deal. You're the most intelligent woman I know."

"Of course I'm intelligent. That's not what I meant."

*She curled closer to him even as she formed the words that would distance him. "I'm not—I don't—I should not marry you. You don't know me."*

*He kissed the top of her head. "Well enough. You've told me all I need to know."*

*"You know nothing. I'm selfish and—Do you know why I first came to your bed? I thought your interest in finding the scroll was waning. I needed to hold you. From the first moment I saw you at the library, I intended to use you to get what I wanted."*

*"I knew that."*

*She sat up and looked down at him in shock. "You knew?"*

*He laughed. "You're very bad at subterfuge, my love."*

*"That's not true," she said indignantly. "I've done quite well at fooling the priests all these years."*

*"Then perhaps I see more because I love you."*

*"Why do you love me?" she asked wonderingly. "I look at myself and I see nothing to love. I'm selfish and sharp-tongued and I've never done anything but use you."*

*"Yes, you've done something else."*

*"What?"*

*"You've loved me," he said simply. "Not at first. But gradually it came."*

*"I do not—" She couldn't finish. She closed her eyes. "I don't know about this love. It's been so long. . . . If I do love you, it feels very rough and strange and hurtful."*

*"It will be better when you become accustomed to the idea. Will you wed me, Layla?"*

*She opened her eyes, but they were still dim with tears. "It's foolish. You won't be happy."*

*"I won't be happy without you. Will you wed me?"*

*She lay down beside him again. "You're right, you wouldn't be happy." Her voice was uneven. "I've probably spoiled you for any other woman. Who could be as clever and witty and—" She had to stop for a moment. "So I suppose it's my duty to marry you. We will do it on the morrow."*

*He smiled. "And wear a blue lotus blossom in your hair."*

*"Flowers don't suit me."*

*"It would please me."*

*And she knew tomorrow the lotus blossom would be tucked in her hair.*

"Layla."

She looked behind her to see Kadar coming down the hall.

He was gazing at her quizzically. "You were lost in thought. I spoke three times to you."

Memories, not thought, and it was just as well he had jarred her from them. "Yes, what do you want?"

"Truce. Even if we cannot agree on the grail, we need to work together."

"You have Tarik." She added ironically, "Why do you need the help of a mere woman?"

"Because that 'mere' woman can cause me innumerable difficulties, if she chooses."

"That's quite true. You're wise to realize that fact and wiser to acknowledge it to me." Her gaze narrowed on his face. "But I've always known you were clever. I just don't know how self-serving you are."

"As self-serving as anyone else. But I do keep my word. The grail is safe."

She nodded slowly. "But how safe is Selene?"

He gazed at her in surprise. "Is that important to you?"

"I'm not without feelings. I've grown to think of Selene as my friend."

"You don't have to worry about Selene. I've cared for her for a long time. That will never change."

"Never?" Her lips twisted. "That may be longer than you think. Have you not been thinking of the possibility of giving Selene the potion?"

"Yes. How could I help it?"

"Even though you're skeptical about Eshe?"

"Yes."

"I thought as much. It's natural to want to play safe with the lives of people we care about. You've been thinking that the potion didn't hurt you and, if you wait until you know for certain that what we told you is true, Selene will be an old woman. So you're wondering, why not give it to her now?"

"Only if she chooses."

"She would always choose you whether it was what she wanted or not."

"Not at the moment. Her mind is on other things." He raised a brow. "Why are you concerned? As I recall, you claim that it would be a great gift."

"It is a great gift." She paused. "But there was Chion. And Selene suffered terribly when Haroun and the babe died. How do I know what effect the years would have on her?" She met his gaze. "You wish my help? You'll have it on one condition. If you decide to give Selene Eshe, you'll first come to me and discuss it."

"Done."

"And there must be choice. Do you understand? No matter how much you're tempted, it's the one rule that must be obeyed."

"Of course."

Relief streamed through her. "Good. And now that's settled, I have to find a servant and tell him to bring food to Selene and me in her chamber."

"I'll do it for you," Kadar said. "Go back and keep her company. She'll need you. She's uneasy tonight."

"Uneasy. A strange term to describe a bride."

"No stranger than the situation." He smiled. "Nor the people surrounding the bride. Including you, Layla."

"I'm not strange. I'm very—" She grimaced and then said grudgingly, "Maybe a little strange. If one is of a boring and unimaginative mind."

He nodded solemnly. "And one wouldn't care about such bores anyway."

He was laughing at her.

And she did not mind, she realized in surprise. His laughter was like Tarik's—no malice, just humor that invited sharing. "Exactly." She turned on her heel. "Nor for those who chatter and don't act. I'll expect a servant bearing food to be knocking on the door of Selene's chamber within the quarter hour."

The priest was murmuring, motioning with his crucifix.

Surely it was almost over, Selene thought. She hadn't remembered Ware and Thea's vows lasting this long. She and Kadar seemed to have been kneeling before the priest forever.

"Stop frowning. It's not been so long," Kadar whispered.

Her gaze flew to his face. He had read her mind, as usual.

He was smiling. "Can't you be a little less grim? Layla is already suspicious. I don't want her running forward and whisking you away before the deed is done."

Her gaze shifted to Layla and Tarik across the chamber. "She's not going to do anything," she whispered. "She spoke very gently of you last night."

"Gently? Layla?"

"Well, more gently than usual. What did you—" She stopped as she became aware that the priest was staring sternly at her. She supposed she was not showing sufficient respect. But Kadar had spoken first, and the priest was not frowning at him. Now that she thought of it, the priest had ignored both her and Layla when he'd arrived at the villa. In the eyes of the Church, a woman was nothing until there was blame to be laid, and then it was always the woman's fault, she thought with annoyance. She deliberately whispered more loudly, "I don't like this priest. He's rude, and I'm becoming very bored."

Kadar smothered a laugh. "I don't believe he considers it his duty to amuse you."

"And this isn't like Ware and Thea's wedding." Dear

God, her voice was trembling. Where had this sudden burst of sadness come from?

Kadar's hand tightened around her own. "Shh, it's all right. This doesn't really have anything to do with us."

How could he say that? Vows were forever. The priest might not be of importance, but the vows loomed so large as to cast a shadow over everything.

"Look at me." He held her gaze, his voice soft but vibrating with force. "Keep looking at me. This is right, Selene. It's always been right. From that very first day I met you at the House of Nicholas."

She couldn't pull her gaze away. She no longer heard the priest's voice. There was no one but Kadar.

Kadar holding her hand in the darkness.

Kadar joking as he sat across from her at the chessboard.

Kadar drawing her down on the couch in the tower chamber.

Kadar...

"It's done," Kadar said. His brilliant smile illuminated his face. "Now, that wasn't so painful, was it?"

"What?" She realized he was talking about their vows. The priest had finished at last. Kadar was standing, lifting her to her feet. "No, I guess not."

He turned her around and gently pushed her toward Tarik and Layla. "I'll join you shortly. I believe I'd best send the priest on his way before he meets with more of your insults. We may have need of the power of the Church before this is over."

"Very well."

"Good God, docility?"

She was as surprised as he. Somehow those last few moments had banished all of her tension and impatience. She did not feel docile but dreamy, warm, and serene.

As serene as when she had learned she was with child.

The thought came out of nowhere. That was what all this was all about. Tonight she would be with Kadar again and there might be another child.

But it wasn't the thought of the child that was making this eagerness and joyous anticipation tingle through her.

"Selene?" Kadar asked.

She smiled at him and then turned and walked toward Tarik and Layla.


"You're sure you wish this?" Layla asked in an undertone. "Just because you took vows doesn't mean you have to bed him."

Selene smiled. "Most people would think that would be a necessary second step."

"But you would not."

"Why are you worrying? It's not as if we haven't coupled before."

"You feel things too deeply. Passion can sway people to do things that aren't good for them. Kadar can be very persuasive."

"Yes, he can."

Kadar in the tower room, moving within her, whispering encouragement.

"You're not listening," Layla said in disgust. "You

look as soft as goose feathers. You might as well go to your chamber. I'll send Kadar to you."

Kadar was still talking to the priest, smiling, mending any anger he might have still felt.

He was her husband. They were joined.

"Go," Layla said. "I dislike the thought of you melting into a puddle before my eyes."

"You exaggerate." But not by much, she thought ruefully. She turned and moved toward the door. "And I tire of your nagging. I'll see you in the morning."

She could feel the soft draping of her gown brush against her body with every step. The touch was sensuous, caressing.

Like Kadar...

Why could she think of nothing else?

She shut the door and leaned back against it.

Soon he would be here.

Her heart was beating hard. She was oddly breathless.

She couldn't just wait. She had to do something.

The room was twilight dim. She crossed the room and lit a candle.

"I like you in that gown."

She whirled to see Kadar standing in the doorway.

She moistened her lips. "It's not really a gown. Layla draped—" She forgot what she was saying as she met his gaze. "The priest left?"

"After Tarik compensated him very generously." He shut the door and came toward her. "He wasn't pleased with you. He commiserated with me on my ill luck in acquiring such a shrew of a bride. He wanted to know if your dowry was enough to compensate me for the misery to come."

"And what did you tell him?"

"I told him that I'd committed a great many sins and you were my penance." He stopped before her, and she could feel the heat of his body. "He said I should have confessed to him and he would never have given me such an atonement."

She could barely make sense of his words. Her knees felt weak and she could only stare at him. What had he been saying? Something about the priest. "He doesn't like women."

"Not a bad thing in a man who took vows of abstinence."

"He should respect—" She inhaled sharply as his thumb touched the hollow of her throat.

"I feel your heartbeat," he said thickly. "But I can feel it more when I'm inside you. It's as if your whole body comes alive and closes around me. Tight and smooth as—" He closed his eyes and his lips tightened with strain. "God, I didn't mean to touch you. I don't know if I can stop."

Of course he'd meant to touch her, and stopping was out of the question. She stepped closer. "You don't need to—I promised that if you—"

"No." His eyes opened and he drew a deep breath. "No, Selene. No ifs. No bargains. No promises." His hand fell away from her and he stepped back. "No excuses why we should come together. When we make love, it has to be because that's what you need, what you want, and because you realize that it can't be any other way."

She stared at him in bewilderment. "What do you mean? You're the one who offered the bargain."

"Because it was the only way I saw that I could protect you."

"You said you wanted a child."

"I do, but I wouldn't bargain for it."

"You lied to me?"

"You're raising walls again. Don't do it, dammit. Don't *hide* from me. I don't know why you've always thought you had to protect yourself against me. I understood that when you were a child, but you're a woman now. Trust me. Belong to me. Let me belong to you. Yes, I lied. I'd do it again if I thought it would help you. I'd do anything to keep you safe and with me." His lips twisted. "I've grown accustomed to taking things and molding them to suit myself. I'll probably not be able to stop. But this is one time when I have to try to step back and let you choose." He gazed directly into her eyes. "I'll give you Nasim no matter what you do. Take me. Reject me. It doesn't matter. I never intended to do anything else. I'd have gone after him even if you begged me not to. Do you think I'd allow him to walk the earth after what he did to you and Haroun?" He turned and moved toward the door. "So think well. You have no bargain, no excuse. This is the last time I'll come to you. If you come to me, it will be because you accept what I am and what you are and that we have to be together."

He was leaving, she realized through the haze of bewilderment surrounding her. "Where are you going?"

"Somewhere far away from you and this villa."

The door slammed behind him.

God, what an idiot.

Kadar strode quickly down the hall, trying to put as much distance between them as possible.

Fool.

She had been willing. There would have been no coercion.

But what of next time? There was more at stake than a night's rutting.

That silky blue gown, clinging to her breasts, revealing the softness of her shoulders.

Stop thinking of her. He was already heavy and hurting.

Would it have harmed anything to have bedded her tonight? So there would not have been honesty between them. He would have been inside her and feeling the heated friction that—

"Where are you going? Why aren't you with Selene?"

He turned to see Layla standing at the door. All he needed was to have to suffer through explanations to her, he thought in exasperation.

He didn't answer as he ran down the steps.


He had left her.

Selene crossed her arms over her chest to still their trembling. He was gone.

Well, good riddance. He had lied to her and—

But hadn't she also lied to herself? Who had been the most at fault?

Excuses. Lies.

"What happened? I saw Kadar leaving the villa." Layla swept into the room without knocking. "I knew you wouldn't send him away unless he did something—You look like a sick cow."

Selene shook her head. She couldn't deal with Layla right now. "He didn't do anything."

"I don't believe it," Layla said flatly.

"I don't care what you believe. Will you leave me?"

Layla frowned. "You're right, it's none of my concern. I just wondered if he'd said anything about—I'll leave you." She didn't move. "But if you want him back, I could send someone to—"

"I don't want him back." She did want him back, but she didn't know what she could say to him. She was confused and hurting and frightened. Kadar's words had resonated with finality and truth.

It was as if he had stripped all the barriers and subterfuges to which she'd clung throughout the years, throughout her entire life.

Leaving what?

"Call if you need me."

Layla was leaving, Selene realized dimly. She barely heard the door close.

*No bargains, no promises.*

*You're a woman now.*

*Trust me. Belong to me.*


"I told you I wouldn't be ready until tomorrow." Vaden leaned back in his chair and gazed quizzically at Kadar. "What are you doing here?"

"This was the farthest I could get from the villa." He sat down at the table opposite Vaden. "I take it this foul place now has sufficient wine to suit you?"

Vaden nodded slowly, his gaze on Kadar's face.

"Well, it may not have enough to suit me."

"Interesting. I'd judge you a man who'd resent losing himself in Bacchus's embrace. What happened?"

"I was wed today."

Vaden threw back his head and shouted with laughter. "By God, that's reason enough for any man. Who is the bride? Lady Selene?"

"Yes."

"A difficult woman, but I didn't think she'd cast you out of her bedchamber."

"The situation is complicated."

"Life is complicated. I have experience with difficult women." He paused. "But I don't believe you came to me solely because I was many miles away from the lady."

"You're right, I'm a cautious man. If I lower my guard, it must be with someone I trust not to take advantage."

"And I'm that person? How strange." He was silent a moment and then held up his hand and motioned to a servant. "Wine for my friend."

Kadar's brows lifted in surprise. "You consider me your friend, Vaden?"

"We're all friends while the wine is flowing." Vaden lifted his goblet in a toast. "And how could I be anything but your most honored friend if you choose to spend your wedding night with me instead of your bride?"

# Chapter Eighteen

THE DOOR OF SELENE'S CHAMBER flew open with a force that sent it crashing against the wall.

"I've brought you a present."

Selene jerked upright in bed and snatched up the sheet to cover her breasts as Vaden strode into the chamber. "What are you—"

Vaden dumped Kadar on her bed and gave a sigh of relief. "He weighs more than I thought. I wouldn't have encouraged him to drink that last goblet of wine if I'd known I'd have to play pack mule. I wanted him dizzy, not unconscious." He swayed as he straightened. "Oh, well, he'd probably have fought me when he saw where I was bringing him. This is probably best."

"You're drunk."

"Very. But not as drunk as your Kadar." He stripped the tunic over Kadar's head and then bent to slip off his sandals. "Not surprising—it's clear he's a man who rarely lets himself overindulge. Those who have purpose usually manage to outdrink me. Your groom had purpose."

"Take him to his chamber."

He shook his head. "That would spoil everything. He said there were complications that kept him from your bed." He rolled Kadar's naked body in the cover. "Behold, no complications." He started for the door. "So simple."

"Wait. You can't—"

It seemed he could. She was talking to air.

Her gaze shifted to Kadar. He appeared so helpless. She had never seen Kadar drunk. As Vaden had said, Kadar was always wary, always in control. He was certainly not in control now. What was she to do with him? she wondered in exasperation. She had thought long into the night, but she was not ready to face Kadar yet. Particularly not a drunken sot of a Kadar.

Ready or not, he was here and she must accept it. She slipped from bed and crossed, naked, to the window. The first rays of dawn were lighting the sky. She didn't have to stay here. She could dress, go and sit in the garden, and then come back after Kadar woke. He might even leave before she returned. It had not been his desire to intrude on her. She could stay out of his way until he—

*Don't* hide *from me.*

Was she hiding, as Kadar claimed? The plan to avoid him had come so easily.

*Accept what I am.*

She wasn't prepared yet. She had to think, to let the thoughts he'd planted come to fruition.

*Trust me.*

How she had battled with that question of trust.

Good God, why was she standing here shivering at the thought? She had never been one to cavil at facing anything else. In truth, the decision had already been made.

She turned and strode back to the bed. She stood there looking down at Kadar for a long moment.

Then she slipped into bed beside him to wait until he woke.

Kadar didn't open his eyes until late afternoon.

Then he immediately closed them. "Good God, my head hurts. . . ."

"It serves you well," Selene said.

His eyes opened again. "What are—" His gaze wandered from her face to her obviously naked body covered by the blanket. "God in heaven."

"Go cleanse your mouth. You stink of wine."

He gingerly sat up and then flinched as he turned his head to look down at her. "What am I doing here?"

"You didn't come on your own, if that's your concern. Vaden brought you. He dumped you on my bed like a limp salmon."

He flinched again as he carefully stood up and moved toward the washbasin. "I hope you didn't use that comparison to Vaden. I've found he has a perverse sense of humor."

"He didn't give me a chance to say anything. He seemed to be too full of glee at ridding you of 'complications' to bother with anything else."

"Instead, he's piled on a mountain more." He splashed water in his face and then rinsed his mouth. "And I can scarcely wait until I'm myself again so that I can go break his neck."

"I'd not go that far. I found his directness to be helpful."

He stopped in midmotion of drying his face. "What?"

Selene drew a deep breath. Don't hide. Honest. Open. "I believe you heard me. Now, if you can come near me without making me intoxicated from that foul odor, I'd like you to come back to bed."

He slowly put the towel back on the washstand. "Why?"

"I wish to couple with you." She moistened her lips. "Though I don't know why when you saw fit to rob me of my wedding night."

"Selene."

"Stop arguing." Her gaze went to his body. "I'm not blind. I can see you're ready for me."

"But are you ready for me?"

He meant the question more than physically. "I think—" She met his gaze and said clearly, "Oh, yes, I know I'm ready for you."

A brilliant smile lit his face. "I suppose I should ask questions and give you an opportunity to question yourself. It would be the noble thing to do." He was across the room in three strides and tearing the cover off her. "But I've been down that path and I'm not going there ever again." He parted her thighs and moved between them. "I've been noble enough to last me for a lifetime."

"I never asked you to be—"

She lost speech and breath as he sank deep and the rhythm started. Her arms closed tightly around him.

Accept. Trust. Belong.

Oh, yes, belong...


"You performed very well." Her lips brushed his shoulder. "I admit I had my doubts. I've never seen you drunk before."

"I was inspired." He lifted himself on one elbow and looked down at her. "And I didn't perform well, I performed magnificently."

"Braggart." She thought about it. "Perhaps the first time."

"I was even better the third time."

She smiled slyly. "I was too weary to notice."

"You wound me." He brushed the hair back from her face with a gentle hand. "But, it's true, I did perceive a lack of enthusiasm in you. I thought I'd taught you that a woman must be as skilled as a man in this—" He inhaled sharply. "Will you—please remove—your hand?"

She squeezed. "Actually, a woman doesn't have to be so skilled. I've found you to be responsive to the simplest things."

"Simple?" He went rigid as her thumbnail caressed

him. "If you don't wish to couple with me again in the next minute, I'd remove your hand."

She laughed and released him. "Not until I've had my supper." She swung her feet to the floor and stood up. "And afterward I wish a hot bath." She carelessly draped the length of blue material around her. Layla was right, this garment had many uses. She liked the feel of the softness against her breasts. Her body felt as sleek and silky smooth as the material. "And then I'll see what other simple things amuse you."

She could feel his gaze on her as she strolled to the window. Night had fallen hours ago, and the moonlight shimmered on the rectangular pool. So serene. She felt serene too. Only minutes ago she had been lost in the most frenzied of passions, yet now she felt as tranquil as that cool, still pool.

"What are you thinking?" Kadar asked.

"That emotions seldom remain the same for very long."

"Some emotions do." He paused. "Love. Hate."

"Yes, but that's not the same." She came back toward him. "And I don't want to think about hate right now." She knelt on the floor beside the bed and laid her cheek on his hand. "I do love you, Kadar," she whispered. "I've loved you for so long." She rubbed her cheek back and forth. She added haltingly, "I thought I could live without you. I thought I'd be fine. I was wrong. I have to be with you."

"Selene."

"So you have to take care of yourself," she said fiercely. "Do you hear me? I won't have you dying on me."

"You won't?" He turned his hand and cradled her cheek in his palm. His voice was uneven. "I'll try to oblige you."

"And you have to promise to love me forever."

"That's an easy task." He lifted her chin and gazed directly into her eyes. "I'll love you until the day I die, Selene."

"I like these vows far better than the ones we gave the priest," she said shakily. "I'll love you until the day I die, too, Kadar."

An indefinable expression flitted over his face for only a second and then was gone. "I thank you." He bent his head and brushed her lips with his own. "I'll try not to violate your trust."

"You'd better not. I've just learned the way of it." She rose to her feet. "But I never do things in small measure. I'll trust you now no matter what you do."

"You will?" There was a strange note in his tone. "Are you sure?"

She smiled. "I'm sure."

"That makes everything much more difficult for me."

"I'd think it would simplify." She looked at him from beneath her lashes. "We've already established my liking for simplicity."

He moved his shoulders as if shrugging off a burden. He grinned. "God bless simplicity. Are you sure you need to eat now?"

"No." The folds of blue silk pooled at her feet. She stepped over it and moved toward him. "We've taken our own vows, and they should be celebrated in some way." She slipped into bed and into his arms. She whispered, "And it need not necessarily be a very simple way. You're very good at complications."


"I've been patient long enough." Vaden strode into Selene's chamber and slammed the door. "Out of bed and into your clothes."

Kadar sat up and quickly pulled the cover over Selene. "It's courteous to knock, Vaden."

"He doesn't know how," Selene said sarcastically.

"Would you have answered my knock? Tarik says you haven't been out of this chamber in two days. Coupling is all very well, but it can't interfere with the business at hand. Since I was the one who threw you into her bed, I felt obligated to allow you some extra time to enjoy her, Kadar, but I—"

"Allow?" Kadar repeated.

"Don't be testy. You wanted my services. You have them. I won't be kept waiting while you pleasure—"

"Get out, Vaden," Kadar said.

Vaden sat down in a chair. "When you do."

"Go on, Kadar," Selene said. "I've no desire to lie here while you argue. Besides, perhaps he's right. Keeping him waiting was discourteous."

Vaden gave her a brilliant smile. "Thank you. It's seldom I meet a woman who is both beautiful and just."

He was the one who was beautiful, and she wondered how many women had melted at that stunning smile. "I'm not beautiful, and I'm not stupid enough to believe such flattery. Take your sweet words out of here while I dress."

He blinked and then rose to his feet. "As you command."

Kadar was throwing on his clothes. "Where are Tarik and Layla?"

"On the terrace. They seemed in no hurry to disturb you. Do I detect a hint of reluctance in them?"

"More than a hint, but it won't affect your fee."

"Of course it won't." He moved leisurely toward the door. "Since I tremble at your lady's wrath, I'll wait outside in the hall for you."

Selene doubted if he had ever trembled in his life and certainly not at any woman's displeasure. She had never seen a cooler, more confident man.

As soon as he was gone, she said to Kadar, "Don't wait for me. I wish to cleanse myself. I'll join you as soon as I'm dressed."

Kadar nodded. "Though we should really keep Vaden waiting. It's not good for him to have his way in everything."

"And have him burst in here again? I'd rather have privacy than give him lessons in manners."

He had finished dressing and bent to brush her lips with his own. "I could break his head," he whispered. "This isn't the way I wanted it to—"

"End?" she finished as he stopped. "Nothing has ended. What are you thinking? We couldn't stay here like this forever." She kissed him long and hard. "Don't settle anything of importance until I join you, no matter how impatient Vaden becomes."

"I wouldn't dare." He smiled and gently touched the hollow of her cheek. "I, too, tremble at the thought of your wrath."

"As well you should." She pushed him away and tossed the blanket aside. "Now go and keep Vaden from attacking Nasim before I manage to make my toilet."

He was gone almost before she finished the sentence. In spite of his words, she could see his eagerness. Sensuality and coupling were all very well, but Nasim was shimmering on the horizon and Kadar could never resist a challenge.

Nasim.

Fear clenched the muscles of her stomach. This was what she had wanted: a final confrontation and Nasim punished for his sins. It was what she still wanted. Right was right.

But, dear God, what of Kadar? She had been so fanatically determined to accomplish her goal that she had barely allowed herself to think of anything else. She had needed his help and told herself she would involve him as little as possible.

But no one could stop Kadar from involving himself if he decided that was what he wanted to do. She should have known that better than anyone else. No argument would sway him. He would just go his own way.

And he could die as Haroun had died, as her baby had died.

She would not allow it. After all they had been through to reach this point, she would not lose him now.

She drew a deep breath to ease the tightness of her chest. She must not panic. Kadar mustn't see either her terror or any reluctance regarding his participation. That child-woman who had helplessly pounded her fists against his resolve was gone and must never return. She must think and plan and find a way to make sure that Kadar survived.

"It's time you joined us." Vaden's smile was as brilliant as sunlight, but his tone was edged. "Very clever of you to send Kadar to pacify my impatience and then tell him not to speak until you arrived." He glanced at Kadar. "I told him he was too new a groom to be so hagridden."

"It's been far less than an hour. Since you roused me out of my bed, it should have taken longer." Selene moved forward and sat down beside Layla. "And better that Kadar have to deal with you than me. He has more patience with such rudeness."

"Ah, yes, patience is one of my prime virtues," Kadar murmured. "That and my passionate love for simplicity."

Rascal. She felt the heat flush her cheeks but refused to look at him. "I'm here now, Vaden." She glanced at Tarik and Layla and deliberately addressed her apology to them. "I regret keeping you waiting."

Tarik nodded. "As you know, I'm in no rush for any of this to come into being. I'd just as soon have Nasim grow impatient, pack up, and set sail."

"He won't grow impatient," Kadar said.

"And I would have known if he'd moved his camp," Vaden said. "I've not gone to all this trouble to have him slip the net."

"What trouble?" Selene asked.

"My men are gathered, armed, and camped south of the city."

"That seems a great deal of trouble for them, not for you."

Vaden grimaced. "I hope Ware had greater fortune with his choice of wife, Kadar. Though I thought I saw the same signs of willfulness."

Kadar smiled at Selene. "I've grown used to it. I wouldn't have her any other way."

"But that's because you're obviously besotted. Is your mind clear enough to put it to such mundane things as a battle plan?"

Kadar's gaze shifted back to Vaden. "We use the grail. I meet with Nasim first and tell him I've managed to steal the grail from Tarik. It's the task he sent me to do, and it won't seem unreasonable to him. Since he no longer has Selene as a hostage, I'll tell him I'm in a position to demand a price for the grail. I'll set up an exchange point to receive payment and give him the grail at a location where he won't be entirely surrounded by his men. I'll argue it would be too easy for him to take the grail and dispose of me as he sees fit. He'll still demand a small protective force and twenty of his men are worth fifty of yours."

Vaden shook his head.

"Believe me, it's true. Nasim's followers are fanatics who would die for him. Would your men die for you?"

"I hope not. I'd rather they live and wreak havoc among my enemies. You mean me to attack his force on the way to the meeting place?"

"That won't be possible. You won't see the assassins

until they want to be seen and he'll probably select the site and then send a message to me after they've arrived. He'll expect me to reconnoiter the area and make certain everything is safe for me, but I'll be watched. You can't come too close."

"It's difficult to attack from a distance," Vaden said dryly.

"You can't attack until I accomplish what I have to do."

"And what is that?"

"Kill Nasim."

Selene had known it was coming, but she still tensed.

Vaden raised his brow. "And what of his guards you say are willing to die for him? What are they going to be doing?"

"I'll have to find a way to get him alone. After I've killed him, I'll signal you to attack."

"I realize Nasim is a most unpleasant fellow, but why can't we attack and you kill Nasim after we've secured the camp?"

"He could slip away. He's not a warrior with a warrior's code. I trained under him. I know him. He'd think nothing of leaving his men to die in an attack, if it meant his survival."

"And what will be the signal?"

Kadar shrugged. "I won't know until an opportunity presents itself."

"It's not as safe a plan as I'd like."

"Nothing is safe with Nasim." Kadar looked at Tarik. "You know Nasim. Can you think of a better plan?"

Tarik shook his head. "What of the grail?"

"It can't be just a lure. I'll have to take it with me and actually show it to him. Otherwise I'll be dead two minutes after I reach the camp."

"And what if Nasim slips away?" Layla asked. "You know he'll take the grail."

"You'll have to trust me to make sure he doesn't slip away."

"And what of me?" Selene asked. "This plan is all you and Vaden. I'm the one who set all of this in motion. Am I to sit and wait and do nothing?"

"The whole reason for the meeting relies on the fact that you're not a hostage and out of Nasim's reach."

"Then think of another plan."

Kadar shook his head.

She turned to Layla and Tarik. "It's too dangerous."

"I agree," Layla said. "Both for Kadar and the grail."

"Then give me another plan that has a chance of working as well," Kadar said.

Silence.

"Don't do this," Selene whispered.

He smiled. "It's not as dangerous as it sounds. There are always opportunities occurring when one least expects them. That's what life is all about."

"I won't let—" It was no use. He had made his decision, and there was nothing she could do to persuade him to abandon it. She wanted to *shout* at him. She should have known he'd concoct a scheme that would shut her out. "This isn't fair." Sweet Mary, that protest sounded puny. It was just the sort of whining she had promised herself she would not do.

"Fairness doesn't enter into it," Kadar said. "It's the only plan that will accomplish what we want."

"It could work." Vaden frowned thoughtfully. "But you're depending considerably on luck."

"Or on brilliance of mind and magnificent execution." Kadar smiled slyly at Vaden. "I doubt if you consider any of your victories based on good fortune."

"Certainly not."

"Well, neither do I."

"When do you go to Nasim?" Tarik asked.

"Tomorrow."

The word struck Selene like a blow. Too soon. How could she find a way to keep him from committing this madness with so little time?

"Good," Vaden said. "I was afraid you'd decide to return to the bridal bower and keep me waiting another fortnight." He turned to Selene. "His prospects are not so dismal. Let's get on with it. It would be foolish to attempt to dissuade him."

"I've no intention of trying to dissuade him." She rose to her feet. "Why should I? As you say, it would be foolish." She didn't look at Kadar as she started for the door. "He's obviously made up his mind."

"Selene."

She didn't stop. She had to get away from them. They were all so cool and reasonable, and panic was tearing through her. She had to gain her composure before she faced Kadar again. She had to think of a plan or an argument that would move him.

That prospect was far from likely.

Then she had to devise a plan of her own to keep him safe.

Tomorrow.

Dear God in heaven, tomorrow.

"She's upset," Vaden said. "But she was more reasonable than I thought she'd be."

"Too reasonable." Kadar was uneasy. He'd expected more of an argument from Selene. There was no question she had been shaken, and yet there had been no explosion. He had to talk to her.

"You're cheating her," Layla said. "She doesn't appreciate you protecting her out of her vengeance."

"I couldn't do anything else." He met her steady gaze and shrugged. "Very well, I won't do anything else."

"Then you have to accept the consequences." Layla changed the subject. "Tarik and I are going with Vaden. I want to be sure we're there if Nasim escapes your net with the grail."

"That's your privilege." Kadar glanced at Vaden. "I want no hint of your presence in the area tomorrow when I meet with Nasim."

"As you like. I've no desire for the assassins to know of my part in this any sooner than necessary. I'll set up camp some distance away and we'll meet after you leave Nasim."

Kadar turned to Tarik. "And I'll want you to bring the grail to the camp tomorrow evening."

"What if Nasim follows you and attacks in force?"

"I'll be careful. Nasim and Sinan taught me never to allow myself to be followed and the ways to avoid it. I doubt if Nasim will even attempt it." His gaze went to the door. "Are we finished here? I need to talk to Selene."

"It will do little good unless you tell her what she wishes to hear," Layla said.

"Go." Vaden's smile was wicked. "I have a challenge for you. See if you can persuade her to give you pleasure. Considering her mood, that would be a true test of 'brilliance of mind and magnificent execution.' "

He wouldn't even consider that challenge, Kadar thought as he strode down the hall. He would be content if he could just make Selene understand that the danger was not as intense as she imagined.

And how was he to do that when it was possibly greater?

"Are you angry with me?"

Selene turned away from the window to see Kadar in the doorway. "No," she said quietly.

She could see the answer disconcerted him. He had obviously come fully expecting to have to pacify her. He didn't realize that this wasn't anger, it was about fear and justice. "I suppose that it was natural for you to try to protect me. It's what you've done ever since we first met all those years ago."

"But it's true, this is the best way."

"Not in my eyes." She met his gaze. "But I can't convince you to do anything else, can I?"

He shook his head. "Tarik and Layla will be accompanying Vaden. You can go with them."

"And be safe?"

"Vaden would argue that point."

"Safe in comparison to what you're doing."

"Perhaps."

"Don't quibble. You know it is. Do you think I don't—" She had to stop to steady her voice. "Don't treat me like a fool, Kadar."

"All right, it's dangerous." He crossed the room to stand before her. "And I want to keep you safe. Is that so terrible?" He reached out and gently touched her cheek. "I'm selfish. I've always been closer to the dark than the light, and when I'm with you all the darkness goes away." The next words were stilted. "You warm me, and I need that warmth. No one else can give it to me but you, and I'm not sure I'd want to survive without it."

Kadar had never spoken to her like this. His manner was pained, the sentences stiff, not at all like Kadar, whose words usually flowed like warm honey. She wanted to reach out and touch him, hold him, surrender to whatever he wanted to take away his pain. She couldn't do it. "No, it's not terrible. I just can't accept it."

He became still. "You said you weren't angry."

She smiled. "Why should I be angry? Do you expect me to reject you? I've committed that foolishness before and I won't repeat it. I'm selfish, too, and I have no intention of losing you. We just cannot agree." She kissed him lightly on the mouth. "But there are things on which we do agree. We should enjoy them in the time we have left. What time do you leave tomorrow to go to Nasim?"

"In the afternoon." He stared at her warily. "Why?"

"Then we have time to walk in the garden, sup,

talk." She smiled teasingly. "And enjoy the simple things of life." He was relaxing. That was good. She wanted no tension this night. "And I promise I'll not try to dissuade you from going tomorrow." She stepped back. "I know better than to waste my time. Now go and bathe and return to me within two hours. I'll do the same and order a meal brought to us."

He smiled. "If that's what you wish."

She smiled back at him. "That is exactly what I wish—for now."

# Chapter Nineteen

THE MOONLIGHT GLITTERED on the waters of the reflecting pool and the breeze ruffling the surface seemed to give movement to the statues surrounding it.

"I don't like those statues," Selene said. "They're too cold." She stepped forward so that her face was mirrored in the water. "But I look cold too. Isn't that strange?"

"Yes. No one is less cold." His grasp steadied her. "But that may change if you topple into the water."

She chuckled. "Would you jump in and save me?"

"Always."

"Well, I doubt I'd need rescuing. The pool is scarce five feet deep."

"Men in armor have been known to drown in a few feet of water."

"And serves them right for making war."

"You're making war on Nasim."

Her smile faded. "That's different."

"And that's what every antagonist says about his war."

She made a face. "I don't want to talk about wars tonight."

"Or Nasim."

"Or Nasim." She moved away from him and sat down on the bench beside the pool. "So talk about something else."

"You're being entirely too serene. You're not planning on going over the wall again?" Kadar asked.

She shook her head. "I don't think Vaden could be fooled as was that guard at Sienbara, and I'm sure you'll warn him to watch me."

He sat down beside her and took her hand. "Of course. But Layla has already given him ample warning. She's learned your temperament very well in such a short time."

"We think a good deal alike. I thought she'd fight harder to keep us from using the grail."

"It was Tarik's decision. Since I had a weapon to use, I bent all my efforts on him."

"What weapon?"

"Guilt."

She frowned, puzzled. "It's Nasim who was guilty, not Tarik. I wouldn't think Tarik would feel any blame."

"Tarik evidently is a man with a conscience."

"That would still not be—" She studied his face. "You're not telling me something."

"Not because I'm trying to keep secrets from you, it's just not the time. I have to make a decision first."

"Is it about the grail?"

He nodded.

"You agreed to protect it for Tarik? Is that why he's letting us use it? You should never have—"

"I promised him only that I'd protect it from Nasim while it was in my possession." He lifted her hand and kissed the palm. "Don't you think it's time we went inside?"

She stared at him in wonder. "I think you're beginning to believe Tarik. How can you? It's impossible."

"Sometimes one is forced to consider the possibility of the impossible." He smiled. "But that shouldn't trouble you. You've already told me that the goal Tarik and Layla worked so hard to accomplish is of no interest to you."

She shivered. "It would be too lonely and strange."

"Perhaps not so lonely. We could make it—" He drew a deep breath and his hand tightened with bruising force. "My God, it's a temptation to try to persuade you. I could do it. I *know* I could do it."

"You're hurting me." And frightening her. "Persuade me?"

His eyes glittered as they held her own. "You say you trust me now. Don't trust me in this. It's too important to me."

"What are you talking about?" Her eyes widened. "Tarik promised you something. Don't believe him. It's madness. This Eshe is a dream."

"What if it isn't?"

"Then it could be a nightmare. Promise me you won't let Tarik talk you into trying to create this Eshe from the directions on the grail."

He was silent a moment. "I promise."

Her relief was tempered by a nagging unease. She could still sense that tension just below the surface.

"And will you promise me that you'll try to forget the nightmare and consider the dream? Because it could be such a—" He muttered an oath and jumped to his feet. "Come, let's go back to the house. We've had enough talk. I can't seem to stop myself from trying to—"

He was striding through the garden away from her, she realized in bewilderment.

She caught up with him as they reached the house. "I think I would rather talk of Nasim," she said breathlessly. "He doesn't arouse such a furor in you."

"We will talk of neither." In the short time it had taken to reach the house, Kadar had changed again. His smile was seductive as he took her hand. "We won't talk at all. I've saved something very special to demonstrate for you from my years in the house of pleasure. I think tonight is just the time to show you."


"That was very wicked." Her breath was coming in short pants as she rolled over on her back. "I'm not sure that you should—"

"Did you enjoy it?" He kissed her shoulder. "Then I should have done it. Rest, and then I'll show you another way."

She had never dreamed of the intensity and sensual skill Kadar had demonstrated tonight. He was always a master, but tonight he had been spellbinding, driven. Her body was tingling, alive, and still wanting more.

"I'm dizzy. I feel as I did in the tower...hashish."

"Pleasure can be as strong as hashish and as addictive." He kissed her breast. "Your body can become so accustomed to it that you can't do without it. I can make you want me like that. Your body will crave mine so much that you—"

"What's wrong?"

He jerkily moved off her. "Nothing." He lay down beside her and turned his back. "Go to sleep."

Go to sleep when he had turned from sorcery to remoteness in the space of a heartbeat? "I will not." Her hand grasped his and she turned him on his back. "What's wrong?"

He drew her down and buried her head in his shoulder. "What's wrong is that you can't trust me even in this," he whispered. "I didn't even know I intended to do this to you. I was tempted, I reached out, and—"

"Don't be ridiculous. I enjoyed it. It was a trifle unusual, but I liked—"

"That's not what I mean."

"Oh, you think you can make a slave of me with your wicked ways?" She bit his shoulder. "You flatter yourself."

"Do I?"

"And why should you want to? A slave would not suit you at all."

"You suit me. And I find I'd want you any way I could get you."

"But you have me already."

"Do I?"

"If you don't get yourself killed by Nasim." She raised her head and smiled teasingly down at him. "And if you don't deny me pleasure because you're so vain as to think you have some sort of magical coupling powers."

"Not magic, skill." He smiled. "And I'm tempted to show you that it's not vanity. You've seriously damaged my self-love."

That almost desperate intensity was gone, she realized with relief. She cuddled closer and nestled her head in the hollow of his shoulder. "Later. I need to gather my strength. Besides, I like this too. Don't you?"

His hand gently stroked the hair at her temple. "Oh, yes. I like everything I do with you, my love."


He was asleep.

She wished she could join him in slumber, Selene thought, as she stared into the darkness. She didn't want to lie here, thinking.

If she had imagined she would lie awake this night, she would have thought the cause would lay at Nasim's feet. Surely Kadar's meeting with Nasim should be more worrisome to her than his strange behavior tonight.

Eshe.

Impossible.

Yet Tarik and Layla were intelligent, reasonable people, and they believed it possible. Kadar was not a man to plunge foolishly to any conclusion, but he was beginning to believe it too.

And she could see how Kadar would be lured by the prospects it presented. It was his nature to question and explore.

What if he decided that he could not resist that ultimate challenge?

But he had promised her he'd not take that challenge.

But did she have the right to ask that promise?

Of course she did. She loved him. Dabbling in the unknown could be dangerous. She had to protect him from that risk.

He was not afraid of risk. But she was afraid for him.

Or was she afraid for herself? When Tarik had spoken of her not being ready, he had been talking about Eshe. He had seen what she knew to be true: She wasn't ready to face the possibility of losing what she had to gain an uncertain future. She had grown up with uncertainty. Now she wanted everything secure and predictable.

Secure? Nothing could be less secure than their immediate future, and that danger was by her will and was her responsibility.

"You're frowning." Kadar's eyes were open, but his voice was thick with drowsiness. "Stop worrying about Nasim and go to sleep."

"I will."

"It will be all right. Nothing will happen to me."

"I know." Because she had already made the decision that there was no chance of anything happening to Kadar. She closed her eyes. "Go back to sleep. You need to garner your strength. I intend to wake you in a few hours and have you pleasure me."

"I'm not that sleepy now."

"But I deserve better."

He chuckled and brushed his lips across her cheek. "As you command."

Not when it came to a choice of her will or protecting her from Nasim.

Well, that was one challenge she was ready to meet. No mysterious Eshe, no groping into the future, just a duty to be done, a debt to be paid.

A life to be taken.


"Why should I believe you?" Nasim's gaze narrowed on Kadar's face. "It would be no small thing to steal the grail from Tarik. What if it's a lie? It could be a trap."

"Why would I want to trap you? I want gold, not blood." He glanced at Balkir hovering by the tent entrance and smiled maliciously. "Well, some blood. I want *him*. That wound in my chest still pains me at times."

Balkir stiffened, his gaze flying to Nasim's face.

Nasim didn't look at him. "I don't have to give you anything. If you've truly stolen the grail, I could torture you until you tell me what I need to know."

Kadar chuckled. "But you won't. It would take too much time. You're the one who taught me to withstand torture. Who knows? I might even die before I told you where I hid it. Wouldn't that be inconvenient?"

Nasim was silent. "How much gold?"

"I want the golden coffer that holds the grail and enough sacks of gold to fill it." His glance went to Balkir. "Perhaps not quite fill it. There should still be room for Balkir's head."

Balkir's face flushed with anger. "The master would not consent to such a bargain."

"No?" Kadar's gaze returned to Nasim and he said softly, "I really do want him, Nasim."

Nasim made an impatient gesture. "You know that's not possible. What else?"

"The *Dark Star* to take me back to Montdhu and your promise that Montdhu will continue to exist."

"A high price."

"Too high for the grail?"

"He thinks to beggar you," Balkir said. "Let me have him. I'll make him give you the grail."

"You interrupt," Nasim said icily. "Leave us."

Balkir's eyes widened. "I did not mean—forgive me. I only wished to—"

"Did I ask for your aid?"

Balkir shook his head and backed quickly out of the tent.

"A fool," Kadar said. "I'm surprised you endure him."

"A loyal fool. Not like you, Kadar. I could always count on your brilliance, never your loyalty."

"Because I'm not a fool. I'd not throw my loyalty down a bottomless pit." He smiled. "Now that he's gone, we can talk freely. I wasn't joking. I want him dead."

Nasim shrugged. "It's an unimportant thing. However, the ship..."

"Is also an unimportant thing." He paused. "When tossed in the balance. Look at me, Nasim: I was a dead man."

He became still. "You know it was the grail?"

"What else? You saw the wound."

Nasim's gaze hungrily raked Kadar's face. "Do you know how fortunate you are? You're *young* and frozen in time. Every year that passed, I knew my body was failing me and I couldn't get my hands on the grail." He frowned. "But perhaps if I drink constantly from the grail, I will reverse in aging. Is that possible?"

He shrugged. "I know little about the grail."

"Tarik does not seem to be getting younger. He only stays the same." His lips twisted. "So I'll take what I can get."

"You agree to the bargain?"

"On my terms. I'll not go unguarded to meet you, and I'll send you word of the meeting place tomorrow afternoon."

"Send it to the old cypress near the stream seven miles from here. I think it best that you not know exactly where I am from now on." He added mockingly, "Not that I don't trust you. But Balkir might be tempted to attack while I'm unaware and run another sword through me. Send a messenger to the cypress at midday and I'll be there."

"You're never unaware." Nasim smiled slyly. "Do

you wish me to send Balkir with the message tomorrow?"

"You *are* annoyed with him. You don't wish to see him alive again?"

"On second thought, I'll send someone else. I won't give you Balkir until I see that golden coffer."

"As you like, but he'd better not live a minute longer."

"No longer than you'll live if you try to betray me." He paused. "And I'll find the woman and kill her too. You cannot hide her forever."

"I'm not worried. When you have the grail, you'll lose interest in both of us."

"That's true." Nasim's eyes glittered in his taut face. "Nothing is more important. Bring me the grail. I *have* to have the grail."

"Tomorrow." Kadar turned to leave. "You won't be disappointed. Just make sure you don't disappoint me."


Vaden's army was camped some fifteen miles east of Nasim's camp on the southern slope of Mount Vesuvius.

Selene, Tarik, and Layla arrived at the camp in the late afternoon.

Kadar strode out to meet them. "You brought it?"

Tarik jerked his head to indicate the mule behind him. "Selene saw that I did. She watched me like a hawk as I loaded it on the mule. She wasn't about to let you go to Nasim without something to bargain with. Did all go well today?"

"As we expected." Kadar turned to Selene with a smile. "You see, all your worry was for nothing."

"I wasn't worried." It was a lie. The relief that had surged through her when she saw him had almost made her dizzy. "I wasn't expecting anything to happen today. I had every confidence you could keep Nasim from killing you as you dangled the prospect of the grail before his nose." She slipped from the saddle. "We both know it's after he gets the grail that you'll be in danger. Is Vaden ready?"

"Oh, I'm always ready," Vaden said as he joined them. "But I'm not sure I'll be given an opportunity to test that readiness. We're too far away."

"Tomorrow after I receive the message about Nasim's new location, you'll move closer. If you can do it without Nasim's guards seeing you."

"I can do it." His gaze went to the chest tied to the mule. "Is that it?"

Layla nodded. "And you'd better be prepared to protect it."

"I'll protect Kadar and do my best to destroy Nasim and his men. That's my only commitment. I wish nothing to do with your grail. I've had my fill of such tripe." He turned on his heel and walked away.

"Vaden is not enamored with objects of power," Kadar said. "You'll have to rely on me." He turned to Selene. "Our tent is over there. Are you ready to eat or would you prefer to refresh yourself?"

"Neither. I'm stiff from the ride." She set out for the perimeter of the camp. "I want to walk."

Kadar caught up with her. "May I go along?"

"If you like."

"But I'm not invited?"

"I won't be good company. I'm in a foul humor."

"I'd rather be with you in bad humor than anyone else in good."

She felt that usual melting at his words. This was not the night to quarrel with him, no matter how tense she felt. She slowed down and they walked in silence for a while. "Do you have any idea where he'll choose to meet you?"

"I have an idea where I'd choose. I've explored the area, and there's a plateau on the western side of the mountain. It's open enough so that you could see an attacking force on one side, and the cliff drops sheer to the valley on the other. I'd be surprised if Nasim chose any other place."

"You can't just ride into his camp with the grail."

"There's a cluster of boulders a short ride away. I'll hide the chest there and try to lure Nasim away from the camp."

"I've been thinking about Balkir. He's always with Nasim."

"I believe I've found a way to rid myself of him. We'll see, tomorrow."

Speculation. All of it was too frighteningly uncertain. She could feel the muscles of her stomach tighten at the thought. Don't think of it. Not yet.

She stopped as they reached an outcropping of the mountain to look down at the ruins below. "Tarik says there are people, a whole city buried beneath all that stone." She shivered. "One night they were alive and happy and the next they were buried. All their plans, all their worries and joys gone."

"Stop brooding. Their situation was nothing like ours. Disasters like that happen once in a thousand years. No volcano is going to rush down and destroy us. We're controlling our fate."

"I know." But she still felt a heavy melancholy as she looked down at the ruins. "But it must have been terrible. Tarik said he heard the sky was black for days."

"I doubt if he heard it secondhand."

Her gaze flew to his face. "Why do you say that?"

He didn't look at her. "He was quite probably here or nearby."

"What?" she whispered. "But that was centuries ago."

"Yes."

"What are you saying?"

"Ask Tarik." He pulled her close. "But not now. I want to hold you."

Centuries, she thought incredulously. "It's not possible. I thought a few decades."

"So did I."

"And Layla?"

"The same." He paused. "I knew it would frighten you, but it was important for you to know. No one should have to make a choice without the full truth."

"It's more unbelievable than ever now."

"Not when you talk to them."

"I don't want to talk to them about this." She stiffened. "What choice?"

"Not now. You're feeling a little desperate, and it wouldn't be fair."

"I want to know."

He shook his head.

Her hands tightened on his arms. She had a chilling idea what choice was to be offered. "Then tell me what choice you're going to make."

"I have no choice."

His words struck her like a blow. "I don't understand."

He put his fingers on her lips. "Shh, no more. Not tonight. I cursed Tarik for doing the same thing, but he was right to go slowly. I just wanted to prepare you."

"You're as bad as they are. I don't have enough to worry about with you going to Nasim tomorrow. You have to boggle my mind with this."

He smiled. "Better to split the worry. You were too somber. You'd have brooded all night about Nasim."

"And you'd rather I brooded over some idiotic choice. Well, I'll not do it. I won't think of you at all." She whirled and strode away from him. "Idiot."

"Does that mean you won't sleep with me tonight?" he called after her.

"Of course I'll sleep with you. Do you think I want to live with guilt if you get your stupid head chopped off? Just stay away from me until I can bear to look at you without wanting to slap you."

"Yes, ma'am," he said meekly. "Fortunately, Vaden isn't so disdainful of my company. He wants to go over the plan this evening."

She didn't answer as her pace quickened. A few minutes later she was inside the tent Kadar had indicated. Imbecile. What made him think introducing a new hazard weakened the impact of the first? It was just like a man to think that a woman could not hold two thoughts in her head at the same time.

*Nasim.*

*I have no choice.*

Panic was rising, and she had to remain calm if she was to get through tomorrow. How could she be calm when she was whirling in the dark?

She strode out of the tent and went in search of Layla.

"You're upset," Layla said warily as Selene strode into her tent. "Did you argue with Kadar?"

"No, he was too busy mumbling idiocies about choices and Pompeii and Tarik and you living for centuries."

"Oh."

"Well, *talk* to me." Selene plopped down on the cushions. "And don't tell me to go slowly or that I'm not ready or I'll throw a pitcher at you."

"I wouldn't want that." Layla smiled. "There's going to be enough violence tomorrow. What did he tell you?"

"Nothing. He's being as cautious and annoying as the rest of you." She bit her lower lip. "He told me he had no choice. What did he mean?"

"It seems he was very clumsy."

"What did he mean?"

Layla dropped down on the cushions across from her. "Shall I start at the beginning?"

"If you don't, I'll strangle you."

"Another threat?" Layla clucked reprovingly. "Since all this is clearly Kadar's fault, I really think he should get the brunt of this." She held up her hand to stem Selene's words. "Very well, I'll tell you all that Kadar knows."

The tent was silent for a long time before Selene whispered, "A thousand years..."

Layla nodded. "It sounds like a long time, but it passes more quickly than you would think."

"Why didn't anyone tell me that Kadar had already taken Eshe?"

"Did you really want to know?" Layla asked. "Kadar said you could think only of Nasim."

She supposed that was true. If she had not been so obsessed, she would have suspected Kadar was keeping something from her. "And I'm the one who gave Kadar the potion."

"You didn't know what it was."

"Tarik did."

"And it saved Kadar's life. Would you have him dead?"

"No." She remembered saying that she didn't care if it was sorcery as long as it cured Kadar. "I'd give it to him again tomorrow if it meant keeping him alive."

"Well, it will keep him alive for a long, long time." Layla paused. "He did not ask you to take it too?"

"No. I don't think he will. I told him—it frightens me."

"More than seeing yourself grow weak and old while Kadar remains young and strong? More than leaving him alone when he needs you?"

"You *want* me to do it?"

"I'm saying it's a decision with which you have to

come to terms. You can't hide your head in the ground and ignore the facts."

"I don't even know if they are facts or if it's some outrageous myth. I don't know anything about Eshe."

"Neither do we. We can't give it to enough people to gather a full picture."

"So you pick and choose?"

She nodded. "What else can we do?"

"On what basis?"

"Do you want me to say we have rules? We don't. Sometimes it's someone who is brilliant and has much still to give to the world. Sometimes it's only someone whom we cannot bear to lose."

"No rules?"

"Choice. They have to agree."

"And what of their families?"

"We aren't monsters, but the quantities are scarce. Each person we choose to receive Eshe is allowed five vials of their own. No more."

"And they have to choose who in their family is to live, who is to die?"

"I never said we were perfect. We do what we can."

"I couldn't do it."

"You could do it. I did."

"You didn't do it. You had no children." She stiffened as the thought sank home. "Children—is the reason you have no children because of Eshe?"

"At first I thought it was, but there have been other women given Eshe who later conceived and gave birth." Her lips twisted. "So I cannot blame it on the potion. I'm just barren."

"And what of the children? Are they frozen in time like you and Tarik?"

"You mean, do they never grow up? Eshe doesn't work like that. Growth takes place the way God intended. When the growth ends, the aging stops."

"But you couldn't know that. You must have taken horrible chances giving the potion to children."

"I didn't give it." She added deliberately, "But I didn't stop it being given. The first child to take it was the eight-year-old son of a Greek woman. His name was Niko, and I was very fond of him."

"Not fond enough to wait until he was grown."

"Do you know how many children die each year? How few reach their full growth? This was the seventh child born to Ariane. The others had died, and Niko was a terribly delicate child. She desperately wanted to make sure she could keep him alive. Did I have the right to stop her?" She met Selene's gaze. "And, yes, I wanted to know if it was safe to give to other children. The only way to find out Eshe's limits was to probe them. I made myself part of her responsibility. Blame me, if you will. But not until you're willing to stand in my shoes."

"I'm not willing. I don't want—" Her hands clenched. "I hope this is all a lie."

"But you're no longer sure it is." Layla smiled faintly. "It's very sobering, isn't it? But you'll become used to the idea."

"Will I?"

"It's a great gift."

"So you say."

"Because it's true. Death, not Eshe, is the enemy."

"Tarik chose Kadar not only to receive Eshe but to protect the grail. I don't think he meant to give him a choice in the beginning."

"It was very difficult for Tarik. Eshe has always been an unbearable burden for him. He must have been desperate to relinquish the grail."

"And you thought he sent me to you because he couldn't bring himself to give me the potion. Would you have done it?"

"Oh, yes. I was desperate too. I've been without Tarik for a long time. I thought he was reaching out to me." She grimaced. "I would have done anything, and I'm far more ruthless than Tarik."

"Yes, you are. For God's sake, if your story is true, I'd think the years would have made you more civilized."

"Souls don't change. I've come to believe we're all born with the soul we take to the grave. We learn, but we cannot change that part of us. If anything, we become more of what we started out to be."

"Then God help us."

"Sometimes He does. Sometimes we help ourselves." Layla paused. "And sometimes we falter and make mistakes. When that happens, you forgive yourself or let it destroy you. I won't let either Tarik or myself be destroyed by what happened to his brother. We just have to go on." She moved her shoulders as if shrugging off a burden. "Enough. I've told you all you asked of me. It's not easy to sit here and have you stare at me and question things I've questioned myself. Now go away and let me have some peace."

Selene wearily rose to her feet. Peace. She wouldn't

know peace this night. Her mind was too full and her emotions too rampant.

"What are you going to do?" Layla asked.

"About Eshe? I don't know." She turned to the tent entrance. "Perhaps there's nothing to be done. Maybe you and Tarik are mad and there's no such thing as Eshe. I can't think any more about it right now. I'm upset enough, and there's Nasim to deal with."

She stopped outside the tent and drew a deep breath. Night had fallen, and the cool air felt good on her hot cheeks. She was shaking, she realized. It was all very well to say she couldn't afford to think of Eshe, but how could she not.

*I have no choice.*

*Five vials . . . No more.*

*You can't hide your head in the ground.*

But she must try not to face it tonight. She had found out what she needed to know. Now she mustn't be distracted from the urgency of Nasim.

Her gaze searched the camp, and she saw Vaden and Kadar in conversation by the fire. Good, she would have time to recover her composure before she set out to do what had to be done.

# Chapter Twenty

KADAR WAS SITTING by the tent entrance when she arrived two hours later.

He stood up. "You were gone long enough. I thought you'd run away."

"No, you didn't. You know I'd not be that foolish. Why would I cheat myself?"

He smiled. "Still, I was uneasy enough to check to make sure your horse was still staked with the others. Where were you?"

"Talking to Layla."

His smile faded. "And?"

"She's not nearly as reluctant or caring of my feelings as you."

"She doesn't love you as I do."

"She doesn't love anyone but Tarik, but I believe

she likes me. Not that her liking would stop her from sacrificing me on the altar. However, she's honest, brutally honest. It's a quality I've grown to value of late." She stepped closer and took his hand. "And now I wish to lie with you. I don't wish to talk of Layla, Tarik, Nasim, or Eshe. I want to hold you and be held. I want you to make love to me. I want to sleep in your arms, and when I wake, I want you to be gone. I don't want to see you again until you return safely from Nasim's camp. Is that understood?"

"Oh, yes." He smiled and drew her into the tent. "By all means, come lie with me, my love."


The tents hugged the side of the cliff that overlooked the western slopes just as Nasim's messenger had told Kadar when he had met him earlier.

Kadar reined in a hundred yards distant.

It was not as formidable a sight as Nasim's full force, but it was dangerous enough.

Kadar could see Nasim and Balkir standing in front of the largest tent, their eyes fixed on him. He could count at least twenty assassins milling about the camp.

Well, he had known it would be so. He would just have to rely on wits and opportunity.

He kicked his horse into a trot.


"Where's the coffer?" Nasim demanded.

"It's close by. Do you really think I'd bring it here?" Kadar's gaze traveled around the circle of men surrounding Nasim. "What would stop you from slicing my throat and taking the coffer anyway?"

"My promise."

Kadar chuckled. "That *is* amusing."

"Where is it?"

"I'll take you there. But only you and Balkir. We'll stay within view of your men, but I'll want a head start once you have the grail." He glanced at Balkir. "Go fetch the bags of gold and tie them to your saddle."

Nasim shook his head. "We're not going anywhere."

"What do you fear?" Kadar gestured toward the steep drop beside which Nasim's camp was situated. "You've seen that no trap is possible. I defy anyone to climb up that cliff." He took his dagger from its sheath and dropped it on the ground. "And I'm unarmed."

Nasim was silent for a moment, then mounted his horse. "Let's go. But we stay in sight of the camp."

"Balkir?" Kadar asked.

"I don't like this," Balkir said.

"Fetch the gold, Balkir," Nasim said.

Balkir hesitated and then went into the tent. He came out a moment later carrying four sacks and tied them to his saddle.

"Very good," Kadar said.

Balkir glared at him as he got on his horse and followed them from the camp.

"Where did you hide the grail?" Nasim asked when they were several hundred yards from the camp.

Kadar nodded toward a clump of boulders in the distance. "Not far."

"I'll not go behind those rocks. I stay in the open, in full view of my men."

"Of course." Kadar nudged his horse to a faster pace. "I didn't expect anything else."

When they reached the boulders, he jumped down from his horse and disappeared behind the rocks. A moment later he returned, carrying the wooden chest. He set it down in front of Nasim. "Both of you get down and look at it."

Balkir slowly dismounted, his gaze on the coffer. Nasim was already off his horse, his face flushed with eagerness. "That's it?" he whispered. "It's really the grail?"

"I'd be a fool to bring you anything else." He opened the chest and pulled off the purple silk cover. The gold of the coffer shimmered in the sunlight.

Nasim reached for the coffer.

Kadar stepped in front of it and glanced at Balkir. "Haven't you forgotten something?" he asked softly.

"Do it yourself," Nasim said impatiently. "You don't need a dagger for such a one."

"Not with every assassin in your camp looking on."

"Oh, very well." Nasim drew his dagger, whirled, and plunged it into Balkir's heart.

Balkir's eyes glazed over, an expression of shock forever frozen on his face.

Nasim watched him fall to the ground before turning back to Kadar. "Satisfied?"

"Yes." Kadar stepped away from the front of the coffer. "Quick. Graceful. But I could have done it better."

"No one does it better." Nasim stared hungrily

down at the box. "Open it. Do you think I'll turn my back on you?"

Too bad. He'd hoped Nasim's eagerness would have overcome his caution. It would have taken only a few seconds to attack from behind and break his neck. "And do you think I'll turn my back on you?"

"It doesn't matter. The grail's not there anyway," Selene said.

Kadar went rigid. He whirled toward the boulders to see Selene walking toward them. "My God," he whispered. "Get out of here, Selene."

"Ah, the woman," Nasim murmured. He drew his sword. "And where is the grail?"

"Here." She pulled the cup from beneath her cloak. The chalice blazed in the sunlight. "Do you want it, Nasim?"

His eyes fixed on the grail. "Yes, I want it."

"Then come and get it." She moved in the direction of the cliff edge. "Or I'll throw it over. It's several hundred feet down, and there must be thousands of crevices. You might find it if you look for a few years."

Nasim gazed warily at Kadar before stepping toward her. "You wouldn't throw such a treasure away."

"It's no treasure to me. Sometimes I wish I'd never heard of it." She met his gaze. "Look at me. Am I telling the truth?"

"You're mad." He glanced at the camp. "My men are stirring. I told them to attack at the first sign of anything unusual. They'll be here in a moment."

"If they get here before you come to me, the grail

will be gone. I won't die and let you have what you want."

"Stupid woman. Do you know what you—stand back." His sword was again pointed at Kadar.

"I haven't moved," Kadar said.

"You were readying."

"Come and get it," Selene repeated. She whirled and ran toward the edge of the cliff, her feet flying over the rough ground.

Nasim cursed and started after her.

Kadar couldn't wait any longer. He pounced and ducked to the left at the same time.

The flat of Nasim's sword crashed into the side of his head.

Darkness.


He was gaining on her.

Selene ran faster.

Her breath was coming hard, painfully, as her lungs labored.

She could hear the pound of hoofbeats.

Nasim's men were tearing toward them from the camp.

Faster. She had to go faster.

Where was Kadar?

She risked a glance over her shoulder but saw only Nasim.

Kadar...

Only a little farther. She had to reach the edge—

Nasim's hand fell on her shoulder.

She jerked away.

So close, and he had the sword.

Terror rained through her.

If her pace slowed, she would die.

"Stop," Nasim muttered.

If she stumbled, she would die.

Wear him out. Make him unsteady.

"Why are you trying to catch me? You're an old man. You're weak. You'll die soon. You'll never have the grail."

She heard an explosion of rage behind her.

All right. It was time.

Her pace slowed. The point of the sword touched her back as he lunged.

She fell to the ground and rolled toward him.

He grunted as he tripped and stumbled over her body.

She heard him scream as he tottered over the edge of the cliff.

He tried to step back.

"No!" She launched herself forward at his knees.

He went over the cliff, his hands clawing, clutching. They closed on her hair. Agony tore through her as strands were ripped from her head.

He fell through space.

And she saw the twisted terror on his face.

"Quick." Kadar was lifting her to her feet. "They're coming!"

*The assassins.*

He dragged her toward the boulders.

Hooves pounding.

Close. Too close.

They darted across the plateau.

But the sound of hooves wasn't behind them any longer.

It was ahead, then all around them.

Vaden.

Relief poured through her.

Kadar jerked her to one side as the stream of riders thundered past him toward the oncoming horde of assassins.

"Get behind the boulders," Kadar said curtly. "You don't want to see this."

She was already seeing it. She shuddered as she saw Vaden's sword decapitate one of the leaders in the charge. She hurriedly looked away and let Kadar lead her toward the boulders where she had hidden and waited.

Death there too.

Balkir.

Kadar dragged her behind the boulders.

She leaned back against the rock and closed her eyes.

"Are you satisfied?" Kadar asked roughly. "He almost killed you."

No one knew that better than she. She had been terrified on that frantic run to the edge of the cliff. She whispered, "I started this. It was my responsibility. He was mine."

"And you couldn't leave it to me."

"No."

"How did you get here? Did you follow me?"

She shook her head. "If the assassins couldn't follow you without you knowing, I knew I couldn't. You told me where you thought Nasim would set up camp. I was here before you and saw you hide the chest."

"But your horse was still staked out when I left."

"Vaden gave me one of his horses."

"Vaden." He muttered a curse. "And what if one of Nasim's guards had seen you?"

"I was careful. They didn't."

Kadar swore beneath his breath. "You don't know how lucky you—"

Her eyes opened. "I was careful, not lucky," she said fiercely. "Now stop *yelling* at me. Do you think I wanted to do it? Was I to leave it all to you? You didn't even have a weapon."

"There are many ways to kill without a sword. I would have been able to do it."

"I couldn't take the chance. I wasn't going to lose you too. Though now I wonder why I cared. You're a fool, and you have no more understanding than—" She was suddenly in his arms, her face buried in his chest. "Let me go."

"No." His voice was muffled. "Never again. You scared me out of my senses. Now be quiet and try to stop shaking."

"I'm not—" She was shaking, she realized. "Why shouldn't I be upset? I've never killed anyone before. His face..." She drew a deep breath. "But it was right. I'd do it a hundred times if it meant—"

"Not like that. I've no desire to have a bald wife. If you must kill someone, remind me to teach you a few better ways."

"I don't want to learn a better way. It was—"

"Shh, I know." He took the grail she was still clutching in her hand and dropped it to the ground.

His hand pressed her head deeper into his chest. "You'll never have to do anything like that again."

She could hear the shouts and other sounds of battle only dimly. More death. When would it be over?

She didn't know how long they stayed locked together as the battle waged. It seemed a long time.

"Good God, can you not wait until you get back to camp to embrace?" Vaden asked. "There should be a certain dignity to war."

She lifted her head and saw Vaden sitting on his horse a few yards away. He had taken off his helmet, and the contrast between that almost angelic beauty and the blood that spattered him was a strange and macabre sight.

Kadar loosed his hold on her and whirled on Vaden. "You bastard, you were supposed to watch her."

"She had other ideas." Vaden smiled. "She came to my tent last night and persuaded me we should not leave it all to you. It didn't take much persuasion when she told me that I was to attack when I saw Nasim die. It was better than having to wait for some vague signal from you. I had no liking for the idea of having no control."

"She almost died, damn you."

"But she didn't, and neither did you. Though judging by that wound on your head, you came closer than she did."

Selene's gaze flew to Kadar. She hadn't even noticed the thin line of blood in the dark hair above his temple.

"It's nothing." Kadar shrugged. "Nasim hit me with the flat of his sword. It only stunned me for a moment."

"You see, you took too much on yourself. What if he'd killed you? I'd be out my fee," Vaden said. "Incidentally, your claim that the assassins were better warriors than my men has proved as false as I knew it to be." Vaden turned his horse. "But I can no longer chat with you. I have to finish my task."

Kadar glanced at the scene of battle. "I'd say you have finished. You left no one standing. No prisoners?"

Vaden shook his head. "Survival. I intend to live a long life, and the only way to do that is to make sure no word is carried back to Maysef of what happened. I'm done here, but I go to attack the main camp." He kicked his horse into a gallop. "And, after that, the *Dark Star*."

Selene shivered as she watched him ride away. "He's rather terrible, isn't he? I had no idea he would start a bloodbath."

"It's a bloodbath that will probably save us all. He's right: The only way to keep any of us safe from the assassins is to make sure no word gets back to Maysef."

Vaden's men had set fire to the tents and smoke curled upward, blackening the clear blue sky.

"It's time to get back to camp," Kadar said. "Where's your horse?"

She nodded at the boulder behind which she had waited those many hours for Kadar.

"I'll get it. Stay here."

She didn't argue with him. Her gaze was fixed in fascination on the burning tents. Death and destruction—and justice.

"It's done, Haroun," she whispered.

Layla and Tarik met them as they rode into the camp.

"The grail is safe." Selene jerked her head at the chest tied to Kadar's saddle. "You can see for yourself."

Neither made a motion toward the chest.

"And how are you?" Layla asked.

How was she? She didn't know. Sad. At peace. "Tired, I suppose." She slipped from the saddle. "I just want to go to sleep."

"Nasim?"

"Dead." She grimaced. "According to Vaden, they'll all be dead before he's through."

"It's safer," Tarik said.

"I know." But she didn't want to think about it. She was exhausted. Her legs felt unsteady as she moved toward her tent.

Kadar was there, his hand beneath her elbow.

"I don't need—"

"Hush. Yes, you do. It's all right to need someone. God knows, I need you."

He was right, she did need him. It was time she accepted that need. She let herself lean against him as he helped her to the tent.

It was dark when she woke, and Kadar was sitting cross-legged on the ground beside her pallet. It was like the night after she had come to Tarik's villa, she thought drowsily. No, not really. Kadar had been strange and forbidding then, and there was nothing threatening about him tonight.

He smiled down at her. "You slept deeply. It's almost dawn. Do you feel better?"

"I think so. I had dreams."

"Nightmares?"

She nodded. "Nasim. He was a terrible man. He deserved to die. Why should he plague my sleep?"

"He shouldn't. The dreams will go away."

She shivered. "I hope so." She sat up and brushed her hair back from her face. "Has Vaden returned?"

"Over an hour ago."

"And?"

"There will be no one returning to Maysef."

"What about the *Dark Star*?"

"It's docked near Rome. It seems we have a ship to take us home to Montdhu. Of course, we'll have to get a new crew."

"Home."

"You do want to go home?"

"Yes." Montdhu. She longed to see it again with aching intensity. She wanted to leave these foreign shores and go back to all that was familiar and beloved. "Don't you?"

He nodded. "But I have a decision to make."

"The grail? Why should you have to care for it? Let Tarik and Layla do it."

"Perhaps." He smiled. "But I'm feeling a small tugging of responsibility."

And he might still choose to do it. "Why should you? You had no choice about taking Eshe."

He became still. "What did Layla tell you?"

"Everything you should have told me." She tossed

aside the cover. "Now, go get me some food. I need to wash and eat before I talk of such matters."

He stood up and pulled her to her feet. "We don't have to talk at all. There's time."

"More time for you than for me." She turned away. "That's why we must talk. Later we will go for a walk and discuss this."

The sky was a glory of pink-scarlet as the dawn broke over the ruins of Pompeii. It seemed impossible that it had only been a day since they had stood on this same spot, Selene thought.

"I was going to tell you," Kadar said.

"When it suited you."

"It seemed better to wait."

She shrugged. "I'm not sure I believe any of this, you know."

"I know."

"But you do?"

"As much as I can with no proof."

She looked away from him. "Then I want you to give me the potion."

He stiffened. "Why?"

"What difference does it make? Just give it to me."

"It makes a considerable difference. I've been struggling to keep myself from persuading you since I was told about Eshe."

"Then stop struggling. The battle's won. Go to Tarik and tell him to give it to me."

He shook his head. "Not because I want it."

"Very well, then do it because I want it."

"But you don't. You told me you'd never choose it."

"I was afraid."

"And you're not afraid any longer?"

"Maybe," she whispered.

He looked at her.

"All right, I'm still afraid. But I'm more afraid of not taking it. I won't leave you alone. You *need* me."

"That's a poor reason."

"I'm not reasonable about this. The entire idea is mad. Why should I be sane?"

"Because I won't let you do this for me. It has to be because you want it for yourself."

"Maybe I do." She moistened her lips. "I was terribly afraid when I was running away from Nasim. I thought every minute I was going to die. I didn't want to die. I wanted to live with you and have your children. I wanted to see Thea again. I wanted to *live*."

"Nothing is sweeter than life when you're close to losing it. You could change your mind."

"I won't change it. Why are you arguing with me?"

"Because it means too much. It's too important."

"You're just being selfish." She tried to smile. "You want me to grow old, ugly, and wrinkled and then you can laugh at me."

"How did you guess?"

She launched herself into his arms and buried her face in his chest. "Give me the potion," she whispered. "Please, Kadar."

His arms closed tightly around her. "I can't," he said hoarsely. "It's killing me, but I can't."

"I'll do it anyway. I'll go to Tarik or Layla and ask them myself."

"And I'll tell Tarik that if he gives it to you, I won't act as guardian for the grail."

"You told me once we had to be together. You said it was meant to be."

"Not like this. I can't force you to—"

"You're not *forcing* me." She pushed away and glared up at him. "Stop being noble. I won't lose you. Not by your death. Not by mine. We're going to be together. Yes, I'm frightened. Yes, I can see a mountain of problems. But I won't let any of them keep me from having you."

His face was pale and taut. "And I won't let you hate me later for rushing you into doing this."

"Rushing? When I can't even convince you to—" She drew an uneven breath. He wasn't going to yield. She would have to handle this differently. "Very well, we won't rush. I'd rather take Eshe now and put the decision behind me, but I can wait. I'm not going to age overnight. You'll probably find me just as desirable a wife in a fortnight."

"Possibly." He smiled faintly. "But a fortnight is still not enough time to make such a choice."

"The choice is made. I just have to persuade you to forget your scruples. I think we'll go away by ourselves for a little while. I don't want you around Tarik. He has far too many scruples of his own."

"You wanted to return to Montdhu."

"Not before I take the potion."

"You're afraid you'll change your mind."

"I won't change my mind. You'll change yours. We'll couple and talk and I'll be so winsome and captivating that you'll not be able to resist me." She took his arm and started back toward camp. "So you might as well forget this stubbornness now and do as I wish."

"It's not stubbornness," he said. "It's desperation. I couldn't bear for you to grow to hate me."

"Do you think me so unfair? Never mind. You're obviously not thinking clearly. You'll be much more reasonable when I get you to myself."

"I shouldn't go with you."

"But you will." She smiled lovingly at him. "Won't you?"

He sighed. "I greatly fear I will."

"You're being very rude," Tarik said as he watched Kadar lift Selene to the saddle. "Are we to at least know where you're going?"

"No," Selene said. "We've had enough intrusions. Go back to the villa. We'll return there when we're ready."

"I don't like this," Layla said.

"Because you aren't controlling us," Selene said. "Don't worry: In this instance, I'm doing exactly what you would want me to do. But I'll brook no interference."

"I still think we should know. What if we need to contact you?"

"Vaden knows where we'll be. I asked him where we could find a safe, quiet cottage near Rome."

Selene grimaced. "And we only hope he hasn't directed us to a hovel like the one where we found him. It would be just like his wicked humor."

"Vaden," Tarik repeated thoughtfully.

"Don't sound so hopeful." Kadar mounted his own horse. "I told him if he revealed our whereabouts to you I'd cut his throat."

"I don't think we deserve this lack of trust," Tarik said.

"Yes, we do," Layla said. "Or I do. Stop arguing, Tarik, it will do no good." She stepped forward and gazed into Selene's eyes. "Be sure. There's no going back."

Selene nodded and turned her horse. The next moment she and Kadar were galloping down the mountain path.

"He's going to try to persuade her to take Eshe," Tarik said as he watched them disappear around the bend of the trail.

Layla shook her head. "No, she's trying to persuade him to let her take it." She made a face. "And I thought it was Kadar I had to warn. I should have known that once she made up her mind she'd throw caution to the winds."

"Why are you concerned?" His tone was mocking. "Eshe is perfect, is it not? Mankind's savior."

"Not perfect, but wonderful. We just have to learn how to use it. You thought the same once." She turned away from him to hide the hurt. "We disrupted their lives. I'm not so lacking in conscience that I'll let them wander about the countryside with no guidance if they need it. I'll go and see if I can find out where they'll be from Vaden."

"He won't tell you. He has a liking for Kadar." He fell into step with her. "But I'll go with you. I have to speak to him anyway. He still hasn't told me his price for destroying Nasim's forces."

"Are you sure you want to know?"

"No." His lips twisted. "But it's better than having it hang over my head like a sword."


Tarik and Layla arrived at the villa two days later. The next day Vaden and his army left and headed north.

"Are you going to do it?" Layla's gaze was on Vaden's retreating figure.

"Do I have a choice?" Tarik asked. "I'd wager Vaden intends I have none."

"You have a choice." She suddenly whirled on him. "Why do you always fool yourself into thinking that anyone controls your destiny but you? You're more like me than you think. You believe you wouldn't have given Kadar the potion if he hadn't been hurt. You would have done it. Otherwise, all of your philosophy and soul-searching would have come to naught. Because you're human, Tarik."

"I never denied it." His lips twisted painfully. "But I try to limit my opportunity for mistakes."

"I know." She tried to control the trembling of her voice. "Who should know better? I was one of your mistakes."

"No, it wasn't—"

"Don't lie." She blinked to rid herself of stinging tears. "I've always known it. Well, you need not put up with my presence any longer. After Kadar and Selene are settled, I'll go away."

He stiffened. "You're going away?"

"Why not? You never wanted me here. You made that—"

She couldn't stay here. She was running through the corridors and out into the garden. Dear God, she shouldn't have lost her composure. She had been so careful not to let Tarik see the pain since she had arrived here. Where was her pride? Lost somewhere in the pain and regret and the—

"You were never a mistake," Tarik said from behind her.

She didn't look at him. "Yes, I was. From the beginning you never really wanted me. Oh, perhaps my body. But you wanted your scrolls and your learned discussions and your peaceful life. Then I came and everything was different. I made you leave the library, I caused you to be crippled and involved you with Eshe...and I gave you no children."

"And you took me out of grayness into sunlight. I had only to look at you and I came alive." He paused. "Just as I did when I walked down that hill and saw you again."

She stiffened. Don't be foolish. Don't begin to hope. "How can you say that? You left me."

"You know why."

"Eshe. But it had nothing to do with us."

"It had everything to do with us. It still does. It's what brought us together. It's what kept us apart."

Past tense? Her heart stopped and then began to race. "I haven't changed. I can't change. Not about Eshe. I've tried. I believe you're wrong, Tarik."

He was silent. "Perhaps we can come to some compromise."

She held her breath. "Why?"

"If you'd turn around and face me, I think you'd know."

She couldn't face him. Not yet. "Why?"

"Because I can't fight it any longer. I don't want to fight it. I thought I wanted peace, but peace can be very dull."

"You say that now. But you left me before."

"Not because I didn't love you. It was that damnable relentlessness. But over the years I've found I'm stronger than I gave myself credit for. I've discovered I can do battle with you if necessary."

"And?"

"Why, I deserve you, Layla. For good or ill, for the rest of our years, I deserve you."

"That doesn't sound like a statement of devotion to me. Ill? Do you insult me? Do you think I'd let anything bad—"

"Look at me, Layla. I tire of staring at your back."

She took a deep breath and turned to face him.

He was smiling at her. He held out his hand.

Joy soared through her. She wanted to run to him.

No, she had always been the aggressor. That had been part of their problem. Compromise. This time he must come to her. "You may be right," she said unevenly. "There's a possibility you do deserve me."

And he took a step toward her.

# Chapter Twenty-one

"YOU'RE BEING VERY STUBBORN." Selene rolled over on her back and straightened her bodice. "What does it take to convince you that you cannot live without me? I'm sure that I must be as proficient now as any of those women in that house of pleasure where you apprenticed."

"You concentrate on seduction of the body, not the mind." Kadar sat up, picked up a blade of grass, and drew it teasingly over her lower lip. "But, by all means, continue."

She knocked his hand away. "Only because you won't talk to me."

"It's too pleasant a day for discussion. The sky is blue, the sun is bright, and you—"

"The sky was stormy yesterday, and you would not

talk then either. It's been over a month and we've done nothing but make love."

He shook his head. "A terrible waste of time."

"It is when I wish to—"

His lips covered hers.

She bit him.

He jumped back, and his hand touched his lower lip. "I take it you're really sincere about this."

"I want to go back to the villa and have you tell Tarik to give me the potion."

He shook his head.

Dear God, he was obstinate. She had not expected to have this much trouble convincing him. "You know you'll do it eventually. I won't have it any other way."

"Perhaps."

"What will it take to convince you?"

"I have to give you time."

"How much time? A week? A month?" When he didn't reply, her eyes widened. "A year?"

"Five years should give you a goodly period to consider the consequences."

"Five—" She vigorously shook her head. "No."

"Have you thought why you're so eager to have this done and over? Are you afraid you'll change your mind?"

"No. I want it over because it will be in contention until it's done. I don't want that between us. No more confusion or conflict, Kadar."

He drew her closer. "I wish I could believe that's the only reason for—"

"I want to *hit* you." She pushed him away and

jumped to her feet. "All right, I don't believe this Eshe is a miracle. But, by heaven, I'm going to take it." She started down the hill.

"Where are you going?" he called after her.

"Away from you. Go back to the cottage, you stupid man. I don't want to see you for at least an hour." She had reached the stand of trees and was enveloped in the shady coolness. She needed that coolness. She was frustrated and annoyed and she saw no way to—

She froze with shock.

No.

*Again.*

She staggered to a nearby oak tree and leaned against it.

*Impossible.*

"You weren't long." Kadar didn't look up from the stew he was stirring in the fireplace. "Does that mean I'm forgiven? Or that you're going to do me bodily— My God, what's wrong?"

"We're going back to the villa."

He was by her side. "You're pale. Are you ill?"

"No. Yes. I don't know." She began to gather her belongings. "We have to go back to the villa."

"Tell me what's wrong."

She shook her head. How could she tell him what she didn't understand herself? "Just take me to the villa."

———

The villa was in turmoil when they reached it a half day later. The courtyard was filled with wagons loaded with boxes and furniture. Heavily laden servants were scurrying to and from the house and the wagons.

"What's going on?" Kadar murmured as he lifted Selene down from her horse. "It looks as if they're abandoning the place."

"Not abandoning." Tarik walked down the steps toward them. "We're merely moving on. It's never wise staying in one place too long. You'll also find that to be true, Kadar."

"Where's Layla?" Selene demanded. "I have to see Layla. Is she still here?"

"Of course. But you caught us just in time." He turned toward the door and raised his voice. "Layla."

"In a moment. I cannot—" Layla appeared in the doorway. "Well, it's about time you returned. We've been waiting for weeks."

"It appears you're waiting no longer," Kadar said dryly. "If we'd come tomorrow, the villa would have been deserted."

"We would have sent word of our location. Vaden is becoming impatient."

"Vaden?" Kadar asked. "What on earth has Vaden to—"

"Stop it. None of this is important." Selene stepped forward. "I have to talk to Layla."

"You don't look well." Layla's gaze was raking Selene's face. "You're very pale."

"I'm with child."

She could sense Kadar stiffening in shock beside her.

A brilliant smile lit Layla's face. "Again? What wonderful news. It will be—"

"Not again. I felt *life*. Thea didn't feel life until she had reached almost her fourth month. It has to be the same child. I did not lose my baby."

"What?" Layla asked, stunned.

"You heard me. How could this be? You told me I'd lost the babe."

"I thought you had. There was bleeding..."

"How much bleeding?"

"Not too much, but you were unconscious and the shock... You *should* have lost it." Her eyes widened as a thought occurred to her. "Unless it was—"

"What?" Selene asked as Layla stopped speaking.

"Nothing. What do I know about babies? I'm no midwife. I've always tried to stay away from—It hurt too much when I couldn't conceive myself."

"Layla," Tarik said.

Layla glanced warily at him. "I thought you wanted it."

"Oh, my God," he whispered.

"Eshe," Kadar said.

"It was the only time I didn't offer choice," Layla said quickly to Tarik. "You'd given it to Kadar, and it was clear you wouldn't want him to be alone. She loved him."

"You put it in my wine that first night," Selene whispered.

Layla's gaze was still fixed anxiously on Tarik's face. "I thought you wanted it."

And obviously that was the only thing of importance in Layla's world, Selene realized in frustration.

Tarik shook his head. "It mustn't happen again, Layla. Not without choice."

"Oh, it won't," she said, obviously relieved. "But it's just as well, don't you agree?"

"No, I don't agree," Kadar said grimly. "You robbed Selene."

"Of choice." Layla turned to Selene. "But you should have lost the child. It had to be Eshe that kept it alive."

"You're sure?" Selene asked.

Layla shook her head. "We don't know enough for me to be sure. I've never given Eshe to anyone carrying a child. I didn't know you were with child when I gave it to you. But it makes sense a potion that would battle disease and strengthen the mother would also strengthen the child, doesn't it?"

"Yes," Selene said dazedly.

"Then I did entirely the right thing."

"You did not," Kadar said through his teeth. "Were you going to deceive us indefinitely into believing she had a choice? Good God, you even made me promise not to give her Eshe without discussing it with you."

"Because I wasn't sure what effect two doses would have on her. We don't know enough about—"

"You keep saying that," Kadar said. "I'd think you'd refrain from reckless acts until you do know."

"Tell me that when you face a similar choice." She turned to Tarik. "I believe we're packed. Are you ready to go?"

He nodded and helped her onto her horse.

"Where are you going?" Selene asked.

"First to the north. Vaden has claimed his price. It seems he wants a piece of property and he has to wed a lady to get it."

"Wed?"

Tarik nodded. "But there are difficulties. The lady is already married." He mounted his horse. "And after that we will probably set sail on the *Dark Star* for Ireland. Neither of us has been there."

"But don't worry," Layla said. "We'll not lose touch. We'll be there to help you when you need us."

"Wonderful," Kadar said.

"You need only send word." Layla ignored Kadar's sarcasm and addressed Selene. "And let me know when the babe is born. After all, I feel a certain responsibility toward it."

"God forbid," Kadar murmured.

"Since we have need of the *Dark Star* for our own purposes, I've sent word to Genoa and my captain will put my ship there at your disposal to take you home to Montdhu," Tarik said as he turned his horse. "I believe that's all. Farewell."

"Wait," Kadar said.

Tarik shook his head. "Now isn't the time to talk. You're too upset with Layla, and I'd feel the necessity to defend her. Much better to let everything settle and let you become accustomed to the situation."

"When? Another hundred years?"

Tarik chuckled. "Much sooner. You'll be surprised." He raised his hand and put spurs to his horse.

Layla lingered a moment. "The babe," she reminded Selene. "Send word."

Selene nodded, still in a daze.

Layla's smile lit her face. "I told you Eshe was wonderful."

The next moment she was riding out of the courtyard after Tarik.

Selene's knees felt suddenly weak. She abruptly sat down on the steps and watched the wagons roll slowly out of the courtyard.

"Are you well?" Kadar asked quickly.

She nodded. "It's just that—I never expected—I thought I'd lost—"

"Idiot woman."

"She's not an idiot."

"No, she's a ruthless, self-absorbed—"

"Hush." She couldn't deny the condemnation, but she felt the need to defend Layla. "She was desperate. She loves Tarik."

"So she gave you no choice. Do you know what a struggle I've had to keep myself from giving in to that temptation? And that blasted woman had already given it to you."

"Why are you so upset? It would have come to the same thing anyway. I'd already told you what my decision would be."

"That doesn't matter. What if you'd changed your mind later?"

She shook her head. "I'm relieved. Now I don't have to put up with your noble restraint for the next five years. I couldn't bear such—"

"I've brought you a present." Vaden galloped into the courtyard. "Though I doubt if you'll like it overmuch. I would not." He got down from his horse and untied the wooden chest. "Tarik said to tell you it was now your responsibility. He was starting anew and there were enough bones of contention to plague him." He set the chest down on the stones of the courtyard. "So here it is."

"Take it back to him," Kadar said.

Vaden shook his head. "I don't want him distracted. I have use for him. That's the only reason I agreed to deliver it to you." He got back on his horse. "Give Ware my greetings."

Before they could protest, he'd galloped out of the courtyard.

Selene stared at the carved chest.

Kadar muttered a curse. "By God, I won't be saddled with this against my will. I'm tempted to ride out of here and leave it sitting there."

"No, you aren't."

"What?"

"It isn't against your will. I think you'd already made up your mind. I think you were looking forward to it."

"And what of you? Was I going to force it on you as well?"

She shook her head. "But you hoped..." She closed her eyes. She felt in a fog, drunk. "Let me think for a moment. Everything has happened too fast. I never dreamed—"

"There's nothing to think about. It's bad enough

that you weren't given a choice about Eshe. You don't want this."

"Don't I?"

"You know you don't."

"I didn't think I did. I only wanted to take the potion because it was the only way we could be together. It seemed there was too much danger of unhappiness...." Her eyes opened and she slowly stood up and moved toward the chest. She put a tentative hand on the carved top. It felt smooth, pleasing beneath her palm. "There's still that danger."

He stood watching her.

"But there's something else too." Her hand moved in a gentle stroking motion. "I told you I didn't think Eshe was a miracle, but if it saved my baby, then it can't be anything else. If it saved my baby, then it's worth protecting. Maybe it's as wonderful as Layla thinks it is."

"May I point out you're thinking with your heart and not your mind?" Kadar asked gently.

"What's wrong with that?" Her palm left the wooden chest and rested on her abdomen. No flutter of life, but it would come again. She was filled with wonder at the realization. Life. Eshe. "Feelings are good. Instinct is good. I'll let you think coolly and calmly. It sounds very boring." She turned and mounted the steps. "Now bring the chest inside. We have to plan on how we're to safely transport it to Montdhu. What if the ship sinks? Nothing must happen to it." She turned as she heard him chuckle. "What's so amusing?"

"You sound like Layla." He picked up the chest and caught up with her on the steps. "And I was wondering if Tarik should have left the grail in your care instead of mine."

"Then you're very foolish." She smiled at him. "Together, Kadar. What must I do to convince you that everything we do must be done together?"

# Epilogue

MONTDHU

"IT'S NOT AS LARGE as I remembered it." Selene rested her arms on the ship's rail, her gaze fixed eagerly on the castle on the hill. "Isn't that strange? In my thoughts Montdhu loomed gigantic."

"It's large enough." Kadar's arm slipped around her waist. "Or is it? Do you wish a castle of your own?"

"And leave Ware and Thea? Why would I want to do that? And what of the babe? It will need company. Children should not grow up alone. Thea's Niall will make a fine companion and kinsman."

"Heaven help him." He paused. "I wasn't suggesting taking you far away. I just thought a little distance might be a wise course."

"Because of the potion?" A little of her eagerness

left her. "You believe it may be dangerous for us to not show signs of age?"

"I believe it's something with which we'll have to contend," he said gently. "We both know that it will come sometime."

"I've been thinking." She didn't look at him. "Who is to say Tarik and Layla are right? Why shouldn't we give more than five vials?"

He shook his head. "There would soon be none left if you give it to the whole glen. I realize how you feel. I feel the same. But Eshe is a responsibility. There have to be limits."

She had known that would be his response, but she still could not consider the limitations of Eshe calmly. It wasn't right. There should be something they could do. "Because of the rarity of the herb that grows along the Nile. Well, surely that herb grows somewhere else. The world is wide. Perhaps wider than we know. We could find it. We *must* find it."

He threw back his head and laughed. "Good God, I should have known that you'd not meekly accept Tarik and Layla's strictures. Tell me, should we turn the ship around and sail out of the harbor in search of this elusive herb?"

"Don't be ridiculous. We can wait awhile. We've just come home."

Home. A rush of emotion overwhelmed her as she gazed mistily at the distant castle. Soon she would see Thea and Ware. "So solid. So peaceful," she whispered. "It's beautiful, isn't it?"

"Very." Kadar's arm tightened around her. "Home

usually is beautiful. I'm glad you're going to allow us to enjoy it for a time."

"You know I'm right about searching for—Oh, look, the gate's opening. They must have caught sight of the ship."

"I'd wager Ware's lookout spotted us some minutes ago."

"Then why—Dear heaven, they're going to attack!" Selene watched in astonishment as soldiers thundered through the gates, with Ware at their head.

"Why are you surprised?" He chuckled. "It's to be expected. This ship is unknown to them, and Ware is a cautious man."

"It's not funny. I did not expect any such thing. We've not come all this way home to be sunk in the harbor by the people we love."

"Then we must make sure they know who we are." He was still laughing as he stepped closer to the rail and waved his arm back and forth, repeating her words, "So solid. So peaceful."

He was right. Montdhu was no more peaceful than any other place, and Selene was not certain she would have it any other way.

Havens were all very well, but they could become boring. When she had made her choice about Eshe, she had rejected her right to hide away from life. She had to go to meet it.

But there was a difference between hiding and putting down roots. She wanted those roots, and by God, she'd find a way to strike a balance and hold what she wanted.

"You're doing this all wrong, Kadar. You look like

you're trying to catch a seagull," she said. "You'll have an arrow in your chest before you get his attention. Let me do it." She stepped forward, and her voice rang over the water to her brother-in-law, who had just reined in at the shore. "Ware, you idiot, don't you dare attack us. Are you blind? It's Kadar and Selene. We've come home."